"Who are you?" Tamara *whispered to the dark stranger who held her in his arms.*

"You don't know?" His voice sent another surge of recognition coursing through her.

"I . . . I feel I do, but . . ." She felt as if some great void within her had suddenly been filled simply by the sight of this man. Words swirled and eddied in her mind, absurd words. *Thank God you've come back. . . . I've missed you so. . . . Please, don't leave me again. . . .*

Tears filled her eyes, and she wanted to turn away so he wouldn't see them. He was staring so intensely, and the feeling that he could somehow see inside her mind struck her with an impossible certainty.

She wanted to turn and run away.

And she wanted him to hold her forever.

Dear Reader,

We're really out to spook you this month—but then, October is the traditional month for ghoulies and ghosties and things that go bump in the night.

Start off your chilling reading experience with Patricia Simpson's *The Haunting of Brier Rose*. This eerie tale is set in the darkly forested Pacific Northwest and features a villain for whom time itself means nothing, a villain who has come from the past to destroy the heroine's future, unless she and the man she loves—the man she has always loved—can find a way to save themselves and preserve their love.

Maggie Shayne is a relatively new author but an extremely talented one, and *Twilight Phantasies* is the first of her "Wings in the Night" duo. You'll love this inside look at the life—and loves—of a man who walks by night and shows his love in a most spine-tingling way.

Next month, keep your eyes open for "New for November," when Shadows will feature two brand-new authors whose way with a spooky tale will impress you just as much as it impressed us. As always, turn on all the lights, draw the shades and lock the doors, then join us for a walk where only Shadows can lead you—to the dark side of love.

Enjoy!

Leslie Wainger
Senior Editor and Editorial Coordinator

MAGGIE SHAYNE

TWILIGHT PHANTASIES

Published by Silhouette Books New York
America's Publisher of Contemporary Romance

SILHOUETTE BOOKS
300 East 42nd St., New York, N.Y. 10017

TWILIGHT PHANTASIES

Copyright © 1993 by Margaret Benson

All rights reserved. Except for use in any review, the reproduction or utilization of this work in whole or in part in any form by any electronic, mechanical or other means, now known or hereafter invented, including xerography, photocopying and recording, or in any information storage or retrieval system, is forbidden without the permission of the publisher, Silhouette Books, 300 E. 42nd St., New York, N.Y. 10017

ISBN: 0-373-27018-6

First Silhouette Books printing October 1993

All the characters in this book have no existence outside the imagination of the author and have no relation whatsoever to anyone bearing the same name or names. They are not even distantly inspired by any individual known or unknown to the author, and all incidents are pure invention.

® and ™:Trademarks used with authorization. Trademarks indicated with ® are registered in the United States Patent and Trademark Office, the Canada Trade Mark Office and in other countries.

Printed in U.S.A.

Books by Maggie Shayne

Silhouette Shadows
Twilight Phantasies #18

Silhouette Intimate Moments
Reckless Angel #522

MAGGIE SHAYNE

and her husband of sixteen years make their home in rural Otselic Valley, nestled in the rolling hills of Southern Central New York. Among her friends, Maggie is known for her quirky sense of humor, a tool she sees as essential in raising her five beautiful daughters.

Maggie has served for two years as secretary and conference coordinator for her chapter of Romance Writers of America. She has written articles for *Romance Writers Report,* and wrote features and humor for all but one issue of *Inside Romance.* In addition, she often writes for her chapter newsletter, *Prose and Cons.* More than anything else, she enjoys writing. She loves to create characters that come alive in her own mind and, she hopes, in the minds of her readers.

To the real "hearts" of New York, the members of CNYRW.

And to the young blond man on the balcony high above Rue Royale.

PROLOGUE

Desires and Adorations,
Wingèd Persuasions and veiled Destinies,
Splendours, and Glooms, and glimmering Incarnations
Of hopes and fears, and twilight Phantasies;
And Sorrow, with her family of Sighs,
And Pleasure, blind with tears, led by the gleam
Of her own dying smile instead of eyes,
Came in slow pomp.

—Percy Bysshe Shelley

March 20, 1793

The stub of a tallow candle balanced on a ledge of cold stone, its flame casting odd, lively shadows. The smell of burning tallow wasn't a pleasant one, but far more pleasant than the other aromas hanging heavily all around him. Damp, musty air. Thick green fungus growing over rough-hewn stone walls. Rat droppings. Filthy human bodies. Until tonight, Eric had been careful to conserve the tallow, well aware he'd be allowed no more. Tonight there was no need. At dawn he'd face the guillotine.

Eric closed his eyes against the dancing shadows that seemed to mock him, and drew his knees closer to his chest. At the far end of the cell a man coughed in awful spasms. Closer, someone moaned and turned in his sleep. Only Eric sat awake this night. The others would face death, as well, but not tomorrow. He wondered again whether his father had suffered this way in the hours before his appointed time. He wondered whether his mother and younger sister, Jaqueline, had made it across the Channel to safety. He'd held the bloodthirsty peasants off as long as he'd been able. If the women were safe he'd consider it well worth the sacrifice of his own pathetic life. He'd never been quite like other people, anyway. Always considered odd. In his own estimation he would not be greatly missed. His thirty-five years had been spent, for the most part, alone.

His stomach convulsed and he bent lower, suppressing a groan. Neither food nor drink had passed his lips in three days. The swill they provided here would kill him more quickly than starvation. Perhaps he'd die before they could behead him. The thought of depriving the bastards of their barbaric entertainment brought a painful upward curve to his parched lips.

The cell door opened with a great groan, but Eric did not look up. He'd learned better than to draw attention to himself when the guards came looking for a bit of sport. But it wasn't a familiar voice he heard, and it was far too civilized to belong to one of those illiterate pigs.

"Leave us! I'll call when I've finished here." The tone held authority that commanded obedience. The door closed with a bang, and still Eric didn't move.

Footsteps came nearer and stopped. "Come, Marquand, I haven't all night."

He tried to swallow, but felt only dry sand in his throat. He lifted his face slowly. The man before him smiled, absently stroking the elaborately knotted silk cravat at his throat. The candlelight made his black hair gleam like a raven's wing, but his eyes glowed even darker. "Who are you?" Eric managed. Speaking hurt his throat after so many days without uttering a word, or downing a drop.

"I am Roland. I've come to help you, Eric. Get to your feet. There isn't much time."

"Monsieur, if this is a prank—"

"I assure you, it is no prank." He reached to grasp Eric's upper arm, and with a tug that seemed to cost him minimal effort at best, he jerked Eric to his feet.

"You—you don't even know me. Why would a stranger wish to help me now? 'Twould be a risk to your own freedom. Besides, there is naught to be done. My sentence is passed. I die on the morrow. Keep your head, friend. Leave here now."

The man called Roland listened to Eric's hoarse speech, then nodded slowly. "Yes, you are a worthy one, aren't you? Speak to me no more, lad. I can see it pains you. You'd do better to listen. I do know you. I've known you from the time you drew your first breath."

Eric gasped and took a step away from the man. A sense of familiarity niggled at his brain. He fumbled for the candle without taking his eyes from Roland, and when he gripped it, he held it up. "What you say is quite impossible, monsieur. Surely you have mistaken me for someone else." He blinked in the flickering light, still unable to place the man in his memory.

Roland sighed as if in frustration, and blocked the candlelight from his face with one hand. "Get that thing out of my face, man. I tell you I know you. I tell you I've come to help and yet you argue. Can it be you are eager to have your head in a basket?" Eric moved the candle away, and Roland lowered the hand and faced him again. "In your fourth year you fell into the Channel. Nearly drowned, Eric. Have you no memory of the man who pulled you, dripping, from the cold water? The eve of your tenth birthday celebration you were nearly flattened by a runaway carriage. Do you not recall the man who yanked you from the path of those hooves?"

The truth of the man's words hit Eric like a blow, and he flinched. The face so white it appeared chalked, the eyes so black one couldn't see where the iris ended and the pupil began—it was the face of the man who'd been there at both those times, he realized, though he wished to deny it. Something about the man struck him afraid.

"You mustn't fear me, Eric Marquand. I am your friend. You must believe that."

The dark gaze bored into Eric as the man spoke in a tone that was oddly hypnotic. Eric felt himself relax. "I believe, and I am grateful. But a friend is of little use to me now. I know not even the number of hours left me. Is it full dark yet?"

"It is, lad, else I could not be here. But time is short, dawn comes soon. It took longer than I anticipated to bribe the guards to allow me this visit. If you want to live, you must trust me and do as I say without question." He paused, arching his brows and awaiting a response.

Eric only nodded, unable to think for the confusion in his brain.

"Good, then," Roland said. "Now, remove the cravat."

Eric worked at the ragged, dirty linen with leaden fingers. "Tell me what you plan, monsieur."

"I plan to see to it that you do not die," he said simply, as if it were already done.

"I fear no one can prevent tomorrow's fate." Eric finally loosed the knot and slid the cravat from his neck.

"You will not die, Eric. Tomorrow, or any other day. Come here."

Eric's feet seemed to become one with the floor. He couldn't have stepped forward had he wanted to. His eyes widened and he felt his throat tighten.

"I know your fear, man, but think! Am I more fearsome than the guillotine!" He shouted it, and Eric stiffened and looked around him, but not one body stirred.

"Why—why don't they wake?" Roland came forward then, gripping his shoulders. "I don't understand. Why don't they wake?" Eric asked again.

The guard pounded on the door. "Time's up!"

"Five minutes more!" Roland's voice boomed, nearly, Eric thought, rattling the walls. "I'll make it worth your while, man! Now go!"

Eric heard the guard grumble, and then his footsteps shuffle away from the door as he called, "Two minutes, then. No more."

"Blast it, lad. It has to be done. Forgive me for not finding a way to make it less frightening!" With those words Roland pulled Eric to him with unnatural strength. He pressed Eric's head back with the flat of one hand, and even as Eric struggled to free himself Roland's teeth sank into his throat.

When he opened his mouth to release a scream of unbridled horror, something wet sealed his lips. It sickened him when he understood that it was a wrist, gashed open and pulsing blood. Roland forced the severed vein to him and Eric had no choice but to swallow the vile fluid that filled his mouth.

Vile? No. But warm and salty. With the first swallow came the shocking realization that he wanted more. What was happening to him? Had he lost his sanity? Yes! He must have, for here he was, allowing another man's blood to assuage his painful hunger, his endless thirst. He didn't even cower when the word rushed through his brain like a chilling breeze. *Vampire.* Fear filled his heart even as Roland's blood filled his body. He felt himself weakening, sinking into a dark abyss from which he wanted no escape.

It was a far better death than the one the dawn would bring. The blood drugged him, and Roland stepped away.

Eric couldn't stand upright. He felt emptied of everything in him, and he sank to the floor. He didn't feel the impact. His head floated somewhere above him and his skin pricked with a million invisible needles. "Wh-what have you d-done to me?" He had to force the words out, and they slurred together as if he were drunk. He couldn't feel his tongue anymore.

"Sleep, my son. When next you wake you will be free of this cell. I promise you that. Sleep."

Eric fought to keep his eyes from closing, but they did. Vaguely he felt cold hands replacing his soiled cravat. Then he heard Roland pound on the door and call for the guard.

"He'll not live long enough for his execution, I fear." Roland's voice seemed to come from far away.

"The hell, you say! He was fine—"

"Look for yourself, man. See how he lies there? Dead before the dawn, I'll wager. I'll send a coach for the body. See to it, will you?"

"For a price, sir."

"Here, then. And there will be more to follow, if you do it precisely as I say."

"Well, now, if he dies, like you say, I'll see he gets in your coach. But if not, I'll be here to see he keeps his other appointment. Either way he ends up the same. In the ground, eh, mister?" Harsh laughter filled the cell and the door slammed.

CHAPTER ONE

In the dream she was running. From something, toward something. *Someone.* She plunged through dense forest woven with vines and brambles that clawed at her legs, snared her, pulled her back. Swirls of smoky mist writhed, serpentlike, around her calves. She couldn't even see where her feet touched the ground. All the while she kept calling for him, but, as always, when she woke she couldn't remember his name.

Jet hair stuck to her face, glued there by tears and perspiration. Her lungs swelled like those of a marathon runner after a race. She dragged in breath after ragged breath. Her heart felt ready to explode. Her head spun in ever-tightening circles and she had to close her eyes tightly against the horrible dizziness. She sat up quickly, pushing the damp hair from her forehead, and glanced at the clock beside the bed and then at the fading light beyond the window.

She needn't have done so. The dream assaulted her at the same time each day, just one part of her increasingly irregular sleep patterns. Nighttime insomnia, daytime lethargy and vivid nightmares that were always the same had become a predictable part of her existence. She'd made a habit of rushing to her room for a nap the second she got home from work, knowing it would be the only sleep she was likely to get. She'd sleep like the dead until just before dusk, only to be wakened by that frightening, lingering dream.

The effects slowly faded, and Tamara got to her feet, pulled on her satin robe and padded to the adjoining bathroom, leaving tracks in the deep, silvery pile of the carpet. She twisted the knob on the oversize tub and sprinkled a handful of bath oil beads into the rising water. As the stream of water bubbled and spurted she heard an urgent knock, and she went to the door.

Daniel's silver brows bunched together over pale blue, concern-filled eyes. "Tam? Are you all right?"

She closed her eyes slowly and sighed. She must have cried out again. It was bad enough to be certain her own sanity was slipping steadily out of her grasp, but to worry the man who'd been like a father to her for the past twenty years was too much. "Of course, I'm fine. Why?"

"I . . . thought I heard you call." His eyes narrowed to study her face. She hoped the circles beneath her eyes didn't show. "Are you sure you're—"

"Fine. I'm fine. I stubbed my toe on the bedpost, that's all."

Still he looked doubtful. "You look tired."

"I was about to take a nice hot bath and then I'm down for the night." She smiled to ease his worry, but it turned to a frown when she noted the coat over his arm. "You're going out? Daniel, it's been snowing all day. The roads—"

"I'm not driving, Tam. Curtis is coming to pick me up."

She felt her spine stiffen. Her breath escaped her in a rush. "You're going to spy on that man again, aren't you? Honestly, Daniel, this obsession you have—"

"Spying! It's surveillance. And don't call it obsession, Tamara. It's pure scientific study. You should understand that."

Her brows rose. "It's folklore, that's what it is. And if you keep dogging the poor man's every step he's going to end up dragging you into court. Daniel, you've followed him for months. You have yet to come up with a shred of evidence that he's—"

"Daniel." Curt's voice cut her off, and in a moment he'd hurried up the stairs to join Daniel outside her bedroom door. "Are you ready?"

"And you!" Tamara rushed on as if he'd been privy to the entire conversation. "I can't believe you're encouraging this witch-hunt. For God's sake, the three of us spend every day in a high-tech, brass-and-glass-filled office building in White Plains. We're living in the nineties, guys. Byram, Connecticut, not fifteenth-century Transylvania!"

Curt stared at her for a moment. Then he tilted his head to one side and opened his arms. She sighed and allowed his embrace. "Still not sleeping nights?" His voice came smoothly, softly.

She shook her head against the damp fabric of his coat.

"I'm worried about leaving her alone," Daniel said, as if she were not there.

"I have experiments to finish in the basement lab," Curt offered. "I could hang around here, if you want to do the surveillance alone."

"I don't need a baby-sitter," she snapped.

Daniel ignored her. "I think that's a good idea," he said. He leaned over to plant a dry peck on her cheek. "I'll be back around dawn."

She pulled from Curt's arms and shook her head in frustration. "Daniel and I know what we're doing, Tam," Curt told her, his tone placating. "We've been in this business a lot longer than you have. DPI has reams on Marquand. It's not legend."

"I want to see the files." She sniffed and met his gaze.

His lips tightened at the corners. "Your security clearance isn't high enough."

It was the answer she'd expected, the same one she got every time she asked to see the data that the Division of Paranormal Investigations had on the alleged vampire, Marquand. She lowered her head and turned from him. His hand on her shoulder stopped her. "Tamara, don't be angry. It's for your own—"

"I know. For my own good. My tub is going to run over." She stepped away from him and closed the door. Curtis would sequester himself in the basement lab and not give her a second thought, she was sure of it. He didn't worry about her the way Daniel did. He did seem to feel he had the right to boss her around more than usual lately. She shrugged, vowing not to worry anymore about Curt's proprietary attitude toward her. She stopped the water in the bathtub and stared down into it for long moments. No hot bath was going to help her sleep. She'd tried everything from warm milk to double doses of a prescription sleep aid she'd pressured her doctor into giving her. Nothing worked. Why go through the motions?

With a frustrated sigh she padded to the French doors. On a whim, she flung them open and stepped out onto the balcony. A purple-black sky, lightening to silvery blue in the west, dropped snowflakes in chaotic choreography. The sun had set fully while she'd been arguing with her insane guardian and his stubborn cohort. She stared, entranced by the simple grace of the dancing snow. All at once she felt she had to be a part of it. Why waste all this nervous energy lying in bed, staring up at the underside of the white canopy? Especially when she knew sleep wouldn't come for hours. Maybe she could exhaust herself into oblivion. How long had it been since she'd been able to put aside her gnawing worry and enjoy some simple pleasure?

She hurried back inside, eager now that the decision was made. She yanked on tight black leggings and a bulky knit sweater, two pairs of socks and furry pink earmuffs. She grabbed her coat and her skates from the closet, dropped them into her duffel bag, shoved her purse in beside them and opened her bedroom door.

For a moment she just listened. The hollow dinosaur of a house was silent. She tiptoed through the hall and down the stairs. She paused at the front door just long enough to stuff her feet into her boots, and then she slipped silently through it.

Crisp air stung her cheeks and her breath made little steam clouds in the falling snow. Twenty minutes of walking and snow-dance watching brought her to the outskirts of Byram. Childish delight warmed her when her destination came into view.

The rink sparkled from its nest amid the town park's shrubbery and carefully pruned elms. Meandering, snow-dusted sidewalks, wrought-iron benches with redwood slatted seats, and trash cans painted a festive green made a wreath around the ice. Tamara hastened to the nearest bench to change into her skates.

When he woke, Eric felt as if his head were stuffed with wet cotton. He'd swung his legs to the floor, landing with unusual clumsiness. He hadn't needed a window to sense the pale blush that still hung in the western sky. It hadn't been the coming of night that had wakened him. Hadn't been that for weeks. Always her cries echoed in his head until he could no longer rest. Fear and confusion were palpable in her wrenching pleas. He felt her need like a barbed hook, snagged through his heart and pulling him. Yet he hesitated. Some preternatural instinct warned him not to act hastily. No sense of imminent danger laced her nightly summons. No physical weakness or life-threatening accident seemed to be the cause. What, then?

That she was able to summon him at all was incredible. No human could summon a vampire. That anything other than mortal danger could rouse him from his deathlike slumber astounded him. He longed to go to her, to ask the questions that burned in his mind. Yet he hesitated. Long ago he'd left this place, vowing to stay clear of the girl for her own sake. He'd hoped the incredible psychic link between them would fade with time and distance. Apparently it had not.

He relaxed for an hour in the comfort of his lair. With the final setting of the sun came the familiar rush of energy. His senses sharpened to the deadly keenness of a freshly whetted blade. His body tingled with a million needles of sensation.

He dressed, then released the multitude of locks on the heavy door. He moved in silence through the pitch-black hall and pushed against a heavy slab of stone at the end. It swung inward easily, without a creak of protest, and he stepped through the opening into what appeared to be an ordinary basement. The door, from this side, looked like a well-stocked wine rack. He pushed it gently closed again and mounted the stairway that led to the main house.

He had to see her. He'd known it for some time, and avoided the knowledge. Her pull was too strong to resist. When her sweet, tormented voice came to him in the velvet folds of his rest, he felt her anguish. He had to know what troubled her so. He moved into the parlor, to the tall window, and parted the drape.

The DPI van sat across from the front gate, as it had every night for two months now. Another reason he needed to exercise caution. The division had begun with a group of pious imbeciles, intent on the destruction of any and everything they did not understand, over a century ago. Rumor had it they were now under the auspices of the CIA, making them a threat not to be taken lightly. They occupied an entire office building in White Plains, according to Eric's information. It was said they had operatives in place

all over the United States, and even in Europe. The one
outside seemed to have made Eric his personal obsession.
As if the front gate were the only way out, he parked there
at dark every night and remained until dawn. He was as
bothersome to Eric as a noisy fly.

He shrugged into a dark-colored overcoat and left
through the French doors off the living room, facing opposite the front gate. He crossed the back lawn, stretching
from the house to the sheer, rocky cliff above Long Island
Sound. He went to the tall iron fence that completely surrounded his property, and vaulted it without much effort.
He moved through the trees, gaining the road several yards
behind the intense man who thought he was watching so
well.

He walked only a short distance before he stopped,
cleared his mind and closed his eyes. He opened himself to
the cacophony of sensations that were usually denied access. He winced inwardly at the bombardment. Voices of
every tone, inflection and decibel level echoed in his mind.
Emotions from terrible fear to delirious joy swept through
him. Physical sensations, both pleasure and pain, twisted
within him, and he braced himself against the mental assault. He couldn't target an individual's mind any other
way, unless that person was deliberately sending him a
message—the way she'd been doing.

Gradually he gained mastery over the barrage. He sifted
it, searching for her voice, her thoughts. In moments he felt
her, and he turned in the direction he knew her to be.

He nearly choked when he drew near the ice rink and
caught sight of her. She twirled in the center of the rink,
bathed in moonglow, her face turned up as if in supplication—as if she were in love with the night. She stopped,
extended her arms with the grace of a ballerina and skated
slowly, then faster, carving a figure eight into the ice. She
turned then, glided backward over the ice, then turned

again, crossing skate over skate, slowing her pace gradually.

Eric felt an odd burning in his throat as he watched her. It had been twenty years since he'd left the innocent, raven-haired child's hospital bed after saving her life. How vividly he recalled that night—the way she'd opened her eyes and clutched his hand. She'd called him by name, and asked him not to go. Called him by name, even though she'd never seen him before that night! It was then he'd realized the strength of the bond between them, and made the decision to leave.

Did she remember? Would she recognize him, if she saw him again? Of course, he had no intention of allowing that. He only wanted to look at her, to scan her mind and learn what caused her nightly anguish.

She skated to a bench near the edge of the ice, pulled off the earmuffs she wore and tossed them down. She shook her head and her hair flew wildly, like a black satin cloak of curls. She shrugged off the jacket and dropped it on the bench. She seemed unconcerned that it slid over the side to land in the snow. She drew a breath, turned and skated off.

Eric opened his mind and locked in on hers, honed his every sense to her. It took only seconds, and once again he marveled at the strength of the mental link between them. He heard her thoughts as clearly as she did.

What he heard was music—the music she imagined as she swooped and swirled around the ice. It faded slightly, and she spoke inwardly to herself. *Axel, Tam, old girl. A little more speed . . . now!*

He caught his breath when she leapt from the ice to spin one and a half times. She landed almost perfectly, with one leg extended behind her, then wobbled and went down hard. Eric almost rushed out to her. Some nearly unheard instinct whispered a warning and he stopped himself.

Slowly he realized she was laughing, and the sound was like crystal water bubbling over stones.

She stood, rubbed her backside and skated away as his gaze followed her. She looped around the far end of the rink. That's when Eric spotted the van, parked in the darkness just across the street. Daniel St. Claire!

He quickly corrected himself. It couldn't be St. Claire. He'd have heard the man's arrival. He would have had to arrive after Eric himself. He looked more closely at the white van, noticing minute differences—that scratch along the side, the tires. It wasn't St. Claire's vehicle, but it was DPI. Someone was watching—not him, but Tamara.

He would have moved nearer, pierced the dark interior with his eyes and identified the watcher, but his foot caught on something and he glanced down. A bag. Her bag. He looked toward Tamara again. She was completely engrossed in her skating. Apparently the one watching her was, as well. Eric bent, snatched up the bag and melted into the shadows. Besides her boots the only thing inside was a small handbag. Supple kid leather beneath his fingers. He took it out.

An invasion of her privacy, yes. He knew it. If the same people were watching her as were watching him, though, he had to know why. If St. Claire had somehow learned of his connection to the girl, this could be some elaborate trap. He removed each item from the bag, methodically examining each one before replacing it. Inside the small billfold he found a plastic DPI keycard with Tamara's name emblazoned so boldly across the front that it hurt his eyes.

"No," he whispered. His gaze moved back to her as he mindlessly dropped the card into the bag, the bag into the duffel, and tossed the lot back toward the place where he'd found it. His heart convulsed as he watched her. So beautiful, so delicate, with diamondlike droplets glistening as if they'd been magically woven into that mane of hair while she twirled beneath the full moon. Could she be his Judas? A betrayer in the guise of an angel?

He attuned his mind to hers with every ounce of power he possessed, but the only sensations he found there were joy and exuberance. All he heard was the music, playing ever more loudly in her mind. Overture to *The Impresario*. She skated in perfect harmony with the urgent piece, until the music stopped all at once.

She skidded to a halt and stood poised on the ice, head cocked slightly, as if she'd heard a sound she couldn't identify. She turned very slowly, making a full circle as her gaze swept the rink. She stopped moving when she faced him, though he knew she couldn't possibly see him there, dressed in black, swathed in shadow. Still, she frowned and skated toward him.

My God, could the connection between them be so strong that she actually sensed his presence? Had she felt him probing her mind? He turned and would have left but for the quickened strokes of her blades over the ice, and the scrape as she skidded to a stop so close to him he felt the spray of ice fragments her skates threw at his legs. He felt the heat emanating from her exertion-warmed body. She'd seen him now. Her gaze burned a path over his back and for the life of him he couldn't walk away from her. Foolish it might have been, but Eric turned and faced her.

She stared for a long moment, her expression puzzled. Her cheeks glowed with warmth and life. The tip of her nose was red. Small white puffs escaped her parted lips and lower, a pulse throbbed at her throat. Even when he forced his gaze away from the tiny beat he felt it pound through him the way Beethoven must have felt the physical impact of his music. He found himself unable to look away from her eyes. They held his captive, as if she possessed the same power of command he did. He felt lost in huge, bottomless orbs, so black they appeared to have no pupils. My God, he thought. She already looks like one of us.

She frowned, and shook her head as if trying to shake the snowflakes from her hair. "I'm sorry. I thought you were..." The explanation died on her lips, but Eric knew. She thought he was someone she knew, someone she was close to. He was.

"Someone else," he finished for her. "Happens all the time. I have one of those faces." He scanned her mind, seeking signs of recognition on her part. There was no memory there, only a powerful longing—a craving she hadn't yet identified. "Good night." He nodded once and forced himself to turn from her.

Even as he took the first step he heard her unspoken plea as if she'd shouted it. *Please, don't go!*

He faced her again, unable to do otherwise. His practical mind kept reminding him of the DPI card in her bag. His heart wanted her cradled in his arms. She'd truly grown into a beauty. A glimpse of her would be enough to take away the breath of any man. The glint of unshed tears in her eyes shocked him.

"I'm sure I know you," she said. Her voice trembled when she spoke. "Tell me who you are."

Her need tore at him, and he sensed no lie or evil intent. Yet if she worked for DPI she could only mean him harm. He sensed the attention of the man in the van. He must wonder why she lingered here.

"You must be mistaken." It tore at his soul to utter the lie. "I'm certain we've never met." Again he turned, but this time she came toward him, one hand reaching out to him. She stumbled, and only Eric's preternatural speed enabled him to whirl in time. He caught her as she plunged forward. His arms encircled her slender frame and he pulled her to his chest.

He couldn't make himself let go. He held her to him and she didn't resist. Her face lay upon his chest, above his pounding heart. Her scent enslaved him. When her arms came to his shoulders, as if to steady herself, only to slide around his neck, he felt he'd die a thousand deaths before he'd let her go.

She lifted her head, tipped it back and gazed into his eyes. "I do know you, don't I?"

CHAPTER TWO

Tamara tried to blink away the drugged daze into which she seemed to have slipped. She stood so close to this stranger that every part of her body pressed against his from her thighs to her chest. Her arms encircled his corded neck. His iron ones clasped tight around her waist. She'd tipped her head back to look into his eyes, and she felt as if she were trapped in them.

He's so familiar!

They shone, those eyes, like perfectly round bits of jet amid sooty sable lashes. His dark brows, just as sooty and thick, made a slash above each eye, and she had the oddest certainty that he would cock one when puzzled or amused in a way that would make her heart stop.

But I don't know him.

His full lips parted, as if he'd say something, then closed once more. How soft his lips! How smooth, and how wonderful when he smiled. Oh, how she'd missed his smile.

What am I saying? I've never met this man before in my life.

His chest was a broad and solid wall beneath hers. She felt his heart thudding powerfully inside it. His shoulders were so wide they invited a weary head to drop upon them. His hair gleamed in the moonlight, as black as her own, but without the riotous curls. It fell instead in long, satin waves over his shoulders, when it wasn't tied back with the small velvet ribbon in what he called a queue. She fingered the ribbon at his nape, having known it was there before she'd touched it. She felt an irrational urge to tug it free and run her fingers through his glorious hair—to pull great masses of it to her face and rub them over her cheeks.

She felt her brows draw together, and she forced her lips to part. "Who *are* you?"

"You don't know?" His voice sent another surge of recognition coursing through her.

"I . . . feel as if I do, but . . ." She frowned harder and shook her head in frustration. Her gaze fell to his lips again and she forced it away. The sensation that bubbled in her felt like joyous relief. She felt as if some great void in her heart had suddenly been filled simply by seeing this familiar man. The words that swirled and eddied in her mind, and which she only barely restrained herself from blurting, were absurd. *Thank God you've come back . . . I've missed you so . . . please, don't leave me again . . . I'll die if you leave me again.*

She felt tears filling her eyes, and she wanted to turn away so he wouldn't see them. The pain in his flickered and then vanished, so she wondered if she'd truly seen it there. He stared so intensely, and the peculiar feeling that he somehow saw inside her mind hit her with ridiculous certainty.

She wanted to turn and run away. She wanted him to hold her forever. *I'm losing my mind.*

"No, sweet. You are perfectly sane, never doubt that." His voice caressed her.

She drew a breath. She hadn't spoken the thought aloud, had she? He'd . . . my God, he'd read her mind.

Impossible! He couldn't have. She stared at his sensual mouth again, licked her lips. Had he read her mind? *I want you to kiss me,* she thought, deliberately.

A silent voice whispered a reply inside her brain—his voice. *A test? I couldn't think of a more pleasant one.*

She watched, mesmerized, as his head came down. His mouth relaxed over hers, and she allowed her lips to part at his gentle nudging. At the instant his moist, warm tongue slipped into her mouth to stroke hers, a jolt went through her. Not a sudden rush of physical desire. No, this felt like an actual electric current, hammering from the point of contact, through her body to exit through the soles of her feet. It rocked her and left her weak.

His hands moved up, over her back. His fingertips danced along her nape and higher, until he'd buried them in her hair. With his hands at the back of her head he pressed her nearer, tilting her to the angle that best fit him, and preventing her pulling away as his tongue stroked deeper, kindling fires in her belly.

Finally his lips slid away from hers, and she thought the kiss had ended. Instead it only changed form. He trailed his moist lips along the line of her jaw. He flicked his tongue over the sensitized skin just below her ear. He moved his lips caressingly to her throat, and her head fell back on its own. Her hands cupped his head, and pressed him closer. Her eyes fluttered closed and she felt so light-headed she was sure she must be about to faint.

He sucked the tender skin between his teeth. She felt sharp incisors skim the soft flesh as he suckled her there like a babe at its mother's breast. She felt him shudder, heard him groan as if tortured. He lifted his head from her, and his hands straightened hers so he could gaze into her eyes. For an instant there seemed to be light in them—an unnatural glow shining from somewhere beyond the ebony.

His voice, when he spoke, sounded rough and shaky. It was no longer the soothing honey that had coated her ears earlier. "What is it you want of me? And take care not to ask too much, Tamara. I fear I can refuse you nothing."

She frowned. "I don't want—" She sucked air through her teeth, stepping out of his arms. "How do you know my name?"

Slowly the spell faded. She breathed deeply, evenly. What had she done? Since when did she go around kissing strangers in the middle of the night?

"The same way you know mine," he said, his voice regaining some of its former strength and tone.

"I don't know yours! And how could you—why did you..." She shook her head angrily and couldn't finish the sentence. After all, she'd kissed him as much as he'd kissed her.

"Come, Tamara, we both know you summoned me here, so stop this pretense. I only want to know what troubles you."

"Summoned you—I most certainly did not summon you. How could I? I don't even know you!"

One brow shot upward. Tamara's hand flew to her mouth because she'd pictured him with just such an expression. She had no time to consider it, though, since his next odd question came so quickly. "And do you know *him?*"

He glanced toward the street and she followed his gaze, catching her breath when she saw Curt's DPI van parked there. She knew it was his by the rust spot just beneath the side mirror on the driver's door. She could barely believe he had the audacity to spy on her. On an indignant sigh she whispered, "He followed me. Why, that heavy-handed son of a—"

"Very good, although I suspect his reason for being posted there is known to you full well. This was a trap, was it not? Lure me here, and then your attentive friend over there—"

"Lure you here? Why on earth would I lure you here, and how, for God's sake? I told you I've never seen you before."

"You call to me nightly, Tamara. You've begged me to come to you until you've nearly driven me insane."

"I don't think it would be a long trip. I told you, I haven't called you. I don't even know your name."

Again his gaze searched her face and she felt her mind being searched. He sighed, frowning until his brows met. "Suppose you tell me why you think that gent would follow you, then?"

"Knowing Curt, he probably thinks it's for my own good. God knows he tosses that phrase around enough lately." Her anger softened a bit, as she thought it through more thoroughly. "He might be a little worried about me. I know Daniel is...my guardian, that is. Frankly, I'm worried myself. I don't sleep at night anymore—not ever. The only time I feel even slightly like sleeping is during the day. In fact, I've fallen asleep at my desk twice now. I take to my bed the second I get home and sleep like a rock, but only until dusk. Just at nightfall I have terrible nightmares and usually cry out loud enough to convince them both I'm losing my mind, and then I'm up and restless all night lo—" She broke off, realizing she was blurting her life story to a perfect stranger.

"Please don't stop," he said at once. He seemed keenly interested in hearing more. "Tell me about these nightmares." He must've seen her wariness. He reached out to her, touched her cheek with the tips of his long, narrow fingers. "I only want to help you. I mean you no harm."

She shook her head. "You'll only agree with me that I'm slipping around the bend." He frowned. "Cracking up," she explained. She pointed one finger at her ear and made little circles. "Wacko."

"You most certainly are not...wacko, as you put it." His hand slipped around to the back of her head and he drew her nearer. She didn't resist. She hadn't felt so perfectly at peace in months as she felt in his arms. He held her gently against him, as if she were a small child, and one hand stroked her hair. "Tell me, Tamara."

She sighed, unable to resist the smooth allure of his voice, or of his touch, though she knew it made no sense. "It's dark, and there is a jungle of sorts, and a lot of fog and mist covering the ground so I can't see my feet. I trip a lot as I run. I don't know if I'm running toward something or away from something. I know I'm looking for someone, and in the dream I know that person can help me find my way. But I call and call and he doesn't answer."

He stopped stroking her hair all at once, and she thought he tensed. "To whom do you call?"

"I think that might be what's driving me crazy. I can never remember. I wake as breathless and exhausted as if I really had been running through that forest, sometimes halfway through shouting his name—but I just can't remember."

His breath escaped in a rush. "Tamara, how does the dream make you feel?"

She stepped away from him and studied his face. "Are you a psychologist?"

"No."

"Then I shouldn't be telling you any of this." She tried to pull her gaze from his familiar face. "Because I really don't know you."

She stiffened as her name was shouted from across the ice. "Tammy!"

She grimaced. "I hate when he calls me that." She searched the eyes of her stranger again, and again she felt as if she'd just had a long-awaited reunion with someone she adored. "Are you real, or a part of my insanity?" *No, don't tell me,* she thought suddenly. *I don't want to know.* "I'd better go before Curt worries himself into a stroke."

"Does he have the right to worry?"

She paused, frowning. "If you mean is he my husband, the answer is no. We're close, but not in a romantic way. He's more like a . . . bossy older brother."

She turned and skated away across the ice toward Curt, but she felt his gaze on her back all the way there. She tried to glance over her shoulder to see if he was still there, but she caught no sight of him. Then she approached Curt and slowed her pace. He'd been hurrying across the ice, toward her.

He gripped her upper arm hard, and marched her off the edge of the ice. On the snowy ground she stumbled on her skates, but he continued propelling her at the same pace until they reached the nearest bench, and then he shoved her down onto the seat.

"Who the hell was that man?"

She shrugged, relieved that Curtis had seen him, too. "Just a stranger I met."

"I want his name!"

She frowned at the authority and anger in his voice. Curt had always been bossy but this was going too far. "We didn't get around to exchanging names, and what business is it of yours, anyway?"

"You're telling me you don't know who that was?" She nodded. "The hell you don't," he exploded. He gripped her shoulders, pulled her to her feet and held her hard. He glared at her and would have frightened her if she hadn't known him so well. "What did you think you were doing sneaking out alone at night like that? Well?"

"Skating! Ouch." His fingers bit into her shoulders. "I was only skating, Curt. You know I can't sleep. I thought some exercise—"

"Bull. You came out here to meet *him,* didn't you?"

"Who? That nice man I was talking to? For God's sake, Curtis, I—"

"Talking to? That's a nice name for it. I saw you, Tammy. You were in his arms."

Anger flared. "I don't care if I had sex with the man in the middle of the rink, Curtis Rogers. I'm a grown woman and what I do is my business. You followed me here! I don't care how worried Daniel gets, I will not put up with you spying on me, and I won't defend my actions to you. Who do you think you are?"

His grip tightened and he shook her once—then again. "The truth, Tammy. Dammit, you'll tell me the truth!" He shook her until her head wobbled on her shoulders. "You know who he was, don't you? You came here to meet him, didn't you? Didn't you!"

"L-let me go... Curt-tis you're-rr... hurt-ting..."

Her vision had blurred from the shaking and the fear that she didn't know Curt as well as she thought she did—but not so much that she couldn't see the dark form silhouetted beyond Curtis. She knew who stood there. She'd felt his presence... maybe even before she'd seen him. She felt something else, too. His blinding anger.

"Take your hands off her," the stranger growled, his voice quivering with barely contained rage.

Curt went rigid. His hands fell to his sides and his eyes widened. Tamara took a step back, her hand moving to massage one tender, bruised shoulder. The heat of the stranger's gaze on her made her look up. Those black eyes had followed the movement of her hand and his anger heated still more.

But how can I know that?

Curtis turned to face him, and took a step backward... away from the man's imposing form. Well, at least she now knew he was real. She couldn't take her gaze from him, nor he from her, it seemed. Her lips throbbed with the memory of his moving over them. She felt as if he knew it. She should say something, she thought vaguely. Sensible or not, she knew the man was about to throttle Curtis.

Before she could think of a suitable deterrent, though, Curtis croaked, "M-Marquand!" She'd never heard his voice sound the way it did.

Tamara felt the shock like a physical blow. Her gaze shot back to the stranger's face again. He regarded Curtis now. A small, humorless smile appeared on his lips, and he nodded to Curt. A sudden move caught her eye, and she glimpsed Curt thrusting a hand inside his jacket, as the bad guys did on television when reaching for a hidden gun. She stiffened in panic, but relaxed when he pulled out only a small gold crucifix, which he held toward Marquand straight-armed, in a white-knuckled grip.

For a moment the stranger didn't move. He stared fixedly at the golden symbol as if frozen. She watched him intently, shivering as her fingers involuntarily touched the spot on her throat, and she recalled the feel of those skimming incisors. Could he truly be a vampire?

The smile returned, sarcastic and bitter. He even chuckled, a sound like distant thunder rumbling from deep in his chest. He reached out to pluck the cross from Curt's hand, and he turned it several times, inspecting it closely. "Impressive," he said, and handed it back. Curt let it fall to the ground and Tamara sighed in relief, but only briefly.

She understood now what the little encounter between her and Marquand had been all about. She resented it. "You're really Marquand?"

He sketched an exaggerated bow in her direction.

She couldn't hold his gaze, embarrassed at her earlier responses to what, for him, had been only a game. "I can appreciate why you're so angry with my guardian. After all, he's been hounding you to death. However, it might interest you to know that I had no part in it. I've argued on your behalf until I'm hoarse with it. I won't bother to do so anymore. I truly appreciate that you chose not to haul Daniel into court, but I would not suggest you attempt to use me to deliver your messages in future."

She saw his brow cock up again, and she caught her breath. "Your guardian? You said so once before, but I—" His eyes widened. "St. Claire?"

"As if you weren't aware of it before your little performance over there." She shook her head, her fingers once again trailing over the tender spot on her throat. "I might even be able to see the humor in it, if I wasn't already on the brink of—" She broke off and shook her head as her eyes filled, and her airways seemed suddenly blocked.

"Tamara, that isn't what I—"

She stopped him by shaking her head violently. "I'll see he gets your message. He may be an ass, Marquand, but I love him dearly. I don't want him to bear the brunt of a lawsuit."

She turned on her heel. "Tamara, wait! What happened to your parents? How did he—Tamara!" She ignored him, mounting the ice and speeding to the opposite side, where she'd left her duffel bag. She stumbled over the snow to snatch it up, and sat hard on the nearest bench, bending to unlace her skates. Her fingers shook. She could barely see for the tears clouding her vision.

Why was she reacting so strongly to the man's insensitive ploy? Why did she feel such an acute sense of betrayal?

Because I'm losing my mind, that's why.

Anger made her look up. She felt it as if it were a palpable thing. She yanked one skate off, stomped her foot into a boot and unlaced the other without looking. Her gaze was on Marquand, who had Curtis by the lapels now, and was shaking him the way Curt had shaken her a few moments ago. When he stopped he released Curt, shoving

him away in the same motion. Curt landed on his backside
in the snow. Marquand's back was all she could see, but she
heard his words clearly, though not with her ears. *If I ever
see you lay hands on her again, Rogers, you will pay for it
with your life. Do I make myself sufficiently clear?*

Sufficiently clear to me, Tamara thought. Curt seemed
to be in no danger of being murdered at the moment. She
put her skates in her bag and slipped away while they were
still arguing.

Pain like a skewer running the length of his breastbone,
Eric stroked the pink fur of the earmuffs she'd abandoned
in her rush to get away from him. She'd left her coat, too.
He carried it slung over one arm as he followed the two.
Rogers had caught up to Tamara only a few minutes after
she'd left. He kept pace with her angry strides, talking
constantly in his efforts to end her anger.

"I'm sorry, Tammy. I swear to you, I didn't mean to hurt
you. Can't you understand I was scared half out of my
mind when I saw you in his arms? My God, don't you know
what could've happened?"

He scanned the bastard's mind with his own, and found
no indication that Tamara was in danger from him. He did
the same after they'd entered Daniel St. Claire's gloomy
Victorian mansion, unwilling to leave her in their hands
until he could be certain. And even then he couldn't leave.

How the hell had St. Claire managed to become her
guardian? When Eric had left her all those years ago she'd
had two adoring parents who'd nearly lost their minds
when they'd thought they might lose her. He could still see
them—the small Miranda, a frail-looking woman with
mouse brown hair and pretty green eyes brimming with love
whenever she glanced at her adorable child. She'd been in
hysterics that night at the hospital. Eric had seen her
clutching the doctor's white coat, shaking her head fast at

what he was telling her as tears poured unchecked over her face. Her husband's quiet devastation had been even more painful to witness. Kenneth had seemed deflated, sinking into a chair as if he'd never rise again, his blond hair falling over one eye.

What in hell had happened to them? He sank to a rotted, snow-dusted stump outside the mansion, his head in his hands. "I never should have left her," he whispered into the night. "My God, I never should have left her."

He remained there in anguish until the sky began to pale in the east. She now thought he'd only used her to make a point to St. Claire. She obviously had no conscious memory of him, nor knowledge of the connection between them. She called to him while in the throes of her subconscious mind—in a dream. She couldn't even recall his name.

She paused outside Daniel's office door to brace herself, her hand on the knob. Last night she'd avoided further confrontation with Curt by pleading exhaustion, a lie he'd believed since he knew how little sleep she'd been getting. This morning she'd deliberately remained in her room, feigning sleep when Daniel called from the doorway. She'd known he wouldn't wake her if he thought she was finally sleeping. She'd waited until he left for DPI headquarters in White Plains, then had got herself ready and driven in late, in her battered VW Bug. Her day had been packed solid with the trivial work they gave her there. Her measly security clearance wasn't high enough to allow her to work on anything important. Except for Jamey Bryant. He was important—to her, at least. He was only a class three clairvoyant in DPI's book, but he was class one in hers. Besides, she loved the kid.

She sighed, smiling as she thought of him, then stiffened her spine for the coming encounter. She gripped the knob more tightly, then paused as Curt's voice came through the wood.

"Look at her! I'm telling you, something is happening and you're a fool if you don't see it."

"She's confused," Daniel said, sounding pained. "I admit, the proximity is having an unexpected effect on her, but she can't be blamed for that. She has no idea what's happening to her."

"*You* think. *I* think she ought to be under constant observation."

She grew angry fast, and threw the door open. "Do you have any idea how tired I am of being talked about like one of your cases?"

Both men looked up, startled. They exchanged uneasy glances and Daniel came out of his chair so fast it scraped over the tiled floor. "Now, Tam, what makes you think we were discussing you? Actually, we were talking about a case. One we obviously disagree about."

She smirked, crossing her arms over her chest. "Oh, really? Which case?"

"Sorry, Tammy," Curt snapped. "Your security clearance isn't high enough."

"When has it ever been high enough?"

"Tam, please." Daniel came toward her, folded her in a gentle embrace and kissed her cheek. He stood back and searched her face. "Are you all right?"

"Why on earth wouldn't I be?" His concern softened her somewhat, but she was still sick and tired of his coddling.

"Curt told me you met Marquand last night." He shook his head. "I want you to tell me everything that happened. Everything he said to you, did to you. Did..." Daniel paled right before her eyes. "Did he touch you?"

"Had her crushed against him like he'd never let go," Curt exploded. "I told you, Daniel—"

"I'd like to hear her tell me." His pale blue eyes sought hers again. They dropped to the collar of her turquoise turtleneck, under the baggy white pullover sweater. She thought he would collapse.

Curtis seemed to notice her choice of attire at the same instant, and he caught his breath. "Tammy, my God, did he—"

"He most certainly did not! Do you two have any idea how insane you both sound?"

"Show me," Daniel said softly.

She shook her head and expelled a rush of air. "All right, but first I want to explain something. Marquand seems to be very well aware of what you two think he is. This meeting at the rink last night, I think, was his way of sending you a message, and the message is lay off. I don't think he was kidding." She hooked her first two fingers beneath the neck of the shirt and pulled it down to show them the blue-and-violet bruise he'd left on her neck.

Daniel gasped. "Look closely, you two. There are no fang marks, just a . . . well, let's be frank about it, a hickey. I let a perfect stranger give me a hickey, which should illustrate to you both just how much stress I've been under lately. Between this sleep disorder and your overprotectiveness, I feel like I'm in a pressure cooker." Daniel was leaning closer, breathing down her neck as he inspected the bruise.

He satisfied himself and put a hand on her shoulder. "Did he hurt you, sweetheart?"

She couldn't stop the little smile that question evoked, even though she erased it immediately. "Hurt her?" Curtis slapped one hand on the surface of the desk. "She was loving every minute of it." He glared at her. "Don't you realize what could've happened out there?"

"Of course I do, Curtis. He could've ripped my jugular

open and sucked all my blood out and left me dying there on the ice with two holes in my throat!''

"If I hadn't scared him off," Curt began.

"Keep your story straight, Curt. It was he who scared you off. You were shaking me until my teeth rattled, if you remember correctly. If he hadn't come to my defense I might have come into work wearing a neck brace today."

Curt clamped his jaw shut under Daniel's withering gaze. Daniel shifted his glance to Tamara again. "He came to your defense, you say?" She nodded. "Hmm."

"And," Tamara went on, almost as an afterthought, "he took the crucifix right out of Curt's hand. It did not even burn a brand in his palm, or whatever it's supposed to do. Doesn't that prove anything?"

"Yeah." Curt wore a sulking-child look on his face. "Proves vampires are not affected by religious symbols."

Tamara rolled her eyes, then heard Daniel mutter, "Interesting." She felt as if she, even with her strange symptoms, was the only sane person in the room.

"I know you think we're overreacting to this, Tam," Daniel told her. "But I don't want you leaving the house after dark anymore."

She bristled. "I will go where I want, when I want. I am twenty-six years old, Daniel, and if this nonsense doesn't stop, then I'm..." She paused long enough to get his full attention before she blurted, "Moving out."

"Tam, you wouldn't—"

"Not unless you force me, Daniel. And if I find either you or Curt following me again, I'll consider myself forced." She felt a lump in her throat at the pained look on Daniel's face. She made her tone gentler when she said, "I'm going home now. Good night."

CHAPTER THREE

Her mental cries woke him earlier tonight than last. Eric stood less than erect and squeezed his eyes shut tight, as if doing so might clear his mind. Rising before sunset produced an effect in him not unlike what humans feel after a night of heavy drinking. Bracing one hand upon the smooth mahogany, his fingertips brushing the satin lining within, he focused on Tamara. He wanted only to comfort her. If he could ease the torment of her subconscious mind, though she might not be fully aware of it, she'd feel better. She might even be more able to sleep. He couldn't be sure, though. Her situation was unique, after all.

He focused on her mind, still hearing her whispered pleas. *Where are you, Eric? Why won't you come to me? I'm lost. I need you.*

He swallowed once, and concentrated every ounce of his power into a single invisible beam of thought, shooting through time and space, directed at her. *I am here, Tamara.*

I can't see you!

The immediate response shocked him. He hadn't been certain he could make her aware of his thoughts. Again he focused. *I am near. I will come to you soon, love. Now you must rest. You needn't call to me in your dreams anymore. I have heard—I will come.*

He awaited a response, but felt none. The emotions that reached him, though, were tense, uncertain. He wanted to ease her mind, but he'd done all he could for the moment.

The sun far above, though unseen by him, was not unfelt. It sapped his strength. He took a moment to be certain of his balance and crossed slowly to the hearth, bending to rekindle the sparks of this morning's fire. That done, he used a long wooden match to ignite the three oil lamps posted around the room. With fragrant cherry logs emitting aromatic warmth, and the golden lamplight, the Oriental rugs over the concrete floor and the paintings he'd hung, the place seemed a bit less like a tomb in the bowels of the earth. He sat himself carefully in the oversize antique oak rocking chair, and allowed his muscles to relax. His head fell heavily back against the cushion, and he reached, without looking, for the remote control on the pedestal table beside him. He thumbed a button. His heavy lids fell closed as music surrounded him.

A smile touched his lips as the bittersweet notes brought a memory. He'd seen young Amadeus perform in Paris. 1775, had it been? So many years. He'd been enthralled—an ordinary boy of seventeen, awestruck by the gift of another, only two years older. The sublime feeling had remained with him for days after that performance, he recalled. He'd talked about it until his poor mother's ears were sore. He'd had Jaqueline on the brink of declaring he'd fallen in love with a man she'd never met, and she'd teased and cajoled until he'd managed to get her a seat at his side for the next night's performance. His sister had failed to see what caused him to be so impressed. "He is good," she'd declared, fanning herself in the hot, crowded hall. "But I've seen better." He smiled at the memory. She hadn't been referring to the young man's talents, but to his appearance. He'd caught her peering over her fan's lacy edge at a skinny dandy she considered "better."

He sighed. He'd thought it tragic that a man of such genius had died at thirty-five. Lately he'd wondered if it was so tragic, after all. Eric, too, had died at thirty-five, but in a far different manner. His was a living death. All things considered, he hadn't convinced himself that Mozart had suffered the less desirable fate. Of the two of them, Mozart must be the most serene. He couldn't possibly be the most alone. There were times when he wished the guillotine had got to him before Roland had.

Such maudlin thoughts on such a delightfully snowy night? I don't recall you were all that eager to meet the blade, at the time.

Roland! Eric's head snapped up, buzzing with energy now that the sun had set. He rose and hurriedly released the locks, to run through the hall and take the stairs two at a time. He yanked the front door open just as his dearest friend mounted the front steps. The two embraced violently, and Eric drew Roland inside.

Roland paused in the center of the room, cocking his head and listening to Mozart's music. "What's this? Not a recording, surely! It sounds as if the orchestra were right here, in this very room!"

Eric shook his head, having forgotten that the last time he'd seen Roland he hadn't yet installed the state-of-the-art stereo system, with speakers in every room. "Come, I'll show you." He drew his friend toward the equipment, stacked near the far wall, and withdrew a CD from its case. Roland turned the disc in his hand, watching the light dance in vivid rainbows of green, blue and yellow.

"They had no such inventions where I have been." He returned the disc to its case, and replaced it on the shelf.

"Where *have* you been, you recluse? It's been twenty years." Roland had not aged a day. He still had the swarthy good looks he'd had as a thirty-two year old mortal and the build of an athlete.

"Ahh, paradise. A tiny island in the South Pacific, Eric. No meddling humans to contend with. Just simple villagers who accept what they see instead of feeling the need to explain it. I tell you, Eric, it's a haven for our kind. The palms, the sweet smell of the night—"

"How did you live?" Eric knew he sounded doubtful. He'd always despised the loneliness of this existence. Roland embraced it. "Don't tell me you've taken to tapping the veins of innocent natives."

Roland's brows drew together. "You know better. The animals there keep me in good stead. The wild boar are particularly—"

"Pigs' blood!" Eric shouted. "I think the sun must have penetrated your coffin! Pigs' blood! Ach!"

"Wild boars, not pigs."

"Great difference, I'll wager." Eric urged Roland toward the velvet-covered antique settee. "Sit. I'll get refreshment to restore your senses."

Roland watched suspiciously as Eric moved behind the bar, to the small built-in refrigerator. "What have you, a half dozen freshly killed virgins stored in that thing?"

Eric threw back his head and laughed, realizing just how long it had been since he'd done so. He withdrew a plastic bag from the refrigerator, and rummaged beneath the bar for glasses. When he handed the drink to Roland, he felt himself thoroughly perused.

"Is it the girl's nightly cries that trouble you so?"

Eric blinked. "You've heard her, too?"

"I hear her cries when I look inside your mind, Eric. They are what brought me to you. Tell me what this is about."

Eric sighed, and took a seat in a claw-footed, brocade cushioned chair near the fireplace. Few coals glowed in this hearth. He really ought to kindle it. Should some nosy human manage to scale the gate and breach the security systems, they might well notice that smoke spiraled from the chimney, but no fire warmed the grate.

Reading his thoughts, Roland set his glass aside. "I'll do that. You simply talk."

Eric sighed again. Where to begin? "I came to know of a child, right after you left last time. A beautiful girl, with raven curls and cherub's cheeks and eyes like glossy bits of coal."

"One of the Chosen?" Roland sat forward.

"Yes. She was one of those rare humans with a slight psychic connection to the undead, although, like most, she was completely unaware of it. I've found that there are ways of detecting the Chosen, aside from our natural awareness of them, you know."

Roland looked around from where he'd hunkered before the hearth. "Really?"

Eric nodded. "All those humans who can be transformed, those we call Chosen, share a common ancestor. Prince Vlad the Impaler." He glanced sharply at Roland. "Was he the first?"

Roland shook his head. "I know your love of science, Eric, but some things are better left alone. Go on with your story."

Eric felt a ripple of exasperation at Roland's tight-lipped stance on the subject. He swallowed his irritation and continued. "They also share a rare blood antigen. We all had it, as humans. It's known as Belladonna. Only those with both these unlikely traits can become vampires. They are the Chosen."

"Doesn't seem like an earth-shattering discovery to me, Eric. We've always been able to sense the Chosen ones, instinctively."

"But other humans haven't. Some of them have now discovered the same things I have. DPI knows about it. They can pinpoint Chosen humans, and then watch them, and wait for one of us to approach. I believe that is precisely what has happened with Tamara."

"Perhaps you need to back up a bit, old friend," Roland said gently.

Eric pushed one hand through his black hair, lifting it from his shoulders and clenching a fist in the tangles. "I couldn't stay away from her, Roland. God help me, I tried, but I couldn't. Something in her tugged at me. I used to look in on her as she slept. You should've seen her then. Sooty lashes on her rosy cheeks, lips like a small pink bow." He looked up, feeling absurdly defensive. "I never meant her harm, you know. How could I? I adored the child."

Roland frowned. "This should not trouble you. It happens all the time, this unseen bond between our kind and the Chosen. Many was the night I peered in upon you as a boy. Rarely to find you asleep, though. Usually, you were awake and teasing your poor sister."

Eric absorbed that information with dawning understanding. "You never told me. I'd thought you only came to me when I was in danger."

"I'm sorry we haven't discussed this matter before, Eric. It simply never came up. You only *saw* me those times you were in danger. There was little time for discretion when a coach was about to flatten you, or when I pulled you spluttering from the Channel."

"Then you felt the same connection to me that I felt for her?"

"I felt a connection, yes. An urge to protect. I can't say it's the same because I haven't experienced what you felt for the child. But, Eric, many young ones over the centuries have had a vampire as a guardian and never even known it. After all, we don't go to them to harm, or transform, or even make contact. Only to watch over, and protect."

Eric's shoulders slumped forward, so great was his relief. He shook his head once and resumed his story. "I woke one night to sense her spirit fading. She was slipping away so steadily I was barely able to get to her in time." The same pain he'd felt then swept over him now, and his voice went lower. "I found her in hospital, her tiny face whiter than the sheets tucked around her. Her lips...they were blue. I overheard a doctor telling her parents that she'd lost too much blood to survive, and that her type was so rare no donors had been located. He told them to prepare themselves. She was dying, Roland."

Roland swore softly.

"So you see my dilemma. A child I'd come to love lay dying, and I knew I alone had the power to save her."

"You didn't transform her! Not a small child, Eric. She'd be better dead than to exist as we must. Her young mind could never grasp—"

"I didn't transform her. I probably couldn't if I'd tried. She hadn't enough blood left to mingle with mine. I saw another option, though. I simply opened my vein and—"

"She drank from you?"

Eric closed his eyes. "As if she were dying of thirst. I suppose, in a manner, she was. Her vitality began to return at once. I was ecstatic."

"You had right to be." Roland grinned now. "You saved the child. I've never heard of anything like this happening before, Eric, but apparently, it worked." He paused, regarding Eric intensely. "It did work, did it not? The child lives?"

Eric nodded. "Before I left her bedside, Roland, she opened her eyes and looked at me, and I swear to you, I felt her probing my mind. When I turned to go she gripped my hand in her doll-sized one and she whispered my name. 'Eric,' she said. 'Don't go just yet. Don't leave me.'"

"My God." Roland sank back onto the settee, blinking as if he were thunderstruck. "Did you stay?"

"I couldn't refuse her. I stayed the night at her bedside, though I had to hide on the window ledge every time someone entered the room. When they discovered the improvement in her, the place was a madhouse for a time. But they soon saw that she would be fine, and decided to let the poor child rest."

"And then?"

Eric smiled softly. "I held her on my lap. She stayed awake, though she needed to rest, and insisted I invent story upon story to tell her. She made me sing to her, Roland. I'd never sung to anyone in my existence. Yet the whole time she was inside my mind, reading my every thought. I couldn't believe the strength of the connection between us. It was stronger even than the one between you and me."

Roland nodded. "Our blood only mixed. Yours was nearly pure in her small body. It's no wonder... What happened?"

"Toward dawn she fell asleep, and I left her. I felt it would only confuse the sweet child to have contact with one of us. I took myself as far away as I could, severed all contact with her. I refused even to think of seeing her again, until now. I thought the mental bond would weaken with time and distance. But it hasn't. I've only been back in the western hemisphere a few months, and she calls to me every night. Something happened to her parents after I'd left her, Roland. I don't know what, but she ended up in the custody of Daniel St. Claire."

"He's DPI!" Roland shot to his feet, stunned.

"So is she," Eric muttered, dropping his forehead into his hand.

"You cannot go to her, Eric. You mustn't trust her, it could be your end."

"I *don't* trust her. As for going to her...I have no choice about that."

Even while Tamara was arguing with Daniel and Curtis, he'd been on her mind. All day she had been unable to get that mysterious stranger—who didn't seem a stranger at all—out of her thoughts. She'd only managed to cram him far to the back, to allow herself to concentrate on her work. Now that she was home, in the secure haven of her room, and now that she'd wakened from her after-work nap, she felt refreshed, energized and free to turn last night's adventure over in her mind.

She paused and frowned. Since when did she wake refreshed? She usually woke trembling, breathless and afraid. Why was tonight different? She glanced out at the snow-spotted sky, and realized it was fully dark. She normally woke from her nightmare just at dusk. She struggled to remember. It seemed to her she *had* had the dream—or she'd begun to. She remembered the forest and the mists, the brambles and darkness. She remembered calling that elusive name. . . .

And hearing an answer. Yes. From very far away she'd heard an answer; a calm, deep voice, full of comfort and strength, had promised to come to her. He'd told her to rest. She'd felt uncertain, until the music came. Soft strains she thought to be Mozart—something from *Elvira Madigan*—soothed her taut nerves.

She allowed a small smile. Maybe she was getting past this thing, whatever it was. The smile died when she wondered if that was true, or whether she was only exchanging one problem for another. The man from the ice rink filled her mind again. Marquand—the one Daniel insisted was a vampire. He'd kissed her and, much as she hated to admit it, she'd responded to that kiss with every cell in her body.

She rose slowly from her bed and tightened the single sash that held the red satin robe around her. She leaned over her dressing table and examined the bruised skin of her neck in the mirror. Her fingers touched the spot. She recalled the odd, swooning sensation she'd experienced when he'd sucked the skin between his teeth, and wondered at it.

Lack of sleep, and too much stress.

But he knew my name. . . .

Simple enough to answer that one. He'd done a little research on the man who'd been harassing him. Daniel was her legal guardian. It was a matter of public record.

Then why did he seem so surprised when I told him that?

Good acting. He must have known. He just assumed I'd be the easiest, most effective way to get his point across.

She frowned at her reflection, not liking the look of disappointment she saw there. She tried to erase it. "He only wanted to scare Daniel into laying off, so he followed me to the rink for that little performance. Imagine him going so far as to actually..."

She pressed her palm to the mark on her throat, and turned from the mirror. She'd failed to convince herself that was all there had been to it. So many things about the man defied explanation. Why did he seem so familiar to her? How had he made her feel as if he were reading her thoughts? What about the way she'd seemed to hear what he said, when he hadn't even spoken? And what about this... this *longing.*

Blood flooded her cheeks and a fist poked into her stomach. Desire. She recognized the feeling for what it was. Foolish though it was, Tamara was lusting after a man she didn't know—a man she felt as if she'd known forever. She had to admit, at least to herself, that the man they called Marquand stirred reactions in her as no other man ever had.

As she stood she slowly became aware of a peculiar lightheadedness stealing over her. Not dizziness, but rather a floating sensation, though her bare feet still connected her to the floor. A warm whirlwind stirred around her ankles, twisting up her legs, swishing the hem of the robe so the satin brushed over her calves.

She blinked slowly, pressing her palm to her forehead, waiting for the feeling to pass. The French doors blew open all at once, as if from a great gust, and the wind that surged through felt warm, heady.... It smelled faintly of bay rum.

Impossible. It's twenty degrees out there.

Yet it lingered; the warmth and the scent. She felt a pull—a mental magnet she was powerless to resist. She faced the heated blast, even as it picked up force. The scarlet satin sailed behind her. It twisted around her legs like a twining serpent.

Like the mist in my dream.

Her hair billowed around her face. The robe's sash snapped against her thighs. She moved toward the doors even as she told herself not to. She resisted, but the pull was stronger than her own will. Her feet scuffed over the soft carpet, then scraped over the cold, wet wood floor of the balcony. The whirlwind surrounded her, propelled her to the rail. She heard the doors slam behind her, and didn't even turn. Her eyes probed the darkness below. Would this unseen hand pull her right over? She didn't think she'd be able to stop it if it wanted to.

God, what is happening to me?

She resisted and the wind stiffened. The sash whipped loose and the robe blew back. No part of her went untouched by this tempest. Like invisible hands it swirled around her thighs, between them. Her breasts quivered. Her nipples stood erect and pulsing. She throbbed with heightened awareness, her flesh hypersensitive to the touch of the wind as it mercilessly stroked her body. Her heart raced, and before she could stop herself she'd let her head fall back, closed her eyes and moaned softly at the intensity of the sensations.

All at once it simply stopped. The warmth and the essence of bay rum lingered, but that intimate whirlwind died slowly, giving her control of her body once more. She didn't know what it had been. A near breakdown? A mental lapse of some sort? Whatever, it was over.

Shaken, she pushed her hands through her hair, uncaring that her robe still hung gaping, having been driven down, baring one shoulder. She turned to go back inside.

He stood so close she nearly bumped into his massive chest. Her head came up fast and her breath caught in her throat. His black eyes seemed molten as they raked her. The mystery wind stirred gently. She could see silver glints behind those onyx eyes, and she felt their heat touch her as the wind had when his gaze moved slowly upward from her bare feet. She felt it scorching her as it lifted, over her legs. The hot gaze paused at the mound of black curls at the apex of her thighs and she thought she'd go up in flames. Finally it moved again, with deliberate slowness over her stomach. She commanded her arms to come to life—to pull her robe together. They did not respond. His eyes seemed to devour her breasts, and she knew her nipples stiffened under that heated stare. The man licked his lips and she very nearly groaned aloud. She closed her eyes, but they refused to stay that way. They opened again, against her will. They focused on his, though she didn't want to see the lust in his eyes. Finally he looked at her throat. The bruise he'd put on her there seemed to come alive with his gaze. It tingled, and she felt the muscle beneath the skin twitch spasmodically. She saw his Adam's apple move as he swallowed. He closed his eyes briefly, and when they opened again they locked with hers, refusing to allow her to look away.

Her arms regained feeling and she jerked the robe together in a move that showed her anger. "You," she whispered. She felt fear and confusion. More than that, she felt sheer joy to see him again. She refused to let him see it. "What are you doing here?"

CHAPTER FOUR

"Waiting for you," he said slowly, watching her.

Her mind rebelled against what that implied. "That's ridiculous. How could you have known I'd come out here?"

The intensity of his gaze boring into her eyes was staggering. "I summoned you here, Tamara . . . just as you've summoned me nightly with your cries."

Her brows drew together so far it hurt. She shook her head in denial as she searched his face. "You said that before. I still don't know what you mean."

"Tamara . . ." He lifted one hand in slow motion. He turned it gracefully at the wrist, and trailed the backs of his long fingers downward, over her face. She closed her eyes involuntarily at the pure rapture his touch evoked, but quickly forced them open again and took a step back. "Listen to your heart. It wants to tell you—"

"Then I *do* know you!" She felt as if there were a bird trapped in her stomach, flapping its wings desperately. Her eyes tugged at his as she tried to pull the answer from their endless depths. "I thought so before. Tell me when we met, Marquand. You seem so . . . familiar to me." *Familiar* wasn't the word that had been on her lips. He seemed precious to her—like someone she'd cherished once, someone she'd lost.

She saw the indecision in his eyes, and a glimmer that might have been pain, before he closed them and shook his head. "You will remember in time. I cannot force it on you—your mind is not yet ready. For now, though, I would ask that you simply trust me. I will not harm you, Tamara."

His eyes opened again, and danced over her face. The way he looked at her made her feel as if he couldn't do so enough to appease him, as if he were trying to absorb her through his eyes. She stilled her responses to the feeling, and reminded herself of the game he'd played with her last night. Her shoulders squared. Her chin lifted.

"Your message was delivered, Marquand. Daniel knows about our meeting and your little . . . performance. I made sure he understood." As she spoke her fingers touched the still-tender skin at her throat. "It probably won't change anything, though. He doesn't listen to me where you're concerned, so you can see how ineffective this conversation will be. Leave me alone. If you have something to say to Daniel, say it to him in person."

He listened . . . so well it seemed he heard her thoughts as well as her words. When she finished he tilted his head very slightly to one side. "You believe I kissed you only to make a point with St. Claire," he stated, his words slow, carefully enunciated and laced with the barest hint of an accent that she had yet to place. "And the thought causes you pain."

She released a clipped sigh and shook her head. "Why would it cause me pain? I don't know you. I don't care—"

"You felt drugged when I kissed you, sweet Tamara. You felt the ground tilt beneath you, and the sky above begin to spin. Your heart raced, your pulse roared in your temples. Your skin came to life with sensation. In those moments, as I held you, nothing else existed. No," he said when she shook her head fast, and parted her lips to blurt angry denials. "No, don't. I know what you felt, because I felt it, too. The touch of your hands, the taste of your mouth, the feel of your body pressed to mine sent me to the very edge of my control."

She felt the blood rush into her face. Her cheeks burned hotter with his every word, and yet the familiar knot of longing formed in the pit of her stomach. She wanted to tell him he was crazy to believe that, but she couldn't seem to form the words.

Again his hand rose to her face, and she didn't pull away this time. She couldn't say why, but she felt like crying. "Tamara, I swear to you, I did not know you were even acquainted with St. Claire until you said the words. I came to you because you begged me to do so. In your dreams you begged me to come."

Her eyes had begun to drift closed as his hand stroked her cheek, but they flew wide now. She searched her brain frantically. How could he know about the dreams? She shook her head quickly. "No, that isn't true."

"What isn't true? That you dream each night before dusk? That the dreams are testing your sanity, Tamara? That you cry out to someone in your sleep and cannot recall the name when you wake? Do not forget, you confided all of these things to me last night."

Relief nearly made her limp. "That's right, I did." She had told him about her nightmares. That explained why he knew.

"The dream was different tonight, though," he said softly.

Again her eyes widened. It had been different. He couldn't know that. She hadn't told him that. She swallowed the lump in her throat. "The name I call, I can't remember what it is, but I know it isn't Marquand. Why do you want to play with my mind?"

"I want only to ease your mind. It is true, you have never cried my surname. It is my first name you call in your sleep." His hand had fallen from her face, to gently stroke her hair.

Breathlessly she whispered, "I don't even know your first name. So it can't be—"

"Yes, you do, Tamara." His gaze took on a new dimension as he stared into her eyes. "You know my name. Say it."

And she did. Just like that, she knew the name she'd cried over and over again in her recurring dream. She knew it as well as she knew her own. The shroud had been lifted from her memory, and she knew. But it couldn't be him. She shook her head. "You aren't—"

"I am." Both his hands rested on her shoulders now, and he squeezed gently. She winced inwardly because he'd put pressure on the spots where Curt had held her last night, and the skin there had bruised. He immediately readjusted his grip on her, as if he'd sensed her discomfort at the instant she'd felt it. "Say it, Tamara."

Choking on unshed tears, she croaked, "Eric?"

He nodded, his face relaxing in an approving half smile. "Yes. Eric. If you require confirmation, I'm certain your St. Claire can provide it."

She looked at the floor, her relief so great the muscles of her neck relaxed. She didn't need confirmation. She knew he told the truth. Why this intense relief, though? And why had she dreamed of him in the first place?

"You've begged me to come to you, Tamara, and I am here." He caught her chin in gentle fingers, and lifted her face to him. "I'm here."

She wanted to fling herself into his arms. She wanted to hold him desperately and beg him not to leave her ever again. But that was crazy. It was insane. *She* was insane. As tears spilled over and rolled slowly down her face, she shook her head. "This isn't happening. It isn't real. I'm hallucinating, or it's just another dream. That's all. It isn't real."

He pulled her against him suddenly, his arms going around her, his hands stroking her back and shoulders, lifting her hair, caressing her nape. "It is real, Tamara. I am real, and what you feel for me is real . . . more real, I think, than anything else in your life." His head turned and she felt his lips pressed to her hair just above her temple...lower, to her cheekbone...lower, to the hollow of her cheek. His voice uneven, he spoke near her ear. "How did St. Claire manage to get custody of you? What happened to your family?"

She found herself relaxing against him, allowing his embrace to warm and comfort her. "I was six when I fell through a plate glass window," she told him, her voice barely audible to her own ears. "I severed the arteries in both wrists and nearly bled to death. They called it a miracle when I pulled through, because they hadn't been able to locate any donors with my blood type. Everyone expected me to die." She drew a shuddering breath. In truth, she remembered very little about the accident, or her life to that point. Daniel had always insisted it was probably best for her not to try to remember. What was blocked out was blocked out for a reason, he'd said. If her mind didn't think she could handle it, she probably couldn't. After all, near-death experiences were traumatic, especially for a six-year-old child.

She released the air she'd taken in, drew a steadier breath and continued. "I was still hospitalized when my parents were taken with an extremely rare virulent infection. By the time the virus was isolated and identified, they...they'd both succumbed."

"I am more sorry for that than I can tell you," he said softly, his breath caressing her skin as he spoke. "I wish I had been there for you."

"So do I," she blurted before she had a chance to consider the words. She cleared her throat. "But Daniel was there. He worked part-time in the research lab at the hospital then. As soon as he heard about the miracle girl upstairs, he came to see me. After that he was there every day. He brought presents with every visit, and constantly went on about how he'd always wanted a little girl like me. By the time my parents got sick, Daniel and I were best friends. When they died he petitioned the courts for custody, and got it. I had no other close relatives. If it hadn't been for Daniel, I would've been alone."

She felt his swift inhalation, and the slight stiffening of his body. "I'm sorry." The words were almost a moan, so much pain came through in them. His arms tightened around her and he rocked her slowly.

God, why did his touch feel like heaven? Why did the wide, hard chest beneath her head and the steel arms around her feel like the safest cocoon in all the world?

His voice only slightly more normal, he said, "It was Daniel who arranged for your employment at DPI, then." She only nodded, moving her head minimally against his chest. "And what do you do there, Tamara? Do you work with St. Claire?"

"No," she mumbled into the fabric of his coat. "My security clearance isn't—" She broke off, stiffening, and jerked away from him. My God, he'd played her well! "DPI is a government agency, a subdivision of the CIA, for God's sake. And you are the subject of one of their most long-running investigations. I certainly don't intend to discuss what I do there with you." She broke eye contact, and shook her head in self-deprecation. "God, you're good. I was actually buying all of this. You just wanted to milk information from me."

"You know better." His deep voice held anger now, and for the first time Tamara felt afraid of him. She backed up another step and felt the iron rail press into the small of her back. Eric Marquand stood between her and the doors. "I only want to discern whether I can trust you. St. Claire is out to destroy me. I cannot dismiss the possibility that you are a part of that plan."

"Daniel wouldn't hurt a fly!" She bristled at the suggestion that her beloved Daniel was anything less than the sweet, loving man she knew him to be.

"I know that to be false. I do not need proof of his intent. I already have it. It is you I need to be sure of, Tamara. Tell me what your duties entail."

He took a step nearer and there was nowhere for her to go. "I won't," she told him. "I can't betray the division...or Daniel."

"You would rather betray me?"

She shook her head fast, confusion muddling her brain. "I couldn't betray you. I know nothing about you."

"You could easily be the instrument of my destruction."

"But I wouldn't—"

"Then tell me. Answer whatever I ask, it is vital—" She shook her head again. He sighed and pushed one hand back through his hair, loosening several black silk strands from the queue in the back. When he looked into her eyes again the intensity had returned. "I can force you, you know."

Fear tiptoed over her spine. "If you touch me, I'll scream."

"I don't need to touch you. I can make you obey my will just as I made you come out here tonight...with my mind."

"I think you need help, Marquand. You're more screwed up than I am, and that's saying something."

One raven brow rose inquiringly. "You doubt what I know to be true?" He stared at her, and she saw an iridescent shimmer, as if the jet irises were suddenly translucent and the swirling light behind them came through. She felt her mind turn to water, and the hot whirlwind began to stir around her ankles, gaining force as it rose until it sur-

rounded her like a twister. Her hair whipped her face. The
satin robe flagellated her legs from calf to thigh. The wind
moved, forcing her forward until only millimeters separated her from him.

He put his hands on her throat, his thumbs caressing the
hollows above her clavicle. His fingers slipped beneath the
material of the robe at her shoulders. The wind whipped the
sash free, seemingly at his command. Slowly he pushed
the scarlet satin from her shoulders, and it fell, to her horror, in a shimmering cascade at her feet. Yet she was incapable of lifting her arms to prevent it. She tried to tell her
body to move. He wasn't holding her to him by force. Her
arms hadn't been pinioned to her sides by his iron grip.
They only hung limply there, abnormally heavy, unable to
move. Her feet seemed to have the same mysterious mal-
ady. She could not make them take her a single step away
from him.

Her eyes had followed the soft red cloth as it fell, but he
caught her chin now and lifted it. He stared down into her
eyes, but his gaze shifted every few seconds to her throat.

Part of her mind screamed in protest. Another, primal
part screamed for his touch. He lowered his head and
caught her earlobe between his lips. He nibbled it so lightly
his touch was almost imperceptible, yet desire shot through
her in fiery jolts. His lips trailed a path around her face and
stopped only when they reached hers. They lingered there,
barely touching. His hands touched the backs of her thighs
and rose slowly, cupping her buttocks, squeezing, parting.
One slipped around her hips, to cup her most intimate
place, while the other remained behind her, to hold her
immobile. She felt his fingers touch lightly, part her, probe
her, and she heard a stifled whimper that must have been
hers. Fire coursed through her veins, heating her blood
until it boiled. She wanted this . . . damn him, he was making her want it!

Both hands flattened against her stomach and inched slowly upward. She trembled violently, knowing what was next. Awaiting it with a burning need that came against her will. Still his lips worked hers, sucking at them, first upper, then lower. Biting them softly, licking them with quick tiny flicks of his tongue, followed by slow, languorous laps that traced their shape. His fingers finally reached her breasts. He positioned a thumb and forefinger at each nipple, barely touching. She moaned low and hoarsely in supplication, and he closed them, pinching, rolling the erect nubs between his fingers until they pulsed like the rest of her.

She realized she'd regained use of her arms when she found them linking behind his head and pulling him closer. Her mouth opened wide to him, and his tongue plunged into it, stroking hers, twining with hers, tugging at it. He pulled it into his own silken moistness, and suckled the way she wished he would suckle her breasts. They throbbed for his mouth.

Before she'd completed the thought his hands were at her back, between her shoulder blades. His lips burned a path of liquid heat down over her chin, over her throat, along her chest. She arched backward, supported by his hands behind her, one at her back, one at her buttocks. He bent over her and unerringly found one swollen crest with his mouth. Mercilessly he worried it, licking until she whimpered, sucking until she cried out and biting until her hands tangled in his hair, holding him to her.

She couldn't catch her breath. She wanted him so badly it was out of control. Her center throbbed with hot moisture, and longed to be filled ... with him.

He lifted his head and eased her upward until she had her balance. At some point during the rapacious seduction he had released her mind. She was unsure when, exactly, but at some time she had been free to object, to pull away, to slap him. She hadn't. Instead she'd responded like an animal. She was angry, with herself, with him and with her mind for refusing to give her the memory she needed to make sense of all of this.

He bent down, retrieved her robe and straightened again, slipping it over her shoulders. "You see?" He said it very softly.

"Why are you doing this to me?" Her voice cracked as she asked the question. She tugged her robe together, yanking the sash tight. She couldn't look him in the eyes.

"Not *to* you, Tamara. I came tonight *for* you. To help you, if you'll permit it."

"Was what you just did to me supposed to help me, too?"

When he didn't answer right away she looked at him. To her surprise his gaze fell before hers. "No," he finally whispered. "I meant to demonstrate.... I did not intend to go so far."

She frowned, looking at him—*really looking* at him—for the first time since he'd peeled his body from hers. His eyes fairly glowed with passion and were still hooded. His breaths came in short, shallow gasps, just as hers did. My God, he'd been as swept away by what had happened between them as she had! He moved past her, his hands trembling as he gripped the iron rail and looked down over it into the blue-black night, and the illuminating snow-covered ground below. His back was presented to her, its broad strength slightly bowed. Nothing prevented her going back inside.

"I am afraid I've handled this badly," he said slowly and carefully, though his voice was still hoarse. "It is not my wish to frighten you, or to make you loathe me. I care for you, Tamara. I have for a very long time."

She allowed his words to penetrate the confusion in her mind. "I think I believe that."

He turned, faced her and seemed to search for the correct words. "I truly came to you because I heard your cries. I had no other motive. Can you believe that, as well?"

She drew a slow breath. "I work with a young boy who has, on occasion, demonstrated some psychic ability. Several operatives have had sessions with him, besides me. But his powers, however slight, are always a good deal more evident when he is with me. I suppose there's a chance I might have some latent clairvoyant tendency that's been enhancing his. Maybe you *did* somehow hear my dreams. I won't say it's impossible."

She was trying to give him the benefit of the doubt, no matter how outrageous his claims seemed to be. Besides, how else could she explain what had been happening?

Encouraged, it seemed, he went on. "I came to you only because of the desperation in your cries. I swear this to you. I had no idea St. Claire was your guardian." He took a step forward, one hand lifting, palm up, a gesture of entreaty. "Try to imagine how I felt when I discovered it, Tamara. The woman who'd been calling me to her, living under the same roof as the man who has doggedly pursued me for months. How could I not suspect a conspiracy to entrap me?"

She listened as he presented his case. She supposed he had a point. She would have thought the same if she'd been in his place. "I suppose you had cause to be suspicious." She looked at the floor, bit her lip. She could reassure him without revealing any sensitive information. The truth was, she knew very little that was classified. "I have a low security clearance. Sometimes I think they invented a new one, just for me, it's so low." She smiled slightly when she said that, and she faced him. "I can't count the number of times I've tried to argue Daniel out of this crazy idea that you're..." Why couldn't she finish the sentence? She swallowed and went on. "He always counters my rationale with the claim that he has loads of evidence to prove his theories. And I always respond by asking to see the files. The answer never changes. My clearance isn't high enough." She studied his face, but it gave no evidence of whether he believed her. He listened attentively. "I never told him about the dreams. I didn't want to worry him."

He nodded. "Is there a chance he might've found out in another way?"

"How could he, short of reading my mind?" She blinked and looked away suddenly. "Unless..." He waited expectantly. She made up her mind. What she had to say couldn't hurt Daniel. If anything, it might help him avoid a lawsuit if she could stay on good terms with Marquand. She tried to avoid the burning knowledge of her own powerful feelings for a man she barely knew. "There were times when I cried out loud, loud enough to alert Daniel and bring him to my room. He always told me he hadn't heard clearly enough to guess what I'd said in my sleep, but I suppose there's a chance he might not have told me if he thought it would add to the problem."

"Or if he knew I would come to you, and planned to lie in wait."

Until that point she'd done her best to see his side of things. Now her head came up fast and she bristled. "You need to get that idea out of your mind. I admit, Daniel follows you, lurks outside your house and watches everything you do. But why on earth would he want to trap you, as you say? What do you suppose he'd do with you when he got you?"

"He specializes in research, Tamara, not surveillance. What do you suppose he'd do with a live specimen of what he considers an unstudied species?"

Tamara's stomach lurched. Her hand flew to her mouth, and she closed her eyes. "That's ludicrous! Daniel would never... He's the most gentle man I've ever known." She shook her head so hard her hair flew around her. "No. No, Daniel couldn't even entertain the thought."

"You don't know him so well as you believe to." He spoke gently, but his words were brutal. "Has it occurred to you that he might have known of the connection between us all along, that it might have been what drove him to take you in from the start?"

Eyes wide, she stared at him, shaking her head in disbelief. "It would never occur to me to think that. Daniel loves me. I love him! He's the only family I have. How can you suggest—" She stopped and tried to catch her breath. Suddenly her head throbbed. The lack of sleep seemed to catch up to her all at once. Every limb of her body ached with exhaustion.

"You have to at least consider the possibility. He knew about me, even then. I can prove it to you, if—"

"Stop it!" She pressed her palms flat to the sides of her head.

"Tamara—"

"Please, Eric," she whispered, suddenly too tired to shout or to argue any longer. "Please don't do this, don't say these things to me. I feel so close to losing my mind I don't trust my own senses anymore. I'm not sure what's real and what's delusion. I can't deal with all of this."

Her head bowed, her eyes tear filled, she didn't see him come closer. He gathered her into his arms and held her. His arms offered only comfort this time. There was no lust in his touch. "Forgive me, Tamara. My thoughtless words cause you pain. Forgive me. I don't wish to hurt you. My concern for you overwhelmed my common sense." He sighed, long and low. "God, but I've bungled this."

She found too much comfort in his arms. She felt too warm and safe and cherished there. It made no sense. She needed to be away from him. She couldn't think when he was so close. She straightened, stepping out of his embrace. "I think . . . I think you ought to leave."

The pain that flashed in his onyx eyes was almost more than she could bear to see. He dipped his head. "If you wish." He met her gaze again, his own shuttered now. "Please do not forget the things I've said to you tonight. If ever you need me, you have only to call to me. I will come."

She blinked, not bothering to argue that his claim was impossible. Perhaps he had picked up on her dreams, but they had been exceptionally powerful dreams. He couldn't possibly think this odd mental link of theirs extended beyond the one isolated incident. He didn't give her time to ask. His hand at the small of her back, he urged her toward the French doors. He opened them for her and gently pushed her through. She stepped inside and stopped, suddenly aware of the cold. Goose bumps rose on her arms and an involuntary shiver raced through her. She stood there a moment, then whirled to ask him how he'd gotten onto her balcony in the first place, a question she'd stupidly not thought of sooner—but he was gone. She shook her head hard and looked around her. It was as if he'd never been there.

CHAPTER FIVE

Jamey Bryant squirmed in his chair, his eyes focused more often on the falling snow beyond the window than on Tamara or the box in the center of the table.

"Come on, Jamey. Concentrate." She felt guilty ordering the boy to do what she found impossible. All day she'd been unable to get Eric Marquand out of her mind. His face appeared before her each time she closed her eyes. The memory of his touch, the way his lips had felt on hers, the security of being rocked in his arms haunted her without letup. The pain she'd seen in his eyes before he'd vanished haunted her more than anything else.

Then again, she still had a tiny doubt he'd been real. He could have been a figment of her imagination, a delusion, a dream. How else could he have vanished from her balcony so quickly? He couldn't have jumped. At the very least he'd have broken a leg. So maybe he hadn't been real. . . .

But he had. She knew he had, and the way he made her feel had been real, as well. Nothing so intense could be imaginary.

Jamey sighed and fixed his gaze on the cube of cardboard between them. He screwed up his face until it puckered and the furrow between his fine, dark brows became three. He leaned forward and his freckle-smattered face reddened until Tamara thought he was holding his breath. Her suspicion was confirmed a moment later when he released it in a loud whoosh and sank back into his chair. "I can't," he said. "Can I go now?"

Tamara tried to summon an encouraging smile. "You really hate this, don't you?"

He shrugged, glanced toward the window, then back to the box again. "I wish I could be like other kids. I feel weird when I know things. Then when I don't know something I think I should, I feel stupid. And then there are times when I get things that don't make any sense at all. It's like I know something, but I don't know what it means, you know?"

She nodded. "I think so."

"So what good is it to be able to know something if you can't make sense out of it?"

"Jamey, you aren't weird and you know you aren't stupid. Everyone has some quality that sets them apart. Some people can sing notes that seem impossible to the rest of us. Some athletes do things that seem supernatural to those who can't do the same. That's exactly what extrasensory perception is, something you do a lot better than most people. It's just not as understood as those other things."

She studied his face, thinking he didn't look much comforted by her pep talk. "Maybe you should tell me what it is that's bothering you."

He blew air through his lips, and shook his head. "You know I'm lousy at this. It's probably nothing. I—I don't want to scare you for no reason."

She frowned. "Scare me? This is about me, Jamey?"

He nodded, avoiding her eyes.

She rose from her seat, walked around the table and dropped to one knee in front of him. Since she'd begun working with Jamey six months ago, they'd formed a tight bond. She couldn't have loved him more if he were her own son. She hated that he was agonizing so much over something involving her. Always, he'd been incredibly sensitive to her feelings. He always knew if she felt upset, or under the weather. He'd known about the nightmares and insomnia, too.

"You are not lousy at this. At least, not where I'm concerned. If you've picked up on something, just tell me. Maybe I can explain it."

His mouth twisted at one side. He looked at her seriously. His intense expression made him look like a miniature adult. "I keep feeling like something's going to happen to you...like someone is going to—to hurt you." He shook his head. "But I don't know who and I don't know what, so what good is it to know anything?"

She smiled softly. "There's been a lot going on with me lately, Jamey. Personal stuff. Stuff that's upset me quite a lot. I think you might be picking up on that."

"You think so?" His dark eyes met hers hopefully, then darkened again with worry. "Is everything okay?"

She nodded hard. "I think so. And, yes, everything is working itself out. The nightmares I'd been having are gone now."

"Good." His frown didn't vanish, though. "But I still get the feeling there are people out to get you." He chewed his lip. "Do you know anyone named Eric?"

Something hard, like a brick, lodged in the center of her chest. She gasped audibly, and rose so fast she nearly lost her balance. "Eric?" she repeated dumbly. "Why? Is there something about him—"

"I dunno. I just keep getting that name floating in at the oddest times. I always feel really sad, or else really worried, when it comes. I think maybe that's what he's feeling like, but like I said, I'm lousy at this. I could be reading it all wrong."

She let the moment of panic recede. She'd thought he might say Eric was the one out to hurt her. She still wondered if it might not be the case, but didn't want to let

Jamey sense it. She drew several calming breaths and tried to compose her face before she looked at him again.

"Thanks for the warning, Jamey, but I think you're overreacting to this danger thing. Look, why don't you open the box? At this point I don't even remember what was inside."

After a last cursory glance, as if assuring himself he hadn't frightened her, he leaned forward, swung one arm out and caught the box, drawing it to him on the follow-through. When he looked inside his eyes widened, and he pulled the video game cartridge out. "Dungeon Warriors! Mom's been looking all over for this—where'd you find it?"

"Your mom didn't look as hard as you thought. I told her not to."

He examined the colorful package eagerly. "Thanks, Tam." He stood, obviously in a hurry to get home and try out the new game.

"Go ahead, Jamey. Your mom's waiting right downstairs." He nodded and started for the door. "Jamey," she called after him. When he glanced back at her she said, "If you get any more of these weird vibes about me, and if they bother you, just call. You have my number. Okay?"

"Sure, Tam." He gave her a broad, dimpled grin that told her his mind had been eased for the moment, and hustled through the door, leaving Tamara alone to contemplate his warning.

She worked late that evening, trying to use her mundane duties to fill her mind. It didn't work. She finally went home to find the house looking abandoned. Of course, it was past dusk, so Daniel and Curtis had already left on their nightly spying mission. Despite his unfounded accusations against Daniel, Tamara felt a little sorry for Eric

Marquand. It must get tiresome looking out his window night after night to see them there.

She bounced in her VW Bug over the curving, rutted driveway. Snowflakes pirouetted over the rambling Victorian mansion, caught in the glow of her headlights. Their pristine whiteness emphasized the age-yellowed paint. Tall, narrow windows stood like sad eyes. Rusty water stains like teardrops beneath each one enhanced that fanciful image. Tamara set the brake and got out to wrench open the stubborn overhead garage door, muttering under her breath. She'd argued for an automatic one every winter for the past three, all without success. Daniel wouldn't budge an inch. What he couldn't do to the old house himself simply wouldn't get done. He didn't want a crew of strangers snooping around and that was final.

She drove her car inside, noting the absence of Daniel's Cadillac. A finger of worry traced a path along her spine. She hoped he wasn't driving tonight. The roads were slippery and, dammit all, she'd never replaced the spare after he'd had that flat two months ago. She imagined Curt was with him, and comforted herself with the thought.

She flicked on lights as she moved through the foyer. The phone began ringing before she'd even sat down to remove her boots. She tracked across the faded carpet to pick it up.

"Tammy, it's about time you got home. Where've you been?"

She bit back the sharp retort that sprang to her lips. "Curtis, are you with Daniel?"

"Yeah, but that doesn't answer the question."

"I came straight home from the office, if you must know. I worked a bit late and the roads are slick. I don't want him driving."

"I'll take care of him. Look, Tam, are you in for the night?"

She frowned hard. "Why?"

He hesitated, started to speak, stopped and started again. "It's just, after that incident with Marquand the other night, Daniel and I both feel it would be best if you, uh, try to stick close to home after sundown. I know how much you resent being told what to do, but it would be for your own—"

"My own good, I know." She sighed and shook her head. "Look, I don't have any plans to leave the house tonight. Besides, I thought you guys were watching Marquand's every move."

"We are, but—"

"Then you don't have anything to worry about, do you? I'm heading for a long soak in a scalding bath, and then straight to bed, if that makes you feel any better."

"It does." He was quiet for a moment. "It's only because we're worried, Tammy."

"Yeah, I know it is. Good night." She replaced the receiver before he could make her any angrier, and headed upstairs to follow her own advice about the hot bath. As for straight to bed, she knew better. At work she'd been on the verge of falling asleep on her feet all day. Now that she was home she felt wide awake and brimming with energy.

She toweled herself dry after a soothing, if not a relaxing, soak, and pulled on a pair of comfortable jeans and a baggy sweater. She wriggled her feet into her heaviest socks and halfheartedly dried her hair, before padding downstairs to hunt for something to fill her empty stomach. She'd just settled on the sofa in the huge living room with a thick bacon, lettuce and tomato sandwich sliced diagonally on a paper plate, and a can of cola, when the doorbell chimed.

Tamara rolled her eyes, lowered the sandwich she'd just brought to her lips and went to open the door. Her irritation disappeared when Eric Marquand stepped over the threshold into the foyer. She slammed the door after giving a fear-filled glance down the driveway, and looked at him agape. "You shouldn't be here, Eric. My God, if Daniel saw you here, he'd have a stroke!"

"He won't. He and Rogers will remain on sentry duty outside my front gate until dawn, as they do every night, I promise you. They did not see me leave. I took great pains to assure that."

She stood still, fighting the bubbling sense of joy she felt at seeing him, arguing inwardly that it made no sense to feel so about a stranger. It was there, all the same.

"After my behavior last night, I half expected you to throw me out. Will you, Tamara?"

She tried to tug her gaze free of his, but was unsuccessful. "I . . . no. No, I'm not going to throw you out. Come in. I was about to have a sandwich. Can I make one for you?"

He shook his head. "I've already dined. If I'm interrupting your dinner . . ."

She shook her head quickly. "No, I mean, you can hardly call a sandwich and a cola dinner." He followed her into the living room and sat beside her on the sofa, despite the fact that she'd waved her arm toward a chair nearby. She reached for the dewy can. "I could get you one."

"Thank you, no." He cleared his throat. "I've come because . . ." He shook his head. "Actually, there is no other reason, except that I couldn't stay away. Tamara, will you come out with me tonight? I give you my word, I will say nothing against your St. Claire. I'll ask you no questions about DPI. I only want your companionship."

She smiled, then stopped herself. Did she dare go out with him? After all the warnings Daniel had given her about him?

Eric took her hand in his, his thumb slowly stroking the tops of her fingers. "If you cannot believe my charges against him, Tamara, you should equally doubt his against me. It is only fair.''

She nodded slowly. ''I guess you're right. Okay. I'll come with you.'' She stood quickly, more eager than she wanted him to see. ''Should I change? Where are we going?''

''You are beautiful as you are, sweet. Would you mind if we simply went driving until something better occurs to us? I don't wish to share you with a crowd just yet.''

''Okay. I'll grab my coat and . . . Driving? I didn't see a car. How will we—''

''Finish your sandwich, Tamara. It is a surprise.''

She couldn't stop herself from smiling fully at that, and for a moment he seemed almost staggered by it. ''I'm not hungry, anyway,'' she told him, rushing past him to the foyer and the closet near the front door. ''I was only eating to fill the loneliness.''

She tugged on her heaviest coat, a long houndstooth check, with a black woolly scarf around the collar and matching mittens in the pocket. She stomped into her boots. When she looked up again he was staring at her. ''Have you been lonely, then?'' he asked softly.

She blinked back the instant moisture that sprang to her eyes at the question. It never occurred to her to lie to him. ''I often think I'm the loneliest person I know. Oh, I've got Daniel, and a few friends at work, but . . .'' She looked into his eyes and knew he'd understand. ''I'm not like them. I feel set apart, like there's an invisible barrier between us.'' She frowned. ''I don't feel that way with you.''

His eyes closed slowly, and opened again. Flustered more than a little bit, she hurried through the room and took the telephone off the hook. Without an explanation she trotted upstairs to her room and spent a few minutes stuffing spare blankets underneath her comforter, to make it look as if she were asleep there. She shut off her bedroom light and closed the door.

When she turned, Eric stood there. One brow lifted as he looked down at her. "For St. Claire's benefit?"

"This way I can relax and enjoy our evening," she said softly, her gaze lingering on his lips for a long moment. She saw his Adam's apple move as he swallowed. When she lifted her gaze to his eyes, she saw they were focused on her lips, and her tongue darted out involuntarily to moisten them.

"I promised myself I wouldn't touch you tonight," he told her in a voice softer than a whisper. "But I don't believe I can prevent myself kissing you."

"You're bound to, sooner or later," she told him, striving to keep her own voice level. "Maybe we ought to get it out of the way now." He stood perfectly still, not a single muscle moving. She stepped forward, tilted her head back and touched his lips with hers. She felt him tremble when she settled her hands on his rock-solid shoulders. She let her eyes fall closed, parted her lips against his and tentatively slid the tip of her tongue over them.

He sighed into her mouth as his arms came around her waist to crush her against him. The pressure of his lips forced hers to part for him, and he tasted every bit of her mouth, even reaching his tongue to the back of her throat in a forceful, thrusting motion that hinted at far greater pleasures to come. His hands moved over her body, one holding her to him while the other tangled in her hair, pulling her head back farther to accommodate that probing tongue more deeply. She felt his hot arousal pressing into her belly, telling her how much he wanted her. She moved her hips against him, to let him know she felt the same mindless need.

When the fire in her blood raged out of control he pulled away, panting. "This is not the way, Tamara. With everything in me, I want to take you right here. I want to lift you to the wall, or take you on the floor, dammit. But it is not the way. You might hate me tomorrow, when the fire no longer burns in your eyes." He stroked the hair away from her face. He pressed his lips to each eye in turn. "Agree with me, before I lose control."

Tamara's body was screaming that she wanted him to lose control. Her mind knew he was right. She didn't know him. She had once, she was certain of it now. But she couldn't remember that. It would be like making love to a stranger, and that would make her feel cheap and ashamed. She stepped away from him. "You're right. I—I'm sorry."

"Never apologize for kissing me, for touching me, Tamara. Your caress is a gift worthy of any king . . . one I will be grateful for whenever you choose to bestow it."

Eric could barely bring himself to stop what she'd started in St. Claire's corridor. He'd only just restrained himself in time. The desire she stirred in him was a beast he could hardly subdue. He had to, though. The blood lust in him intertwined with sexual desire. The two were so closely linked among his kind that there was no separating them. If he took her, he'd take her blood as well as her body. She'd know the truth then, and she'd despise him forever.

Or worse . . .

No. he refused to believe she could be party to Daniel St. Claire's machinations.

Refusing to believe it does not make it impossible.

If she was plotting his destruction, he'd know, he reminded himself as he descended the stairs beside her. He'd see it in her mind.

Vampires can learn to guard their thoughts. Why not her?

She is no vampire, he thought angrily. I've never known a human to be capable of such a thing.

You've never known a human like Tamara.

At the bottom of the stairway Eric glimpsed a light glowing beyond a doorway at the far side. She'd flicked off every other glaring electric light she'd come to, so he touched her shoulder now, and pointed. "Do you wish to shut that light off, as well?"

She shook her head quickly, opened her mouth to explain, then seemed to think better of it. Not before Eric heard what was in her mind, however. To go through that door was forbidden to her. St. Claire's basement lab lay at the bottom of the staircase there, and he'd deemed it off-limits. Eric would have liked to go down there now, to examine the ruthless scientist's files and equipment. But he'd given Tamara his word that he'd come here only to be with her. How could she believe him if he betrayed her trust in such a way?

He'd spoken the truth when he'd spoken those words, yet he could've told her more. He wanted to be with her because he feared for her safety. That St. Claire had known of the connection between them from the start was obvious. He'd orchestrated events to gain custody of the child, Eric felt certain of it. Whether to brainwash her into helping him in his plots or to use her as unwitting bait remained to be seen. Either way, though, Tamara was no more to St. Claire than a pawn in a high-stakes game. She could not be safe with him. That Eric had to leave her side by day had him at his wits' end, but what choice did he have? He would stay by her side when he could, and he'd try to learn exactly what St. Claire had on his mind. He'd protect Tamara if he had to kill the bastard himself. In the three times Eric had seen her since returning from his travels, he'd learned one thing he hadn't fully realized before. He still adored her.

The emotions had changed, radically. She was no longer the small child in need of bedtime stories and lullabies. She was a woman grown, a woman of incomparable beauty and incredible passion... a woman capable of setting his pulse throbbing in his temples, and his blood to boiling for want of her. He knew what he felt for her. He understood it. Constantly he needed to remind himself that she did not. She couldn't, nor could she fathom her own feelings for him. To her, he was a stranger... at least until her memory returned, and until she became aware that she could know anything about him simply by searching his mind. Now, though, at this moment, he was a stranger.

He hoped to remedy that to some extent tonight.

She locked the door, pocketed the key and turned toward him. Eric allowed himself the pleasure of encircling her shoulders with his arm. No matter how good his intentions, it seemed he couldn't prevent himself from touching her, holding her close whenever possible. Her coat was too thick for his liking. He could scarcely feel the shape of her beneath it. He urged her down the curving driveway, and felt her start in surprise when she caught sight of the vehicle that awaited her there. One horse's ears pricked forward and his head came up at the sound of their approach.

Tamara stopped walking to turn wide eyes toward Eric. He smiled at the delight he saw in them. "I thought a sleigh would be more enjoyable than any other mode of transportation," he said.

Her smile took his breath away, and she hurried forward, sending a powdery blizzard ahead of her as she plowed through the five inches of new snow on the ground. She stood in front of the black, speaking softly, for the horse's ears only, and stroking his muzzle. He blew in appreciation. Eric joined her there a second later. "This is Max. He's a gelding, and I think he's as enchanted by his first glimpse of you as I was."

She glanced up, meeting his eyes, her own acknowledging the compliment, before Eric continued. "And this—"

he moved toward the golden palomino beside Max "—is Melinda, his partner."

Tamara stepped to the side and stroked Melinda's sleek neck. "She's beautiful—they both are. Are they yours, Eric?"

"Unfortunately, no. I was able to rent them for the night." He watched the emotions in her face and felt those in her mind as she touched and caressed one horse, then the other. "I'm thinking of buying them, though," he added. It was true. The moment he'd seen her joy at the sight of the animals, he'd wanted to own them.

"Oh?" Her attention was, at last, on him again. "Do you have a stable?"

"I'll have one built," he announced. She laughed as he took her arm and led her around the horses, to help her into the sleigh. Eric climbed in beside her and picked up the reins.

"I've always loved horses. When I was a little girl I wanted to own a ranch, where I could raise them by the hundreds."

Eric nodded. He remembered her love of horses. He'd hoped it still existed. He snapped the reins lightly and clicked his tongue. The sleigh jerked into motion, and Tamara settled back against the cushioned seat. He took them off the paved road as soon as possible, onto a snow-coated side road that was barely more than a path. He watched her more often than the road ahead. She remarked on everything with little sighs of pleasure—the full moon glistening on the snow, making it sparkle as if it held tiny diamonds just beneath the surface, the ice-coated branches that made ugly, bare limbs turn into sculpted crystal. The crisp, clean air that touched her face, and the scent of the horses' warm bodies.

Eric nodded in agreement, but in truth he was aware of none of it. It was her scent that enveloped him. It was see-

ing the way the chill breeze played with her hair and reddened her cheeks and the tip of her nose that entranced
him. He felt only the warmth of her body, pressed alongside his own, and saw the moonlight glistening in her eyes,
rather than upon the snow. Beyond the rhythmic thudding
of the horses' hooves he heard the music in her voice.

Her arm was wrapped around his, and her head rested
upon his shoulder. "This is wonderful, Eric. It's the most
fun I've had in..." She blinked and considered a moment. "I can't remember when I've enjoyed a night this
much."

"Nor I," he whispered, certain it was true. "But you
must tell me if you grow tired, or I'll likely keep you out all
night."

"I don't get tired at night. Not ever. I haven't slept a
night through in over a month...closer to two. So if you
want to keep me out all night, I'll be more than willing."

She seemed so exuberant and happy. Yet he worried
about this sleeplessness. She'd mentioned it before. "Are
you able to sleep by day, then?"

"No, I have to work. I usually catch a few hours in the
afternoon, though." She tipped her head up and saw his
frown. "Do I look like I'm suffering from exhaustion to
you?"

"Quite the opposite," he admitted.

She settled against him again, then straightened, snapping her fingers. "It's French, isn't it?"

"What?"

"Your accent."

"I wasn't aware I had one." God, she was beautiful. Her
eyes in the moonlight seemed luminous, and he noticed
again the thickness of the lashes surrounding them.

"It's very slight. I barely notice it myself. I've been trying to place it. Am I right?"

He nodded. "I was born in France."

"Where?"

He smiled down at her, amazed that she even cared to ask. "Paris. I haven't been back there in...years."

"You sound as if you'd like to go, though," she said, studying his face. "Why haven't you?"

"Bad memories, I suppose. My father was murdered there. I nearly suffered the same fate, save for the intervention of a good friend." He saw her eyes widen. He'd vowed to be as honest with her as he could without giving away the secret. He wanted her to feel she knew him.

Her hand clutched his upper arm more tightly. "That's horrible."

He nodded. "But a long time past, Tamara. I'm recovered."

"Are you sure?" He met her intense scrutiny. "Have you talked it out with someone, Eric? These things have a way of festering."

He tilted his head, considering his words. "It was... political...and utterly senseless. It left me without any family at all, and if not for Roland, I'd have been without a friend, as well." He looked down to see her listening raptly. "I never had many to begin with, you see. I always felt separate—set apart from my peers."

"You didn't fit in. I know exactly what you mean."

He looked deeply into her eyes. "Yes, I imagine you do."

"Tell me about your friend. Do you still keep in touch?"

He chuckled. "It is sometimes a long time between letters, or visits. But Roland happens to be staying with me at the moment."

Her head came up, eyes eager. "Could I meet him?"

He frowned. "Why would you want to?"

She had to give her answer a long moment's thought before speaking it. "You...said he saved your life. I..." Her gaze fell to her hand, resting on her knee. "I'd like to thank him."

Eric closed his eyes at the warmth her words sent through his heart. "He's a recluse. Perhaps I can arrange it, though. Unlike me, he still has a residence in France, though he rarely lives there. He owns a sprawling medieval castle in the Loire Valley. He hid me there for a time after we fled Paris."

When he glanced at her again it was to find her gaze affixed to his face as it had been through most of the ride. "You are a fascinating man," she whispered.

"I am a simple man, with simple tastes."

"I'd love to see your home."

"Another time, perhaps. If I took you there while my reclusive friend was in residence, he'd likely throttle me." He slipped his arm around the back of the seat, and squeezed her to his side. "It is furnished almost exclusively in antiques. Electric lighting is there, of course, but I seldom use it. I prefer the muted glow of oil lamps to the harsh glare of those white bulbs, except in my laboratory."

"You're a scientist?"

"I dabble in a few projects that interest me."

Her lovely eyes narrowed. "You are being modest, I think."

He shrugged, gave a tug on the reins to stop their progress and reached beneath the seat for the thermos he'd brought along. "You told me once, a very long time ago, that your favorite beverage was hot chocolate. Is it still the case?"

For the first time in years Tamara felt completely at ease with another person. The hours of the night flew past almost without her knowledge. They talked incessantly, touching on every subject imaginable, from music and art to politics. He fascinated her, and the more she learned about him the more she wanted to know.

Through it all she was constantly aware of the physical attraction that zapped between them. She'd deliberately sat close to him, so her body touched his. She liked touching him, so much so that she felt cold and alone when they hit a rough spot in the road and she was jarred away from his side. Without hesitation she resumed her former position. He seemed to share her need to feel her close. He touched her often. He kept his hard arm around her, managing the reins with one hand. When they passed beneath an overhanging branch and a handful of snow dusted her, he stopped the sleigh and turned to brush it away from her shoulders and her hair. Their eyes met, and she felt the irresistible pull of him. He leaned forward and pressed his lips to hers with infinite tenderness. He held himself in check, though. She sensed his forced restraint and knew he was determined to go slowly with her . . . to give her time to adjust to what was happening between them.

She wondered exactly *what was* happening between them. She knew that it was intense, and that it was real. She knew that she'd never felt this way toward another human being in her life. And she knew that whatever it was, she didn't want it to end. She wanted to tell him so, but didn't quite know how.

He left the sleigh in the same spot near the end of the driveway when they returned to the house. He walked her to the door, and stopped as she fit her key into the lock. Her heart twisted painfully at the thought of leaving him. The lock released, but she didn't open the door. She turned and gazed up at him, wondering if he knew.

"I'd like to see you again," she said, suddenly shy and awkward with him, which seemed strange considering all that had passed between them before.

"I think it would be impossible for me to go a night without seeing you, Tamara," he told her. "I will come to you again . . . do not doubt it."

She bit her lower lip, searching his face. "I'm a grown woman. It's silly to have to sneak around this way. You know you could end this foolish notion Daniel has about you, if you wanted to. Just come to the house during the day. He'd have to realize then—"

"He would only assume I had some protection against the daylight, sweet. Nothing can change his opinion of me." He looked away from her briefly. "I have my own schedule—one that is vital to me. Should I alter that to accommodate the whims of a man determined to persecute me?"

"No, I didn't mean it like that!" She sighed, feeling deflated. "It's just that I hate deceiving him."

"If you tell him you're seeing me, Tamara, he'll find a way to prevent it." She met his gaze again, and saw the hint of impatience vanish as he regarded her. "Let me amend that. He would try to find a way. He would not succeed."

She believed that he meant it. "I'm glad you said that," she admitted.

She knew he would kiss her. She saw the heat come into his luminous eyes in the instant before his arms imprisoned her waist. Her lips parted as his descended. The restraint he'd shown earlier dissolved the instant her arms encircled his corded neck and her body pressed to his. His lips quivered as they covered hers, and she accepted his probing tongue enthusiastically. Even with her heavy coat between them she was aware of the heat of him touching her, as if his hands touched her naked skin. He explored her mouth, and his fingers moved lightly over her nape, sending exquisite shivers down her spine.

She'd experimented with sex. In college, though she'd lived at home at Daniel's insistence, there had been plenty of opportunities and no shortage of eager tutors. Her times with men had been few, though, and inspired more by curiosity than passion. Tonight, with Eric, she wanted it. A hunger like nothing she'd known existed made a cavern inside her—a vast emptiness that only he could fill. It gnawed at her mercilessly, and the longing made her groan deep in her throat.

He straightened, and she knew he saw the need in her eyes. His own closed as if he were in pain, and his arms fell away from her. "I must go," he rasped. He reached past her and threw the door wide. There was no tenderness in his touch when he pushed her through it.

She felt tears stinging her eyes when he turned and walked away.

CHAPTER SIX

At 7:00 a.m. she sat across the table from Daniel, nursing a strong cup of coffee and a pounding headache. "It's probably just a bug," she repeated. "I'm tired and achy. I'll spend the day in bed and be myself again by tomorrow morning."

His lips thinned and he shook his head. "I'll call in, make arrangements to work at home today. That way—"

"I don't need a baby-sitter."

"I didn't say you did. I only think I should be here, in case—"

Tamara slammed the half-filled cup onto the table, sloshing coffee over the rim, and got to her feet. "Daniel, this has to stop."

"What? Tam, I'm only concerned about you."

"I know." She pushed a hand through her hair, wishing she could ease the throbbing in her temples. She felt like a wrung-out rag this morning, and in no shape for a confrontation. "I know it's love that motivates you, Daniel— I know you care. But for God's sake, look at me. I'm not an orphaned little girl anymore." She kept her voice level, and moved around the table to press her hands to his shoulders. "You and Curtis are smothering me with all this *concern.* You hover over me as if I'm Little Red Riding Hood and there are wolves behind every tree."

Daniel looked at the floor. "Have we been that bad?"

"Worse." She squeezed his shoulders gently. "But I love you, anyway."

He met her gaze, and slowly shook his head. "I'm sorry, Tam. It's not that I think you need watching, like a child. It's...it's this thing with Marquand, dammit. I'm terrified he'll try to see you again."

She let her hands fall away from him, and straightened. Eric had said he believed Daniel knew of the connection between them. Could he have been right? "Why would you think that?"

He sighed as if she were stupid. "Tamara, you're a beautiful woman! Curtis said the man was obviously attracted that night at the rink. He'd have to have been blind not to be. These creatures have a sex drive like rutting animals. Even one as old as he is."

She turned away from him, trying not to laugh. Eric was not a "creature," nor was he old. The skin of his face was smooth and tight. He moved with a grace beyond anything she'd seen before, and yet his strength was obvious. His body rippled with hard muscles and kinetic energy.

Shaking her head, she reached for her coffee. "Just how old is he?"

"Two hundred and thirty something. I've traced him to the French Revolution, when he was imprisoned and should have been beheaded in Paris. His father was, you know."

Tamara had lifted her cup to her lips, but now she choked on the sip she'd taken. Eric had told her his father was murdered in Paris! He'd said it was "political." My God, could Daniel possibly be right—no. No, that was utterly ridiculous.

But I've never seen Eric during the day.

She shoved the doubts aside. This was nonsense. Absolute nonsense.

"He's dangerous, Tam. Clever as a wizard, too. I wouldn't put it past him to use you to get to me.

And he says you're using me to get to him, she thought. Aloud, she only said, "I'd never let that happen."

"I know, Tam. But promise you'll tell me if he tries to make contact. We have to be careful. He's evil—"

"Yes, you've told me. He's the devil himself. Okay, I'll let you know. Happy?" He studied her face before he nodded. "Go to work," she told him playfully. "He can't bother me during the day, right?"

She tried not to let his words replay in her mind, over and over again all morning. She only wanted to go back to bed and get some much-needed rest. That was impossible to do, though. She supposed she wouldn't act so impulsively if she'd had a decent amount of sleep in the past several weeks. If she'd been in a normal, relatively sane frame of mind, nothing could have convinced her to do what she suddenly decided she must do. Unfortunately, her sanity was in question, and she thought if she didn't answer the questions in her mind once and for all, it would slip away from her completely.

She had to prove to herself that Eric Marquand was not a vampire. She thought that made about as much sense as trying to prove the earth was not flat, or that the moon was not made of green cheese. Yet several hours later she sat in her pathetic excuse for a car alongside the road in front of Eric Marquand's estate.

She glanced at her watch. Only an hour or so left before sunset. Part of her wanted to put this off until tomorrow. Part of her wanted to put it off permanently. Still, she was here, and she knew if she didn't go through with this now, she never would.

Getting the address hadn't been easy. She couldn't possibly have asked Daniel or Curt without sending them both into hysterics. She couldn't show up at work and tap the DPI computers. Her security clearance wasn't high enough to get her the correct access codes. She'd spent most of the day at the county seat, scouring the records deemed "public domain." She'd struck out on birth certificates. He didn't seem to have a driver's license, or a car registered in his name. He did, however, have a deed to his home. She found the information she needed in the property tax files. His address was there, and she frowned to note it was only a few miles southeast of Daniel's house, on the northern shore of the sound.

She'd spent the entire drive back arguing with herself. Was she about to shore up her sanity, or had it already been buried in an avalanche? Would any sane person visit a man's home during the day to prove he wasn't a vampire?

Too late now, she thought, pulling her car around a bend in the road and easing it close to the woodlot on the opposite side. I'm here and I'm going in. She left the keys in the switch, and walked back to the towering wrought-iron gate. She peered between the bars and the crisscrossing pattern of vines and leaves writhing between them, all made of flattened metal. The pattern was the same as far as she could see in either direction. Beyond the fence a cobblestone driveway twisted its way toward the house. Huge trees lined the driveway, so she had to move around a bit to get a glimpse of the building beyond them.

When she did she caught her breath. The house towered at least three stories high. It was built of rough-hewn stone blocks, each one too big for three men to lift. The windows—at least, the ones she could see—were arched at the tops, and deep set. They reminded her of hooded eyes, watching but not wishing to be seen. She touched the gate and at the same instant noticed the small metal box affixed to a post just inside. A tiny red light flashed in sync with her pulse. This was no antique fence, but a high-tech security device. She drew her hand away fast, wondering how many alarms she'd set off simply by touching it. She waited and watched. No sound or movement came from within.

When she could breathe again she glanced up. The spikes at the top of each of the fence's bars looked real, and sharp.

Climbing over would be impossible. But there had to be another way inside. She squared her shoulders and began walking the perimeter.

It seemed like a mile as she pressed through tangles of brush and a miniature forest, but it couldn't have been that much. The fence bowed out, and curved back toward the house in the rear. She didn't find a single flaw in it, and she bit her lip in dismay when she reached the end. The last spiked bar of black iron sank into the ground at the edge of a rocky cliff. Below, the sound roiled in whitecapped chaos. The wind picked up and Tamara shivered. She had to do something. Go back? After all this?

She eyed the final spear of the fence. The ground near its base didn't look too solid. Still, she thought, if she gripped the fence tightly she might be able to swing her body around to the other side. Right?

She gripped a filigree vine with her right hand, the right side of her body touching the fence. She faced the sound and the biting wind that came off it. She had to lean out, over, and twist her body in order to grip the same vine on the other side of the fence with her left hand.

Bent in this awkward, painful pose, she glanced down. Points of slick, black rock jutted sporadically from water of the same color. They appeared and disappeared with each swell. They winked at her, like supernatural, unspeakably evil eyes. Her hair whipped around her face. Her nose and cheeks burned with cold, and her eyes watered. She edged forward until her toes hung over, then drew a breath and swung her left leg out and around, slamming it down again on firm, solid earth.

She couldn't stop her gaze from slanting downward once more as she straddled the iron fence, one arm and one leg on either side while her rear end jutted into space. A wave of dizziness, almost exactly corresponding to the waves of seawater moving below, temporarily swamped her brain.

She had to close her eyes to battle it. She swallowed three times in quick succession before she dared open them again.

Grunting with the effort, she released her right hand from the outside of the fence and brought it around to cling to a bar on the inside. She clung for all she was worth. All that remained was to move her right leg around to this side now. She lifted it, drew it backward, out over the water, and jerked it in again, slamming her foot down on the ground near the edge. But the ground she stood on dissolved like sugar in hot coffee. *Too near the edge,* she had time to think. Her right foot scraped down over the sheer face of the cliff until the entire leg, to the thigh, made an arrow pointing to certain death on the rocks below. Her left leg lay flat, heel down, on the ground so she was almost doing a split. She still clung to the fence with her left hand. Her right had been torn free when she'd slipped so hard and so fast.

The filigree vine she gripped began slowly to cut into her fingers. They burned, and in moments they throbbed incessantly. She knew she couldn't hold on another second with each second that she held on. The muscle in the back of the thigh that lay flat to the ground felt stretched to violin-string proportions.

Frantically she dug at the stone face with her toe, knowing as she did that it was useless. She was going to die on those rocks beneath the angry black water...and all for the chance to prove to herself that Eric Marquand was not a vampire.

Her fingers slipped. Her thigh throbbed with pain. She slid a couple more inches. Then her toe struck a small protrusion in the cliff face. She pressed onto it, praying it would hold. It did, and she was able to lever herself higher, and get a grip on the fence with her free hand. She pulled, scraping her foot along the sheer stone, wriggling her body up until she was completely supported by the solid, snow-dusted ground. For a long moment she remained there, hands still gripping the cold iron bars, face pressed to them, as well. Her body trembled and she wished to God she'd never embarked on this crazy mission.

Fine time to change my mind, she thought. I'm certainly not leaving here the same way I came. She sighed, lifted her head and pulled herself to her feet. She'd just have to go inside, confess her lunacy to Eric and hope he wouldn't laugh her off the planet. Then she sobered. He might not find her intrusion funny at all. He might resent her snooping as much as he resented Daniel's.

She brushed snow and damp earth from her jeans, wincing and drawing her hand away. A thin smear of blood stained the denim and she turned her palm up to see spiderweb strands of scarlet trickling from the creases of her fingers. She fought the tiny shiver that raced along her spine, balled her hand into a fist and shoved it into her pocket, then strode over the snowy ground toward the rear of Eric's house. She knocked at a set of French doors similar to her own. When no response came she thumped a little harder. Still no one answered.

He wasn't home. And she was stuck in his backyard until he *got* home, she thought miserably.

The wind howled off the sound, battering the house and Tamara with it. Her jeans were dampened from the snow and the wet ground. Her hand was throbbing. She had no idea when he'd return, or even if he would tonight. She couldn't stand here much longer or she thought she'd suffer frostbite. No, she had to get inside. Eric could be as angry as he wanted, but she'd left herself with few options. She wasn't about to tempt the sound again by trying to leave as she'd arrived. The French doors seemed like an omen. If they'd been any other type, she would have had *no* options. But French doors she could open. She'd had to force her own a time or two when she'd misplaced the key.

She dipped into her coat pocket hoping to find—yes! A small silver nail file presented itself when she withdrew her fist and opened it. She turned toward the doors, and hesitated. Another gust exploded from the sound, and suddenly wet snow slanted across the sky, slicing her face like tiny shards of glass. She huddled into her coat and moved more quickly. She slipped the file between the two panels, nimbly flicked the latch and opened them.

She stepped inside and pulled the doors together behind her. She thought it wasn't much warmer here than outside, then saw the huge marble fireplace facing her, glowing with coals of a forgotten fire. She tugged off her boots, shrugged free of the coat and hurried to the promise of warmth. A stack of wood beside the hearth offered hope, and she bent to toss several chunks onto the grate, then stretched her nearly numb hands toward the heat. She stood for just a moment, absorbing the warmth as the chills stopped racing around her body. Tongues of flame lapped hungrily at the logs, snapping loudly and sending tiny showers of sparks up the chimney.

After a time she lowered her hands and glanced around her. She had the urge to rub her eyes and look again. It seemed she'd been transported backward in time. The chair behind her was a profusion of needlepoint genius. Every scrap of material on the thing had been embroidered with birds, flowers, leaves. The wooden arms and legs had scroll-like shapes at their ends. A footstool of the same design sat before it, and Tamara bent to run one fingertip reverently over the cushion. All of the furniture was of the same period. She was no expert, but she guessed it was Louis XV, and she knew it was in mint condition. Marble-topped, gilded tables with angels carved into their legs were placed at intervals. Other chairs similar to the first were scattered about. The sofa . . . no, it was more like a settee, was small by today's standards. Its velvet upholstery of deep green contrasted with the intricately carved wooden arms and legs.

She examined the room itself, noting a chandelier of brass and crystal suspended high overhead. Yet at one end of the room shelves had been built to hold thousands of dollars worth of stereo equipment, and rows of CDs, LPs, and cassettes. Nearby, a rather ordinary-looking bar seemed out of place in the antique-filled room, with the parquet floors. She saw oil lamps on every stand, yet a light switch on the wall. The sun sank lower, and she walked toward the bar, snapped on the light and licked her lips. She could use a drink. She was still shivering intermittently, despite the warmth filling the room. If Eric could forgive her for breaking into his home, she reasoned, he ought to be able to forgive her for stealing a small glass of—of whatever he had on hand.

She went behind the bar and ducked down to look at the nearly-empty shelves underneath. Not a single bottle rested there. Glasses, yes. A couple of expensive cut-crystal decanters. She stood, frowning, turning only when she heard the almost silent hum of the small refrigerator, built in to the wall behind her.

Smiling at her own oversight, Tamara gripped the handle and tugged....

A tiny chunk of ice placed itself in the center of her chest, and slowly grew until it enveloped her entire body.

Her jaw fell. She took a step back, blinking, unable to believe what she was seeing. Blood. Plastic bags filled with blood in two neat stacks. She felt as if she'd been dropped into the fury of a cyclone. She saw nothing all at once, except a thin red haze, heard nothing but a deafening roar. Mindlessly she shoved at the small door. It swung, but didn't quite close, and slowly it slipped back to its wide-open position. Tamara didn't notice. She turned away, face buried in her hands, fingertips pressing into her eyelids as if she could erase what she'd seen.

"It wasn't real. It couldn't have been real. I'll turn around. If I turn around and look again it won't be there because it wasn't real."

She didn't turn around, though. She lifted her head, focused on the French doors and hurried toward them. She wanted to run, but couldn't. Just walking in her socks seemed absurdly loud on the parquet floor. She felt eyes on her, seemingly from everywhere. Her own gaze darted about, like a bird flitting from branch to branch on a tree, in constant motion. She couldn't shake the feeling that someone was right behind her, no matter which way she turned. She moved forward, then whirled and walked backward a few steps. Only a yard to go. She'd grab up her boots. She'd snatch her coat as she ran outside. She wouldn't wait to put them on first. Another step. An invisible finger of ice traced a path up her backbone.

"Too crazy," she whispered, turning fast and walking backward again. "It's all too crazy—this place—me. *I'm* too crazy." Her mind cartwheeled out of control and she pivoted once more, ready to make a lunge for the door. Her path was blocked by a broad, hard chest covered in crisp white cotton.

She automatically drew back, but Eric's hands clamped down on her shoulders before she'd moved a half step. Frozen in place, she only stared up at him as her breaths began coming too quickly and too shallowly. Her head swam. Against her will she studied his face. His eyes glistened, and she knew more than just bald terror of this man. She felt a sickening sense of loss and of betrayal. Daniel had been right all along.

"What are you doing here, Tamara?"

She tried to swallow, but her throat was like a sandy desert. She pulled against his hands, surprised when he let them fall from her shoulders. A strange voice behind her made her whirl between heartbeats. "Snooping, of course. I told you not to trust her, Eric. She's DPI." The man standing near the bar waved a hand toward the opened refrigerator. That first glimpse of him nearly extinguished the small spark of reason she had left. He was dressed all in black, with a satin cloak that reached to the floor all but blanketing him. He moved like a panther, with inconceivable grace and latent power. He exuded a sexual magnetism that was palpable. His dark good looks were belied by the ageless wisdom in the depths of his smoldering jet eyes. As she watched he lifted a decanter to the bar, and then a matching glass. He reached into the open fridge and took out a bag.

Tamara had never fainted in her life, but she came very close then. Her head floated three feet above her shoulders and her knees dissolved. For just an instant black velvet engulfed her. She didn't feel herself sink toward the floor. Eric moved even before she knew what was happening. He scooped her up as soon as she faltered, carried her to the settee and lowered her carefully. "That was unnecessary, Roland!" She heard his angry shout, but knew he hadn't moved his lips. Her sanity slipped another notch.

She sat with her back against one hard wooden arm. Eric sat beside her, his arms making walls around her. His right hand braced against the back of the settee, his left against the arm on which she leaned. She cringed into the warm green velvet. "Get away from me." Her words tripped over each other on the way past her lips. "Let me go home."

"You will go home, Tamara. As soon as you tell me what you are doing here. Is Roland correct? Have you been sent by your employers? Perhaps by St. Claire himself?"

CHAPTER SEVEN

Deny it, Eric thought desperately. *Deny it, Tamara, and I'll believe you. If it costs my existence, I'll believe you.* He watched her chalky face go even paler. He honed his senses to hers and felt a shock of paralyzing fear. Fear... of *him.* It hit him painfully.

"Tamara, you needn't be afraid. I'd sooner harm myself than you." He glanced toward Roland. "Leave us for a time." He spoke aloud to be certain Tamara understood.

He had no doubt Roland did so for the same reason. Slanting a derogatory gaze in her direction, he said, "And if she would lead a regiment of DPI forces to the back door?" He stepped out from behind the bar and came nearer. "Well, girl? Speak up. Have you come alone? How did you get in?"

Eric shot to his feet, his anger flaring hot. "I am warning you, Roland, let me take care of this matter. You are only frightening her."

"*I?* Frightening *her?* You think I felt secure when I woke and sensed a human presence in this house? For God's sake, Eric, for all I knew I was about to be skewered on a stake!"

"Th-then it's true." Tamara's voice, shaking and sounding as if every word were forced, brought Eric's gaze back to her. "You're—you both are, are—"

"Vampires," Roland spat. "It isn't a dirty word, at least, not among us."

She groaned and put her head in her hands. Roland shook his head in exasperation and turned away. Eric took his seat beside her once more. He wanted to comfort her, but wasn't certain he knew how. He pulled one of her hands into his own, and stroked her palm with his thumb. "Tamara, look at me, please." She lifted her head, but couldn't seem to meet his gaze. "Try to see beyond your fear, and the shock of this revelation. Just see me. I am the same man I was last night, and the night before. I am the same man who held you in my arms...who kissed you. Did I frighten you then? Did I give you any reason to fear me?"

Her eyes focused on his, and he thought they cleared a bit. She shook her head. More confident, he pressed on. "I am not a monster, Tamara. I'd never harm you. I'd kill anyone who tried. Listen with your heart and you'll know it to be true." He reached one hand tentatively, and when she didn't flinch or draw away he flattened one palm to her silken cheek. "Believe that."

Her brows drew together slightly, and he thought she might be thinking it over. Roland cleared his throat, her head snapped around and the fear returned to her eyes. "If it is me you fear, you need not. I do not choose to trust you as my dear friend does, but neither would I lift a finger to harm you. My anger at finding you here is directly related to my wish to continue existing." The last was said with a meaningful glance at Eric.

"Tamara." When he had her attention again, he continued. "There are those who would like nothing better than to murder us in our sleep. We both thought my security system infallible. Please, tell me how you breached it."

She swallowed. Her throat convulsed. "Where the fence ends," she said hoarsely. "At the cliff." Her gaze flew to Roland. "I didn't bring anyone here. I didn't even tell them where I—" She bit her lips before she could finish the sentence, but Eric had barely heard her words.

"At the cliff?" he repeated. For the first time he looked at her closely. Her denims were damp and caked with dirt. A streak of mud marred her high cheekbone, and her hair was wild. The scent of blood reached him from the hand he held, and he spread her fingers wider with his own. Drying blood coated her palm. Fresh trickles of it came from narrow slices at the creases of three fingers. It pulsed a bit harder from the fourth. "How did this happen?"

"I—I fell. I had to cling to the fence, and the vine patterns are sharp. They cut—"

Roland swore softly and whirled to leave the room. Eric could clearly see what she described. He sensed what had happened, her fear, her panic and her pain. The memory embedded itself in his mind as firmly as it had in hers, and it shook him to think of her coming so close to death while he slept, helpless to save her. Roland returned, dropped to his knees beside the settee and deposited a basin of warm water on the table beside it. He squeezed a clean white cloth and handed it to Eric. As Eric gently cleaned her hand, Roland looked on, his face drawn as if he, too, could envision what had happened.

The wounds cleansed, Roland produced a tiny bottle of iodine. He took Tamara's hand from Eric's, and dabbed each cut liberally with the brownish liquid. He recapped the bottle, and took another strip of white cloth from some hidden pocket beneath his cloak. Carefully he began to wrap her four fingers at the knuckle.

"It—it's only a couple of scratches," Tamara croaked, watching his movements in something like astonishment.

Roland stopped, seeming to consider for a moment. He grinned then, a bit sheepishly. "I sometimes forget what century this is. You've likely been vaccinated against tetanus. There was a time when even minor scratches like these could have cost the entire hand, if not treated." He shrugged and finished the wrapping with a neat little knot.

He glanced up at Tamara, caught her amazement and frowned. "You assumed we would go into a frenzy at the scent of your blood, like a pack of hungry wolves, did you not?"

"Enough, Roland," Eric cut in. "You cannot blame her for misconceptions about us. She's been reared by a man who loathes our kind. She only needs to see for herself we are not the monsters he would have her believe." He studied Tamara, but found she wasn't looking at either of them. She was staring at the white bandage on her hand, turning it this way and that, frowning as if she didn't quite know what it was, or how it had got there.

His stomach clenched. She'd had a scare out there at the cliff, and now another shock, in learning the truth about him. She was shaken. He'd have to go gently. "Tamara," he said softly. When she looked up, he went on. "Will you tell me why you came here?"

"I . . . had to know. I had to know."

He closed his eyes and made himself continue. "Then St. Claire doesn't know you've come to me?"

Some of the fear returned to her wide, dark eyes, but to her credit she answered honestly. "No one knows I'm here."

He swallowed, and squared his shoulders. He had to ask the next question, no matter how distasteful. "Did you come to discover my secrets, and take them back to your guardian, Tamara?"

She shook her head emphatically, straightening up in her corner of the settee. "I wouldn't do that!" When she met his gaze again, her eyes narrowed. The fear seemed to be shoved aside to make room for another emotion. "I was honest with you, Eric. I found myself telling you things I had never told anyone, and every one of them was the truth. I trusted you." Her voice broke, and she had to draw a shaky breath before she could continue. In that instant

Roland nodded toward Eric, indicating he was satisfied that she posed no threat, and would leave them alone now. Roland vanished through a darkened doorway. Tamara found her voice and rushed on.

"I told you about the nightmares, about how I thought I might be going insane. I bared my soul to you, and the whole time you were deceiving me. Daniel was right. You were only using me to get closer to him!"

Eric felt a shaft of white-hot iron pierce his heart. All she wanted at this moment was to get away from him. He swallowed his pain. "I never deceived you, Tamara."

"You deceived me by omission," she countered.

"And I would have told you the rest of it, in time. I didn't think you were ready to hear the truth."

"The truth? You mean that you've been plotting to rid yourself of an old man's harassment, and you were using me to do it?"

"That I am not like other men. I had no idea you were under St. Claire's hand until you told me yourself, and after that my only goal was to protect you from the bastard!"

"Protect me? From *Daniel?*"

Eric let his chin drop to his chest. "If I was lying to you, you would know it," he told her slowly, carefully, enunciating each word and giving each time to penetrate her mind. She was angry now. He didn't suppose that should surprise him. He met her probing, questing eyes. "We have a psychic link, Tamara. You cannot deny that. You've felt its power. When you called to me in your dreams, when I summoned you out onto the balcony. Have you realized yet that you can cry out to me, across the miles, using nothing but your mind, and that I will hear you?"

She shook her head fast. "The dream was a fluke, and beyond my control. I couldn't do it at will."

"You could. Put it to the test, if you doubt me."

"No, thank you. I just want to go home . . . and—"

"Do not say it, Tamara. You know it is untrue," Eric cut in, sensing her declaration before she uttered it.

She met his gaze, her own unwavering. "I don't want to see you again. I want you to leave me alone. I can't let myself be used to betray Daniel, or DPI."

"I would never ask you to do either one. I haven't yet, have I?" He grabbed her shoulders when she would have stood, and held her where she was. "As for the rest, now you are the one lying, Tamara—to yourself and to me. You do not wish for me to leave you alone. Quite the opposite, in fact."

She shook her head.

"Shall I prove it to you, yet again? You want me, Tamara. With the same mindless passion I feel for you. It goes far beyond the past we share. It exceeds this mental link. I would feel it even if you were a stranger. Our bond only strengthens it, and vice versa."

She stared into his eyes, and her own dampened. "I can't feel this way for you. *I can't,* dammit."

"Because I'm a vampire?"

She closed her eyes against the glycerin like tears that pooled there. "I don't even know what that means. I only know you despise the man I hold more dear to me than anything in the world."

"I despise no one. It is true that I distrust the man. But I wish him no harm, I swear to you." Her eyes opened slowly, and she studied his face. "I could not long for something that would cause you pain, Tamara. To harm St. Claire would also harm you. I can see that clearly. I'm not capable of causing you pain."

She shook her head. "I don't know what to believe. I— I just want to leave. I can't think clearly here."

"I can't let you go in this frame of mind," he said softly. "Stop trying to rationalize, Tamara. Let yourself feel what is between us. You cannot make it disappear." His gaze touched her lips, and before he could stop himself he fastened his hungry mouth over them, enfolding her in his arms and drawing her to his chest.

She remained stiff, but he felt her lips tremble against his. Barely lifting his mouth away, he whispered, "Close your mind and open your heart. Do not think. *Feel.*" His lips closed the hairbreadth of space again, nudging hers apart, feeding on the sweetness behind them. With a shudder that shook her entire body Tamara surrendered. He felt her go soft and pliable, and then her arms twined around his neck and her soft mouth opened farther. When his tongue plunged deeply into the velvet moistness, her fingers clenched in his hair. One hand fumbled with the ribbon that held his customary queue. A moment later the ribbon fell away, and she swept her fingers again and again through his hair, driving him to greater passion.

He pressed her backward until she lay against the settee's wooden arm and still farther, so her back arched over it. His own arm clutching her to him rested at the small of her back, protecting her from the hard wood. His other arm stretched lengthwise, up her spine so his hand could entangle itself in her hair. His fingers spread open to cradle her head. He moved it this way and that beneath his plundering lips to fit her to him. His chest pressed hard on hers. He drank in the honeyed elixir of her; he tasted every wet recess his tongue could reach. He caressed the roof of her mouth, the backs of her teeth and the sweet well of her throat.

She groaned, a deep, guttural sound that set an inferno blazing through him. She shifted beneath him so that one leg, bent at the knee, pressed into the back of the settee, while the other still hung off the side, onto the floor. He responded instantly and without thought, turning into her, pressing one knee to the cushion and lowering his hips to hers. He brought one hand down, sliding it beneath her firm backside and holding her to him while he ground against her. He throbbed with need, and he knew she could feel his hardness pushing insistently against her most sensitive spot, as his hand kneaded her derriere. He felt her desire racing through her, and the knowledge that she wanted just what he did added fuel to the fire incinerating his mind.

He trailed a burning path over her face with his lips, moving steadily lower, over her defined jawbone, to the soft hollow of her throat. Her jugular swelled its welcome, and her pulse thundered in anticipation. He tasted the salt of her skin on his stroking tongue, and the stream of her blood rushing beneath its surface tingled on his lips. His breathing became rapid and gruff. His own heart hammered and the blood lust twined with the sexual arousal, enhancing it until both roared in his ears as one entity.

Another moment—another of her heated, whimpering breaths bathing his skin, or one more shift of her luscious body against his straining groin—and it would take over completely. He'd lose control. He'd tear her clothing off and he'd take her. He'd take her completely. He'd bury himself inside her so deeply she'd cry out, and he'd drink the nectar from her veins until he was sated.

She arched against him then, pressing her throat hard against his mouth, and her hips tighter to his manhood. She shivered from her toes to her lips. Even her hands on his back and in his hair trembled, and she moaned softly—a plea for something she wasn't even fully aware of craving.

He gathered every ounce of strength in him and tore himself from her so roughly he almost stumbled to the floor. He whirled away from her, bent nearly double, holding the edge of the table for support.

He heard her gasp in surprise, then he heard the strangled sob that broke from her lips, and when he dared look at her, her knees were drawn to her chest, her face pressed to them. "Why—" she began.

"I'm sorry. Tamara, you make me forget common sense. You make me forget everything except how badly I want you."

"Then . . ." She paused for a long moment and drew a shuddery breath. "Then why did you stop?"

He had to close his eyes. She'd lifted her tearstained face to search his for an answer. When he opened them again, she was dashing her tears away with the backs of her hands. "I came to you to help you, to protect you. You called to me for help. You thought yourself slipping away from sanity. I had to come to you. But not for this—not to satisfy my own unquenchable lust."

She shook her head in obvious confusion. He stepped forward, extended his hands, and she slipped her feet to the floor, took them in her own and rose.

"There are still many things you do not fully understand. No matter how badly I want you—and I do, never doubt that—I cannot let my desire cloud my good judgment. You are not ready."

She glanced up at him, and very slightly her lips turned up. "I don't know anything about you, and yet I feel I know you better than anyone. One thing I do know is that you were right when you said you were different from other men. Any other man wouldn't have stopped himself just now. The hell with what was best for me." She sighed and shook her head. "When I'm with you, even I say the hell with what is best for me. Sensation takes over. It's as if I lose my will. It frightens me."

His lips thinned and he nodded. He well understood what she was feeling. The powerful feelings seemed beyond her control. Well, they seemed beyond his, as well. But he'd keep himself in check if it killed him.

"Will you tell me yet, how I know you? When did we get so close? Why can't I remember?"

He reached out, unable to resist touching her again. His body screamed for contact with hers. He lifted her hair away from her head, and let it fall through his fingers. "You have had enough to deal with tonight, Tamara. Your mind will give you the memory when it can accept and understand. It grieves me to refuse anything you ask of me, but, believe me, I feel it is better for you to remember on your own. Ask me anything else, anything at all."

She tilted her head to one side, seeming to accept what he said. Then, "You told me your father was murdered in Paris. Was it during the revolution?"

He sighed his relief. He'd thought she would run from him. Even the strength of their passion hadn't frightened her away...yet. He slipped an arm around her shoulders, and she walked beside him easily. He drew her into the corridor, and through it to the library, where he flicked the switch, flooding the room with harsh electric light. Normally he wouldn't have bothered. He'd simply have lit a lamp or two. He waved a hand to the huge portrait of his parents on the wall. It had been commissioned shortly after their marriage, and so had captured them in the bloom of youth and the height of beauty.

"Your parents?" She caught her breath when he nodded. "She's so beautiful, such delicate features and skin like porcelain. Her hair is like yours."

At her words Eric felt a rush of memory. He saw again his petite mother, remembered the softness of her hair and the sweet sound of her voice. She'd spurned the trend of leaving the child rearing to the nurse. She'd tucked him into bed each night, and sung to him in that lilting, lulling voice.

He hadn't realized Tamara stared at him, until she suddenly clutched his hand and blinked moisture from her eyes. "You must miss her terribly."

"At least she escaped the bloody terror. Both she and my sister, Jaqueline, lived out their lives to the natural end, in England. My father wasn't so fortunate. He was beheaded in Paris. I would have been, too, if not for Roland."

"That's when you were...changed?" Eric nodded. "And afterward, when you were free, why didn't you join your mother and sister in England?"

"I couldn't go to them then, Tamara. I was no longer the son or the brother they remembered—the awkward, withdrawn outsider who never fit in and lacked confidence enough to try. I was changed, strong, sure of myself, powerful. How could I have explained all of the differences in me, or the fact that I could only see them by night?"

"It might not have mattered to them," she said, placing a hand gently on his arm.

"Or it might have made them despise and fear me. I couldn't have borne that...to see revulsion in the eyes of my own mother. No. It was easier to let them believe me dead and go on with their lives."

The night was a revelation. What at first had frightened and shocked her she soon found only one more unique thing about Eric Marquand. He was a vampire. What did that mean? she wondered. That the sun would kill him, the way inhaling water would kill a human? It meant he needed human blood in order to exist. She'd seen for herself how he acquired it. Not by killing or maiming innocent people, but by stealing it from blood banks.

As the hours of the night raced past he told her of the night he'd helped his mother and sister escape France, and been arrested himself. At her gentle coaxing he'd shared more of his past. He'd related tales of his boyhood that made her laugh, and revealed a love for his long-lost mother that made her cry. He might not be human, but he had human emotions. She sensed a pain within him that would have crippled her had it been her own. How many centuries of a nearly solitary existence could one man bear?

She found herself likening her solitude to his, and feeling another level of kinship with him. By the time he walked her to her car the feeling that she'd known him forever had overwhelmed her confusion over his true nature.

Until she arrived home, after midnight, to find Daniel and Curtis waiting like guard dogs. "Where have you been?" They snapped the question almost in unison.

"Here we go again," she muttered, keeping her bandaged hand thrust into her pocket. "I was out. I had some thinking to do, and you both know how much I enjoy crisp wintry nights. I just lost track of time."

She was shocked speechless when Curtis gripped her upper arm hard and drew her close. His gaze burned over her throat, and she knew what he sought. "You saw Marquand tonight, didn't you, Tammy?"

"You think I'd tell you if I did? You are not my keeper, Curt."

He released her, turned away and pushed a hand through his hair. Daniel took his place. "He's only worried, just as I am, honey. I told you before we suspected he'd try to see you again. Please, you have to tell me if he did. It's for your own good."

If she told Daniel the truth he'd probably have a coronary, she thought. She swallowed against the bile that rose at the thought of telling him the truth. But lying was equally distasteful. "I didn't see anyone tonight, Daniel. I'm confused and frustrated. I needed to be alone, without you two hovering." She'd done it. She'd told an out-and-out lie to the man she loved most in the world. She felt like a Judas.

Curtis faced her again. He took her arm, gently this time, and led her to the sofa, pushing her down. "It's time you heard a few harsh truths, kid. The first one is this. I do have the right to ask. I love you, you little idiot. I always assumed you'd realize that sooner or later, and marry me. Lately, though, you've been acting like I'm a stranger. I'm tired of it. I've had enough. It ends, here and now. I won't let Marquand come between us."

"Come between—Curtis, how can he? There is no *us*."

He sighed in frustration, looking at her as if she were dense. "You see what I mean?" He made his voice gentler, and he sat down beside her. "Tamara, no matter what he's told you, you have to remember what he is. He'll lie so smoothly you'll hang on every word. He'll convince you he cares about you, when the truth is, he only cares about eliminating any threat to his existence. And at the moment the threat in question is Daniel. Don't let his words confuse you, Tammy. We are the ones who love you. We are the ones who've been here for you, who know you inside and out."

She wanted to answer him, but found herself tongue-tied.

"I know what's happening," Curt went on. "They have an incredible psychic ability. He's pulling one of the oldest tricks in the book on you, Tammy. I'd bet money on it. He's planting feelings in your mind, making you think you know him. You feel like you are intimate friends, but you can't remember when you met or where. You trust him instinctively—only it isn't instinctive. It's his damn mind commanding yours to trust him. He can do it, you know. He can fill your head with all these vague feelings for him, and make you ignore the ones that are real."

My God, could he be right?

"You're confused, Tam," Daniel added slowly, carefully. "He's keeping you awake nights by exerting his power over you. That's why you feel as if you can sleep during the day. He rests then. He can't influence your mind. By using the added susceptibility caused by the lack of sleep, his power over your mind can get stronger and stronger. Believe me, sweetheart, I've seen it happen before."

She stared from one of them to the other, as a sickening feeling grew within her. What they'd said made perfect sense. Yet she felt a certainty in her heart that they were wrong. Or was that in her mind—put there by Eric? How could she tell what she felt from what he was making her feel?

"What reason would I have to lie to you, Tam?" Daniel asked.

She shook her head. She couldn't bring herself to tell the truth. She'd feel as if she were betraying Eric if she did. But she felt she was betraying them by keeping it from them. She had a real sensation of being torn in half. "It doesn't matter, because you're wrong. I haven't seen him since the night at the rink. He hasn't been on my mind at all, except when you two hound me about him. And my insomnia was just from stress. It's gone now. I'm sleeping just fine. In fact, I'd like to be sleeping right now."

She rose and made her way past them, and up the stairs to her room. She collapsed on the bed and pushed her face into the pillows. She wouldn't close her eyes until dawn. Was it because of Eric? Was he trying to take over her mind? Oh, God, how could she ever know for sure? She herself had said that she couldn't think clearly when she was with him. And hadn't he demonstrated how he could take control of her that night on the balcony?

She sat up in bed, eyes flying wide. How could she stop it?

"I can't see him anymore," she whispered. "I have to stay away from him and give myself a chance to see this without his influence. I need to be objective." The decision made, her heart proceeded to crumble as if it were made of crystal and had just been pummeled with a sledgehammer. "I can't see him again," she repeated, and the bits were ground to dust.

CHAPTER EIGHT

"She despises me." Eric drew away from the microscope at the sound of his friend entering the lab where he'd ensconced himself for the third night running.

"She might fear you, Eric, but it's as you pointed out. She's been reared by a man who thinks us monsters. Give her time to adjust to the idea."

"She's repulsed by the idea." Eric pressed four fingertips to the dull ache at the center of his forehead. "There is nothing I can do to change that. The fact remains, though, that she is in trouble."

Roland frowned. "The nightmares have returned?"

"No, and she no longer cries out to me. But she hasn't slept since last I saw her. I feel her exhaustion to the point where it saps my own strength. She cannot continue this way."

"Not since you saw her? Eric, it's been three nights—"

"Tonight will make four. She's on the verge of collapse. I want to go to her. But to force my presence on her if she's not yet able to handle it could do more harm than good, I think. Especially in her present state of mind."

Roland nodded. "I have to agree. But it's killing you to stay away, is it not, Eric?"

Eric sighed, his gaze sweeping the ceiling as his head tilted back. "That it is. What is worse is that I am not certain I can help her when she's ready to accept my assistance. Why does she not sleep? Is it simply the blocked memory of our encounters keeping her from her rest, or something more? Is it possible that my blood changed her in some way—that its effect is felt even now, after all this time? Or is it only when I'm near she suffers this way? Would she be better off if I left the country again?"

"Use a bit of sense, Eric! Would you leave her without aid in the hands of that butcher who calls himself a scientist?"

Eric shook his head. "No. That I could never do. If these things have occurred to me, they must have occurred to him, as well. I'd not be surprised if he decided to use her for his experiments."

"Are you certain he hasn't?"

"I'd know if she were in pain, or distress."

"Perhaps he has her sedated, unconscious," Roland suggested.

"No. She doesn't summon me, but I feel her. I feel the wall she's erected to keep herself from me. She resists the very thought of me." An odd lump formed in his throat, nearly choking him, and an unseen fist squeezed his heart.

The nights were the hardest. She'd taken to staying late at the DPI building in White Plains. Her reasons were multiple. One was that she got a lot more work done after sunset. No matter how physically and emotionally drained she became, the energy surged after dark. She wondered why Eric would want to torture her this way. She couldn't give in to her body's need for rest during the day. She'd convinced Daniel that she was better, and for the moment it seemed he believed her. At least he wasn't hovering over her constantly. Then again, she hadn't left the house except to go to work and come home again, in days.

Curtis was another problem altogether. He checked in on her three or four times every day while she was at work, and it was an effort to appear wide awake and bright eyed at his surprise visits. He hadn't mentioned again his outrageous suggestion that she marry him. She was grateful for that. She knew he didn't love her, and still had enough acumen in her dulled mind to understand what had prompted his words. He wanted to protect her from the alleged threat of Eric Marquand. He wanted her under his thumb twenty-four hours a day, and especially those hours after dark. He saw that she was outgrowing his and Daniel's ability to control her. As her husband, he assumed he could keep her in line. She couldn't hate him for it. After all, it was only because he cared so much and was so concerned about her that he had spoken at all.

She gathered up the files on her desk and carried them toward the cabinet to put them in their places. The sun had vanished. She felt wide awake. It frightened her. How much longer could she go on without sleep?

Another question lingered in the back of her mind, one more troubling than the first. She avoided it when she could, but at night found it impossible. Why did she feel so empty inside? Why did she miss him so? It was foolish, she barely knew the man. Or did she? She found it difficult to believe that her sense of knowing him in the past had been planted there by some kind of hypnosis. The familiar sense of him didn't seem based in her mind, but in her heart, *her soul*. And so was the aching need to see him again. She longed for him so much it hurt. How could this feeling be false, the result of a spell she was under?

"Tamara?"

She looked up fast, startled at the soft voice intruding on her thoughts. She blinked away the burning moisture that had gathered in her eyes, and rose, forcing a smile for Hilary Garner.

Hilary smiled back, but her chocolate eyes were narrow. "You look like you've been ridden hard and put away wet," she quipped. "And you've been doing a great impression of a recluse lately, Tam. Haven't even been coming outside for lunch. I've missed it.''

Tamara sighed, and couldn't meet the other girl's eyes. Hilary was the closest friend she had, besides Daniel and Curtis. They used to do things together. Lately, Tamara realized, she'd had no thought for anyone other than Eric. "It wasn't intentional," she said, and shrugged. "I've had a lot on my mind."

A soft hand, the color of a doe and just as graceful, settled on Tamara's shoulder. "You want to tell me about it?"

Tears sprang anew, and her throat closed painfully. "I can't."

Hilary nodded. "If you can't, you can't. You aren't going home to that mausoleum to brood on it all night, either, unless you're going through me." The mock severity of her voice was comforting.

Tamara met her gaze, grateful that she didn't pry. "What, then?"

"Nothing wild. You don't look up to it. How about a nice quiet dinner someplace? We'll get your mind off whatever's been bugging you."

Tamara nodded as all the air left her lungs. It was a relief that she could put off going home, pacing the hollow house alone while Daniel and Curt either huddled over their latest "breakthrough" in the off-limits basement lab, or took off to spy on Eric for the night.

Daniel appeared in the doorway and Tamara flashed him a smile that was, for once, genuine. "I'm going to dinner with Hilary," she announced. "I'll be home later and if you waste your time worrying about me I'll be very upset with you."

He frowned, but didn't ask her not to go. "Promise me you'll come straight home afterward?"

"Yes, Daniel," she said with exaggerated submissiveness.

He dug in his pocket and brought out a set of keys. "Take the Cadillac. I don't want you stranded in that old car of yours."

"And what if *you* end up stalling the Bug alongside the road somewhere?"

"I'll have Curt follow me home." He held the keys in an outstretched hand and she stepped forward and took them. She dropped them into her purse, extracted her own set and handed them to Daniel. He gave her a long look, seemed to want to say something, but didn't. He left with a sigh that told her he didn't like the idea of her going out at night.

It was worth it, though. For three wonderful hours she and Hilary lingered over every course, from the huge salad and the rich hot soup to the deliciously rare steaks and baked potatoes with buttery baby carrots on the side, and even dessert—cherry cheesecake. Tamara ordered wine with dinner. It was not her habit to imbibe, but she had the glimmering hope that if she had a few drinks tonight, she might be able to sleep when she got home. She allowed the waiter to refill her wineglass three times, and when dinner was over and Hilary ordered an after-dinner seven-seven, Tamara said, "Make it two."

The conversation flowed as it had in the old days, before the nightmares and sleepless nights. For a short time she felt as if she were a normal woman with a strong, healthy mind. The evening ended all too soon, and she said goodbye reluctantly in the parking lot outside and hurried to Daniel's car. She took careful stock of herself before she got behind the wheel. She counted the number of drinks she'd had, and then the number of hours. Four and four. She felt fine. Assured her ability was not impaired, she started the car, pulled on the headlights and backed carefully out of the lot.

She'd take her time driving home, she thought. She'd listen to the radio and not think about the things that were wrong in her life. When she got home, she'd choose a wonderful book from Daniel's shelves and she'd lose herself in reading it. She wouldn't worry about vampires or brainwashing or insane asylums.

The flat tire did not fall in with her plan, however. She thanked her lucky stars she was near an exit ramp, and veered onto it, limping pathetically along the shoulder. She stopped the boat-sized car as soon as she came to a relatively sane spot to do so, and sat for a moment, drumming her fingers on the steering wheel. "I never replaced the spare," she reminded herself.

She looked up and spotted the towering, lighted gas station sign in the distance, not more than three hundred yards from her. With a sigh of resignation she wrenched open the car door, and hooked the strap of her purse over her shoulder with her thumb. She spent one moment hoping the attendant would be a chivalrous type, who'd offer her a ride back to the car... and maybe even change the tire for her.

She almost laughed aloud at that notion. She knew full well that a few minutes from now she'd be heading back to her car, on foot, rolling a new tire and rim along in front of her. Oh, well, she'd changed tires before. She walked along the shoulder, glad of the streetlights in addition to the moon illuminating the pavement ahead of her. Her cheerful demeanor deserted her, though, when a carload of laughing youths passed her, blasting heavy metal from open windows despite the below-freezing temperature, and came to a screeching halt. Two men—boys, really—got out and stood unsteadily. Probably due to whatever had been in the bottles they both gripped.

She turned, deciding it would be better to drive to the station, even if it meant ruining the rim. As soon as she did, the rusted Mustang that seemed to have no muffler lurched into Reverse and roared past her again. It stopped on the shoulder this time and the driver got out. He came slowly toward her. The object in his hand that caught and reflected the light wasn't a bottle. It was a blade.

She stiffened as they closed in on her, two from behind, one dead ahead. No traffic passed in those elongated seconds. She considered darting off to the side, but that would only put her in a scrub lot where they'd be able to catch her, anyway. Better, she decided, to take her chances here. Any second now a car would pass and she'd wave her arms...step in front of it, if necessary.

She glanced over her shoulder at the two youths. One wore tattered jeans and a plaid shirt, unbuttoned and blowing away from his bare, skinny chest in the frigid wind. The other wore sweats and a leather jacket. Both looked sorely in need of a bath and a haircut, but she couldn't believe they'd hurt her. She didn't think either of them was old enough to have legally bought the beer they were swilling down.

She caught her breath when her arm was gripped, and she swung her head forward. The one who held her was no kid. His long, greasy hair hung to his shoulders, but was rooted in a horseshoe shape around a shiny pate. He was shorter than she and a good fifty pounds overweight. He grinned at her. There were gaps in his slimy teeth.

Without a word he took her purse, releasing her arm to do so, but still holding the knife in his other hand. She took a step back and he lifted it fast, pressing the tip just beneath one breast. "Move it and lose it, lady." He tossed her purse over her head, where the two boys now stood close behind her. "Her big Caddy has a flat. You two get it changed, and we'll have ourselves a little joyride."

"There is no spare," she took great pleasure in telling him, thinking it might thwart his plan to steal Daniel's car.

"But you were on your way to buy one, right, honey?" She didn't answer, as the boy in the leather jacket pawed the contents of her purse. "Ninety-five bucks and change in here."

The man with the knife smiled more broadly. "Take it and go to the station. Take the Mustang. Bring the tire back here and get it changed." He traced her breast with the tip of the knife, not hard enough to cut, but she winced in pain and fear. "I'll just keep the lady company while you're gone."

She heard the patter of their feet over the pavement, then they were past her, on their way to the noisy car. They spun the tires as they headed for the gas station. The man turned her around abruptly, twisting one arm behind her back. He shoved her down the slight slope toward the brush lot. "We'll just wait for 'em down here, outta sight."

"The hell we will." She struck backward with one foot, but he caught it with a quick uplift of his own and she wound up facedown in the snow with him on her back.

"You want it right here, that's fine with me," he growled into her ear. She cried out, and immediately felt the icy blade against her throat. Her face was shoved cruelly into the snow, and then his hand was groping beneath her, shoving up inside her blouse, tugging angrily at her bra. When he touched her, her stomach heaved.

My God, she thought, there was no way out of this. Daniel wouldn't worry. He thought her out with Hilary. Even if he did come looking for her, he'd never look here. She'd only used this exit because of the flat. Her normal route home was three exits farther on the highway. His breath fanned her face. With one last vicious pinch he dragged his hot hand away from her breast, and tried to shove it down the front of her jeans, while his hips writhed against her backside.

He's going to do it, she thought. White panic sent her mind whirling, and she fought for control. She couldn't give up. She wouldn't allow herself to feel the hand that violated her. She refused to vomit, because if she did, she'd likely choke to death. She needed help.

Calm descended as Eric's face filled her mind. His words, soothing her with the deep tenor of his voice, rang in her ears. *I'd never harm you. I'd kill anyone who tried.* She closed her eyes. Had he meant what he'd said? *Have you realized yet,* his voice seemed to whisper in her mind, drowning out the frantic panting of the pig on top of her, *that you can cry out to me, across the miles, using nothing but your mind?*

Could she do it? Would he answer if she did?

If you need me, Tamara, call me. I will come to you.

He had managed to unbutton her jeans. The zipper gaped. He rose from her slightly, removing his filthy, vile hand, to fumble with his own fly. She squeezed her eyes tight and tried to make her thoughts coherent. *Help me, Eric. Please, if you meant what you said, help me.* At the sound of his zipper being lowered she felt the oddest sensation that her mind was literally screaming through time and space. It was a frightening feeling, but not unfamiliar. She'd felt it before . . . in her dreams. The urgency of her thoughts pierced her brain with a high-pitched pain. *I need you, Eric! For God's sake, help me!*

Eric paused in swirling the liquid in the test tube, and his head tilted to one side. He frowned, then shook his head and continued.

"So what's this hocus-pocus?"

He glanced at Roland, one brow raised. "I am trying to isolate the single property in human blood that keeps us alive."

"And what will you do then? Develop it in a tiny pill and expect us to live on them?"

"It would be more convenient than robbing blood banks, my friend." He smiled, but it died almost instantly. His head snapped up and the glass tube fell to the floor and shattered.

Roland jerked in surprise. "What is it, Eric?"

"Tamara." He whipped the latex gloves from his hands as he moved through the room. The white coat followed and then he raced through the corridors of the enormous house, pausing only to snatch his coat from a hook on the way out. By the time he reached the gate he was moving with the preternatural speed that rendered his form no more than a blur to human eyes. He used the speed and momentum to carry him cleanly over the barrier, and sensed Roland at his side. He honed his mind to Tamara's and felt a rush of sickening fear, and icy cold.

Minutes. It took only minutes to reach her, but they seemed like hours to Eric. He stood still for an instant, filling with rage when he saw the bastard wrench her onto her back and attempt to shove her denims down her hips as his mouth covered hers.

Her eyes closed tight, she twisted her face away, and sobbed his name. "Eric... oh, God, Eric, please..."

He gripped the back of the thug's shirt and lifted him away from her, to send him tumbling into the snow. He bent over the stunned man, pulled him slightly upward by his shirtfront and smashed his face with his right fist. He drew back and hit him again, and would have continued doing so had not her soft cry cut through the murderous rage enveloping him. He turned, saw her lying in the snow and let the limp, bloody-faced man fall from his hands.

He went to her, falling to his knees and pulling her trembling body into his arms. He lifted her easily, cradling her, rocking her. "It's over. I'm here. He can't hurt you now." He pressed his face into her hair, and closed his eyes. "He can't hurt you. No one can. I won't allow it."

She drew one shuddering, slow breath, then another, and yet another. Suddenly her arms linked around his neck. She turned her face into the crook of his neck and shoulder and she sobbed—violent, racking sobs that he thought would tear her in two. She clung to him as if to a lifeline, and he held her tightly. For a long while he simply held her and let her cry. He whispered into her hair, words of comfort and reassurance. It was over now. She was safe.

With an involuntary spasmodic sob she lifted her head, searched his face, her eyes brimming with tears and wide with wonder. "You came to me. You really came to me. I called you . . ."

He blinked against the tears that clouded his vision, and pushed the tangled hair away from her face. "I could not do otherwise. And you should not be so surprised. I told you I would, did I not?"

She nodded.

"I cannot lie to you. I never have, and I swear to you now, I never will." He studied her, knowing she believed him. Her blouse had been torn, and hung from one shoulder in tatters. The fastenings of her denims hung open. She was wet from the snow, and shaking with cold and with reaction, no doubt. He carried her up the slope to the pavement. Roland moved around the automobile. Eric saw that the tire lay on the pavement. Roland had the jack and its handle in his hands and he tossed them into the open trunk.

When he reached the car he glanced down at Tamara once more. She still clung tightly. "Are you injured? Can you stand?"

She lifted her head from his shoulder. "I'm okay. Just a little shaky."

Eric lowered her gently to the pavement, and opened the passenger door of the car. He kept hold of her shoulders as she got in. Roland had just tossed the flat tire into the trunk and slammed it down. Eric called to him. "Where are the others?"

Roland answered mentally, not aloud. *Ran like rabbits, my friend.*

You let them go? Roland, you ought to have thrashed them for this, Eric answered silently, falling into the old habit of speaking that way with his friend.

What of her attacker? Did you kill him?

Not yet. His anger returned when he thought of how close the bastard had come to raping Tamara. *But I intend to, and then those sorry curs that helped him.*

Murder doesn't suit you, Eric. And the other two were mere lads. Leave this as it is. It will be for the best.

Tamara rose from her seat in the car, and Eric realized he hadn't closed the door. Her hand came to his shoulder, and with surprising calm she said, "Roland is right, Eric. They were just kids. When they see the shape you left their friend in, they'll realize how lucky they were tonight. And you know you can't go back there and murder that man in cold blood. It isn't in you."

Both men glanced at her, Roland's gaze astonished. He lifted his brows and spoke aloud. "This will require getting used to. It is odd to think a human can hear my thoughts, although I assume it only occurs when I am conversing with you, Eric. She hears what you hear."

Eric nodded. He slipped his coat from his shoulders, and arranged it over her like a blanket. "She hears what I hear," he repeated. "She can feel what I feel, if she only looks deeply enough. She can read my thoughts and my feelings. I can keep nothing from her." He spoke to Roland but his words were for Tamara's ears. He longed to have her trust. "I'm going to drive her home. Care to ride along?"

Roland took a step away from the auto as if it might bite him. "In that?"

Tamara smiled. Her gaze slid to Eric's and he smiled, as well. She would be all right.

"I am glad you both find my aversion to these machines so highly amusing. I shall manage to travel under my own power, thank you." With a dramatic whirl of his black cloak he vanished into the darkness.

Eric closed Tamara's door, circled the car and got in beside her. For a long moment he simply looked at her, drinking in the familiar beauty of her face. Her eyes moved over his in like manner, as if she, too, had craved the sight of him.

He dragged his gaze away, and searched the car's panel. "It's been a while," he told her, frowning. "But I assume you still need a key."

Her smile sent warmth surging through him. She glanced around, and pointed into the rear seat. "It was in my purse."

He glanced where she pointed and spotted her handbag, spilling over the back seat. He leaned over, located the keys and returned to the correct position. It took him a moment to locate the switch. The last time he'd driven a car the switch had been on the dashboard, not the side of the steering wheel.

He inserted the key, turned it on and jerked at the mechanical hum the car emitted. She laughed aloud, the sound like music to him. He felt some of her tension leaving her with that laughter.

"How long has it been?" she asked him, amusement in her voice.

Smiling, he looked at her. "I don't recall, exactly. But fear not, I am a quick study. Now then . . ." His feet did a little tap dance on the floorboard. "Where's the clutch?"

"It's automatic." She slid across the seat, closer to him, and pointed to the pedals on the floor. "There is the brake and that's the accelerator. Now hold your foot on the brake."

He slipped an arm around her shoulders and drew her closer to his side. He pressed his foot onto the pedal she indicated. She put her finger on the indicator. "Look. Park, Reverse, Neutral, Drive. Put it in Drive." He did, smelling her hair, then jerking his head around when the car began to move.

He eased it onto the street and moved it slowly until he got a feel for the thing. Soon he maneuvered the car easily, finding the correct ramp and bringing them onto the highway.

"You said you could never lie to me," she said softly, settling close to him. "Is it true?"

"I could attempt to lie to you, but if I did, and you paid attention, you would know." He tightened his arms on her shoulders. "But I'd never have reason to lie to you, Tamara."

She nodded. "I don't want to go right home. Could we stop somewhere? Talk for a while?"

CHAPTER NINE

She didn't need to tell him that the first thing she had to do was to wash the memory of the vile man's touch away from her body. It amazed her that he could read her so well, but he did. He took her to his home, parking the Cadillac within the fence, and around a bend in the driveway, so it couldn't be seen from the highway. He then suggested she call Daniel with a plausible explanation for her lateness. She told Daniel that she and Hilary were heading to a nightclub after dinner, and that she didn't know how late she'd be. He grumbled, but didn't throw too much of a fit. She had to give him credit. He was trying.

When she replaced the receiver of the telephone, Eric reentered the living room, carrying a tray with a bottle of brandy and a delicate-looking long-stemmed bubble glass. She eyed it, unconsciously rubbing one palm over her breast where the pig had touched her.

"His filth can't touch you, Tamara. You're too pure to be sullied by one so vile."

She realized what she'd been doing and drew her hand away. "I feel dirty...contaminated."

"I know. It is a normal reaction, from what I understand. Would you feel less so if you bathed?"

She closed her eyes. "God, yes. I want to scrub myself raw every place he—"

"I sensed as much. I drew a bath for you while you spoke to St. Claire."

Her eyes opened then. "You did?"

He lowered the tray, poured the glass half-full of brandy and brought it to her. One arm around her shoulders, he led her down a long, high-ceilinged corridor, and through a door.

The room glowed with amber light from the oil lamps, and the tall, elegant candles that burned on every inch of available space. A claw-footed, ivory-toned tub brimmed with bubbly, steaming water. He took the brandy from her unresisting hand and set the glass on a stand near the tub. He picked up what looked like a remote control from the same spot, thumbed a button, and soft music wafted into the room, as soothing as the steam that rose from the water, or the halo glows of light around the myriad of tiny flames.

She leaned over the tub, touched an iridescent bubble and felt the spatters on her wrist when it popped. His hand touched her shoulder and she turned, staring up at him in wonder. "I can't believe you did all this."

"I want to comfort you, Tamara. I want to erase the horror that touched you tonight. I want to replace it with tenderness. I cherish you. Do you know that?"

She felt a lump in her throat. His words were so poignant they made her eyes burn.

"I won't lose control. I couldn't unleash my passions on you after what you've experienced tonight. I only want to pamper you, to show you..." He closed his eyes, lifted her hand to his lips. He kissed her knuckles, one by one, then opened his eyes and turned her hand over and pressed his lips to her palm.

She gave her consent, without parting her lips. He heard it, it seemed. He gently removed her tattered blouse, and set it aside. He reached around her, unhooked her bra in the back and then drew the straps down over her shoulders. Her right breast was bruised, and she felt the marks of the other man's fingers would never go away completely.

"The marks are only skin-deep, and they will fade." He pushed her still-damp jeans down, lifted his hands and she held them, to balance while she stepped out of them. She removed the panties herself. She didn't want him to look down at her body. She still felt dirty, despite his words. He kept his gaze magnetized to hers, holding her hands as she lifted one foot, then the other into the bubbly water. She sank slowly down, leaning back against the cool porcelain and closing her eyes.

She felt the touch of the chill glass in her palm and she closed her hand on it. "Sip," Eric instructed. "Relax. Let the tension ebb. Hear Wolfgang's genius."

She tasted the brandy, not opening her eyes. "Mmm. This is wonderful."

"Cognac," he replied. She heard the trickle of water, then felt a warm cloth moving over her throat, and around to the back of her neck.

She frowned, still keeping her eyes closed. "There used to be a legend about vampires and running water...."

She heard his low chuckle. The cloth left her skin to plunge into the water. He squeezed it out, lathered it with soap and returned to his gentle cleansing—of her soul, it seemed. "Completely false." He moved slowly over her chest, washing her breasts as her heartbeat quickened. But he didn't touch her in passion, only in comfort. "And so is the one about the garlic, or wolfsbane. And, as you already know, the crucifix."

"But sunlight..."

"Yes, sunlight is my enemy. It is one of the things I try to work out in my laboratory. The how of it, and the why. What I might do to change it." He sighed, and lathered her stomach and abdomen. "I can't tell you how much I miss the sun." His hand, covered by the wet cloth, moved over her rib cage beneath the water, and down her side.

"The wooden stake?"

"It isn't the stake that would do me in. Any sharp object could, if used properly. A vampire is almost like a sufferer of hemophilia. We could bleed to death quite easily." He ran the cloth between her legs all too briefly, and then moved on to rhythmically massage her thighs.

"Why do we have this mental link?" She took another long, slow drink of the cognac and opened her eyes to watch his face as he answered.

"I will try to begin to explain it to you. You see, not just any human can become a vampire. There are, in fact, very few who could be transformed, all of whom have two common traits." He moved to her calf, kneading the back of it as he soaped it for her. "One is the bloodline. It traces back to a common ancestor, but I suspect it goes back much farther, even, than that."

"Who?"

He captured one of her feet in both his soapy hands and lifted it from the water to rub and caress and massage it until the foot and his hands were invisible beneath a mound of suds. "Prince Vlad the Impaler...better known as—"

"Dracula," she breathed, awestruck.

"Exactly. The other trait—" he rubbed her big toe between his thumb and forefinger "—is in the blood itself. There is an antigen called Belladonna."

She sat up fast. "But I have the Belladonna antigen." He turned his face toward her, his gaze momentarily locking onto her breasts, jiggling with the sudden movement just above the water's surface, bubbles clinging, sliding slowly down.

He licked his lips. "Yes, and you have the ancestor, as well. Such humans with both traits are rare. We call them the Chosen. Always there is a mental link between us and them, though in most cases the humans are unaware of it. We know if they are in danger, and we do our best to protect them. The incident in Paris was not the first time Roland had saved my life, you see." He forced his head to turn away again, she noticed, and he went to work, with his magic hands and fingers, on her other foot. "That is where our link began. It became much stronger, and that part of it you must remember on your own."

She lowered herself into the water again. She believed him. She no longer doubted what he'd told her. The sensation of being able to see what was in his mind was awesome to her, but very real. She knew, for instance, that it would do her no good to insist he tell her more of their past and this link. He wouldn't. For her sake, he wouldn't. And she knew, right now, the effort it was costing him not to jerk her roughly into his arms and to kiss her until her head swam with desire. He held himself in rigid check, knowing the terror she'd felt tonight. For her sake, he held back.

He loved her.

His love was like a soft, warm blanket, enveloping her and protecting her from the world. Nothing could touch her with this feeling around her. It was heaven to be loved so much. Cherished, as he'd told her. The emotions touched her almost physically. Their warmth was palpable.

"Roll over," he said, his voice very deep and soft in the tiny room. She did, folding her arms on the tub's rim to make a pillow for her head. His powerful hands worked the soapy cloth over her back and shoulders. He massaged and caressed and washed her all at once, and his every touch was pure ecstasy. God, she wondered. What would it be like to make love to him?

He shuddered. She felt his hands tremble with it. He heard her thoughts. With her face averted she found the courage to speak them aloud. "Why do you always...hold back?"

His sigh was not quite steady. "This is not the wisest subject to discuss with you naked, wet and plied with brandy."

He kneaded her buttocks with soapy hands, but removed them soon. She rolled over, studying his face in the candlelight. "Do you want me?"

His jaw twitched as he studied her. "More than I want to draw another breath."

"Then why—"

"Hush." The command was bitten out. He rose from his crouching position beside the tub and pulled a blanket-sized towel from a rack. He held it wide open and waited. "It is for your own good, Tamara," he told her.

Tamara got up, stepped out of the bath and onto the thick rug beside the tub. His towel-draped arms closed around her, then moved away, leaving the towel behind. "I'll leave you to dress—"

"You didn't leave me to undress," she snapped. She wasn't certain what made her angrier—the knowledge that she wanted him or the fact that he refused to oblige her.

"Your blouse is ruined." He nodded toward the stand where he'd placed her clothes after she'd discarded them. "There is one of my shirts for you to wear." He turned from her and strode out of the room.

"For my own good," she fumed after he left her. She reached down into the bubbly water and jerked the stopper out. "Why is everything I hate always supposedly for my own good? It's like *I* don't know what's good for me and what isn't."

She roughly adjusted the towel under her arms, and tucked the corners in to hold it there. She knew what was good for her. She was an adult, not a child. She wanted him, whatever he was. And he wanted her, dammit. All of this honorable restraint bull was making her crazy. The only time she felt right anymore was when he held her, when he kissed her.

Tonight . . . tonight more than ever she needed that feeling of rightness, of belonging. She moved very slowly through the door, down the hallway and back into the living room. Eric's back was to her. He knelt in front of the fireplace, feeding sticks into it. She made no sound as she moved barefoot over the parquet floor, onto the colorful Oriental rug, but he knew she approached. She felt it. She stopped when she stood right behind him, and she placed her damp hands on his shoulders. He'd removed his jacket when they'd arrived here, and rolled his shirt sleeves up when he'd bathed her. His arms, bare to the elbows and taut with tense muscles, stilled at her touch.

Slowly he rose. He turned, and when he looked down at her, his eyes seemed almost pain filled. "You are not making this easy."

His white shirt's top two buttons were open. She touched the expanse of his chest visible there. "Make love to me, Eric."

So hoarsely she wouldn't have known his voice, he answered. "Don't you know that I would if I could?"

"Then tell me why. Make me understand—"

"I'm not human! What more do you need to know?"

"Everything!" She curled her hand around his neck, her fingers moving through the short, curling hairs at his nape, then playing at the queue. "You want to love me, Eric. I feel it every time you look at me. And don't start telling me what's best for me. I'm a grown woman. I know what I want, and I want you."

His eyes moved jerkily over her face. She felt his restraint, and her bravado deserted her. She began to tremble with emotion, and she went all but limp against him. Eric's arms came around her. His hands stroked her shoulders above the towel, and the damp ends of her hair. "Oh, Eric, I was so afraid. I've never been so afraid in my life. He held my face down in the snow—I couldn't breathe— and he—was on me—his—his hands—"

"It's over now," he soothed. "No one will hurt you again."

"But I see him. In my mind I see him, and I can still—smell—God, he stank!"

"Shh."

"Make me forget, Eric. I know you can." She spoke with her face pressed into the crook of his neck. Her hands moved over the back of his head, and she turned her face up. She saw the passion in his black eyes. "I need you tonight, Eric."

His lips met hers lightly, trembling at the fleeting contact. They lifted away. His gaze delved into her eyes, and she saw the fire's glow reflected in his. He moaned her name very softly, before his mouth covered hers again. She tilted her head back, parted her lips to his voracious invasion. His tongue swept within her, as it had done before, as if he would devour her if he were able. It twined around her tongue, and drew it into his mouth to suckle it. She responded by tasting as much of his mouth as he had of hers, as her eager fingers untied the small black ribbon at his nape. She sifted his shining jet hair, pulled a handful around to rub its softness over her cheek. She tugged her lips from his to bury her face in his long hair and let its scent envelop her, drowning out the memory of the other. She turned then, to kiss his neck, and then a warm, wet path down it, to the V of his shirt.

He trembled, his hands tangling in her hair. She brought her own down, to clumsily unbutton and shove aside the cotton that stood between them. She flattened her palms to his hard, hairless chest. She moved them over its broad expanse, her lips following the trail they blazed. She paused at a distended male nipple and flicked her tongue over it, nearly giddy with delight when he sucked his breath through clenched teeth. Her hands moved lower, over the pectorals that rippled beneath taut skin, to his tight, flat belly. Her fingertips touched the waistband of his trousers, and she slid them underneath.

A moment later her hand closed around his hot, bulging shaft. Eric's head fell backward as if his neck muscles had gone limp. He groaned at her touch and she squeezed him and stroked him, encouraged by his response. His head came level again, his eyes fairly blazing when they met hers. He brought one hand around to the front of her and caught the corners of the towel she'd wrapped herself in. With a flick of his fingers the thick terry cloth fell to her feet. His arms slipped around her waist and pulled her body to his, flesh to flesh. The sensation set her pulse racing. His hard, muscled chest and tight, warm skin touching her soft breasts. His strong arms around her, his big hands moving over her bare back, crushing her to him. She clung to his shoulders, further aroused at the sinewy strength she found there.

Attacking her mouth once again, Eric lowered her gently to the floor. She lay on her back, stretched before the fire, and he lay on his side beside her, one arm beneath her, pillowing her head for his plundering mouth. His other hand moved hotly over her body. He cupped and squeezed her breasts, gently pinching her nipples until they throbbed against his fingers. He moved his hand lower, trailing fingertips over her belly, and then burying them in the nest of hair between her thighs.

With a slowness that was torture he parted the soft folds there. She closed her eyes when he probed her, and felt the growing wetness he evoked from her. She wanted him. She parted her legs and arched toward his exploring fingers, to tell him so. She closed her eyes when he took his mouth from hers and lowered it to nurse at her breast. She felt him tremble when his teeth scraped over her nipple, and she pressed his head to her with one hand and fumbled for the fastenings of his trousers with the other.

He helped her push them down, and then he kicked free of them, lying naked as she was. She opened her eyes to look at him in the firelight. She thought him the most beautiful man she'd ever seen. Every inch of him was tight, hard, corded with muscle. His skin was smooth and taut, elastic and practically hairless. Her gaze moved down his body, up it again, and met his smoldering eyes. *Are you certain?* he seemed to ask, though he never said a word.

In answer she fastened her mouth to his, pulling his body to her. He covered her gently. Instinctively she planted her feet, bent her knees and opened herself to him. Slowly he filled her, and she caught her breath at the feeling. This was more than sex, she thought dimly, as he pushed gently deeper. This was a completion of some cosmic cycle. He belonged here with her, and she with him. This was right. He withdrew, so careful not to hurt her, and began to slide inward again. She gripped his firm buttocks and jerked him into her. The fullness forced the breath from her lungs, but she arched to meet his next powerful thrust.

His pace quickened, and Tamara knew nothing for a time, except for the sensations of her body. His mouth moved over her throat, her jaw, her breasts. He suckled and licked and bit at her, setting her blood to boiling. His hands had moved beneath her to cup her buttocks and lift her to him. They kneaded her, caressed her and rocked her to his rhythm. His rigid shaft stroked to her deepest recesses, no longer hesitant, but hard and fast. She felt a tension twist within her. His movements inside her drew it tighter, and she trembled with the force of it. Tighter, and he caused it. He sensed her body's responses and he played upon them, adjusting his movements to draw out the exquisite torture. She bucked beneath him, seeking a release that hovered just beyond her reach, and she felt a similar need in him.

He moved within her more quickly now, his breaths coming short and fast. His mouth opened, hot and wet against her throat, and she felt her skin being drawn into it. She felt the skim of his incisors and the answering thrum of her pulse. She knew a craving she'd never known before, and she arched her throat to him just as she arched her hips to meet his. She screamed aloud with her mindless need, gripped the back of his head and pressed him harder to her neck.

The tension drew tighter, so tight she thought she'd soon explode with it. He withdrew slowly, and she whimpered her plea. "Please...now, Eric...do it now!" He drove into her, withdrew and drove again, the force of his thrusts beyond control, it seemed. He plunged so violently it would have lifted her body from the floor if he hadn't held her immobile, forcing her to take all of him, with all the strength he could muster. And she wouldn't have drawn away if she'd been able. She wanted this...and more. Another rending thrust and she felt herself reach the precipice. He let her linger there, drawing it out until her cries were like those of a wounded animal. His teeth closed on her throat. She felt the incisors pricking at her skin and she clutched him closer.

They punctured her throat as he plunged into her again, driving her over the edge. The pain was ecstasy in the throes of the climax that rocked her. She convulsed around him, and then harder as she felt him sucking at her throat. Her body milked his, and she trembled all over, violently, with spasms of pleasure she hadn't known could exist. He bucked inside her, and she knew he'd reached the peak, as well. She felt his hot seed spill into her as her own climax went on and on. His mouth open wide at her throat, his tongue moving greedily to taste her, he shook with the force of his own release. He groaned, long and low, and then collapsed on top of her with one last, full body shudder. He carefully withdrew his teeth.

He started to move off her, but she quickly wrapped her arms around him. His head was pillowed on her breasts, and she held him there. "Don't move yet," she whispered. "Just hold me."

He pulled free despite her words, and rolled to the floor beside her. He sat up, gazing down at her, his eyes glistening, mirroring the fire. His fingers touched her throat, and he squeezed his eyes closed. "God, what have I done?" His words were no more than a choked whisper. "What kind of monster am I that I would allow myself—"

"Don't say that!" She started to sit up, but his hands came fast to her shoulders.

"No, you mustn't move. Lie still. Rest." He moved one hand through her hair, over and over again. "I'm so sorry. So very sorry, Tamara."

She frowned, shaking her head. "You didn't hurt me, Eric. My God, it was incredible—"

"I *drank* from you!"

"I know what you did. What I don't know is why you act like you've stabbed me through the heart. I've lost more blood than that when I cut myself shaving!" She made her voice more gentle when the pain didn't leave his eyes. She reached up and stroked his face with her palm. "Eric," she whispered. "What ill effects will there be? Will I become a vampire now?"

"No, that requires mingling of—"

"Will I be sick?"

"No. Perhaps a bit dizzy when you get up, but it will pass."

"Then why are you so remorseful?" She sat up slowly, angled her head and pressed her lips to his. "I loved what you did to me, Eric. I wanted it as badly as you did."

"You couldn't—"

"I did. I feel what you feel, don't forget. I understand now why you held back before. It's a part of the passion for you, isn't it? It's another kind of climax.'' His eyes searched hers, as if in awe. ''You see, I do understand. I felt it too.''

He shook his head. ''It didn't repulse you?''

''Repulse me? Eric, I love you.'' She blinked and realized what she'd just said, then looked him in the eyes. ''I love you.''

CHAPTER TEN

Two in the morning. She lay staring up at the white underside of her canopy, wishing to God she could close her eyes. Eric had insisted on bringing her home after she'd blurted that she loved him. He had seemed shocked speechless for a few moments. Then he was awkward, as if he didn't quite know what to say to her. She was confused. What did he want from her, a physical relationship without emotions? But there already had been emotions between them, deep, soul-stirring emotions she was only beginning to understand. And she'd thought he loved her. He'd implied it. He'd said he had love for her. Was that the same thing?

She turned restlessly onto her side and punched her pillow. Again she glanced at the cognac on the bedside stand. He'd insisted she take it with her, since she'd remarked on how wonderful it was. No wonder, she thought now. The stuff was bottled in 1910. It was probably worth a fortune. And here she was swilling another glassful in hopes of using it as a sleep aid. If she didn't get some sleep soon she was going to collapse at work, in front of everyone, and then what would Daniel do? Probably check her into a rest home.

She wandered into the bathroom, still wide awake a half hour later. What was she going to do about Eric? Daniel would die if he knew the truth. She loved the old coot. She would hate to hurt him. God, her mind was spinning with too much tonight. She opened the medicine cabinet and

rummaged until she found the brown plastic prescription
bottle. She'd tried the damned sleeping pills before. Single
doses, double doses, even once a triple dose. She hadn't
even worked up a good yawn. She twisted the cap and
poured four tiny white capsule-shaped pills into the palm
of her hand. She popped them into her mouth with a cynical glance at her reflection. Who was she kidding? She
wouldn't close her eyes until dawn.

A glass of water rinsed the caplets down. She wandered
back to bed, realized she still held the worthless bottle of
tranquilizers in her fist and dropped it carelessly on the
stand.

"Kill him for this."

Daniel? Was that Daniel's voice tickling the fringes of
her consciousness? He sounded angry, and strained.

"I tried to tell you." Curtis's voice was louder, more
level. "She should have been under constant surveillance.
If we'd followed her, we'd have had the bastard."

"If your tranquilizer works. It hasn't been tested, Curtis. You can't be certain it will immobilize him."

"And how the hell do you suggest we test it? Send out a
notice asking for volunteers? Look, I've done everything I
can think of. All signs are, it will work. There's nothing left
to do but try it."

Try what? On whom? And why were they both so angry?

"He raped her, Curtis." Daniel's voice warbled on the
words. "It wasn't enough to take her blood, he had to have
her body, as well. The son of a bitch raped her...left bruises
on her skin. My God, no wonder she couldn't bear to face
us in the morning."

"I never thought Tammy would be the kind to try this
way out. Pills and brandy!" Curt's voice sounded harsh or

her ears. "Why the hell didn't she tell us and let us handle it?"

Raped? Tamara remembered the pig on the highway ramp...his hands on her, his filthy breath on her face. But he hadn't raped her. Eric came and—Eric—my God, they thought Eric had put these bruises on her body. She struggled to open her eyes. Her lips moved but no sound came from them. She had to tell them!

"She's coming around." Daniel's presence lingered closer. She forced her heavy lids to open. Nothing focused and the attempt left her dizzy, with a sharp pain in her head. She felt his hands on her forehead, but it seemed her forehead was not attached to her. Everything seemed distorted.

"Tamara? It's all right, sweetheart. Curtis and I are with you now. Marquand can't hurt you now."

Frantically she tossed her head back and forth on the pillows. Pillows that were too plump and stiff, with cases too starched and white. Not her own pillows. "No... Eric...not...him..." Damn, why couldn't she make her mouth form a coherent sentence?

"Eric," Curtis mocked. "I told you she remembered. It's all been an act. I wouldn't be surprised if she went to him willingly, Daniel. We always knew he'd come for her, didn't we? And I always said she'd never be one of us. You brought her right inside DPI. For Christ's sake, I wonder how many secrets she's passed already?"

"She wouldn't betray us to him, Curt," Daniel said, but his voice was laced with doubt.

"Then why did she mix those pills with the booze? It's guilt, I'm telling you! She sold us out and couldn't face it."

"What could she possibly have told him? She doesn't know anything about the research!"

"That we know of," Curtis added, his words meaningful. "He would like nothing better than to murder the both of us, Daniel. We're the leaders in vampire research. He gets rid of us, he sets the entire field back twenty years or more.''

''You think I don't know that?''

She struggled against the darkness she felt reaching out to her, but it was a worthless fight. She whispered his name once more before she sank into the warm abyss. The voices of the men she loved grew dimmer.

''He'll come to her...just like before.''

''We'll be ready. Get the tranquilizer and meet me back here.''

Eric paced the room yet again, pushing a hand through his hair, adding to its disarray. ''Where is she? I attune my mind to hers, and yet I feel nothing!''

''She's probably managed to get some sleep. Do not disturb her.''

Eric shook his head. ''No. No, something is wrong. I feel it.''

Roland's brows creased with worry, despite his feigned sigh of exasperation. ''This ingenue of yours is becoming a bit of a bother. What trouble do you suppose she's got herself into this time?''

''Wish to God I knew.'' He turned, paced away toward the fireplace, spun on his heel and came back. He stopped and met Roland's gaze. ''I shouldn't have let it happen. She was already in a fragile state of mind. When she realized what she'd done in the cold light of day she likely felt soiled, infected by my touch, made—''

''Shut up, unless you can say something reasonably intelligent, Eric. If she didn't mind it last eve, she won't mind it now. You think the girl doesn't know her own mind? My interpretation of events is this: your blood, given her so many years ago, altered her to some degree. It sealed the bond between you, and made her feel a natural aversion to sunlight, an abounding exuberance by night. It is a logical guess, then, that she would not be as repulsed by the taking of a few drops in a moment of passion, as a normal human might.''

Eric sighed long and loud. "She thinks herself in love with me. Did I tell you that?''

"Only a hundred or so times since we rose a mere hour ago, Eric...not that I'm keeping count. What's so surprising in that? You fancy yourself in love with her, do you not?''

"I don't fancy myself anything. I do love her. With everything in me.''

"Who's to say she doesn't feel the same?''

Eric closed his eyes slowly, and left them that way. "I hope to God she doesn't. It is enough that I will have to bear the pain of our eventual separation. I wouldn't wish such agony on her.'' He opened his eyes and met Roland's frown. "It is inevitable.''

"It is anything but that. She could be—''

"Do not even think to suggest it.'' Eric turned away from his friend, his gaze jumping around the room, settling nowhere. "This existence has been my curse. I wouldn't wish it to be hers, as well.''

Roland's voice came low, more gruff. "If it is the loneliness of which you speak, Eric, no one understands better than I.''

"Your solitude is self-imposed. It's as you want it. Mine is an unending sentence of solitary confinement. I don't interact because I cannot trust in anyone—not with DPI always seeking a way to destroy me.''

"My solitude—'' Roland cut himself off, and simultaneously closed his mind to Eric's curiosity. When he began his voice was steadier. "Is not the matter we were discussing. Your existence would not be lonely if you had someone with whom to share it.''

Eric closed his eyes and shook his head. "I have already considered this question, Roland. I've made my decision."

"The decision, my friend, is not yours to make."

Anger flared within Eric. His head came up, and he slowly turned to tell Roland exactly what he thought of that remark, when the scent slowly twisted around his mind. He gripped it the way a drowning man would grip a lifeline, and he concentrated, focusing his entire being on that one sensation coming to him from Tamara. The scent...he frowned harder...clean...sterile. Sickeningly familiar.

His eyes wide, he faced Roland. "My God, she's hospitalized!"

Eric lunged for the door, but Roland leapt into his path. "A moment, Eric. You tend to lose all sense of caution where Tamara is concerned." He reached for his satin cloak and flung it about his shoulders with a long-practiced twist of his arms. "I dare not imagine what sort of mess you'll end in without me along."

"Fine." Eric paused as he reached for the door. "Roland, you can't wear that to a hospital. You look as if you've stepped out of the pages of that Stoker fellow's book."

"I have no intention of going inside. Can't bear the places, myself."

True to his word, Roland lurked in the shadows outside while Eric followed his sharpening sense of Tamara to the proper floor. He took the stairs, and he sent the probing fingers of his mind out ahead of him, ever on the alert for St. Claire or Rogers. Before long he caught a hint of their presence, very near Tamara's, though he felt it nowhere near as strongly as he felt hers.

He glanced up and down the fourth-floor corridor and quickly spotted the room. He'd have known it without help, but the burly man in the dark gray suit posted outside her door made it obvious. Eric didn't recognize him, but knew at once he was DPI. If he was going to see Tamara he'd need to find another way. Already he felt reassured. Her stamina reached from her mind to his, though he sensed she might still be groggy. She was well. He felt it.

His relief was so great he very nearly didn't notice the hinged metal folder on the counter where nurses milled. A strip of white tape across the front bore the words in black ink. Dey, Tamara. Eric stiffened. He had to see that folder. Only then would he know the extent of her injuries, and exactly what had transpired to land her here. He closed his eyes.

Roland? Are you still out there?

Where else would I be? came the bored reply.

I could use a distraction, Eric told him.

Done.

Eric waited for about thirty seconds, uncomfortably watching both directions, half expecting St. Claire to appear at any second. Then a bloodcurdling scream came from a room in another corridor and every nurse stampeded. A male voice echoed through the halls. "It was *grinning at me*—right through my window! I swear! And it, it had fangs—and its eyes—"

Eric grinned slightly, against his will. He hurried to the desk and flipped open Tamara's folder. He didn't need to scan it long. According to the physician who'd examined her, Tamara had been rushed in early this morning, unconscious and with vital signs that were barely discernible. She'd ingested a large amount of tranquilizers, combined with alcohol. According to the doctor's examination, she had recently had sexual intercourse. He further noted the bruises on her torso, and concluded that she'd been raped sometime the previous night. The pills and alcohol had been, in his opinion, a suicide attempt.

The sheet swam before his eyes. His stomach churned. Had he been alone he'd have roared like a wounded lion. As it was, he had to hold his anguish in check. It wasn't rape that had driven her over the edge, he alone knew that. It was something far more damaging to the soul. She'd made passionate love to a monster. Hadn't he known it would be more than she could face when the fire died down? Nearly blind with pain, he closed the folder and headed back the way he'd come.

Roland had just leapt down from the ledge. "Did you hear that fool bellow?" He laughed hard. "I haven't had such fun in years." He halted his chuckles and cleared his throat. "So, how did you find our girl? Did you see her? Eric—my God, you look like hell. What is it?"

Eric swallowed hard and forced the words to come. It wasn't easy. His throat was so tight he could barely inhale, and when he did it burned. "I . . . couldn't see her. A guard is posted outside her room. DPI." He spotted a bench nearby and went to it. He needed to sit. It was as if he'd been hit by a train. "She tried to take her own life, Roland."

"What!" Instantly Roland sat beside him, his arm at Eric's back. Eric barely felt it.

"I told you she'd regret what we—what I did to her, when she could think clearly. But I had no idea it would repulse her so that she couldn't go on living!"

"You are wrong!"

The violence in Roland's voice didn't penetrate the wall of pain around Eric. "Sleeping pills mixed with alcohol. It's all on her charts."

Roland gripped both of Eric's shoulders and forced him to look him in the eye. "No. She wouldn't do it."

Eric shook his head. "You barely knew her."

"True, but I know the despondency it takes to drive one to that extreme! Eric, I've been witness to such, firsthand. I've seen all the signs." His voice softened. "I only wish I had known them in time." He shook himself then. "Eric, do not accept less than her own words to confirm this theory. I know it to be wrong. See her. Talk to her.''

Eric shook his head for the hundredth time. ''I am the last person she would wish to see.''

''If so, she will tell you so and you will have your answer. If not, you'd do her a grave injustice to leave her in that room with a DPI guard preventing her leaving.''

Eric's shoulders stiffened where before they'd been slumping. ''I suppose I could go in through the window. But I fear St. Claire and Rogers might be in the room with her.''

''Give me a moment,'' Roland said, dropping his brutal grip from Eric's shoulders and rising to pace away. ''I'll think of something.''

She blinked the haziness away slowly, and realized Daniel sat close to her, holding her hand. She wondered why she seemed to be in a hospital room, and bits of the conversation she'd heard earlier began surfacing in her mind.

''You're awake.'' Daniel leaned nearer. ''They said you'd be coming around soon. You shouldn't have been out as long as you were, but we all figured the rest would do you good, so we let you be.''

It had done her good, she thought as her mind cleared more and more. She felt the energy surge and longed to toss the covers back and go outside. She licked her parched lips. ''It's night, isn't it? My God, how long have I slept?''

''I found you in your bed this morning.'' He swallowed. ''I thought you were asleep at first, but then I saw the pills, and the brandy.'' He repeatedly pushed one cool palm up over her forehead. ''Baby, you should have just told me. I wouldn't have blamed you. It wasn't your fault.''

She sat up in bed so fast his hand fell away. Fully now, she recalled the words she'd only dimly been aware of at the time. They all thought she'd tried to kill herself. Moreover, they thought she'd been beaten and raped, by Eric, no less. They'd seen the marks his unbridled passion had left on her throat.

"Daniel, I have to tell you what happened last night."

"Don't torture yourself, sweetheart. I already know. I—" A sob rose in his throat, but he fought it down. "I'll kill him for what he did to you, Tam. I swear to God, I will."

"No!" She came to her feet all at once. "Daniel, you have to listen to me. Just…" A wave of dizziness swamped her, and if Daniel hadn't been there to steady her she'd have sunk to the floor. "Just listen to me, please."

"All right. All right, honey, I'll listen if you feel you need to talk it out. Just get back into the bed first, okay?"

She nodded, clinging to his soft shoulders and easing herself back down. When she was once again settled back against the pillows, she focused on staying calm. "Where is Curtis?"

"Outside. He walks the perimeter once very hour. We're not going to let Marquand get near you again, honey. Don't worry on that score."

She rolled her eyes. "Curt should hear this, too, but it can't wait. You'll tell him everything I tell you. Promise?"

He nodded. She cleared her throat and tried to summon courage enough to be honest with him. She should have been from the start. "I've seen Eric Marquand several times since that night at the rink," she blurted at last. Daniel opened his mouth but she held up two hands. "Please, let me get through this before you say anything." She licked her lips. "He's taken me on a sleigh ride, and fed me hot cocoa and fine cognac—in fact, the cognac I had last night was a gift from him. I've been to his house, too. We sat before a fire and talked for hours. He's not a monster, Daniel. He's a wonderful, caring man."

"My God…"

"Last night after I left Hilary I had a flat tire. I had to pull off an exit and was going to walk to a service station. I was—" she closed her eyes at the memory "—attacked. I fought him, but it was no use. He was very strong. I think he would've killed me when he'd finished. But Eric came just in time." Her eyes opened now that she'd gotten past the most horrid memory of last night. "He pulled the man off me, and beat him unconscious. He carried me to the car. He covered me with his own coat, and then he drove. He would have brought me directly home, but I asked him not to. I needed time to calm myself." She reached for his hand. "Daniel, Eric saved my life last night."

Daniel stared at her for a long moment. "But, how could . . . I don't—"

"He's not the monster you keep telling me he is," she told him. "He's more human than a lot of men I know."

For a moment Daniel appeared uncertain, but then his eyes narrowed. "You can't deny the marks he left on your throat. That's proof of what he is."

She lowered her eyes. "I won't deny them, but I won't lie about them, either. I'm not going to tell you things that are none of your business, Daniel. But you have to know that everything that happened between Eric and me last night happened because I wanted it to happen. I wanted it, even knowing what he is. He didn't hurt me, and he never will."

"Tamara, what are you saying? You admit he's a vampire and still you defend him?"

She met his gaze without flinching. She would not be ashamed of her feelings for Eric. But she thought she'd given her guardian enough shocks for one evening. "I'm saying that you don't need to worry about me. No harm will ever come to me with Eric around." She put a hand on his arm and squeezed. "I want you to think about something, Daniel. For a long time you've assumed that because his kind is different, they are inherently evil. You've been wrong. You need to sit down and realize how bigoted that mind-set is.''

He shook his head and got to his feet. His eyes on her seemed to hold an unvoiced accusation. ''Haven't Curtis and I warned you about the mind control he might exercise over you? Haven't I begged you to tell me if he tried to see you again? Tamara, you cannot believe his lies! He would kill me if he had an opportunity, and you are just the one to give it to him! He's using you to get to me, Tamara. You'd have to be blind not to see that!''

She drew in a sharp breath at the fury in his voice, and in his face. It was as if she'd betrayed him. She'd never seen him so angry. ''Daniel, you're wrong—''

She was interrupted by a mechanical beep coming from Daniel's belt. He pushed a button and it stopped instantly. ''I have to go. Curtis—'' He bit his lip.

''Curtis what?'' Tamara felt a chill go up her spine. It had something to do with Eric, she was certain of it. Daniel had said Curtis was out searching the grounds, or something like that. Had he spotted Eric? What would they do to him if they caught him? Daniel didn't answer, but moved quickly through the heavy wooden door. As he did, she saw the guard posted outside it, and her heart raced all the faster. She couldn't get out to try to warn Eric that they were out for blood. My God, what if they got to him?

The door closed and she paced the room, battling the dizziness that tried to return sporadically. She shut her eyes and tried to call out to Eric as she'd done before, with her mind. *Eric, if you're out there, be careful! Daniel and Curt—*

Her thoughts came to a halt as a chill breeze rushed over her body, and a familiar voice spoke softly. ''Are presently being led a merry chase by Roland, all in order to clear them out of here.'' As her eyes flew open, he swung his legs over the windowsill, landing gracefully on the floor. He stood still for a moment, as if waiting for her permission to come any closer.

Tamara raced toward him and threw herself into his arms. "Eric!" His arms around her seemed hesitant, and then he pushed her from him and eased her back into the bed. His face, she now noted, was a study in misery. Lines were etched deep between his brows and on both sides of his mouth. His eyes were moist and searching. He dropped to one knee beside the bed, and his voice thickened with every word he uttered. "Sweet Tamara, I never meant... My God, I never meant to bring you to this. I swear it to you. If I'd known—but I should have known, shouldn't I? I should never have done what I did." He choked on the words and a single tear slipped slowly down his face.

Her heart wrenched as she reached out to touch it, absorbing it into her fingertips. "Don't think what you're thinking, Eric. Not even for a minute. This was an accident, nothing more." His gaze met hers, and she saw the doubt there. "Look into my mind, since you're so talented at that sort of thing. Better yet, look into my heart. How could you think I'd want to leave you?" She felt him doing just what she'd suggested, and as he probed her mind she explained what she'd done. "I knew I wouldn't close my eyes all night, and I had to go to work, or else Daniel would know something was wrong. I sipped the cognac, but it didn't help. A bit later I tried the sleeping pills that have been sitting in my cabinet for over a month. I'd taken them before without any ill effects at all. The problem was that I wasn't thinking clearly, and didn't stop to consider the consequences of mixing them with alcohol. That's all, Eric. I promise, that's all."

He gathered her into his arms and she felt the shuddering breath he released as it bathed her neck. "I thought you'd awakened to regret having given yourself to me. If ever you do, Tamara, you must tell me. I will not be the cause of your despair. I will leave you now, if you tell me to do so.''

Her arms clenched tighter and she whispered, ''No. Don't leave me, Eric. Don't . . .'' Frowning with a sense of déjà vu so strong it made her light-headed she pulled away from him. ''My God, I've said that to you before. In a hospital bed just like this one. I begged you not to leave me . . . but you did.''

He nodded, his eyes studying her carefully. ''I honestly thought it best for you. I was wrong. I won't make that mistake again. If you ordered me to stay away from you, I'd never go so far as I did then. You'd have my protection. I'd watch over you, as I should have done before. St. Claire never would have got his hands on you if I'd been wiser then.''

''Then it was when I had the accident. That was when I knew you? All these memories and familiarity stem from the time I was six years old?''

''Yes. It is coming back to you now. Soon the rest will, as well, and you will understand better.''

She nodded, wishing she understood now. She wouldn't press him on it, though. He shouldn't be here. It wasn't safe. ''Eric, I had to tell Daniel it wasn't you who attacked and bruised me, but I couldn't very well hide the marks on my throat.'' His eyes moved to that spot and she felt their heat. An answering warmth spread within her, but she forced herself to ignore it. ''I told him that I went to you willingly, that you forced nothing on me. He still insists you have me under some kind of spell, though. Eric, he's furious. It isn't a good idea for you to be here.''

His lips thinned, and he studied her for a long moment. ''You love this man, and I've tried to restrain myself from speaking against him, for your sake, Tamara. Tonight I cannot. It is better to risk your anger than to allow you to continue in your blind trust of him. It is no more safe for you to remain than it is for me. Especially now that he knows of our intimacy.''

She stroked his face lovingly. ''Old habits die hard. He's so used to thinking the worst of you, he can't do otherwise, and I think you have the same problem. Daniel loves me, Eric.''

He covered her hand with his own, closed his eyes and turned his face to press his lips to her palm. ''It kills me to hurt you, Tamara. The traits I explained to you, the ones that make you different from other humans—''

''The Belladonna antigen and the common ancestor?''

He nodded. ''St. Claire knew of them even then.''

She frowned at him, blinking. ''He did? But why hasn't he ever told me?''

Eric held her hand in his own. ''Tamara, there is a good possibility that he only took you in because he knew you were one of the Chosen. He knew of your connection to us, and he knew that as long as he had you, one of us might come near enough to be captured.''

''Captured?'' She searched his face, his mind, as he spoke, but she saw no sign that he was lying to her. ''For...what?''

His lips parted, but closed again. He shook his head. ''I am afraid for you,'' he told her. ''Believe me that is my only motive for telling you these things.''

She shook her head, blinking as hot tears pooled in her eyes. ''I know you mean it, you believe all of this...but it's wrong. You're wrong. Daniel loves me like his own daughter.'' She lowered her gaze and shook her head. ''He has to. He's the only family I've had for all these years. If all of that was a lie—no. You're wrong.''

Eric sighed, but nodded. ''I will not press the matter. But Tamara, he is not the only family you have any longer. You have me. No matter what else might happen, you always will. Do you believe me?''

She nodded in return, but her eyes didn't focus. She was searching her mind, realizing that Daniel must've known Eric had visited her in the hospital all those years ago. It was the only explanation for his overprotective behavior now.

Something niggled at her mind, and she squinted hard, trying to remember. "Eric, when I came around earlier, they were saying something about a . . . a tranquilizer. . . ." She heard their voices replay in her mind, and had the confirmation she'd dreaded. *He'll come to her, just like before.* And then Daniel. *We'll be ready. Get the tranquilizer and meet me back here.* Her stomach clenched.

"No tranquilizer known has any effect on vampires, Tamara."

She shook her head hard. "I got the feeling this was something new, something Curt's been working on." She met his gaze then, her fear for him overcoming her own lingering doubts. "I know I'm safe with them, Eric, but as things stand, you aren't. Please leave before they come back."

"I won't cower in fear of them—"

"But Roland might not be safe, either. If there is some kind of drug, and he lets them get too close . . ."

He frowned then, and nodded. "I'll go, then—this time." Once again he pulled her upper body to him, and kissed her neck, then the hollow just below her ear, then the ear itself. "I find it unbearable to leave you, though."

She closed her eyes and let her head fall back to give his mouth better access. The sensations he sent through her body would overwhelm her common sense in a few seconds. Her fingers tangled in his hair, and her breath caught in her throat. His lips kissed a path to hers, and then he feasted on her mouth and her tongue as if it were to be his last meal. When he lifted himself from her she clung. She pressed wet lips to his ear. "I wish you could stay. I want you so much it hurts." She felt him tremble in response to her words and her touch.

"It is too soon—you've been through so much." Gently he pushed her until she lay amid the pillows. "I will leave you, but not to go far. If anyone tries to harm you, call to me. You know I will hear you."

"I know."

He left the way he'd come, and Tamara thought it felt as if he'd taken a part of her with him.

CHAPTER ELEVEN

She closed the window, returned to her bed and feigned sleep, though she was wide awake and jittery with restlessness. Daniel returned a few minutes after Eric had left her, and took a seat near the window. Tamara ignored him. She wasn't yet ready for a confrontation, but she knew one had to come. She needed to hear from his own lips that the things Eric suspected were wrong.

Dawn approached and Tamara couldn't avoid sleep's clinging vines. They gradually encircled her and tugged her down into slumber. When her eyes flew wide only a moment later, it was to see the final splash of the sun's orange light slowly receding from the sky. Daniel's chair was empty.

She waited, lying still and lazy as the life seemed to filter back into her body. Amazing that she'd slept all day two days running now, so deeply she hadn't been aware of the time ticking past. Refreshed and energized, she flung the covers back and started opening drawers and closet doors in search of her clothes. She'd had enough of this confinement. The only clothing she found were her nightgown and her long houndstooth-check coat. She sighed relief that her boots rested on the closet floor.

There was no guard now. She guessed Daniel assumed she'd only needed guarding after sundown. She caused quite a stir when she announced to the nurses at the crowded desk in the main corridor that she was checking herself out. Forms needed to be signed and the doctor notified. She couldn't just leave. She coolly requested that whatever forms needed signing be handed over at once. She'd already phoned for a cab, and fully intended to be ready when it arrived.

Less than half an hour later she marched through the imposing front door of the neglected house she'd called home for the past twenty years. Daniel stood just beyond the door, pulling his coat on. He looked up, surprised to see her. His smile died slowly when she didn't return it.

"We need to talk" was all she said in greeting.

His faded cornflower eyes turned away from her probing dark ones. He nodded, and exhaled slowly.

"I left a cabby waiting outside. I'll just go get my purse, and—"

"I'll take care of it." Daniel moved past her and out the door before she could argue the point. She heard the vehicle move away, its tires crunching over the packed snow on the road. Daniel returned a moment later. He removed his coat, draped it on a rather wobbly coat tree and gently helped her out of hers. She'd already toed off her boots.

"You ought to go upstairs and lie down, Tam. We can talk in your room."

She faced him squarely. "Is there a DPI guard outside my door?" His gaze dropped so fast there was no doubting his surge of guilt. "Why was I under guard, Daniel?"

He sighed, his shoulders slumping. "I won't lie to you. I was afraid Marquand would try to get to you there."

"Because he came to me once before in a hospital?"

Daniel's head snapped up, eyes widening. "You—you remember?"

She turned from him, stalking though the foyer and into the huge living room. She knew he followed. Her long, quick stride and stiff spine showed her anger almost as well as her words and tone of voice. She faced him again. "No, Daniel. As a matter of fact, I don't remember. For the past few months I've been slowly, systematically losing my mind because I can't remember. I'm trying..." Her throat threatened to close off, and she bit her lips, swallowed twice and forced herself to go on. "You've known about this—this link between Marquand and me all along, though, haven't you? For God's sake, Daniel, how could you keep something like this from me?"

His brows lifted, creasing his forehead. "Tam, I was only doing what I thought was best for you. Trying to protect you—"

"By watching me go insane? My God, the nightmares, the sleeplessness—you had to know it all revolved around Eric. You knew, and you never said a word."

"You were in a fragile state of mind! I couldn't say anything to make it worse."

"Of course not. You couldn't say anything to ease my fears, either, could you, Daniel? Not the way Eric did. You couldn't simply tell me that it was all right, that I wasn't going crazy—that there was a reason for all I was going through and that I'd understand it as soon as my mind was ready to let me remember. You couldn't comfort me that way, could you?"

Daniel couldn't have looked more shocked if she'd slapped him. "He—"

"But you didn't want me to remember, did you, Daniel? Because you knew. You knew how close Eric and I had become, and you knew he'd come to me some day. All these years you've been waiting, watching."

She waited for a furious denial, but saw only remorse in Daniel's leathery face. She had to press it further. She had to ask the final question, though she dreaded hearing the answer. "Is that why you took me in all those years ago, Daniel? Was I just the perfect bait to lure him to you?"

For a long time he didn't answer. When Tamara turned away from him in disgust, his soft hand shot out to grip her arm and turn her back toward him. "I was blind with ambition twenty years ago, Tam. There was nothing in my life except my work. I'd have done anything to get to Marquand...then. But not now." His hand fell from her arm, and he paced away from her slowly, eyes on his feet, but not seeing. "I grew to love you, sweetheart. How could I not? And it wasn't very long at all until I stopped looking forward to the day he'd come back. I started fearing it. I was terrified he'd come and take you away from me."

She held the tears in check. She wasn't certain where she got the strength to do it. "My entire life has been a lie. From the second you came to my hospital room you were enacting a cold, calculated plot." She shook her head. "What were you going to do with Eric when you caught him?"

There was no remorse in his eyes when he faced her this time. Only the frigid gleam of hatred. "Don't pity him, Tam. He's no better than an animal—a rabid wolf who has to be stopped before he can spread his disease. Oh, I had big plans once. I was going to learn the answers to every question I had about him—his kind. Now all I want is to keep him from hurting you."

"Hurt him, and *you'll* be hurting me, Daniel." He stepped closer to her, slowly shaking his head from side to side as his eyes searched her face. "I love him," she said.

Daniel's eyes closed tight and he released a guttural grunt as if he'd been punched hard in the stomach.

She didn't show mercy. She felt none after what he'd said about Eric. "You say you love me, but I don't think that's true. I think you've used me all along and just can't admit it to me now."

Again he shook his head. "That isn't true. I do love you—couldn't love my own child more than I love you."

"Prove it." He faced her, standing stock-still as if he knew what she would ask of him.

"Tamara, I—"

"Drop the research, Daniel. Give up this plan to capture Eric, or any of them." She took a step toward him, and realized she was willing to beg if it would help. "He isn't what you think. He's kind and sensitive and funny. If you met him on the street you wouldn't know he was different at all. He doesn't want to hurt anyone, only to be left alone. If you want your questions answered, Eric would probably be willing to answer them, once he sees he can trust you."

"That's absurd! If I got within his reach I'd be a dead man. Tamara, you're the one who doesn't know this man. He's cunning and ruthless. You accuse me of using you, but he's the one using you . . . to get to me, I think."

She blinked slowly. "I can see I'm not getting through to you." Feeling her heart had been bruised beyond repair, she turned and moved to the curving staircase.

"Where—"

"I'm going to shower and change. Then I'm going out. Tomorrow I'll come back and pick up my things."

"You can't go to him, Tam! My God, don't do this—"

"I can't stay, not unless you agree to what I've asked. Keep in mind the way you've deceived me all this time, Daniel. How much have I ever asked from you? If you love me, you'll do this for me. If not, then it won't kill you to see me go."

She moved up the stairs, and did exactly what she'd said she would. Daniel didn't try to stop her. When she left by the front door he was not in sight.

She sank into his arms when he opened his door to her. Eric had sensed her turmoil as she approached, and he felt a burgeoning anger toward those responsible. St. Claire and his protégé, no doubt. He held her, and her tears flowed into his shirt. Beyond her, through the open doorway, he felt eyes upon him, and he kicked the door closed. Rogers, he realized slowly. He'd followed her. Eric felt the man's rage like a blistering desert wind, and not solely directed toward him. The heat of his anger was aimed toward Tamara, as well, and the knowledge shook Eric. He knew when the van moved away. The sense of hatred faded, and Eric put it aside for later consideration. Tamara needed to be the center of his attention now.

He held her tighter, and pulled her with him into the parlor, where a cheerful fire and a pot of hot cocoa awaited her. He settled himself on the settee, pulling her across his lap as he might do a small child. He cradled her head to his shoulder, stroking her hair and feeling the painful throbbing in her temples and the dampness of tears on her skin.

"Oh, Eric, you were right. Daniel knew about us all those years ago. He knew you'd come back some day, and that was the only reason he took me in when my parents died." He felt her shuddering breath.

"He admitted it to you?"

She nodded. "He could—could barely look me in the eye."

Eric released a sigh, wishing he could choke the life out of the heartless bastard for causing Tamara this kind of grief. "I am so sorry, sweet. I wish I had been wrong."

The air kept catching in her throat, making each breath she took like a small spasm. "It hurts to know the truth. I love him so much, Eric."

Love him, not loved him. Eric frowned.

She lifted her head from his shoulder. "I can't stop myself from loving him just because he lied to me. I think...in his own way...he loves me, too."

"I keep forgetting how well you read my thoughts," he told her. "How can you believe he cares for you after—"

"I have to believe it. It hurts too much to think he's been acting the part all these years. He says he came to love me, and that his motives for keeping me with him changed." She blinked away the remaining tears, and gently brushed his white shirt with her fingertips. "I got you all wet."

"I would gladly catch every tear you shed, if you'd permit it, Tamara."

Her lips turned up slightly at the corners, but still they trembled. "I'm giving him one more chance." Eric's brows lifted, one higher than the other, as he was prone to do when puzzled. "I told Daniel that if he truly loves me he'll drop his research, and the investigation of you."

"Sweet, trusting Tamara," he said, lifting a lock of hair with his forefinger and tucking it behind her ear. "Do you believe he'll agree? He's made me his life's work, you know. He was tracing my every movement even before you were born."

"I don't know if he'll agree. But, Eric, if he doesn't I think you should go away from here. I'm terrified of what he has planned."

He smiled fully. "I am well aware of what he has planned for me. And no, I will not give you new nightmares by sharing it with you. You needn't fear for me, Tamara. With vampires, age is strength. I am over two hundred years strong. A mere human—or even a pair of them—pose no threat to me."

"But this tranquilizer I heard them mention—"

"It matters not. I'll not leave you again."

She gazed into his eyes with so much love Eric nearly winced. "I wouldn't ask you to. I'd go with you."

She'd go with him, and he knew she'd stay with him. For the span of her mortal life he would be allowed to cherish her and adore her. And then she would leave him to die of heartbreak. He wouldn't have her for more than a moment in time—a mere twenty more years, at best. For though he hadn't shared the knowledge with her, he was painfully aware that humans with the Belladonna antigen rarely live beyond their forty-fifth year.

Perhaps, he thought, Roland had been right. Perhaps the decision wasn't his to make. But could he sentence her to an eternity of darkness? Would she even want it?

Her hand at his face broke his line of thought, and he looked into her eyes. "What is it?" she asked. "I feel sadness but I couldn't tell what you were thinking."

"I was thinking that you must leave me in the morning." She had enough to deal with tonight. Let the question of her mortality wait for another time. "I wonder if it is wise, now that St. Claire and Rogers know the nature of our relationship? I do not like to think of you within reach of their wrath."

"Unless Daniel changes his attitude, tomorrow will be the last time I set foot in that house." She looked at him and smiled very softly. "Unless I'm jumping the gun. You haven't invited me—"

"Shall I come to you on my knees? Shall I beg you to stay with me?"

"You only need to tell me you want me." Her voice came out lower than a whisper, and he saw the glimmer left by the tears turn into a soft glow, put there by passion.

"In my existence I have seen women of such beauty it was said they could drive a man beyond reason. Beside you, they would fade as a candle's flame beside the heart of the sun. Never has a woman stirred me as you have done." He lowered his head, tilting her chin with one hand to settle his lips over hers. Softly he sipped them, suckled them, first upper, then lower. He lifted only enough to speak, and to be able to watch her glorious face as he did. "To say that I want you is not enough. Might as well say that the parched and barren desert wants the kiss of the rain. You are the part of myself that's been missing for more than two centuries."

The shimmer in her eyes now had nothing to do with her earlier pain. "Eric, you make love to me with your words as thoroughly as you do with your body." She pressed her mouth to him, parted her succulent lips and invited his tongue's invasion. He accepted eagerly, and her taste aroused him even more than the last time he'd kissed her. Eventually he lifted his head to breathe. "I can't say it as well as you can," she told him, breathless now. "But I feel the same. My life was so empty. I thought I'd never stop wondering why. Then I found you and I knew. I don't know what went between us before, Eric. I don't know why we are this close, but whatever it was, it bound us together. You are a part of me, as vital to my existence as my own heart. If you leave me again..." She stopped there. The sob that involuntarily blocked her words came without warning, he knew.

He lifted her in his arms as he rose from the settee. "Leave you? *Leave you?* Look into my heart with yours. See what is there, and end your doubts. I would swim naked through a pool of shredded glass for you. I'd crawl on my belly over hot coals—through hell itself—to get to you. You are in me, woman, like a fever in my blood. All I find myself wanting these days is more of you."

He took her mouth fiercely; plundered it as she'd been longing for him to do. He knew she had. He'd heard her silent begging. Even as he took her mouth he moved with her, to the staircase and up it. By the time he reached the top he was panting, as she was. Her fingers twined and tugged at his hair. Her tongue dipped and tasted him, then wrapped around his and drew it back into her moistness. She suckled it as if it were some rare, prized fruit—something she needed in order to live.

He kicked open the bedroom door, carrying her through it, certain she only vaguely noted the candles and oil lamps that cast their flickering, amber glow over the bed he'd prepared for her. He laid her gently upon the high mattress, then straightened, allowing his gaze to devour her. He'd never thought highly of the denims today's women favored. On her, however, he found them alluring, the way they hugged her form like an outer skin. Then again, on her he thought he'd find a burlap sack alluring.

She blinked and broke eye contact, glancing around the room. The satin coverlet on which she lay was fortunate enough to receive a long, appreciative stroke from her equally soft hand. She regarded the oversize four-poster bed and the hand-tooled hardwood, then the masses of candles and the two lamps burning scented oil. "You did all of this for me?"

He nodded, watching her face. "You approve?"

Her smile was her answer. She held his eyes prisoner as her delicate fingers began to release the buttons of her blouse. He took a step toward her. She stopped him with a small shake of her head. Eric swallowed hard, but obeyed her silent request. He stood where he was, as the fire inside him burned out of control.

She shrugged so that the blouse fell from her shoulders, and he saw the creamy-colored silk garment beneath it. She slid from the bed, releasing her button, then her zip. She pushed the denim down over her hips, down her long, bare legs, and daintily stepped out of them. She looked to him like a confection prepared especially for him to savor. Cream-colored lace touched her thighs, and the exposed mounds of her breasts. As he fought to form words she repeated his earlier ones. "You approve?"

A low growl was all he managed before he had her in his arms, crushed against him. When his hands lifted the scanty lace to cup her hips he found them bare to his touch. For him, she'd done this. To please him. To arouse him to the point of madness, he thought. He moved his hips so the aching bulge that strained his own zipper nudged her center. He brought one hand up to push the flimsy strap aside and expose her breast to his rough exploration. As his hand teased her nipple to a taut pebble hardness he spoke, moving his lips upon her throat. "You wish to drive me mad, woman? I hope you're certain you want this. I believe you've pushed me beyond the point of return."

He lifted her, hands on her silk-clad sides, and dropped her onto the bed. She watched him struggle with his shirt. He didn't hesitate, but removed his trousers and shorts, as well. He couldn't wait to be inside her luscious body. He saw her eyes focus on his erection, and he clambered onto the bed beside her, eager to mount her. Then he stopped himself. She was his for the entire night, he reminded himself. He needn't take her in haste. He could love her slowly, drive her as wild as she'd already driven him.

She reached for him, eyes glazed with passion. "Are you in such a hurry, sweet Tamara? Would you deny me the chance to savor you first?"

"You want to drink from me again?" Her words were merely sighs given form. "Do it, Eric. I am your slave tonight. Do what you want."

"What I want is to devour you. Every succulent inch of you. At my leisure. Will you lie still and allow it, I wonder?"

He knelt on the mattress beside her, and reached for her tiny foot. He lifted it, kissing a hot path around her ankle, nipping the bone with gentle teasing scrapes of his teeth, then sliding his tongue over it, tracing its shape. She breathed faster, and he moved his head. His mouth trailed very slowly up the soft flesh of her inner calf. He lifted her leg, flicking his tongue over the sensitive hollow behind her knee. She shook violently, and he glanced up to see that her eyes were closed tight. *Oh, yes, my love. Tonight I'll show you the meaning of pleasure.* His mind spoke to hers, since his mouth was too busy carrying out the promise. He nibbled and tasted and licked at her thigh, moving higher slowly and steadily so she couldn't mistake his intent. By the time he reached the heart of her, her need was so great she whimpered with each breath she released. One flick of his tongue over her, and she cried out. *Open for me, love. Give me your sweet nectar.*

She did. He slipped his hands beneath her quivering buttocks and tilted her up, and then he gave her what she silently begged him for. He ravaged her with his mouth, and his teeth. He plunged into her with his tongue. Her taste intoxicated him. He shook with feeling, for her sensations were his, as well. She gasped for breath, tossing her head back and forth on the pillows, her hips writhing beneath him. He pushed her ruthlessly to the precipice, and then forced her over it. She screamed in ecstasy—and still he persisted. She shuddered uncontrollably and pushed his head away, gasping.

"No, no more—I can't—"

"Oh, but you can. Shall I show you that you can?" He lifted himself and moved until his body fully covered hers. He nudged her opening with his hardness. So wet, and still pulsing with her climax. He drove into her without warning. She shivered beneath him as he withdrew and drove again, and yet again. He gave her no time to recover from the first shattering explosion. He forced her trembling body beyond it, and toward another. He anchored her to him with his arms, forcing her acceptance of his every thrust. He covered her mouth with his, and forced his tongue inside, still coated with the taste of her. He plunged harder, faster, and he knew when her fists clenched and her nails sank into the flesh of his back that she was once again on the brink. He swallowed her cries this time when she went over, and she swallowed his, for he fell with her. His entire body shook with the force of his release. He clung to her, relaxing his body to hers.

Aftershocks of pleasure still rippled through him when he began to move inside her again.

CHAPTER TWELVE

Too soon, she thought, when she knew dawn approached. She studied his profile as he lay beside her, and she thought again she'd never known a man so handsome. No shadow of beard darkened his jawline. In fact, his face was as smooth as it had been earlier. He caught her gaze on him and smiled. "I shall have to leave you soon," he said, giving voice to her thoughts.

She snuggled closer, wishing he didn't. "Where do you go? Do you rest in—in a coffin?"

He nodded, sitting up slightly and reaching for his shirt. "Does the idea repulse you?"

"Nothing about you could ever repulse me, Eric." She sat up, too, as he poked his muscled arms into the white sleeves. She pushed his hands away when he began to button the shirt, and leaned over to button it herself. "I don't think I'd like seeing you in it, though. Why a coffin, anyway? Is it some kind of vampire tradition? Why not a bed, for God's sake?"

He laughed, tipping his head back. Tamara found her gaze glued to the corded muscles in his neck. She leaned nearer and pressed her lips to it. He stroked her hair. "It is for protection. There are more humans who know of our existence than you would believe. Most would like nothing better than to terminate it. We could sleep in vaults, or behind locked doors, I suppose. But nothing offers more protection than a coffin, which locks from the inside and has a trapdoor built beneath it."

"Trapdoor?" She finished with his last button and looked up, interested. "Are you conscious enough to use it?"

"The scent of imminent danger would rouse me even from the deepest slumber. Not much, mind you, but I only need move one finger. The button is placed in the spot where my hand rests. When I touch it the hinged mattress swings down, dumping me into a hidden room below. It springs back into place on its own. The only side effects are a few aches from being dumped bodily."

"You feel pain, then?"

"Not while I'm holding you." As he spoke he pulled her into his arms. "But that is not the answer you wanted, is it? In truth, I feel everything more keenly than a human would. Heat, cold, pain..." His fingers danced over her nape. "Pleasure," he whispered close to her ear. "Pain can incapacitate me, but whatever injuries I might sustain are healed while I rest. It's a regenerative sleep, you see." His lips moved over her temple. He kissed her eyelids, her cheeks and then her mouth, thoroughly and deeply. "I believe I will be in need of it after this night."

She smiled at his little joke, but the smile died when she realized that the sky beyond the window was beginning to lighten. She looked at his heavy-lidded eyes, and she felt his growing lethargy. "You need to rest." She pulled from his embrace, reached for their clothes and handed his to him. "Come on, it'll be light soon."

"Too soon," he told her. But he took the trousers from her, and slid off the bed to put them on. "I still dislike the thought of you going back to St. Claire today."

"I know." She fastened her jeans, and walked around the bed to stand close to him. "I have to, though. And I love you more for not trying to tell me what to do. I know you don't think highly of Daniel, but just like he's wrong about you, you're wrong about him, Eric. He isn't all bad."

In the distance the sky began to turn from gray to pink. Eric's shoulders lost their usual spread. His chin wasn't as high as it had been. She put an arm around his waist, and he draped one over her shoulders. She was beginning to feel tired, as well. They descended the stairs side by side, and all too soon stood locked together in the open doorway as Eric kissed her one last time.

She fought her sleepiness as she drove back home. She thought she might have time to catch an hour or two of sleep before she'd have to force herself awake and head in to work. She'd decided to resign. She couldn't continue working for DPI, knowing how they'd sponsored Eric's constant harassment over the years. Besides, it now was a blatant conflict of interest. She was in love with the subject of their longest-running investigation.

She let herself in, and caught her breath. Daniel, fully dressed, lay sprawled on the sofa, one arm and one leg dangling. A blanket had been tossed over him, but he'd only twisted himself up in it. His hair looked as if he'd been outside in a strong wind. When she drew nearer, the odor of stale alcohol assaulted her, and she saw the empty whiskey bottle on the floor.

"Well, finally made it home, did you?"

She caught her breath and looked up fast. Curtis lounged in the doorway that led into the huge dining room, a cup of coffee in his hand. "What are you doing here, Curt?" She glanced quickly at the clock on the wall. It was only five-forty-five.

"You've been with him all night, haven't you?"

There was something in his eyes, some coldness in his voice, that frightened her. "I'm an adult, Curt. Where I go is my business."

He straightened, came across the room and slammed the cup onto a table. "Can't you see how perverted this is? He's a frigging animal! And you're no better—acting like a bitch in heat. Christ, Tammy, if you'd needed it that bad all you had to do was ask—"

She reached him in two long strides and brought her hand across his face hard enough to rock him back on his feet. "Get out!"

"I don't think so." He stood facing her, and she saw absolute hatred in his eyes. How had she ever thought she had a true friend in this man? He blinked, though, and altered his tone of voice. "You're under some kind of spell, Tammy."

"What went on here last night?" She took a step to the side and went past him, through the dining room, knowing he'd follow. In the kitchen she got a cup of coffee for herself, and added sugar, hoping it would give her an energy boost.

"Daniel drank himself into a coma. What does it look like?" She turned, cup in hand, and frowned at him. "He called me around midnight, babbling about you and Marquand. I couldn't make sense of half of it. By the time I got here he'd drained the bottle. He was slurring something about dropping the research, or losing you forever. Is that the game plan, Tam? You use emotional blackmail on a guy who's been like a father to you? Force him to give up forty years of work, just so you can have your kinky fling?"

She felt no anger at his remarks. Only joy. "He said he was going to drop it?"

Curt's glare was once again filled with loathing. "He was too drunk to know *what* he was saying. But let me tell you something, Tam. I'm not going to drop it. Daniel has taught me everything he knows, so if he's ready to throw in the towel, I'll pick it up. You won't manipulate me the way you do him."

She opened her mouth to hurl a scathing reply, but saw Daniel standing weakly beyond Curt, making his way into the kitchen. "You, Curtis, will do what I tell you. I got you this far in DPI, and I can just as easily have you tossed out.''

He made it to a kitchen chair, leaned on the back of it for a moment, head down, then pulled it out and sat down. "Daniel, are you okay?" She turned to pour a cup of coffee, and then set it before him. "Can I get you anything?" He looked at her for a long moment, seemingly searching for something. Finally he shook his head, and stared into the coffee cup.

"I owe her, Curtis. You know it as well as I do. We're dropping it.''

"You're falling for her game, hook, line and sinker, aren't you?" Curt paced the room, shaking his head, pushing his hands through his hair. "Can't you see she's sold you out? She's joined the enemy, Daniel. She's the one we should have been studying all this time. I always told you she was more vampire than human!''

"What is that supposed to mean?" Tamara set her coffee down, spilling half of it.

"You mean to tell me you still don't know?"

"Don't know what?''

Daniel struggled to his feet, one hand massaging his forehead. "That's enough, Curtis. I think you ought to leave now. Tamara and I need to talk.''

Curtis eyed Tamara narrowly. "You mark my words, Tammy. You go through with this sick liaison and we'll all end up dead. You'll have my blood on your hands." He nodded toward Daniel. "And his. You just remember that I warned you." He turned on his heel and strode away. A second later the front door slammed, rattling the windows.

Daniel returned to his seat, shaking his head. "He'll get over it, Tam. Give him time.''

She sat across from him and slipped her hand over his. "He's wrong, Daniel. Eric is the gentlest man I've ever known. I want..." She drew a steadying breath and plunged on. "I want you to meet him. Talk to him. I want you to see that he's not what you think."

He nodded. "I figured you would, and I suppose I have to. I don't mind telling you, Tam, I'm afraid of him. The scientist in me is excited, though. To be that close..." He nodded again, and went on. "The biggest part of me knows this is inevitable. I'll do my best to make my peace with him, Tam. I've been over it a million times, all night long. It boils down to one thing." He reached up and cupped her face with one hand. "I don't want to lose you." Slowly he closed his eyes. "Bringing you into this house, into my life changed everything for me, Tamara. Before that I was..." He opened his eyes and she was surprised to see tears brimming in them. He shook his head.

"Go on. You were what?"

"A different man. A bastard, Tamara. More of a monster than Marquand could ever be. And I'm sorry for it... sorrier than you'll ever know."

She shook her head, not certain what to say. She felt this to be the most honest moment they'd ever shared.

She finished her coffee and went to bed, and Daniel didn't wake her. In fact, she was roused by the phone, shocked when she blinked her clock into focus and saw the time. She groped for the phone when it shrilled again, and brought it to her, wondering why Daniel hadn't answered it himself.

"Tam?"

At the familiar voice, her irritation dissolved. "Jamey?" She frowned and checked the clock once more. "Why aren't you in school?"

"I cut out. Tam..." He sighed and it sounded shaky. Tamara sat up in bed. "Something's wrong."

"Are you sick?" Her alarm sent the lethargy skittering to a dark corner of her mind. "Did you get hurt or something? Do you want me to call your mom?"

"No. It's not like that, it's something else." Another shuddering sigh. "I'm not sure what it is."

"Okay, Jamey, calm down. Just tell me where you are, and—"

"I took a cab. I'm at a pay phone in Byram. I didn't want to come to the house."

At least that was normal. The rambling Victorian had always given Jamey a case of the creeps. "I'll be there in ten minutes."

"Hurry, Tam, or we'll be too late."

Fear made her voice soft. "Too late for what, Jamey?"

"I don't know! Just hurry, okay?"

"Okay." She replaced the receiver with shaking hands. Something was terribly wrong. She'd heard the terror in Jamey's voice. Along with her gut-twisting concern was a flare of anger. Whoever was responsible for upsetting him this much would have to answer for it. She yanked on jeans and a sweatshirt. She pulled on socks and sneakers, then a jacket. She took a hairbrush from her purse and jerked it through her hair on the way down the stairs. Daniel was just coming up from the basement.

"What is it, hon?"

"Jamey. He's all out of sorts about something. I'm going to meet him in town, buy him a burger and talk him through it." She hugged Daniel quickly, then shoved the brush back into her bag and pulled out her keys.

Five minutes later she picked Jamey up. He was tugging on the Bug's door before it came to a full stop. He climbed in, looking pale and wide-eyed. "I think I'm goin' crazy," he announced.

Her instinct was to tell him that was nonsense, but she'd felt the same way recently—too often not to take his fear seriously. "I've thought that a time or two myself, pal." She searched his young face. Eleven years old was far too young to have such serious troubles weighing on him. "Tell me about it."

"You know before, when I asked you if you knew someone named Eric?" She stiffened, but nodded. "Well, I hope you know where he lives. We have to go there."

She didn't question Jamey. She put the car in gear and moved quickly down the street. "Do you know why?"

Jamey closed his eyes and rubbed his forehead as if it ached. "I think somebody's trying to kill him."

"My God." She pressed the accelerator to the floor, shifting rapidly.

"It's been coming in my head ever since I hung up the phone. It won't leave me alone until we go there—but it doesn't make sense."

"Why?"

"Because . . . I get the feeling he's already dead."

She drove the Bug as fast as it would go, and it vibrated with the effort. Even then, it took twenty minutes to reach the tall gate at the end of Eric's driveway. Tamara almost cried out when she saw Curt's car, pulled haphazardly onto the roadside nearby. She slammed on her brakes, killed the motor, wrenched the door open. She ran to the gate with Jamey on her heels.

It had been battered with something heavy. The pretty filigree vines were bent, some broken. The gate hung open and the electronic box inside was crushed. Pieces of its insides littered the snow. A single set of footprints led over the driveway, toward the house.

"Eric!" Tamara's scream echoed in the stillness as the reality of what was happening bludgeoned her mind. A small, firm hand caught hers and tugged her through the gate.

"C'mon, Tam. Come on, hurry!"

She blinked against the tears but they continued to fall unchecked. She couldn't see where her feet were coming down as she ran headlong, guided only by that strong grip. Eric's castlelike home loomed ahead, a tear-blurred mound of rough-hewn blocks. In a matter of seconds they were at the door, which stood yawning.

She swiped her eyes and hurried through. The living room looked as if a madman had raged through. Maybe that was exactly what had happened. The priceless antique furniture lay toppled. Some had been smashed. One of the needlepoint chairs had a leg missing. Vases lay in bits on the parquet floor. Heavy, marble-topped tables lay like fallen trees.

She stumbled almost blindly onward, through the formal dining room, where a candelabra had been hurled through a window, into the kitchen where cupboard doors had been ripped from their hinges. The sounds of breaking glass reached her and she turned, glimpsing the door she hadn't noticed. It hung open wide with a stairway that could only lead to the cellar. The sounds came from the darkness below, and a hand of ice choked her. She had no idea where Eric's coffin was, but if she'd had to hazard a guess she would have guessed the cellar. She approached the door.

A hand on her shoulder made her jump so suddenly she almost fell down the stairs. Jamey's other hand steadied her. "I called the police," he told her softly.

"Good. Stay by the front door and wait for them, okay?"

He looked up at her, but didn't agree. He remained at the top, though, as she slowly descended the stairs. Her foot on a different surface told her when she'd reached the bottom. The air was thick with blackness and the strong aroma of spilled wine. Glass shattered and she forced herself to move toward the sounds. "Curtis!" She shouted his name and the noise abruptly stopped. She stood still. "Stop it, Curt. Just stop it—this is crazy."

She waited while her eyes adjusted to the dark. She finally made out his shape. It grew clearer. He stood near a demolished wine rack, and he held a double-bitted ax. Broken bottles littered the floor around him. He stood in puddles of wine. The rack's wood shelves hung in splinters.

"Get the hell out of here, Tammy. This isn't your business. It's between me and Marquand!" He lifted the ax again.

Tamara threw herself at his back, latching onto his shoulders from behind to keep him from doing more damage. He dropped the ax to the floor and reached back, grabbing her by the hair and yanking her from him. She stumbled, hit the wine-soaked floor, but scrambled to her feet again. She faced him, panting less from exertion than fear. "The police are on their way, Curt. You'll wind up in jail if you don't get out of here, right now."

He reached for her so fast she didn't have a chance to duck. He grabbed the front of her coat, bunching the material in his fists. He whirled her around, and slammed her back against what once had been the wine rack. The back of her head hit a broken shelf and red pain lanced her brain. "Where is he, Tammy?"

She blinked, feeling her knees weaken. She pressed her hands to the wall behind her for support, then she froze. She felt a hinge beneath her palm. This was no wine rack. It was a door. What the hell would a vampire want with wine, anyway? Why hadn't she guessed sooner? And when would it hit Curt?

She sucked air through her teeth. "He's not—here."

The back of his hand connected with her jaw, and his knuckles felt like rocks. "I *said*, where is he? You damn well know and you're damn well going to tell me."

Involuntarily a sob escaped. Tears burned over her face. Curtis let go of her coat, but gripped her shoulders. "Christ, Tammy, I don't want to hurt you. You're under his control, dammit. You'll never see him for what he is until he's gone. If I don't do it, he'll kill us all."

She faced him squarely and shook her head. "You're wrong!"

"He's not even human," he told her.

"He's more human than you'll ever be!"

Curt's hand rose again, but it was caught from behind. "Leave her alone," Jamey shouted.

"What the hell?" Curt looked back, shaking Jamey's grip away effortlessly. Then he turned on him. "You little—"

"Curtis, no!" But before he could hit the boy, Jamey lowered his head and plowed into Curt's midsection like a battering ram. Both went down in a tangle of arms and legs and broken bottles. Tamara grabbed Curt's arm and tried to pull him away.

"Hold it right there!" A strong light shone down the stairs, and footsteps hurriedly descended. A police officer took Tamara's arm and pulled her away, while another lifted Curt, none too gently, then bent over Jamey. "You all right, son?"

"Fine. I'm the one who called you." He pointed an accusing finger at Curtis. "He broke in . . . with that." He angled his finger toward the ax on the floor.

The cop whistled, helping Jamey to his feet, and turned back to Curt. "Izzat right?" He took Curt's arm and urged him up the stairs, while the second officer herded Tamara and Jamey ahead of him. At the top, in the better light, her officer tugged her into the living room and told her his name was Sumner.

"You the owner?"

"No. I . . . he's out of town and I was keeping an eye on the place for him," she lied easily. Jamey stood aside, not saying a word.

"I'll need his name and a number to reach him." He'd pulled a stereotypical dog-eared notepad from his pocket.

"He's en route," she said. "But he should be back tonight."

He nodded, took down Tamara's name, address and phone number, then bent his head and frowned, his eyes fixed to her jawline. "Did he do that?"

Tamara's fingers touched the bruised flesh. She nodded, and saw anger flash in the officer's green eyes. "I need to take Jamey home, and . . . get myself together. I know you need a full statement, but do you think I could come in later and give it to you then?"

He scanned her face, and nodded. "You want to press assault charges?"

"Will it keep him jail overnight?"

He winked. "I can guarantee that."

"Then I guess I do." The officer nodded, took Eric's name down and advised her to have herself looked at by a doctor. Then he went into the dining room and spoke to his partner. Moments later Curtis was led toward the front door with his hands cuffed together behind his back.

"You'll regret this," he repeated again and again. "I'm a federal officer."

"One without a warrant, which in our book makes you just another breaking and entering, vandalism and aggravated assault case." Sumner continued lecturing as they went out the door and along the driveway.

Jamey looked to be in shock. Tamara went to him and ran one hand through his dark, curly hair. "You have guts like I've never seen, kiddo." He looked up but didn't smile. "I hate to admit it, Jamey, but I'm awfully glad you were here with me."

A smile began beneath hollow eyes. "What's going on? Why did Curtis want to kill Eric?"

She looked at him, not blinking. "A lot of reasons. Jealousy might be one, and fear. Curt is definitely afraid of Eric." She wouldn't lie to Jamey. She wasn't certain why, but he was a part of all of this. "Eric is different—not like everyone else. Some people fear what they don't understand. Some would rather destroy anything different, than learn about it." He still looked puzzled. "Do you know about the Salem witch trials?" He nodded. "Same principle is involved here."

Jamey sighed and shook his head, then grew calmer, and got the adult expression on his face that told her he was thinking like one. "Fear what's different, destroy what you fear."

She sighed, awed at the insight of the child. "Sometimes you amaze me." She walked with him out the door, and pulled it closed. She propped the gate with a big rock, so it would at least look like a deterrent. "You think it'll be all right until I get back?"

Jamey frowned at her. "I don't have any more weird feelings jumping in and out of my brain, if that's what you mean." He smiled fully for the first time.

"You know, Jamey, you probably saved my life in there. If you hadn't called the cops..." She shook her head. "And you likely saved Eric's, too, as well as his friend, Roland."

He looked back at the house, with one hand on the car door. "They're in there, aren't they?" He didn't wait for an answer. "They would've helped us, but they couldn't. If Curt had found them, he'd have killed them."

He didn't ask Tamara to confirm or deny any of it. He just slid into the car and rode home in silence.

Tamara told Kathy the bare facts, while trying to gloss over the worst of it. Jamey envisioned a break-in at a friend's house. He and Tamara arrived just in time to prevent it. The suspect was in custody and all was well with the world. Tamara kept the bruised side of her face averted, and made excuses to hurry off without coming inside for a visit. Kathy Bryant, while flustered, took it all in stride.

Tamara arrived back at Eric's front gate a little after 5:00 p.m.

CHAPTER THIRTEEN

Eric opened his eyes and slowly became aware of the smell of dirt surrounding him. He rested in an awkward position, not upon his bed of satin but on the rough wood floor of the secret room beneath it. He frowned, his head still cloudy, and squeezed the bridge of his nose between thumb and forefinger. He recalled the sudden sense of danger that had roused him from the depths of his deathlike slumber to a state hovering near wakefulness. He'd automatically flexed his forefinger on the hidden button, dumping himself into this place. He was safe and the feeling of mortal danger had passed.

Eric stood on the small stool, placed here for just such a purpose, and reached above him to the handle on the underside of his mattress. He pulled downward, then reached higher to release the lock on the lid. A moment later he swung himself over, landing easily on the floor. He attuned his senses, felt no threat and moved across the room to the coffin Roland had set upon a bier. He tapped on the lid, not surprised when Roland emerged from a concealed door in the bier itself, rather than through the polished hardwood lid.

He straightened, brushed at his wrinkled clothing. "What in God's name has been happening?"

"I'm not certain." Eric stood motionless. "Tamara is here."

Roland too, concentrated. "Others have been. Three—no, four others. Gone now."

Nodding, Eric unlocked the door. They moved quickly through the darkened passage, and Eric unlatched and pushed at the wine rack that served as its entrance. It gave a few inches, then jammed. He shoved harder, forcing it open. Both men took pause when they stepped into the cellar.

The electric light bulb above glowed harshly. What had been a well-stocked wine rack was now a shambles, with only a bottle or two remaining intact. The aroma assaulted Eric, pulling his head around until he saw the plastic pails on the floor, filled to the brim with broken glass and bits of wood. An old push broom and a coal shovel were propped against one pail. The floor beneath his feet was damp with wine. Another scent reached Eric's nostrils and he whirled, immediately spotting the slight stain on the wall near the hidden door, and knew it was blood. Tamara's blood.

He flew up the stairs then, and through the house, skidding to a halt when he entered the parlor.

Tamara lowered the two far legs of a heavy table to the floor. She ran her fingers over the chipped edge, sighed deeply and bent to retrieve an old gilded clock. She brought the piece to her ear, then placed it gently on the marble table. Eric took in the scene around her, realizing she'd already righted much of it. She turned slightly, so he saw the dark purple skin along her jaw, and picked up a toppled chair, setting it in its rightful place.

"Tamara." He moved forward slowly.

She looked up at the sound of his voice, and rushed into his arms. He felt her tears, and the trembling that seemed to come from the center of her body. No part of her was steady. He closed his arms as tightly as he dared around her small waist, and held her hard. Roland had stepped into the room and stood silently surveying the damage.

"Who is responsible for this?" Eric stepped back just enough to tilt her chin in gentle fingers, and examine her bruised face.

"It was... it was Curtis, but Eric, I'm all right. It isn't as bad as it looks."

Eric's anger made the words stick in his throat. "He struck you?" She nodded. He reached around to touch the back of her head gently, and knew when she winced that he'd found the cut. "And what else?"

"He..." She looked into his eyes and he knew she'd considered lying to him, then realized it would be useless. "He shoved me against the wall and I hit my head, but I'm fine."

He sought the truth of that statement, probing her mind, wondering if she was truly all right.

"Must have come through here like a raging bull," Roland remarked.

"I've never seen him so angry," Tamara said.

"Nor will you ever see it again." Eric let his arms fall away from her and took a single step toward the door. Roland blocked his path quickly and elegantly. Eric knew he had little chance of moving his powerful friend aside.

"I believe we should hear the tale before any action is taken, Eric."

Eric met Roland's gaze for a moment, and finally nodded. "Remember, though," he said. "He was warned what would happen if he harmed her." Eric turned to Tamara, and noted that as she came to him her gait was wobbly. He slipped his arms around her and helped her to the settee. Roland left the room, and returned in a moment with one of the remaining bottles. He took it to the bar, poured a glassful and brought it to Tamara.

"Take your time," he said softly. "Tell it from the start." He sat in an undamaged chair, while Eric stood stiffly, waiting, wishing he could reach the bastard's throat in the next few seconds.

Tamara sipped the wine. "I guess the start isn't all that bad. I convinced Daniel to drop the research. He agreed when I told him I'd leave forever if he didn't."

Eric frowned. "He agreed?"

"Yes, and that's not all. I asked him to meet you, talk to you. I want him to see you the way I do, and know you would never hurt me. He agreed to that, too."

Eric sat down hard. "I'll be damned—"

"I'm not at all convinced this is a good idea," Roland said. "But I'll leave that for later. Go on with the story, my dear."

Eric saw Tamara sip again, and her hand on the glass still wasn't steady. He sat closer to her. "When Daniel told Curtis he was dropping the research, Curt was furious, but defiant. He said he'd continue with or without Daniel's help. Daniel told him to drop it, or lose his job at DPI. Curt left madder than ever...but I still never thought he'd come here."

Eric frowned and shook his head. "How did you know?"

"It was Jamey, the boy I work with. He's something of a clairvoyant, though it's a weak power except where I'm concerned. He knew your name, Eric. He picked up on my nightmares, too. He called me, frantic, and when I picked him up he insisted we come here. He said someone was trying to kill you."

Eric glanced up at Roland, and both men frowned hard. Tamara, not noticing, went on with her story.

"When we got here I heard Curt down below, smashing things. Jamey called the police and I went down to stop Curt. I was terrified your resting place was down there somewhere." She closed her eyes, and Eric knew she had truly been afraid for his life. "I told Jamey to stay by the front door, but he came down, too."

"Stubborn lad," Roland observed.

Tamara's eyes lit then, and her chin came up. "You should have seen him. He charged Curt like a bull, took him right to the floor when Curt tried to hit me again."

"Was the boy injured?" Again it was Roland who spoke. Eric was busy watching the changing expressions on Tamara's face, and reading the emotions behind them. It changed again now, with a silent rage. He felt it rise up within her, and its ferocity amazed him. He hadn't known she was capable of a violent thought.

Her voice oddly low, she said, "If Curt had hurt Jamey, I'd have killed him."

Eric shot a puzzled glance toward Roland, who seemed to be studying her just as intently. Tamara seemed to shake herself. She blinked twice, and the fire in her eyes died slowly. "The police arrived then. I pressed assault charges. He'll be in jail overnight, so you'll have time to regroup." She placed a hand on Eric's arm. "I'm sorry the police got involved. They expect both of us to show up tonight, to give statements."

"I should be angry with you, Tamara, but not for calling the police. For risking your life. You could have been killed."

"If he'd killed you, I'd have died, anyway. Don't you know that yet?" As she spoke she leaned into his embrace, and settled her head on his shoulder. "You have to get this place fixed up. Curt will flash his DPI card around and get himself out by morning."

"Unfortunate for him, should he decide to give up the protection of a jail cell so soon."

"Eric, you can't...do anything to him. It would only give those idiots at DPI more reason to hound your every step."

"You think I care?"

"I care." She sat up and stared into his eyes. "I intend to be with you from now on, Eric, wherever you go. I'd like it if we were free to come and go as we please, and I could visit Daniel from time to time. I want to enjoy our life together. Please, don't let your anger ruin it before it's even begun."

Her words worked like ice water on his rage. The points she made were valid, and while he still thought St. Claire a moral deviate, he knew she loved the man. He glanced helplessly toward Roland.

"I wouldn't want to square off against her in a debate," he said dryly.

Eric sighed. There was no way in God's earth he could allow Curtis Rogers to get away with what he'd done. But he supposed he'd have to plot a fitting retribution later. There was no use arguing with Tamara. She hadn't a vengeful bone in her beautiful body—except where this boy, Jamey, was concerned. And that puzzled him.

"As for the gate and the door," he said, sensing her lingering worry for his safety, "I can make a few calls tonight and have a reliable crew here by first light."

"But he got in once, Eric," Tamara said.

"Dogs!" Roland stood quickly. "That would solve it. We'll acquire ten—no, twelve—of those attack dogs you hear about. Dobermans or some such breed. Tear a man to shreds."

"I think a direct line to the police department will be just as effective." Eric couldn't keep the amusement from his voice. Roland did possess a brutal streak. "An alarm that alerts the police the moment security is breached. I admit, I hate depending on them for security, but it will only be necessary until—" he stopped, and slanted a glance at Tamara "—until I think of something better. Meantime, why don't we visit the police station and get the unpleasantness

over with. We may still salvage what remains of the night.
I had such plans...."

How he managed to make her laugh after what she'd
been through tonight, she couldn't imagine. But he did. By
the time they left the police station he was behind the wheel
of what he referred to as her "oddly misshapen automobile," and she was splitting a side over his shifting tech-
nique.

The house had been restored to order as much as possible. Roland had left a fire blazing brightly, and a vase stood
in the room's center, filled with twelve graceful white roses.
A card dangling from one stem drew her attention. She
lifted it and read, "My thanks for your earlier heroism.
Roland."

She shook her head, and turned when she heard strains
of music filling the room. Mozart again. "Your friend is
certainly chivalrous."

"You inspire that sort of thing in a man," he told her.

She smiled and went into his arms. "What about these
plans you mentioned earlier?"

"I thought you might like to dance."

She tilted her head back and kissed his chin. "I would."

"Oh, no. I couldn't possibly dance with you dressed like
that."

She frowned, stepping away from him and looking down
at her jeans and sweatshirt. "I admit, I'm not exactly elegant tonight, but—"

"I've a surprise for you, Tamara. Come." He turned her
toward the stairs and urged her up them. He led her into the
bedroom she'd seen before, and left her waiting inside the
doorway while he lit two oil lamps. He turned to a wardrobe, gripped its double handles and opened it with a
flourish.

Curious, she moved forward as he reached into the dark confines and removed a garment carefully, draping it over his arms. When he turned toward her Tamara's heart skipped a beat. It was something made for Cinderella. The jade-colored fabric shimmered. The neckline was heart shaped, the sleeves puffy and the skirt so fully flared she knew there must be petticoats attached. The green satin was gathered up from the hemline and held with tiny white bows at intervals all along the bottom, to show the frilly white underskirt.

Her mouth opened, but only air escaped. "It belonged to my sister," Eric told her. "She used to cinch her waist with corsets, but she wasn't as petite as you. I suspect it will suit you without them."

She forced her eyes away from the dress and back to him her heart tightening. "Your sister...Jaqueline. And you've kept it all this time."

"I supposed I am a bit sentimental where my little sister is concerned. She wore that gown the night she accompanied me to a performance of young Amadeus, in Paris."

Her eyes had wandered downward to the glittering silk, but snapped up again. "Mozart?"

"The same. She was not overly impressed, as I recall." He smiled down at her. "I should like to see you in the gown, Tamara."

She gasped. "Oh, but I couldn't—it's so precious to you. My God, it must have cost a fortune to keep it so well preserved all this time."

"And no good deal of fuss, as well," he said. "But nothing is too precious for you, my love. It will make me happy to see you wear it. Do it for me."

She nodded, and Eric left the room. She was surprised, but didn't question it. She shimmied out of her own clothing, including her bra, since the upper halves of her breasts would be revealed by the daring neckline. She touched the

dress reverently, and stepped into it with great care, terrified she'd rip it while putting it on. She slid her hands
through the armholes, and adjusted the shoulders. "Eric!"

At her call he returned, and she presented her back to
him. Wordlessly he tightened the laces and tied them in
place. He took two steps backward, and she turned slowly
to face him. His gaze moved over her, gleaming with emotion. He blinked quickly and shook his head. "You are a
vision, Tamara. Too lovely to be real. I could almost wonder if you would disappear, should I blink."

"Does it really look all right?" It felt tight, and her
breasts were squished so high they were fairly popping out
of the thing.

Eric smiled, took her hand and turned her toward the
wardrobe doors, which still stood open. She hadn't noticed the mirrors on the inside of the doors, but she did
now. He left her standing there and turned to lift a lamp,
better for her to see her reflection.

She caught her breath again. It wasn't Tamara Dey
looking back at her. It was a raven-haired eighteenth-
century beauty. She couldn't believe the transformation.
And the dress! It was more like a work of art than a piece
of clothing. She glanced gratefully up at Eric, then froze,
and looked back toward the mirror again. "It's true! You
have no reflection!"

"An oddity I still seek to solve, love." He closed the
doors and took her hand. "Now, about the dancing . . ."

He led her back downstairs into the roomy parlor,
thumbed a button and the piano sonata stopped abruptly.
A moment later a minuet lilted from the speakers. Eric
faced her, pointed one toe and bowed formally. Tamara
laughed, picking up his thoughts. She dropped into a deep
curtsy, imitating those she'd seen in movies. He took her
hand and drew her to her feet.

"Look at me as we turn," he instructed moments later. "The eyes are as important to the dance as the feet."

She fixed her gaze to his, rather than keeping it on her bare toes peeping from beneath the hemline. She tried to imitate his pace as they circled one another.

"That's it." His voice was soft but his gaze intense as the flames in the hearth. "You're a quick study."

"I have an excellent teacher." She met him as he stepped forward, then retreated just as he did. "You must have danced with every beautiful girl in Paris."

His lips quirked upward. "Hardly. I always loathed this type of thing." He lifted her hand in his, high above their heads, placed his other hand on her buttocks and urged her to turn beneath their joined fingers. "Perhaps one needs the right partner."

"I know what you mean. I never liked dancing before, either, even in high school." She stopped abruptly.

"Now you've broken the rhythm. We shall have to begin again."

"No. I think it's my turn to be the teacher." She stepped away from him and hurried to the stereo, fiddling with buttons until she'd stopped the CD, and turned on the FM stereo. She scanned stations until she heard the familiar harmony of The Righteous Brothers on the oldies station. "Perfect." She went back to Eric, slipped her arms around his neck and pressed her body as close to his as the full-skirted dress would allow. "This is the way my generation dances . . . when they find the right partner. Put your arms around my waist and hold me close." He did, and she settled her head on his shoulder and very slowly began to sway their bodies in time to "Unchained Melody."

"Your method does have its merits. Is this all there is to it? Certainly easily learned."

"Well, there are variations." To demonstrate, she turned her face toward him and nuzzled his neck with her lips. He moved his hands lower, cupping her buttocks and squeezing her to him. He lowered his head and nibbled her ear. "You're a quick study," she told him, repeating his compliment.

"I have an excellent teacher," he replied. He lifted his head slowly, moving his lips to her chin and then capturing her mouth with his. He kissed her deeply, leaving her breathless and warm inside. His hands at the small of her back, he bent over her and moved his tantalizing lips down the front of her throat to kiss her breasts.

She arched backward, her hands tangling in his hair. Her fingers nimbly loosened the ribbon and threaded in the thick jet waves. One of his hands came around her, to scoop a breast out of its satin confines and hold it to his mouth. He flicked his tongue over the nipple, already throbbing and hard, then closed his lips around it and suckled her roughly. She didn't realize he'd moved her until she felt her back pressed to a wall. She opened her eyes, forcing words despite the sighs of pleasure he was evoking. "Eric...what about...Roland..."

"He knows better than to interrupt." He had to stop what he was doing to speak, but he quickly returned to the business of driving her crazy with desire. When she strained against his mouth he responded by closing his teeth on her nipple. She shuddered with pleasure. He anchored her to the wall with his body and used his hands to gather the voluminous skirts upward in the front, no easy task. Nonetheless, he soon had them arranged high enough to allow his hands ample access to her naked thighs and the unclothed moistness between them.

His hand stilled when it found no scrap of nylon barring its way. She'd seen no need for panties, knowing instinctively where the night would lead. His fingers moved over her, opened her and slipped inside, stroking her to a fever pitch. When they finally moved away it was only to release his own barriers, and then his manhood, hot and solid, nudged against her thigh. His hands slipped down the backs of her legs, and he lifted her. He speared her with a single, unerring thrust, and Tamara's head fell backward as the air was forced from her lungs. That action put her breasts once again in reach of his mouth and he took advantage.

She locked her legs around his body, her arms around his neck, and she rode him like an untamed stallion. He drove into her, his hands clutching her buttocks like a vise and pulling her downward with every upward thrust. In minutes he trembled, and she hovered near a violent release. His teeth on her breasts clamped tighter, and rather than pain she felt intense pleasure. That other kind of climax enticed her nearer. Her entire body vibrated, her every nerve ending tensed at the two places where they were joined. Closer and closer he drove her, until she writhed with need.

Even when the spasms began, she craved more. "Please," she moaned, he fingers raking through his hair. It was all the encouragement he needed. She felt the prick at the tip of her breast, and then the unbearable tingling as he sucked harder. With his first greedy swallows she exploded in sensation, both climaxes rocking her at once. Her entire body shook with pleasure, even as she realized he'd stiffened, plunged himself into her one last time and groaned long and low against her heated skin.

As if his knees had weakened he sank slowly to the floor, taking her with him. He brought her down on top of him, still not withdrawing from her. He released her breast and cradled her to his chest, rocking her slowly. "My God, woman," he whispered into her hair. "You take me higher than I knew was possible. You thrill me to the marrow. Have I told you how very much I love you?"

"Yes, silently. But I won't mind if you tell me again."

His lips caressed her skin, just above her temple. "More than my own existence, Tamara. There is nothing I wouldn't do for you. I would die for you."

She licked her lips. "Would you meet with Daniel?"

He hesitated, and she felt the tightening of his jaw. "It will not change anything."

"I think it will." She lifted her upper body slightly, and regarded his face. "It would mean so much to me."

He cupped her head to pull her down to him again, buried his face in her hair and inhaled its scent. "If it is so important to you, I will do it. When you return to St. Claire at dawn, tell him I'll come just after nightfall."

She found his hands with hers, and laced her fingers through his. "Thank you, Eric. It will make a difference. You'll see." She lifted her head and pressed her lips to his. "But I'll call him. I don't want to leave at dawn."

She felt his body stiffen and knew he'd argue the point. "Eric, they'll only keep Curtis overnight. What if he comes back here while you rest?"

"No doubt you'd like to meet him at the door with claws extended, my tigress. But I'll not have you in harm's way to protect me. What kind of man do you take me for?"

"You'd be defenseless if he found you during the day."

"Tamara, the workmen will be here at first light, and the repairs completed by noon. They will be under instructions to notify police of any intruders, and to arm the new security system before they leave. No one will disturb my rest."

"I'll leave when they do, then."

His eyes flashed impatience. "You will leave at dawn."

She shook her head from side to side. "I won't go."

"I won't have a woman taking my place in battle."

The harshness in his voice brought burning tears springing to her eyes. "I'm not just a woman. I am the woman who loves you, Eric. I'd sooner peel every inch of flesh from Curt with my nails and teeth than to let him near you during the day." A sob rose in her throat, but she fought it down. "You don't know how I felt when I realized he was in here today...that he might have already murdered you. My God, if I lost you now, I couldn't go on."

The hands that came back to her shoulders and nape were gentle, not angry. "And you do not know, my love, how I felt when I woke to find you had been beaten while I lay only a short distance away, helpless to defend you. How could I bear it if I woke to find you murdered in my own home?"

"But that would never happen. Curt couldn't really hurt me. He only acted so crazy because he cares so much."

Eric's long fingers caught her chin and turned her slightly, so his eyes could scan the bruise. "And I suppose this is a token of his undying esteem."

"He was in a rage. He regretted it as soon as he realized what he'd done."

"No doubt he'd regret killing you the instant the deed was done, as well."

"But he wouldn't—"

"My love, you trust too freely, and too deeply. As much as I hate being forced to do so, I can see I must give you an ultimatum. You will leave here at dawn, or I will not meet with St. Claire. And before you agree, with the intent of stealing back here as I rest, you should be aware that I will sense your presence. I know when you are near, my love." His voice softened, and he touched the skin of her cheek with his fingertips.

She blinked away the stupid urge to cry. One tear spilled over despite her efforts, and he leaned up to catch it with his lips. "Do you truly wish to spend what remains of this night bickering?"

She shook her head, unable to sustain her anger. He only wanted to protect her, just as she wanted to protect him.

She understood his motivations all too well. She lowered her head until her pliant lips had settled over his coaxing ones, and she tasted the salt of her own tear.

Eric stood in the doorway long after she'd driven out of sight, heedless of the growing light in the eastern sky.

"Stand gaping like that another five minutes and you will be there permanently, my lovestruck friend." Roland came around Eric, shoved the heavy door closed and eyed the broken lock. "I suppose your men will arrive within the hour to repair that?"

Eric nodded mutely.

"For God's sake, man, snap out of it!"

Eric started, glanced at Roland and grinned foolishly. "Isn't she something?"

Roland rolled his eyes ceilingward, and shoved a glass into Eric's hand. "You're whiter than alabaster. You haven't been feeding properly. The few sips you allow yourself are no doubt sweet, Eric, but not enough to sustain you."

Eric scowled at Roland's rather crude observation, but realized he was right. He felt weak and light-headed. He drained the glass, and moved to the bar to refill it.

"Tell me," Roland said slowly. "Has anything been decided?"

"Such as?" Eric sipped and waited.

"You know precisely what I refer to, Eric. The decision to be made. Has our lady voiced an opinion?"

"You cannot think I'm considering passing my curse on to her."

Roland sighed hard. "When did you begin seeing immortality as a curse?"

"That is what it is." Eric slammed the glass down on the polished hardwood surface. "It's been unending hell for me."

"And what kind of hell has it been these past days, Eric?" Eric didn't answer that, knowing Roland had a valid point. "I thought to save your life two centuries ago in Paris, not curse it. Eric, I live in solitude because it is the only way for me. I had my chance at happiness centuries ago, and lost it. I don't expect another. But you... you are throwing yours away."

Eric bowed his head and pressed his fingertips to his eyes. "I don't know if I could do it to her." He heard Roland's sigh and raised his head. "I have made one decision, though. I've agreed to meet with St. Claire."

"You can't be serious."

"Quite serious. It means a great deal to Tamara that St. Claire be reassured of her safety. She seems to think I can accomplish that by talking with the man. I have my doubts, of course, but—"

"The only thing to be accomplished by such a meeting is your destruction. Think about it, Eric. Wittingly or not, Tamara has lured you into the spider's web, just as St. Claire planned from the start. Once in, there will be no escape."

Eric stood silent, contemplating Roland's words. The idea that the whole meeting scheme might be a trap had niggled at him since Tamara had first broached the subject. Of course, he knew she was no part of it. And if it was a trap, what better way to show Tamara the true nature of those she trusted? Providing, of course, he was able to escape.

Reading his thoughts, Roland bristled. "And suppose you prove this valuable point to the girl, and lose you own life in the process?"

"I won't. I can't, for Tamara's sake. Without me she'd be as she was before. At their mercy."

Roland grimaced. "At the moment, my friend, I fear it is you who are at hers."

Eric smiled. "I can think of no place I'd rather be."

CHAPTER FOURTEEN

As the sky glowed with the rising sun, Tamara peered into Daniel's bedroom. He lay atop the covers, fully dressed, snoring loudly. A half-empty bottle was on its side, on the floor near the bed. The cover wasn't screwed on tightly. Moisture dotted the neck and a few drops of whiskey dampened the worn carpet. A glass lay toppled in an amber puddle on the bedside stand.

She frowned as she moved silently into the room, picked up the bottle and the glass, and retreated again. What was driving him to drink himself in oblivion every night? In all the years she'd known him she'd never seen Daniel drink more than a glass or two at a time. She'd never seen him drunk. She returned with a handful of tissues and mopped up the spills, then dropped a comforter over Daniel and tiptoed away. Something seemed to be eating at Daniel— something more than just the knowledge that she was spending her nights with his lifelong enemy.

She forced the troubling thought out of her mind, determined to concentrate only on the good things to come. Tonight Daniel and Eric would meet. She had no doubt they'd become friends, in time. And Curtis would see reason. He may have lost his head for a time, but he was intelligent. He'd recognize the truth when it was staring him in the face.

The future loomed up before her for a moment as she soaked in a steamy, scented bath. Like a giant black hole, with a question mark at its center, it hovered in her mind. She ignored it. She had all she could deal with at the moment, just trying to keep the present running on an even keel. She'd worry about her future later, when things settled down.

Her plan was to bathe, put on fresh clothes and drive back to Eric's to see if the workers had arrived as he'd promised. With the brilliant sun, glinting blindingly off the snow outside, came physical and emotional exhaustion. She fell asleep in the bath, quite against her will, and for once she didn't sleep soundly. Her dreams were troubled and her sleep fitful. She saw herself old, with white hair and a face deeply lined. Then the dream shifted and she saw a cold stone marker with her name engraved on its face. She saw Eric, bent double with grief, standing beside it, surrounded by bitter cold on a bleak wintry night.

She woke with a start, and realized the now-cold water around her body might have aided in the seeming vividness of the dream. Still, she couldn't shake the lingering images. "It doesn't have to be that way," she said aloud, and firmly. And she knew she was right. Eric had explained to her what it meant to be what he called Chosen. She could be transformed. She could be with him forever. The thought rocked through her, leaving her shaken like a leaf in a storm. She could become what he was....

She pressed a palm to her forehead, and shook herself. Later. She'd consider all of this later. It was more than she could process right now. She toweled herself vigorously, to rub the cold water's chill from her goose-bumped flesh, and dressed quickly. A glance at the clock near her bed chased every other thought from her mind. Noon! By now Curt could have...

She took the stairs two at a time, shocked into immobility when she reached the bottom and saw Curt, comfortable in an overstuffed chair, sipping coffee. Daniel, now awake and sitting with Curt, rose, and she felt his bloodshot gaze move over her still-damp hair and hastily donned clothing.

His gaze stopped at her bruised face, and he spun around to glare at Curtis. "You did that to her?"

He looked at the floor. "You don't know how bad I feel, Tammy. I'm sorry—more sorry for hurting you than I've ever been for anything in my life. I was out of my head yesterday. I— Can you ever forgive me?"

She stepped down from the lowest stair and moved cautiously toward him, scanning his face. She saw nothing but sincere remorse there. He met her gaze and his own seemed to beg for understanding. "I'm still afraid for you," he told her. "I'm afraid for all of us, but—"

"I know you're afraid, Curtis, but there's no reason to be. If Eric had meant to hurt you, he'd have done it by now. Don't you see that? In all the months you two have harassed him, he's never lifted a hand against either of you."

Daniel cleared his throat and came closer to the two of them, forming a circle that seemed intimate. She noticed he'd shaven and taken pains to dress well, in a spotless white shirt and knife-edged trousers, brown leather belt and polished shoes, a dark blue tie held down with a gold clip. Did he want to keep his excessive drinking a secret, then? How could he think she'd not know?

"I have to admit," he began, "it's damn tough for me to consider that I might have been wrong all this time, after the lengths I've gone to." She saw him swallow convulsively and blink fast before he went on. "As scientists, Curtis, we have to consider every possibility. Because of that, and because I love Tamara, I'm going to give the man the benefit of the doubt."

"I can't believe you're going to meet with him, Daniel," Curtis blurted, shaking his head. "But I suppose if you've made up your mind—"

"Has he agreed, Tam?" Daniel interjected.

She nodded, glancing apprehensively toward Curtis.

"Tonight? Here, and not long after dark? He agreed to all of it? I'm not about to meet him anywhere else, even with all your assurances."

"I didn't have to tell him your preference to meet here." She spoke defensively, before she could stop herself. "He suggested that himself."

Daniel nodded, while Curtis let his head fall backward, and stared at the ceiling. Blowing a sigh, he brought his gaze level again. "Okay, if this is unavoidable, then I want to be here."

"No!" Tamara barked the word so loudly both men jumped. She forced her voice lower. "After yesterday, Curt, I don't want you anywhere near him."

Curt blinked at her, his eyes going round with apparent pain. "You don't trust me?" He searched her face for a long moment, then sighed again. "I don't suppose I can blame you, but..." He let his gaze move toward Daniel, but his words were addressed to Tamara. "I hope to God you're right about Marquand."

"I am," she told him. "I know I am." She glanced toward the door, recalling her hurry to leave. She still wanted to check on the repairs at Eric's even though it now seemed Curt had come to his senses. "I have to go out for a while."

Curt caught her arm as she turned. "You haven't said you forgive me for being such an idiot yesterday." His gaze touched her bruise, then hopped back to her eyes. "I feel sick to my stomach when I think of what I did."

She closed her eyes slowly. She wanted no more anger and hard feelings. She wanted nothing bad to interfere with her happiness. "It's been a tense week, Curt. I knew you didn't mean it. I forgave you almost as soon as it was over."

"You're one in a million, Tam."

She hurried away, glad to be alone behind the wheel of her Bug and headed toward Eric's house.

She found two pickup trucks and a van lining the roadside. Young, muscular men worked in shirt sleeves, despite the snow on the ground. She pulled her car to a stop behind the van, and settled into the seat more comfortably. She wasn't planning to leave here until she knew the place was secure. Despite Eric's threat, she knew he wouldn't stay angry with her.

Twice during her vigil she felt her eyelids drooping, and forced them wider. She got out and walked in the biting winter air to stay awake. The crews didn't pack up to leave until well after four-thirty. In an hour the sun would begin to fade, and Eric would wake. Still she waited until the last man had left, gratified to see him look suspiciously at her car before he drove away. She was certain he'd jotted the plate number. Eric had said they were dependable. He was right. Then she pulled away, too. She wanted to have time to change into something pretty and perhaps do something new with her hair before Eric arrived for his talk with Daniel.

She knew something was wrong with her first glimpse of Daniel's frowning face. "What is it?" She hurried toward him, not even shedding her jacket or stomping the clinging snow from her boots. "Tell me. What's happened?"

"I'm sure it's nothing, Tam. I don't want you to get worried until we know for su—"

"Tell me!"

Daniel looked at the floor. "Kathy Bryant called about an hour ago."

"Kathy B—" Tamara's throat went dry, and her stomach felt as if a fist had been driven into it. "It's Jamey, isn't it?"

Daniel nodded. "The school officials claim he left at the normal time, but . . . he never made it home."

"Jamey? He's missing?"

* * *

Jamey sat very still, because it hurt when he tried to move. His arms were pulled tightly behind him, and tied there. A blindfold covered his eyes and there was some kind of tape over his mouth. It felt like duct tape, but he couldn't be sure.

He'd left school to walk home just as he always did, cutting through the vacant lot behind the drugstore. Someone had grabbed him from behind. A damp cloth had been held over his nose and mouth and Jamey had known it was chloroform. He hadn't recognized the smell or anything, but he'd seen enough movies to know that's what they hold to your nose and mouth when they grab you from behind. Never fails. Chloroform. It stank, too. He'd felt himself falling into a black pit.

Now he was here, although he had no idea where *here* was. He couldn't see, and he could barely move. He assumed he was inside, because of the flat, hard surface he sat on and the one at his back. A floor and a wall, he guessed. He was in an old kind of place, because he could smell the old, musty odors. Inside or not, though, it was cold. Breezes wafted through now and then and he felt no kind of warmth at all. He was glad he'd zipped his coat and pulled on his hat when he'd left school. He sure couldn't have done it now. He couldn't do much of anything now.

Except think. He'd been thinking a lot since he had come around and found himself here. Mostly what he thought about was who had grabbed him. He'd felt a clear sense of recognition flash through his mind the second the guy—and he was sure it had been a guy—had grabbed him. He'd been on the brink of total recall when the chloroform had got to him. If he'd had just a few more seconds...

But maybe it would come to him later. Right now his main concerns were two—his empty stomach, and the dropping temperature.

* * *

Tamara listened, numb with worry, as Daniel related the details of Jamey's disappearance. He'd left school to walk home at three-thirty. His mother had been over his route, as had the police, and found nothing. His friends had been questioned, but nothing of any use was learned.

She knew she should remain where she was and wait for Eric. He could meet Daniel when he arrived, and then she'd explain what had happened and ask him to finish the talk another time. He'd help her find Jamey. Rationally she knew that would be the wisest course of action. But her emotions wouldn't allow it. Despite Kathy Bryant's lack of panic when Tamara phoned her, she felt it building within her own mind. Kathy had the assurances of the police, who saw this type of thing all the time, that Jamey would turn up safe and sound within a few hours. But Tamara had her own, sickening intuition that something was terribly wrong. When she closed her eyes and tried to focus on Jamey she felt nothing but coldness and fear. She had to find him, and she couldn't wait. He was cold, afraid and alone, and...

"I can see you want to go, Tam," Daniel said, placing a gentle hand on her arm.

She shook her head. "I can't. Eric will be here before long, and I know how nervous you are."

He shook his head. "To tell you the truth, I was thinking it might be better for the two of us to have a private talk. You go on, go see to the boy. I'll explain to Marquand when he gets here."

She hesitated. "Are you sure?"

"Go on," he repeated.

She hugged his neck. "Thank you, Daniel." She pressed her trembling lips to his leathery cheek. "I love you, you know."

She whirled from him and rushed to her car, then changed her mind and took his, knowing he wouldn't object. It would be faster.

She got the same story when she talked to Kathy face-to-face. The poor woman seemed to grow more concerned each time she glanced at the clock. Her confidence in the official prediction that Jamey was perfectly all right must be fading, Tamara thought.

Tamara ignored the gathering darkness, knowing Eric would soon meet with Daniel, and probably come looking for her as soon as he was told the reason for her absence. She wasn't worried about his ability to find her. He'd know where she was without thinking twice. She wished her psychic link to Jamey was that strong. If she could just close her eyes and *know*... She shook her head. She couldn't, so why waste time wishing? She spent some time in his bedroom, going through things to see if there was a note or some clue... knowing all the while there wouldn't be. He hadn't left of his own accord. Her link was strong enough to tell her that much.

She had Kathy draw her a map of his usual route home, and she went to the school, parked the car and walked it, all of her mind honed for a hint of him. The police had been over the path he would've taken, and found nothing. Kathy had, as well, but Tamara felt certain she would find something they'd missed... and she did.

Something made her pause when she began to walk along the sidewalk past the drugstore. She stopped, lifted her head and waited. Her gaze turned of its own accord to the lot behind the store, a weedy, garbage-strewn mess that any parent would forbid her child to cross. Just as Kathy had probably forbidden Jamey. Yet she detected a meandering path amid the snowy brown weeds, broken bottles and litter. From her bag she pulled the flashlight she'd asked Kathy to lend her, and checked the hand-drawn map. To cross the lot would save several minutes of his walk home. She folded the map and pocketed it, aimed the beam and moved along the barely discernible path. Little snow had managed to accumulate here, and the wind that whipped through constantly rearranged what there was.

Bits of paper and rubbish swirled across her path as she moved behind the flashlight's beam. Crumpled newspaper pages skittered, and a flat sheet of notepaper glided past. She sought footprints but saw none and knew that if there'd been any the wind would have obliterated them by now. Pastel bits of tissue blew past, and then a tumbling bit of white that looked like cloth. She frowned and followed its progress with the light. Not cloth. Gauze. A wadded square of gauze.

The breeze stiffened and the scrap tumbled away. She chased it a few yards, lost sight of it, then spotted it again. She picked it up, careful to touch only a corner of the material, and that with her nails. She turned it in the beam of light. It hadn't been used on an injury. There was no trace of blood anywhere. Slowly, like a stalking phantom, the odor made its way into her senses. She wrinkled her nose. Was that...?

"Chloroform," she whispered, but the word was lost in the wind.

Eric walked up the front steps of St. Claire's house and pressed the button to announce his arrival. He shuffled his feet as he waited, and frowned when no one answered the door. He'd told himself repeatedly that he could handle whatever kinds of surprises St. Claire might have in store. Still, his mind jangled with warnings. He pressed the button again.

"I tell you, something is amiss!" Roland came from his hiding place among the shrubbery and stood beside Eric at the door.

"And I told you to stay out of sight. If he sees you, he'll be convinced we've come here to murder him."

"Have you not noticed, my astute friend, that no one answers the bell?"

Eric nodded. "Patience, Roland. I'll summon Tamara." His brows drew closer as he honed his senses to hers, but he felt no hint of her presence within the house. The wind shifted then, and the unmistakable scent of blood came heavy to them both. Eric's startled gaze met Roland's, and then both men sprinted around the house, toward the source.

They paused in the rear, near an open window with curtains billowing inward. Without hesitation Eric leapt onto the ledge and then over, dropping lightly to the floor inside. The smell was all-encompassing now, and when he glanced around the room he had to quell the jarring shock. St. Claire lay sprawled on the floor, in a virtual pool of his own blood. It still trickled from a jagged tear in his throat, but from the look, there was little left to flow.

"Decided to join my party, Marquand? You're a little late. Refreshments have already been served, as you can see."

Eric glanced up and saw Curtis Rogers standing in a darkened corner. "You," he growled. He lunged at the man, but Curtis ducked his first attack, flinging something warm and sticky into Eric's face. Blood. And he'd tossed it from a glass. Automatically Eric swiped a sleeve over his face, and an instant later he had the laughing little bastard by the throat. A sharp jab stabbed into his midsection. Not a blade, he thought. It was... *Oh, hell, a hypodermic.*

He flinched at the pain but caught himself, withdrawing one hand from Curtis's throat, clenching it into a fist and smashing it into his face. Rogers went down, toppling a table on the way, breaking a lamp. Eric walked toward him, aware now that Roland had come inside. He felt his friend's hand clasp his shoulder from behind.

"It's a trap, I tell you. We must go, now, before—"

"No!" Eric shook Roland's hand free and took another step toward the man on the floor, who made no move to get away. Suddenly Eric knew why. A wave of dizziness assaulted him. He fell to one knee as Rogers scurried backward like a crab. He felt his mind grow fuzzy, and his head suddenly seemed too heavy to hold upright.

Vaguely he felt Roland gripping him under the arms. He saw Rogers get to his feet and pull another hypodermic from somewhere. He tried to mutter a warning, but couldn't hear his own slurred voice. Roland let him go with only one hand when Rogers approached. He backhanded the bastard almost casually. Curtis sailed through the air, connecting with a bookshelf before slumping to the floor amid an avalanche of literature. Even drugged, Eric marvelled at Roland's strength.

"He's drugged you, Eric!" Roland's voice came from far away. "Fight it, man. Get up."

He tried, but his legs seemed numb and useless. Roland lifted his upper body and half dragged him to the window. Eric knew his thoughts. He suspected Rogers would have an army of DPI agents, possibly all armed with syringes of this new drug, converging on the place at any moment. Yet in his hazy mind all Eric could think of was Tamara. Why wasn't she here? Could she bear the grief of losing St. Claire this way? My God, she adored the man.

But she was here! His mind was suddenly pummeled with her aura. He tried to call out to her, but Roland was already pulling him through the window. "Nnno," he tried to say, unsure if he'd actually made a sound.

As Eric felt himself pulled to the ground he heard her steps, and the opening of a door. He lifted his head and tried to see her. He did. She appeared unfocused, a blurry silhouette, but her eyes found his and connected, just for an instant. Then they moved downward, and he heard her agonized screams.

"Have...to...go...to her."

He slumped into unconsciousness as Roland carried him away.

CHAPTER FIFTEEN

Tamara felt the shock like a physical blow. She'd glanced up automatically when she'd opened the library door. She'd felt Eric's presence like a magnetic force on her gaze. She'd seen him. He'd looked at her briefly, and his face had been smeared with something red. She'd glimpsed scarlet stains on his normally pristine-white shirt cuff, as well, before he'd moved away from the window. She let her puzzled gaze travel downward, drawn there by some inner knowledge she couldn't credit. The scream of unbridled horror rose in her throat of its own volition when she saw the spreading pool beneath Daniel's body...the gaping rent in his throat.

She threw herself to the floor, heedless of the blood, and drew his limp head into her lap, stroking his face as her vision was obscured by tears and her mind went numb, unable to face reality. She mumbled soft words of comfort, unaware of what she said. Her mind slipped slowly, steadily from her grasp.

Curt's hands on her shoulders gripped hard, and shook her. He said something in short, harsh tones, but she refused to hear or acknowledge. "Call an ambulance," she told him with the slurred speech of a drunken person. "He's hurt, he needs help. Go call an ambulance."

"He's dead, Tamara." He released his hold on her, and tried instead to move Daniel's head from her cradling arms. She clung to him more tightly, closing her eyes as her vision cleared. She didn't want to see. "He's dead," Curt repeated loudly.

She kept her eyes closed and shook her head. "He's only hurt. He needs—"

Curt's hands closed on either side of her face, tilting it downward. "Look at him. Open your eyes, dammit!"

The increased pressure made her comply and she found her gaze focused on deathly gray skin, slitted, already-glazing eyes and the ragged tear in Daniel's jugular. She shook her head, mute, her mind trying to go black. Her body slowly went limp and Curt jerked her to her feet the moment she relaxed her grip on Daniel. She slipped and nearly fell. When she looked down she saw that the floor was wet with blood. Her clothing soaked in it, Daniel's body drenched. Insanity crept closer, its gnarled hands gripping her mind and clenching.

"I told you this was how it would end."

She blinked and looked at him.

"You saw him yourself, Tam. It was Marquand. When I heard Daniel scream I kicked the door in. I couldn't believe what I saw. Marquand was...he was sucking the blood out of him. I jumped on him, but he'd already severed the vein—tore it right open. Daniel bled to death while I fought with Marquand."

Her face blank, she looked again toward the window, recalling her fleeting glimpse of Eric...the blood on his face. No. It wasn't true, it couldn't be. Mentally she cried out to him, closing her eyes and begging him to tell her the truth, to deny Curtis's words. He didn't respond. His silence drove her beyond control, and while she felt curiously detached, she watched as a blood-soaked woman wearing her body gave way to insanity. She tore at her clothing, raking her own face with bloodied nails, tore at her own hair and screamed like a banshee. Curtis had to backhand the woman twice before she crumpled to a quiv-

ering, sobbing heap on the floor. He left the room, but re
turned in a moment and injected her with something. Th
proportions of the room became distorted, and voices ech
oed endlessly. She had to close her eyes or she knew sh
would be sick.

When she opened them, the unmistakable glint of early
morning sun slanted through her window and across he
bed. Her head throbbed, but she was clean and dressed i
a soft white nightgown. Her face hurt, and a glimpse in th
mirror showed her another deep purple bruise comple
menting the one on her jaw. This one rode high on he
cheekbone. She shook her head, dropped the hand mirro
onto the stand and slipped from the bed. The bruise cam
from Curt's knuckles, landing brutally across her face whe
she'd lost her mind last night. But none of that had bee
real, had it? It hadn't really happened. . . .

Silently she moved through her doorway, over the fade
carpet in the hallway and down the stairs. All the way sh
kept thinking it had been a nightmare, or a delusion. Sh
stopped outside the tall double doors to Daniel's librar
and paused only a moment before she pushed them ope
Her eyes moved directly to the carpet in the room's cente
A pungent, metallic odor reached her at the same insta
she recognized the bloodstains, and saw the masking-tap
outline of Daniel's body.

"Tammy?"

She turned and looked up at Curt, wondering why sh
was so numb. Why wasn't she wailing with grief? Danie
was dead.

"Honey, I don't want you to let yourself be consume
with guilt. You had no way of knowing he was using you a
along. The bastard must have planned this for months
Even Daniel believed him."

That's right, she reminded herself. Eric had never love
her. He'd seduced her. He'd used her to get to Daniel an

then he'd brutally murdered a helpless old man. She'd practically caught him in the act. Hadn't she?

No. It isn't possible. I can't believe... I won't believe it.

"This has to be handled delicately and quickly," Curt went on, apparently unaware of her jumbled thoughts. "DPI doesn't want any local cops poking around."

She blinked, searching her brain for rational thought... logic. "But he was murdered."

"It's going down as a heart attack."

She looked back to the bloodstained carpet and shook her head. "A heart attack?"

"Our own forensics team will take care of Daniel. He's being cremated this morning... on the premises, right after Rose Sversky has a look at him. We'll have a memorial service this afternoon."

Tamara frowned at the mention of DPI's top forensic pathologist. Dr. Sversky's patients were kept in cold storage in a sublevel lab. She closed her eyes as she thought of sweet Daniel down there.

"I hate to leave you on your own, Tam, but there's a lot to do. We want to move fast before anyone has a chance to ask any questions. Word of this leaks out, Byram will turn into a circus. Be at St. Bart's at two for the service."

The telephone shrilled as Tamara tried to digest what he was telling her. There would be no burial in a grave she could visit. Daniel would be reduced to ashes within the next few hours. He'd been ripped from her so suddenly, so violently she felt nothing now but shock. As if she'd lost a limb.

Curt turned toward the phone in the living room, ignoring the closer one in the library. "Stay out of there for now, Tam. A cleanup crew will be here this afternoon."

Oh, yeah, she thought. DPI's good old "cleanup crew." When they finished you wouldn't be able to find a blood cell with a microscope. Cleanup would be more aptly named cover-up, but what the hell?

Curt's voice cut through the dark shroud over her heart. "No, Mrs. Bryant, I'm afraid Tamara isn't up to a phone call just now, but I will pass along the—"

She bolted at the sound of "Bryant," and jerked the phone out of Curt's hand before he could finish the sentence. How, even with all that had happened, could she have forgotten about Jamey? "Kathy? I'm right here. Is there any... There isn't?" She sighed in dismay when she learned Jamey still hadn't been found. She listened as the woman poured out the frustrations of a long, sleepless night. When she finally began to run out of steam Tamara cut in. "I'm going to find him, Kathy. I promise you, I will. I'll check in later, okay?"

She closed her eyes and stood still for a long moment after she hung up. A moment ago she'd wanted nothing more than to crawl into a hole and pull the hole in after her. She'd wanted to sit in a corner and cry until she died. Now she had a purpose to keep her focus. For today, she would do her utmost to find Jamey Bryant. Tonight she would go to Eric and hear what he had to say. She wouldn't believe he'd killed Daniel until she heard it from his own lips. She couldn't believe it... nor could she deny what she'd seen with her own eyes. So she'd give credence to none of it, for now. For now, she'd simply focus on Jamey, and hopefully remain sane long enough to sort out the rest.

Curt was behind her as she moved toward the stairs. "So to anyone who asks, it was a heart attack. Don't forget. The only people who know the truth are Hilary Garner—she came over and helped get you into bed last night—and Mil Kromwell, Daniel's immediate superior. And, of course, Dr. Sversky. Are you sure you'll be all right?"

She nodded, wanting nothing more than to get started doing something that would absorb all her concentration.

She was upstairs and in her room dressing before Curt's car left the driveway. She checked her jacket pocket when she pulled it on, and nodded when she felt the bit of gauze still there.

Jamey knew it was morning because he felt the sunlight gradually warming his stiff body. Thank God for the sleeping bag. He'd have frozen to death for sure if it hadn't been for that. The creep had shown up in the middle of the night with the bag, and slipped it up over him. He'd brought a ham sandwich, too, and a cup of chicken soup and some hot chocolate. He'd untied Jamey's hands so he could eat, but the blindfold had stayed put. He had ripped the tape off so roughly it had felt to Jamey as if his lips were still attached to it. Something cold and tubular had been pressed to his temple and a gruff, phony voice had rasped close to his ear, "One sound and I blow your head off. Got that, kid?"

He'd nodded hard. He fully believed Curtis Rogers would do it. Any guy who'd slug a woman the way Curtis had slugged Tamara wouldn't give a second thought to blowing away a kid. And he knew it was Curtis now. He hadn't seen him, or heard him speak without the phony voice, but he knew. So he'd nodded like a good little hostage and had eaten his soup without seeing it. He had been allowed to relieve himself in a pail before he was tied again, arms behind him just like before, tape back over his mouth.

Damn, he hated that tape. After Curt had left, sometime during the long, cold night, Jamey's nose had started to clog up. He'd felt sickening panic grip him. How would he breathe if his nose clogged up and he had tape over his mouth? One thing was sure, Jamey didn't intend to spend another night here to find out. Curt had rasped that he'd be back in the morning, so Jamey would wait. He had a plan.

It wasn't much of a plan, he figured, but it was better tha
nothing.

He didn't have to wait long. Before the sun had bee
shining very long, Curtis showed up with another cup o
cocoa and a cheese Danish from a fast-food joint. He didn'
say much this time, and Jamey didn't have the nerve to as
questions. He ate, did his business and sat calmly while h
was retied and taped. But when Curt left this time, Jamey'
senses were honed like razors. He listened carefully, mem
orizing the sounds of Curt's steps across the floor as he lef
He waited then, just to be sure Curt wouldn't come back
Then he slid himself across the floor in the direction Cur
had gone. He humped and slithered on his rear end. Hi
feet pointed the way. He bent his knees and pulled himsel
along by digging his heels into the floor. He made goo
progress, too, until he hit a wall.

He sat there, confused for a moment. Then he realize
there must be a doorway. Not a door, since he hadn't hear
one open or close. But there must be a doorway. He wrig
gled around until his back was to the wall so he could ru
his hands along it as he humped sideways. He figured he'
worn his pants down to the thickness of tissue paper an
implanted about a hundred slivers in his backside by th
time his hands slipped off the flat wall and into empt
space.

The doorway! He'd found it!

He was so excited he didn't even bother turning aroun
again. He just pushed off with his feet and went backwar
through the opening . . . and into space.

*Not a doorway, you idiot, a stairway. Oh, damn, a stair
way. . . .*

Rose Sversky was a tiny sprite of a woman with shor
white hair in a close-to-the-head haircut and Coke-bottl
glasses. She looked as if she'd be more at home cuttin

cookies than corpses. Tamara sat in a hard chair amid the organized chaos of chrome and steel and sheet-draped tables, painfully aware that one of those tables had supported Daniel's body only hours earlier. Maybe only minutes earlier.

Dr. Sversky handed the bit of gauze, now safely encased in a plastic zipper bag, across the desk to Tamara. "You were correct about the chloroform. Unfortunately, gauze is a poor receptacle for fingerprints. I couldn't find a hint of who took him." Tamara sighed hard and swore, but Rose wasn't finished. "There was a small trace of blood. Most likely the boy's though I can't be certain without something to compare it to. Do you know his type?"

Tamara frowned. "No. It's probably in his records, but it'll be easier just to ask his mother. I'll get back to you. It's funny, though, I didn't see any blood."

"I don't think you could have without a microscope. It was just a trace. Probably bit his tongue when he was grabbed." She sat silent behind her huge desk for a long moment, then reached across it to cover Tamara's hand with her own. "I'm sorry you're going through so much at once, dear. Daniel was a good man. I'll miss him."

Tamara blinked. She hadn't wanted to think about Daniel now...here. Still, she couldn't keep her gaze from jumping to the nearest table. "You're doing the death certificate, aren't you?"

"Yes. I've fixed them before, and I imagine, as long as I stay with DPI, I'll fix them again."

"It doesn't bother you, changing a cause of death from something as violent as this to a simple heart attack?"

Rose frowned. "Actually, unless anyone's already heard the rumor, it's going down as an accident." Tamara looked up and Rose hurried on. "It's always better to stick as close to the truth as possible. When I found that blow to the back of the head, I figured we might as well use it as the cause of death.''

Tamara stared at her. "I wasn't told about any blow to the head.''

Sversky removed her glasses and pinched the bridge of her nose. "I hope it eases your mind to know this. He was hit with a blunt object hard enough to render him unconscious before the laceration to the jugular. He probably never even felt it." She shook her head. "I've never autopsied a victim of—of a vampire attack before. It's nothing like I thought. You always see two neat little puncture marks on victims in the movies. This was—" She broke off and shook her head. "But you don't need to hear about that.''

No, Tamara thought. She didn't need to hear it because she'd seen it. She rose slowly, thanked Rose Sversky and left. As she rode up in the elevator her fingers touched the tiny marks on her neck. They were barely noticeable now. She frowned as the doors opened on the ground floor, and she walked out to the Cadillac as if in a daze.

She'd wasted most of the day talking to people who lived along Jamey's route home from school, and more of it waiting while Rose Sversky examined the gauze pad. Mechanically she drove home, showered and changed into a black skirt with a white silk blouse Daniel had bought her one Christmas. As she did, her head pounded and her heart ached. She wanted so badly to find some answer to Daniel's death other than the obvious one. Her mind kept offering hopeful hints as reasons to doubt Eric's guilt, but she had to wonder if she was only seeing what she wanted to see. The fact that Curt claimed to have heard Daniel scream, and kicked the door in to see Eric biting him, was in conflict with what Rose had said about Daniel being unconscious when his jugular was slashed. But Curt might be confused, or might have heard Daniel scream just before he was knocked out. The fact that Eric would not need to cause such a bloody mess could be valid, or perhaps he'd just been as cruel as possible in eliminating his tormentor.

Eric? Cruel? Never.

She did what she could to repair the ravages of emotional upheaval with a coat of makeup, then went to the church in downtown Byram and sat in the front pew for a brief, pat sermon. It was, she figured, an all-purpose sermon they kept on hand for people whose names remained on the rolls but who'd given up attending services long ago.

When it was over she sat with a plastic smile firmly in place, and accepted condolences of all in attendance. Mostly co-workers, she noted. Daniel's work had been his life. It would have been more appropriate to hold the service in his office, or his basement lab.

When it was over, Curt came to her, took her hands and drew her to her feet. She'd been aware of him sitting a few seats away and watching her pensively all through the service. "Going home?" he asked.

She nodded. "I'm exhausted. I don't think any of this has sunk in yet."

"How's the hunt for the kid progressing?"

She sighed. "It isn't. I'm going to ask Kromwell to get the FBI involved. He has friends there."

"So do I," Curt said quickly. "Why don't you let me do that for you?"

Her eyes narrowed briefly. His smile seemed false, somehow. Then again, hers probably did, too. Hers *was* false. "Okay. I'll take any help I can get." She swallowed as the uneasiness she felt niggled harder. "It was sweet of you to stay with me last night, Curt. But if you don't mind, I'd kind of like to be alone tonight. I need . . . to sort things out. Do you understand?"

He nodded. "Call if you need me." He leaned over, pressed a brief kiss on her lips and squeezed her shoulders.

She watched him leave, and pulled on her jacket. She was headed for the door herself when a soft hand on her arm stopped her. She turned, and at the sympathetic look on Hilary's face she instantly burst into tears.

Hilary hugged her hard and they stood that way until Tamara had cried herself out. She felt cleansed, and was grateful for a friend she could cry with. Hilary dabbed at her own damp eyes. "You know if you need anything..."

"I know." Tamara nodded, and swiped her wet face with an impatient hand.

"Is there any word on the little boy?"

Tamara met Hilary's doe eyes and felt another good cry coming on. She sniffed, and fought the fresh tears. "No, nothing yet. I found a piece of gauze with traces of chloroform on it near the spot where he was last seen. There was a trace of blood, too, and I'll be able to confirm it was his as soon as I check with his mother about his type."

"Why would you have to do that?"

Tamara only frowned.

"You're telling me you don't know Jameson Bryant's blood type?"

"No, I don't. I suppose it's in his records, but—"

"I *guess* it's in his record. It was one of the first things put in his records. It's the same as yours, Tamara. That Belladonna thing. I can't believe you didn't know."

"Belladonna?" Tamara couldn't believe what she was hearing. "Hilary, how do you know this?"

"I was the one who got the order to enter all of his medical records into DPI computers under level one. I remember thinking that was pretty high for simple medical records, but—"

"Who gave the order?"

Hilary frowned. "I don't know, it came down through channels. Look, I probably shouldn't be discussing any of this with you, Tam. I mean, it is filed under level one, and your security clearance—"

"Isn't high enough," Tamara said slowly. Tamara left then, with Hilary frowning after her. She got into the car and drove away from the church, barely paying attention to traffic. "He has the antigen," she mumbled to herself. "Does he have the lineage, too?"

"Of course he does. That's why his psychic link with me is stronger than with anyone else."

Whoever ordered those records at level one deliberately classified them beyond her security clearance, she realized slowly. They didn't want her to know.

"But they knew. They knew we were close and they knew that if Jamey was in trouble, I'd go after him." She blinked fast. "Jamey was taken to get me out of the house . . . and then Daniel was murdered."

Eric could never harm a little boy. Besides, Jamey had been taken in broad daylight. Eric hadn't killed Daniel. But someone had . . . someone with access to level one data. Someone who wanted it to look like the work of a vampire.

"And someone who knew about the meeting between Daniel and Eric," she whispered. She bit her lip. "Curtis?"

She almost missed the driveway. She hit the brake and jerked the wheel. She killed the engine near the front door, got out to run inside, and locked the door behind her. "My God, is it true? Was Curt angry enough to murder Daniel?" She pressed her fingertips to her temples. "What on earth has he done with Jamey?"

She swallowed a sob and ran up the stairs to Daniel's room. She found his keys in a matter of minutes and hurried back down with them, jangling in the silent house like alarm bells. She didn't hesitate at the basement door. If she did, she'd never go down. She inserted a key, turned it and shoved the door open.

It was still only late afternoon. Outside, the sunlight glinted off the surface of the snow so brightly it was painful to see. Here a dark chasm opened up at her feet. She couldn't even see the stairs. Yet the answers to all her questions were likely a few steps below her. She had no choice but to go down.

CHAPTER SIXTEEN

Jamey shook his head to clear it, but it only brought excruciating pain. He'd been out cold...he knew he had, but had no idea how long. He was on his back and his arms, still tied behind him, had gone completely numb. He tried to sit up, and the pain that knifed through his chest was like nothing he'd ever felt. He thought it would tear him in half. He stopped with his body half sitting up and half lying down. But remaining like that hurt still more so he drew a breath to brace himself, and that sent more pain through him.

Grating his teeth, he shoved himself farther up, relieved when he felt a wall to his right. He leaned against it, then sat still and let the pain slowly recede. It didn't go far. As the blood rushed into his arms, they throbbed and tingled and prickled unbearably. He'd have yelled if he could, but the tape remained over his mouth. His eyes were still covered, and his ankles still bound. His lungs felt funny, and it was more than just the stabbing pain that hurt every time he inhaled. They felt the way they feel after you go swimming and get a little bit of water in them. He kept having the urge to cough, but he was terrified to give in to it. If he coughed, with this tape over his mouth, he'd probably choke to death—especially if that weird feeling in his lungs was what he thought it was. He thought it felt as if something were sticking right into his chest. A blade, a sharp-edged board he'd hit on the way down, something like that. And he thought that whatever kept trying to choke up into his throat might be blood. If it was, he knew he was in a lot of trouble.

She flung the file to the floor in disgust, and turned to leave the small office she'd discovered. She hadn't even made it to the lab itself, which she suspected lay beyond the padlocked door to her right. She needed no more of the revelations she'd found here. In Daniel's files she'd found what he'd termed "case studies." In truth these were detailed accounts of the capture and subsequent torture of three vampires.

Two had been taken in 1959, by Daniel and his then partner, William Reinholt. The pair were described as "young and therefore not as powerful as we'd first assumed." They were "relieved of a good deal of blood to weaken them, thus assuring the safety of my partner and myself. However, they were unable to sustain the loss, and expired during the night." Another study noted was of a woman who called herself only Rhiannon, and who was "entirely uncooperative, hurling insults and abuse constantly." Due to their last efforts, they took less blood from her, leaving her too strong to deal with.

Daniel returned to the lab after hours of "tests and study" to find his partner dead, his neck broken, the bars torn from the window and the "subject" gone.

Tamara felt like cheering for the mysterious Rhiannon. She felt like crying for the man Daniel had been. A monster, just as he'd told her. She hadn't realized just how accurate that confession had been.

She stopped herself from leaving, as appalling as she found the notes. She had to continue scouring the files if she wanted to find a clue as to where Jamey had been taken. She hoped to God there was one to find. She was beginning to think this her last chance. She had a terrible certainty in the pit of her stomach that if she didn't find Jamey soon, it would too late.

She returned to the file cabinet and pawed through more files. There was none with Jamey's name on it, but she halted, her blood going cold, when her fingers touched one with her own. Slowly she withdrew the file. It was thicker than any of the others. Something inside her warned her not to open it and look inside, but she knew she had to.

Moments later she wished she hadn't. Thumbing through the pages, she'd paused when she'd seen her parents' names on one, her eyes traversing a single passage before they became too blurred to read farther.

It has been decided that I should seek to gain custody of this child. She will act as a magnet for Marquand and possibly others of the undead species. The parents, as expected, refuse to cooperate. They are, however, expendable, and of less value than the countless lives which will be saved if this experiment bears fruit. A rare viral strain has been chosen. Their exposure will be carefully contained. Death will occur within twenty-four hours.

"No," she whispered. "Oh, God, no..." The file fell from her nerveless fingers and sheets spread over the floor. Tamara gripped the edge of the open file drawer, her head bowed over it. Daniel had killed her parents. For a moment she conjured their images in her mind, ashamed that they were blurred and indistinct. She barely remembered them. Her memories of them, too, had been stolen from her. Daniel's refusal to discuss them...to allow her to keep mementos of them...his constant advice that her mind didn't want her to remember, that she was better off forgetting.

She drew several short, panting breaths, and forced her eyes open. She blinked the tears away and glimpsed the polished grips of a handgun, protruding from beneath the files in the drawer. Just as she reached for it a hand closed on her shoulder and pulled her backward.

She whirled. "Curtis!"

His narrow gaze raked her, then the open drawers and scattered files. "Been doing a little exploring, Tammy?"

Why had she doubted Eric, even for a second, she wondered silently. Why hadn't she gone straight to his home when she realized it must have been Curt who killed Daniel? He'd have helped her find Jamey. But it was too late for hindsight now. There was still an hour before full dark. And she still had to know where the boy was. "What have you done with Jamey, Curt?"

His brows shot up. "You have been busy. What makes you think I took the kid?"

She shook her head. "I don't think, I know. Where is he?"

"He's safe. Don't worry, I wouldn't hurt the kid...right away. I'd like to study him a little. Later. When I've finished with you and Marquand. Does that reassure you?"

She shook her head so hard her hair billowed around her like a dark cloud. "If you hurt him, Curtis, I swear to God—"

"You'd be better off worrying about yourself, Tammy." He took a step nearer her and she backed up. He took another. So did she. In a moment she realized he'd backed her up to the padlocked door. She stiffened. He pulled a key from his pocket, held it out to her. "Open it."

She shook her head again. "No."

"You want to see the kid, don't you?"

"Jamey?" She glanced furtively over her shoulder at the door. "He's in there?"

"Where else would I put him?"

Relief washed over her and she snatched the key from him, stabbing it into the lock and twisting. When it sprang free she jiggled it loose and shoved the door open. If she could just get to Jamey, she thought, they would be all right. It would be dark soon, and Eric would come for them. She moved into the darkened room. "Jamey? It's Tam, I'm here. It's all right...Jamey?"

The door closed and her heart plummeted when she heard locks being slid home. A flick brought a flood of light so brilliant she had to squint to see. She scanned the room, certain now that Jamey was not here. There was a table in the room's center, with straps where a person's ankles and wrists would rest, another at the head. Beside the table a chrome tray lined with gleaming instruments. Above it, a dome-shaped surgical lamp. She swallowed hard against the panic that rose within her. Beside it was the sickening realization that this was the room where the two young vampires had died at Daniel's hand, and where Rhiannon had been tortured to the point of a murderous rage before she'd made her escape.

She turned to face Curtis when she heard his approach, and in an instant he gripped her upper arms mercilessly. He pushed her backward, oblivious to her feet kicking at his shins, or her thrashing shoulders. When her back hit the table she sucked in her breath. "My God, Curt, what are you doing?"

He brought her wrists together, held them in one hand and reached for a bottle with the other. He twisted the cap off with his teeth, then held it under her nose. She twisted her head away from the frighteningly familiar scent, but her mobility was limited and his reach was long.

When her head swam and her knees buckled he set the chloroform down and shoved her roughly onto the table. A moment later she found her ankles and wrists bound tight.

She blinked away the dizziness, then averted her face fast when he held pungent smelling salts to her nose.

"That's a good girl. Don't go passing out on me, now. It would defeat the whole purpose." She tried to bring the whirling room into focus, relieved when it stopped tilting and spinning. "You can summon him mentally, am I right?"

She pursed her lips, and refused to look at him.

He gripped her chin and made her face him. "Don't answer me, Tammy. I'm betting that you can. We'll soon find out, won't we?" He read her expression correctly and smiled. "You think I'm afraid of him, Tammy? I want you to call him. When he gets here, I'll be ready and waiting."

She shook her head. "I won't do it."

Curtis smiled slowly and Tamara felt a cold chill race up her spine. "I think you will," he said, bending over her to fasten the strap over her forehead, leaving her virtually paralyzed. "I think you'll be screaming for him to come by the time I'm finished." He reached to the tray, and she tried to follow his movements with her eyes. He lifted a gleaming scalpel, looked at it for a long moment, then twisted his wrist to glance at his watch. "Another twenty minutes ought to do it, honey."

Eric went completely rigid in his coffin as a shock of pain shot through him. Eyes wide with sudden alacrity, he flicked the latch and flung the lid back. He was on his feet in a moment, brow furrowed in concentration. He focused on Tamara. He called to her. He waited for a response but felt none.

For a brief instant he wondered if it was possible she believed what Rogers had intended she believe—that he had murdered her beloved St. Claire. He dismissed the notion out of hand. She knew him too well. She was fully aware she need only look into his mind to know the truth. She wouldn't believe his guilt without giving him a chance to explain. Which was why he'd fully expected to find her waiting upstairs when he rose this evening. Instead, he sensed only emptiness. No doubt she was beside herself with grief, but he would not allow her to shut him out. He'd help her through, whether she wanted him to or not. Again he called to her. Again he received no response.

Roland rose with his usual grace, but when Eric glanced at his friend he saw an unfamiliar tension in Roland's face. He ceased his summoning of Tamara to ask, "What is it?"

"I am not sure." Roland visibly shook himself. "Have you had word from our Tamara?"

"She doesn't heed my call."

"Go to her, then. She may be out of sorts after last night, but I have no doubt she'll see the truth when you tell it. If you—" He stopped, cocking his head to one side as if listening. "Damnation!"

Eric cocked one brow, waiting for an explanation, but Roland only shook his head. "I'm still uncertain. I shall go out for a time, see if I can puzzle it out. Will you be able to manage this on your own?"

"Of course, but—"

"Good. Give my regards to our girl."

Roland spun on his heel and left as Eric watched him go, wondering what on earth was the matter. Shrugging, he returned his concentration to Tamara. *Why do you ignore me, my love?*

He felt no reply, then suddenly another spasm of pain shot through him, stiffening his spine. He blinked rapidly, realizing the pain must be hers in order to make itself so completely known to him. *Tamara! If you refuse to answer, I will come to you. I must know what—*

No!

Her answer rang loudly in his head, and he frowned. *You are in pain, love. What has happened to you?*

Nothing. Stay away, Eric. If you love me at all, stay away. Again, intense, jarring pain hit, nearly sending him to his knees, and he knew someone was deliberately hurting her. Rogers?

"I should have killed the bastard the first time I set eyes on him." He fairly ripped the door from its hinges in his haste to get to her. He gained the stairs, and then the frigid night air. His preternatural strength gave him the speed of a cheetah, and beyond. He raced toward her, and would have gone right through the front door had not a quavering train of thought pierced his mind. *It's a trap, Eric. Stay away. Please, stay away.*

He paused, his heart thudding, not with exertion but with rage and fear for Tamara. A trap, she'd said. He used his mind to track her down, then moved slowly around the house, seeking another way in. He finally knelt beside a barred window, obscured from view by shrubbery.

Tamara lay strapped to a table beneath a blinding light. Her blouse had been sliced up the center, as had her brassiere. She still wore a dark skirt. Her feet were bare. Hot pink patches of tissue oozed blood the way a sponge oozed water, in various spots over her torso. One was on the breast from which Eric himself had tasted her blood. Another, at the same spot on her throat. Rogers had amused himself by taking tissue samples, Eric realized. He now stood aside, laying a prodlike instrument down and picking up what looked like a drill.

"Even that baby didn't make you call him, huh, Tam? Well, I have other tricks in my bag. I could really use a bone marrow sample." He depressed the trigger, and the drill whirred. He release it, held it poised over her lower leg. "What do you say, Tammy? Do you call or do I drill?"

Tamara's face was deathly white. Her jaw quivered, but she looked Rogers in the eye. "Drop dead," she rasped.

Shrugging, Rogers lowered a pair of plastic goggles over his eyes and lowered the drill. With a feral growl Eric smashed the glass and ripped the first bar he gripped free of the window. In a second he was inside.

"Eric, no! Go away, hurry!" Her voice was unrecognizable. The stringy bark of an ancient cherry tree, the voice of sandpaper.

Eric lunged for Curtis, who dropped the drill and lifted something that looked like an odd sort of gun. Too fast, the dart plunged into his chest. He jerked backward, gaping like a fish out of water, and fell to his knees. He gripped the dart, pulled it from his flesh and held it up, looking first at it, and then beyond it, at Rogers's triumphant leer. The drug. He'd been expecting a syringe, not a gun. He forced himself to his feet and took an unsteady step toward Rogers. "You...will...die for this," he gasped. He took another step, then sank into a bottomless pool of black mists.

Roland moved in the night like a shadow, speeding over darkened streets, then stopping, listening and moving on. Ever closer to the boy. The faint sense of the boy had niggled at him since he'd arrived on Eric's doorstep. But it had been *so* faint he'd barely been aware of it, much less able to pinpoint the source. Naturally, he understood that the Chosen usually "connect" only with a single vampire. He was the only one who'd sensed Eric as a child. Others would have recognized him, had they encountered him, of course. But no others heard him calling. They didn't feel the pull. Just as with Tamara, Eric had been the one drawn. Roland felt her only through Eric.

This boy called out to someone...not to Roland. If he'd been summoning Roland the entire matter would have been so much simpler. As it was, with the faintest trace of a signal to go by, and the boy not even aware of transmitting it, he'd be lucky to find him in time.

That was the hell of it, Roland thought as he paused again to try to feel the signals the child was sending. They grew weaker with each passing moment. The knowledge that the child's life was ebbing overlapped the pull of him like an alarm sounding in Roland's head—like one of Eric's security contraptions. If only his sense of the boy was clearer! If only the boy was reaching those invisible fingers out to him instead of someone else—someone who apparently wasn't listening. Roland hadn't known it was possible for one of his kind to ignore the desperate cries of a child, a child likely to expire before this night's end.

Eric opened his eyes and found himself strapped to the same table Tamara had previously occupied. His hands, feet and head were bound just as hers had been. Unlike her, he was still fully clothed. No doubt the bastard had been uncertain how long his drug would be effective, and was unwilling to risk personal injury. He hadn't wanted Eric waking until he was fully restrained . . . as if these measly straps would make a difference. Eric pulled against them, shocked when the effort left him limp and even dizzy.

He's drawn vials of blood from you, Eric. It's why you're so weak.

The explanation came to his mind from Tamara's, and with it a lingering pain, a weak, shaken feeling and utter desolation. He wanted to see her, but couldn't turn his head. He tried to attune his groggy senses to hers and they finally began to sharpen. He knew Curtis was still in the room. It was why she hadn't spoken aloud.

What has the bastard done to you?

Nothing so terrible, came the weak reply. *I'll be all right.*

I feel your pain, Tamara. I cannot see you, and keeping things from me only frightens me further. Tell me. Tell me all of it.

He felt her shudder, as if it had passed through his own body. *He...took little patches of skin. It burns, but the scrapes aren't deep. He drew blood from me, too.*

Eric sensed her pain, certain there was more. The jolts of pain he'd felt earlier hadn't been caused by superficial abrasions. *He had an instrument when I arrived—a rod-shaped device he brandished over you. What was it?*

She hesitated for a long moment. *It is...charged...with electricity.*

Rage flooded through Eric. He would kill Curt Rogers for this, he vowed silently, even as Tamara continued. *He killed Daniel. He wanted me to believe it was you, but I could never believe that. He's taken Jamey, Eric. I don't know what he's done with him—*

Her thoughts ceased abruptly with Curtis's approaching footsteps. He leaned over Eric. "Finally awake? Drug didn't last quite as long as I'd hoped, but then, it's still experimental."

"You push me too far, Rogers."

"Not a hell of a lot you can do about it at the moment, is there? I am going to need some samples from you, too, you know. A little bone marrow, some cerebral fluid. Then we'll see just how much sunlight is bearable."

Eric felt the terror Tamara experienced as Rogers described his plans in explicit detail. He also felt the weakening effects of the drug waning. His strength began to seep back into his limbs.

"Curt, you can't do this to him. Please, for God's sake, if you ever cared about me, let him go."

Rogers stepped away from the table. Eric couldn't turn to look, but he knew the bastard was touching her. He felt her shiver of revulsion, and he heard the chilling words. "You haven't figured it out yet? I never did care about you...except as a research subject. A half-breed vampire, Tam. That's what you are. The only thing you're good for is scientific study. Oh, maybe you're good for a few other things, too. I intend to find out before I'm finished with you."

She sobbed involuntarily, and Eric jerked against his restraints. The movement brought Rogers back quickly. "Hmm, you're still a little too lively for my tastes," he drawled, rattling instruments on a tray. A moment later Eric flinched as a needle was driven into his arm. He felt the life force slowly leaving his body with every pulse of blood that rushed into the waiting receptacle. In moments he was sickeningly dizzy, and too weak even to flex his fingers. He felt himself slipping from consciousness. His heavy lids fell, and vaguely he heard Tamara crying, "Stop it, Curtis, please. My God, you're killing him...."

Tamara struggled against the straps he'd tied around her, but it was useless. Her hands were bound behind the chair, her ankles tied to the chair legs. Her entire body pulsed with pain, due to the dozens of scrapings he'd taken from her skin. She was dizzy from the loss of the blood he'd drawn, and weak and shaken from the jolts of electricity he'd sent through her to try to force her to summon Eric. She'd refused, but it had done no good. Eric had felt her pain and rushed to her side. She should have known he would. He'd come to help her, and now all she could do was sit and watch while Curt drained the blood from him. Eric grew whiter and perfectly limp. Finally Curt removed the needle. He lifted Eric's eyelids and flicked a penlight at them, then nodded, satisfied.

She was surprised when Curt glanced at his watch, and then moved to close the shutters. "I think it will be safer to work on him during the day, don't you, Tam?" He brushed away the broken glass, seemingly unconcerned about the bar Eric had wrenched free. He turned to a cupboard, pulled out a fresh bottle and syringe, and Tamara flinched automatically. "Easy, now," he said softly. "I want to get a few hours' sleep. I know he isn't going anywhere, but I have to make sure you stay put, too, don't I?" He gripped her arm and sank the needle, far more deeply than was necessary, into her flesh. She stiffened, trying to resist the drowsiness that began creeping up on her. Curt let his hand move over her breasts before he drew away. She would have pulled her tattered blouse together if she'd been able to move her arms. His touch made her want to vomit.

"I hate you...for this," she managed, before she was unable to resist the lure of sleep any longer. Her head fell forward.

She had no idea how much time had passed when she lifted it again. The dark spaces between the shutters showed gray now, rather than black as before, so she feared dawn was approaching. Her arms ached from being pulled behind her, and her head throbbed so forcefully she could barely focus her vision.

When she did, she saw Eric lying exactly as he had been earlier, as pale and still as... No. She wouldn't complete the thought. He was all right. He had to be. She mustered all of her strength and hopped her chair toward him. "Eric. Wake up, Eric, we have to get out of here." That he didn't respond in the slightest did not deter her. She reached the table, and turned so her back was at his side. She bent almost double and strained her legs until she managed to lift the chair on her back. She groped with her fingers, felt his at last and gripped them. "Do you feel me touching you? Wake up, Eric. Untie me. Come on, I know you can do it. You wake enough to push your damned hidden button, you can wake enough to loosen a simple knot. Our lives depend on it, Eric. Please." She sucked in a breath when she felt his fingers flex. "Good. That's it." She angled her hand so the knot touched his fingertips, and continued speaking to him softly as she felt his fingers move. She knew it was a terrible effort. She felt the energy he forced into just moving his fingers. And then she felt the strap fall away from her hands, and she heard him exhale.

Instantly she bent and freed her feet. She stood, turned to Eric and reached down to release the straps that bound his ankles, then his wrists. When she bent over his head, releasing the final strap, she stroked his cool face with her palm. "Tell me what to do, Eric." She wanted to help him, but wasn't certain how. Hot tears rolled down her face to drop onto his.

His eyes fluttered, then remained open. "Go," he whispered. "Leave me..." The lids fell closed again. "Too late," he finished.

"No, it isn't. It can't be. Don't do this, Eric, don't leave me."

She caught her breath as a memory surged like a flash flood in her mind. In her imagination it wasn't Eric lying on the table. It was Tamara, a very young Tamara, small and pale and afraid. Her wrists were bandaged and she knew that the bandages wouldn't help. She was going to die. She felt it.

Until the tall, dark man had appeared beside her bed. She knew his face, even then. She didn't know his name, but it didn't matter. He was her friend... she'd seen him before, even though she'd pretended she hadn't. She sensed he didn't want to be seen, and she didn't want to frighten him away. He used to come and look in on her at night. He made her feel safe, protected. She knew that he loved her. She felt it, the way you can feel heat from a candle if you hold your hand near the flame.

She was so glad to see him there with her. But sad, too, because he was crying. He stayed beside the bed for a long time, stroking her hair and feeling very sad. She wanted to talk to him, but she was so weak she could barely open her eyes. After a while he did something. He hurt himself. There was a cut on his wrist, and he pushed it to her lips.

At first she thought he wanted her to kiss it better, the way her mommy used to kiss her hurts sometimes. But as soon as the blood touched her tongue she felt something zap through her...just like when she'd touched the frayed wire on the lamp once. Except this didn't hurt and it didn't scare her the way that had. It zapped just the same, though, and all at once she knew he was giving her the medicine that would make her better, and she swallowed it.

She felt herself get stronger with every sip. A long time later he pulled it away, and wrapped a clean white handkerchief around his wrist. He slumped in the chair near the bed, and he was almost as white as the hanky. He felt weak and tired, and she felt strong and better. She knew she would be okay. And when she looked at him again, she knew his name. In fact she knew all about him, somehow. She sat up in bed, and listened as he told stories and sang lullabies. He was her hero and she adored him. It broke her heart when he finally had to go.

Tamara shook herself, and brushed at the tears. "I remember," she told him. "Oh, Eric, I remember."

His only response was a slight flicker of his eyes. His lips formed the word *Go*.

"Not without you," she told him.

"Too...weak." It cost him terribly just to utter the words. His face showed the strain. "Go on."

"Never," she whispered. "Not if I have to carry you on my back, not if I have to crawl, Eric. I'd sooner slit my own wrists than leave you here with—" She broke off there.

He forced his eyes open once more, and met her gaze. "No. You...too weak...could lose too...much." Ignoring him, Tamara brought her gaze to the tray, and snatched up a scalpel. "No..." He put as much force as he had behind the word. "Could...die—"

She grated her teeth and pulled the blade over her fore-arm. She forced the small cut to his mouth. Too weak to fight her, Eric had no choice but to swallow. Her blood flowed into him slowly, but with the samples Curt had already taken, she soon felt weak and dizzy. Her head swirled and the room slowly began to spin. Eric shoved her away from him, snatching up the strap that had bound her before, and jerking it tight around her arm, above the cut.

She vaguely heard the door open, just before she was jerked away from Eric. Curt spun her around and slammed a fist into her temple, sending her to her knees. Blinking slowly as the ceiling rotated above, she tried to see what was happening. Eric was on his feet. Curt was snatching a hypodermic from a shelf. He stood crouched and ready. Eric fell into a similar stance and they circled one another, wary, each ready for the other to spring.

She had to help Eric, she thought through a haze. He didn't stand a chance against Curt's new drug, and if Curt got the best of him this time, she didn't doubt he'd kill him. She couldn't just sit here and watch to see which of them was still breathing after this battle. Eric could not lose. It was that simple. If he did, they would both die here, in this chamber of horrors. And what would become of Jamey?

Unnoticed by either man, she slid backward across the floor toward the door Curtis had left wide. When she reached it she gripped the knob and hauled herself to her feet. Dizziness swamped her and she staggered, but with a desperate lunge she made it to the file cabinet, praying it was still unlocked. She heard something crash to the floor in the laboratory. She heard shattering glass and clanging metal. She yanked on the top drawer and it slid open. She reached inside, groping blindly as she looked over her shoulder, certain Curt would emerge at any second. Her hand closed on the smooth walnut grips and she slowly withdrew the handgun. Stumbling, she made her way back to the doorway. Curt's back was toward her. He stood between her and Eric, who was backed to the far wall, facing her. She thumbed the hammer back.

"That's enough, Curtis. Put the syringe down or—Curtis!" He lunged at Eric, making a sweeping attack with the syringe. Tamara's finger clenched on the trigger, and before she was aware of it, she'd shot twice.

Curt jerked like a marionette whose strings are tugged suddenly, then slumped slowly to the floor and lay still.

Eric slammed flat against the wall as if he'd been punched. Tamara saw the blood spreading across his chest, and then he, too, slumped to the floor.

"Eric!" she shrieked, and dropped the weapon. "My God, Eric!"

Outside an abandoned, crumbling building Roland paused. The boy's signal had been stronger than ever only a second ago. Now it had faded completely. Had the child died? In desperation Roland went inside, his night vision showing him the small form lying weakly against a wall.

He knelt beside the boy, a flick of his fingers snapping the ropes that bound his wrists and ankles. He took the blindfold away, and gently peeled the tape from pale lips. He gathered the child up in his arms and strode from the building, even as his senses sharpened to ascertain the problem.

The child was slipping into what modern medical people call shock, his blood pressure dangerously low, his skin cold and clammy. He was bleeding internally from a lung, punctured by a broken rib. He had a bruise on his brain—a concussion, that is—but Roland didn't believe that injury to be serious.

Cradling the child in one arm, he removed his cloak with the other, and quickly wrapped the boy in it. Warmth was vital. As was speed. He raced with the child to the nearest hospital. As they sped through the night the boy opened his eyes. "Who are you?" was all he said, and that softly.

"I'm Roland, child. Don't worry. You'll be fine."

"Eric's friend?"

Roland frowned. "You're Tamara's Jamey, aren't you?"

He nodded and settled a bit, then his eyes flew wide. "Is she okay?"

"Eric is with her," Roland replied.

They sped into the emergency room, and were immediately surrounded by nurses, with forms to be filled out and endless questions. One took the boy from him and placed him on a table. "Call my mom," Jamey said softly. Roland nodded, searching his memory for the child's last name. Bryant, he recalled Tamara saying. He went to the desk and asked for a telephone.

As he waited, he realized that Tamara must be the missing link. It was she the boy had been unconsciously summoning. She hadn't heard. She wasn't even one of them. Perhaps, though, she was meant to be.

CHAPTER SEVENTEEN

Tamara fell to her knees beside Eric and pulled his head up. She thought he'd be dead. Her weakness and dizziness, as well as her sore arm, were ignored, beaten into submission by her grief. She was amazed when he spoke through clenched teeth. "It isn't the bullets, Tamara. It's...the bleeding."

"Bleeding." She frowned. "The bleeding!" Of course. She remembered now that he'd told her how easily he might bleed to death. She shoved him flat and tore his shirt open with her right hand, then struggled to her feet. Weaving and dizzy, she made her way to the row of cupboards, ripping open three doors before she found rolls of bandages, gauze and adhesive tape. With her arms full, the left one still throbbing, she staggered back to him. Clumsily, one-handed, she wadded bunches of gauze to pack into the two small wounds. He grunted as she worked. He felt pain more keenly than a human would, so she knew this must be excruciating. Still, she made herself continue until it seemed the bleeding had stopped. She wrapped long strips around him to hold the gauze in place. She pulled them tight and taped them there.

Dizziness hit her anew, but Eric sat up and gripped her shoulders when she would have fallen. He made her sit beside him, and carefully he bandaged the small wound on her forearm, padding it thickly and then removing the strap he'd tied around her arm.

They helped each other to stand and slowly made their way out of the lab, around Curtis's still body and up the stairs. When they emerged outside into the paling light of the early predawn sky, Roland appeared in the driveway, and came toward them.

"I had a feeling you might need me. I can see I was mistaken." He eyed them both. "Rogers?"

"Dead," Eric said bleakly.

"I shot him." Tamara made herself say the words. "And my only regret is that he won't be able to tell me what he did with . . . with Jamey." Her voice broke, and she felt tears stinging her eyes.

"The boy is being attended now. I took him to the emergency room."

Tamara's head went up fast, and Eric's arm tightened around her. "Go to him, love. You need your arm stitched, anyway."

"I'm not leaving you until I know you're all right." She glanced up at the sky and frowned. "We'd better hurry or both of you will be in trouble."

Roland put a hand on her shoulder. "I give you my promise, child, that Eric will be as good as new by nightfall. We can make it to the house in less time than you could drive in your car. Go, see to the boy."

She looked up at Eric, and his arms closed around her. His lips, though pale and cool, captured hers and left them with a promise. "Go, love. Until tonight."

She nodded, and hurried to her car. She found a jacket in the back seat and zipped it on to cover her torn blouse before she left. There was nothing that could persuade her to go back inside that house. She noticed that Eric and Roland remained, watching until she drove out of sight, before they went their own way.

* * *

Hours later, her arm stitched and bandaged, the police's questions temporarily answered, her head mercifully clear, Tamara knelt before the fire in Eric's living-room hearth and added logs to the glowing embers. She felt safe here, knowing he was nearby. She hadn't felt this safe, she realized, since she'd been a child of six, in a hospital bed, clinging to the hand of a tall, handsome stranger, who wasn't a stranger at all.

When she'd absorbed enough heat to remove the chill from her body, she wandered to the stereo and slipped a CD into the player. Mozart's music filled the entire house, and Tamara moved from room to room, lighting every lamp. The day was beginning to wane. Night approached and she was too filled with anticipation to sit still and await it. She took her time in the downstairs bathroom, luxuriating in a hot scented tub. When she finished, she didn't resist the impulse that sent her to the bedroom upstairs for the dress he had given her. She put it on carefully, located a brush and stroked her hair to gleaming onyx. When she returned to her seat by the fire the sun rested on the horizon, about to dip below it.

In the hidden room beyond the cellar Eric looked down at his torn, bloodied shirt and grimaced.

"Not much time to clean up before retiring, was there, Eric?" Roland's grin irritated him still further.

"I suppose you find this amusing?"

"Not at all. In fact, I took it upon myself to make a few preparations after I dropped you into your coffin this morning." Roland waved a hand to indicate the fresh suit of clothes that hung nearby, and the basin of water on the stand near the fire.

Eric's temper dissolved. "Only a true friend would think of such trivial necessities."

"No doubt I will ask that you return the favor one day."
Eric washed quickly, knowing she waited upstairs. He
donned the clothes in haste, and hurried up the stairs to join
her. Roland tactfully took his time in following.

She waited by the fire. She was wearing the gown, and
Eric felt a lump in his throat. She stood quickly when she
heard him, and eyed him with obvious concern. "Eric. Are
you—"

"Fully recovered, love. I told you the sleep is regenerative, didn't I? You haven't been worrying about me, I
hope."

"I've been worrying about a lot of things," she admitted, but relaxed into his arms, resting her head on his
shoulder.

He held her hard for a long moment, eyes closed, relish-
ing her nearness, her scent and the feel of her body so close
to his. Then he straightened, took her hand in his and examined her wounded arm. "It's been stitched?" She nodded, and Eric tilted her chin in his hand and searched her
face. "And the other injuries? Are you still in pain?"

Her smile was his answer. "I'm fine."

"Looks a good deal better than fine to these eyes," Roland boomed as he joined them in the parlor. "A sight to
take a man's breath away, if ever there was one."

Tamara smiled at Roland and lowered her lashes. "Are
all you eighteenth-century men so gifted at idle flattery?"

"I am a good deal older than that, my dear, so my flattery can be nothing but genuine." Just when Eric felt the
slightest twinge of jealousy, Roland went on. "I can see you
two have important matters to discuss, and I have an appointment of my own to keep, so I'll be on my way."

"I know about your appointment," Tamara said. Eric
glanced down at her as she stepped out of his embrace,
walked over to Roland and linked her arm through his.

"What's this?" Eric kept his tone jovial. "You two have been sharing secrets?"

"None that I know of, Eric." Roland looked at Tamara as she led him to the settee and pushed him to sit down. "Have you begun reading my mind, as well, little one?"

"No, but I spoke to Jamey's mother today." Roland nodded as if he understood. Eric, however, was still completely in the dark. Tamara returned to him, pulled him to the settee, as well, and joined him upon it. "Roland saved Jamey's life last night. Curtis had kidnapped him because he's like me, one of what you call the Chosen. That's why we've always been so connected, Jamey and I. I've been going nuts wondering what I could do to be sure Jamey would be safe...that some lunatic like Daniel wouldn't decide to further science by murdering his mother and adopting him. That's what Daniel did, you know. My parents' deaths were not accidental."

Eric nodded. For some time he'd had a lingering suspicion that had been the case. She eyed Roland. "Kathy says you've asked her to travel to one of your estates in France. That you need a live-in, full-time manager there and that you would like her to do it. She says you offered her more money than she could turn down." Tamara shook her head. "She would have done it for nothing after you brought Jamey back safe and sound."

"He was hardly that when I last saw him," Roland commented. "How is the boy?"

"He's going to be fine."

Eric frowned hard. "I'm not following all of this. If the boy is one of the Chosen, then where was his protector when he was in all of this trouble?"

Roland sent Eric a meaningful glance. "I wondered the same, until I realized the truth. The boy is fortunate to have a guardian such as Tamara, Eric."

"What are you saying?"

Tamara seemed unaware of the currents running between the two. She reached for Roland's hand and gripped it. "Thank you, Roland. Jamey means so much to me. You'll make sure they leave right away, won't you? Before anyone sees a connection between Jamey and Curtis, and starts poking around."

"You have my word, young one. And now, I'd best take my leave before my best friend becomes my executioner." He sent Eric a wink. "Do not think to oppose the fates, Eric. These cards were drawn long ago, I think." He left them without another word.

Tamara stood abruptly, and paced restlessly toward the fire. "We'll have to leave right away, as well, Eric. When Curt's body is found I'll be a suspect because I lived there and didn't report it. You'll be one, too, because of the break-in. We should go away from here." She stopped in front of the glowing hearth, and turned to face him. The fire made a halo of light around her, so she seemed ethereal, truly a vision. "But first there is something else, and I think you know it as well as I do."

Eric rose, went to her and gazed down into her face. She was more beautiful, more precious to him than the most flawless diamond could be. God, but he loved her beyond reason. More than anything, he wanted to keep her with him, always. He swallowed. "It is an endless, lonely existence, Tamara. An existence of endless night. A world without the sun."

"How could it be lonely if we were together?" She gripped his lapels in her fists. "If it's a choice between you and the sun, Eric, I choose you without a moment's hesitation. Don't you feel the same about me?"

His throat tried to close off. He forced words. "You know I do. But, Tamara, immortality is not a gift. It is a curse. You will live to see all those you love return to the dust—"

"Everyone I've ever loved is gone, except for two. You and Jamey. And as much as I adore him, he's not a part of my life. He has his mother, his own life to live." She blinked as her eyes began to moisten. "Please, if you deny me, I'll truly be alone. What must be done, Eric?"

Her tears caused his own eyes to burn. "You need time to consider."

"What have I had for the past twenty years if not time?" A waver crept into her voice. "I've been wandering aimlessly in a world where I never belonged. I was never meant to be there, Eric, I was meant to be with you. To be *like you*. Roland knows it. You heard what he said, the decision isn't ours to make. My fate—" she lifted a trembling hand to the side of his face, tears streaming now down her own "—is right here in front of me."

The glow of the firelight made the satin gown seem like a soft green blaze. Her hair glistened, and even her skin seemed aglow. Her scent caressed him as truly as her hand did. She cleared her throat, and he knew she was forcing herself to go on. "I know... you have to drink from me," she whispered. "But that's only part of it, is that right? That you have to drink from me, Eric?"

He could not prevent his eyes from fixing themselves on her exposed throat, or his tongue from darting over his lips. "And... and you from me," he answered. Just saying the words had the blood lust coursing through him, singing in his veins, gaining intensity until it throbbed both in his temples and in his loins.

She stood on tiptoes, encircled his neck with her arms and offered up her parted lips. He obliged her, and his desire for her became all consuming, just as his love for her had long since become. Her nimble fingers worked loose his shirt buttons and her hands spread themselves wide upon his chest, then slipped around it, so her lips could pay him homage.

"All my life," she whispered, her lips moving against his skin, her breath hot and moist upon it. "All my life has been spent for this moment...for you. Don't deny me, Eric. I'm already more of you than I am of this world."

"Tamara," he moaned. She tilted her head up and he captured her lips again, feeding from the sweetness of her mouth. He gathered her skirts in his fists and lifted them, his hands then running eagerly over her naked thighs and buttocks. "My God, how I want you. You are a fire in my heart, and each time the flame burns hotter, not cooler. I fear it will never cool. You are an unquenchable thirst in my soul."

Her hand slid between them to the fastenings of his trousers. In seconds she'd freed him, and she caressed his shaft with worshiping hands. "I'd like to have eternity to quench that unquenchable thirst, Eric. Say you'll give it to me."

The heat she stirred in him raged to an inferno. His hands slipped down the backs of her legs to the hollows behind her knees and he lifted her off her feet. She linked her ankles at his back, clung to his shoulders and closed her eyes as he sheathed himself inside her. So deeply he plunged that a small cry was forced from her wet lips, and even then he knew it would not be enough. Not this time.

She rode him, not flinching from his most powerful thrusts, and he held her to him, his hands tight on her soft derriere. She threw her head backward, arching the pale, satin skin of her throat toward him, a hairsbreadth from his lips. He kissed her there, unable to do otherwise. Her jugular thudded just beneath the skin. Her fingers tangled in his hair, pulling him nearer. His tongue flicked out, tasting the salt of her skin, and as he drew that skin between his teeth she moaned very softly. When he closed his teeth on her skin she shuddered, and her hands pressed harder.

"Make me your own, Eric. Make me yours forever, please."

He groaned his surrender, opening his mouth wider, taking more of her throat into his hungry mouth. The anticipation brought a new flood of desire and he tried to plunge more deeply, though he was already inside her as far as he could go. He withdrew and sank himself into her, again and again. His fever seemed mirrored in her, because her responses were just as ardent. Her legs tightening around him, she pressed down to meet his every upward thrust, arching toward him to take him further.

She arched in unspeakable ecstasy. His thrusts inside her matched the pulse of her heart pumping the very essence of herself into his body. The feel of him suckling at her throat sent tingles racing through her.

She felt herself begin to fade, to weaken. She was vanishing like mist under a searing sun, until she no longer existed apart from this feeling . . . this ecstasy.

Only vaguely did she notice when he raised a hand to his own throat, and then, while his mouth was still clamped to her, he pushed her face to his neck. Vibrations seemed to reach the core of her soul. A hunger such as she'd never known enveloped her and she closed her mouth over his neck and she drank.

They were locked together; he moved deep within her, while his teeth and lips demanded all she could give. His hands held her hips to his groin and her head to his throat. His movements became more powerful, and she knew hers did, as well. The approaching climax was like a steaming locomotive, about to hit them both. She moaned, then screamed against his throat again and again as she felt herself turn into the brew in a bubbling cauldron, and slowly boil over. Eric shook violently, groaning and sinking to his knees, still holding her to him.

They remained as they were as the waves of sensation slowly receded, leaving them warm and complete. She knew they'd exchanged ounce for ounce, drop for drop. They were sated ... and they were one.

Carefully Eric unfolded his legs and lay back, keeping her on top of him, cradling her like something precious. She relaxed there, only moving enough so her feet were not behind him when he lay down. The strangest sensations were zipping through her. Her skin tingled as if tiny electrical charges were jolting from nerve ending to nerve ending. Her head reeled with sensory perceptions. Everything seemed suddenly more acute. The firelight, brighter and more beautiful than ever before. She'd never realized how many different colors there actually were in a flame, or how she could smell the essence of the wood as it burned.

"Eric, I feel so strange ... like I'm more alive than I've ever been and yet ... so sleepy." Her eyes widened. Even her own voice sounded different.

He laughed softly, stroking her hair. She swore she could feel every line of his palm as it moved over her tresses. "Thank you for convincing me, my love. I couldn't have gone on without you, you know."

"Is it done?" She struggled to stay awake.

"It is nearly done. You must sleep. I've waited two centuries to find you, Tamara. Only you, I know that now. I can wait now, through one more night, one more day. When you wake again, it will be done."

She burrowed her head into his chest. "Tell me...."

"You'll be stronger than ten humans." His hands stroked her hair, her back, and his hypnotic voice carried her like a magic carpet. "You'll get stronger as you grow older, but that will be the only sign of aging you'll see. Your senses will be altered, heightened, more so than they already are. And there are psychic abilities, too. I will teach you to control them, to use them. I'll teach you so many things, my Tamara. You will live forever."

"With you," she muttered, barely able to move her lips now.

"With me. Always with me, love."

*　　*　　*　　*　　*

SILHOUETTE® Shadows™

NEW! FOR NOVEMBER

IT ALL BEGINS AT NIGHT....

The dark holds many secrets, and answers aren't easily found. In fact, in some cases the truth can be deadly. But Silhouette Shadows women aren't easily frightened....

Brave new authors Cheryl Emerson and Allie Harrison are about to see how scared *you* can get. These talented authors will entice you, bemuse you and thrill you!

#19 TREACHEROUS BEAUTIES by Cheryl Emerson
Widowed Anna Levee was out to discover who had mysteriously murdered her brother. Trouble was, the best suspect was slowly stealing Anna's heart. What if Jason Forrester decided he wanted her life, as well?

#20 DREAM A DEADLY DREAM by Allie Harrison
Kate McCoy assured herself it was just a dream. The erotic fantasies she remembered were strictly her imagination. But when Jake Casperson knocked on her door, Kate discovered her nighttime visions were about to become reality....

Pick up your copy of our newest Silhouette Shadows books at your favorite retail outlet...and prepare to shiver!

SSHNEW

Take 4 bestselling love stories FREE

Plus get a FREE surprise gift!

Special Limited-time Offer

Mail to Silhouette Reader Service™

    P.O. Box 609
    Fort Erie, Ontario
    L2A 5X3

YES! Please send me 4 free Silhouette Shadows™ novels and my free surprise gift. Then send me 4 brand-new novels every other month, which I will receive months before they appear in bookstores. Bill me at the low price of $2.96 each plus 25¢ delivery and GST*. That's the complete price and—compared to the cover prices of $3.50 each—quite a bargain! I understand that accepting the books and gift places me under no obligation ever to buy any books. I can always return a shipment and cancel at any time. Even if I never buy another book from Silhouette, the 4 free books and the surprise gift are mine to keep forever.

315 BPA AKZJ

Name	(PLEASE PRINT)	
Address	Apt. No.	
City	Province	Postal Code

This offer is limited to one order per household and not valid to present Silhouette Shadows™ subscribers.
*Terms and prices are subject to change without notice.
Canadian residents will be charged applicable provincial taxes and GST.

CSHAD-93   ©1993 Harlequin Enterprises Limited

SILHOUETTE.... Where Passion Lives

Don't miss these Silhouette favorites by some of our most popular authors!
And now, you can receive a discount by ordering two or more titles!

Silhouette Desire®

#05751	THE MAN WITH THE MIDNIGHT EYES BJ James	$2.89	❏
#05763	THE COWBOY Cait London	$2.89	❏
#05774	TENNESSEE WALTZ Jackie Merritt	$2.89	❏
#05779	THE RANCHER AND THE RUNAWAY BRIDE Joan Johnston	$2.89	❏

Silhouette Intimate Moments®

#07417	WOLF AND THE ANGEL Kathleen Creighton	$3.29	❏
#07480	DIAMOND WILLOW Kathleen Eagle	$3.39	❏
#07486	MEMORIES OF LAURA Marilyn Pappano	$3.39	❏
#07493	QUINN EISLEY'S WAR Patricia Gardner Evans	$3.39	❏

Silhouette Shadows®

#27003	STRANGER IN THE MIST Lee Karr	$3.50	❏
#27007	FLASHBACK Terri Herrington	$3.50	❏
#27009	BREAK THE NIGHT Anne Stuart	$3.50	❏
#27012	DARK ENCHANTMENT Jane Toombs	$3.50	❏

Silhouette Special Edition®

#09754	THERE AND NOW Linda Lael Miller	$3.39	❏
#09770	FATHER: UNKNOWN Andrea Edwards	$3.39	❏
#09791	THE CAT THAT LIVED ON PARK AVENUE Tracy Sinclair	$3.39	❏
#09811	HE'S THE RICH BOY Lisa Jackson	$3.39	❏

Silhouette Romance®

#08893	LETTERS FROM HOME Toni Collins	$2.69	❏
#08915	NEW YEAR'S BABY Stella Bagwell	$2.69	❏
#08927	THE PURSUIT OF HAPPINESS Anne Peters	$2.69	❏
#08952	INSTANT FATHER Lucy Gordon	$2.75	❏

AMOUNT	$	_____
DEDUCT: **10% DISCOUNT FOR 2+ BOOKS**	$	_____
POSTAGE & HANDLING	$	_____
($1.00 for one book, 50¢ for each additional)		
APPLICABLE TAXES*	$	_____
TOTAL PAYABLE	$	_____
(check or money order—please do not send cash)		

To order, complete this form and send it, along with a check or money order for the total above, payable to Silhouette Books, to: **In the U.S.**: 3010 Walden Avenue, P.O. Box 9077, Buffalo, NY 14269-9077; **In Canada**: P.O. Box 636, Fort Erie, Ontario, L2A 5X3.

Name: _____

Address: _____ City: _____

State/Prov.: _____ Zip/Postal Code: _____

*New York residents remit applicable sales taxes.
Canadian residents remit applicable GST and provincial taxes.

SBACK-OD

▼ Silhouette

"I Know What You Want!"

"And what might that be?" His voice was low as he drew her closer to him.

"You're hoping I'll fall under your spell. Well, I won't. I know all about you."

"What do you know about me?" His hands traced a pattern of fire down her back.

"You have a reputation for getting your way with women." She fought the reactions he aroused in her. "I meant what I said. You may be able to make my body respond to you, but that's all of me you'll ever have!"

"It may just be"—he smiled mockingly—"that I'm not interested in anything else."

JOANNA SCOTT
is a former teacher who gave up that career to follow her dream: writing. She has traveled widely, researching her novels, but is especially fond of California, the state that she and her husband of twenty-three years call home.

Dear Reader:

Silhouette Romances is an exciting new
publishing venture. We will be presenting the
very finest writers of contemporary romantic fiction
as well as outstanding new talent in this field.
It is our hope that our stories, our heroes and our
heroines will give you, the reader, all you want
from romantic fiction.

Also, you play an important part in our future
plans for Silhouette Romances. We welcome any
suggestions or comments on our books and I invite
you to write to us at the address below.

So, enjoy this book and all the wonderful
romances from Silhouette. They're for you!

Editor-in-Chief,
Silhouette Books,
330 Steelcase Road East,
Markham, Ontario L3R 2M1

JOANNA SCOTT
The Marriage Bargain

Silhouette **Romance**

Published by Silhouette Books New York

Distributed in Canada by PaperJacks Ltd., a Licensee
of the trademarks of Simon & Schuster, a division of
Gulf+Western Corporation.

Other Silhouette Romances by Joanna Scott

Dusky Rose
The Marriage Bargain

SILHOUETTE BOOKS, a Simon & Schuster Division of
GULF & WESTERN CORPORATION
1230 Avenue of the Americas, New York, N.Y. 10020
In Canada distributed by PaperJacks Ltd.,
330 Steelcase Road, Markham, Ontario.

ISBN: 0-671-57068-4

First Silhouette printing March, 1981

10 9 8 7 6 5 4 3 2 1

The Marriage
Bargain

Chapter One

Cindy walked through the milling crowd and scanned the vast sea of unfamiliar faces, searching for her mother's friendly countenance. Mrs. Templeton had promised to attend her daughter's graduation exercises, and she had never yet broken her word. All the other graduates of the California Institute of Fine Arts seemed to have found their families and were standing in small groups around the campus quadrangle where the commencement ceremonies had just been held.

Cindy's relationship with her mother was more intimate than that of most girls, since her father had died two years ago, leaving Mrs. Templeton to care for Cindy and her older brother, Richard. Luckily, Mr. Templeton's business interests still generated sufficient income to permit Cindy to continue with her education and to allow Richard to start medical school. Now Cindy had completed her studies and was ready to get a job, which would ease her mother's financial burden while Richard pursued his medical degree.

The last two years had been lonely ones for both Cindy and her mother, and Cindy was eager to share the triumph of her graduation day with the person who had done so much to make it all possible. She stepped up onto a field chair and, shielding her eyes against the glaring sun, attempted to view the crowd more clearly. Her high-heeled spectator pumps made her balance precarious, and she clasped the back of the chair with her free hand while her raised hand tautened the clinging fabric of her mauve cowl-necked silk jersey blouse against the swelling curves of her figure. She lowered her hand from the back of the chair to stop the wind from whipping her knife-pleated white linen skirt around her long suntanned legs but her blazer remained open, giving the tall, dark-haired man walking toward her an excellent view of her feminine assets.

"Are you looking for us?"

The deep masculine voice startled Cindy and she lost her balance, falling off the chair and into a pair of strong outstretched arms which easily caught her, tightened their protective circle and drew her up against a broad, muscular chest. The man's dark brown eyes hypnotized her gaze with the same steely strength with which his powerful arms held her body. Her slender limbs grew as rigid as her taut nerves as she felt herself firmly locked in his unyielding embrace. The spicy scent of his cologne drifted to her nostrils, enticing her with its clean masculinity.

"What are *you* doing here?" she asked, pressing her palms against his chest in an attempt to free herself.

"I came to see you," he said, tightening his arms around her waist. "And now that I've found you, I'd like to be the first to kiss the new graduate." One hand left her waist and slid slowly up her back to gently lift her long blonde tresses and lightly caress the nape of her neck before combing through her hair and tilting her face to his. The powerful hand held her head immobile while he casually lowered his lips to hers, capturing them authoritatively with his own.

She tried to twist away but was prevented by the

tenacity of the vise in which he held her. The coolly passionate demands of his kiss reduced her to a state of complete helplessness and she felt herself go boneless in his arms, no longer strong enough to fight him as he molded her soft curves to his own unyielding firmness. Then, like a beast of prey sensing victory, he relaxed his arms and let his fingertips tenderly massage the small of her back while his insistent lips gradually grew more sensual, moving deftly over hers.

Time stopped as Cindy clung to his embrace; then he suddenly released her, holding her away from him so that he could view the effects of his effortless conquest. Cindy remained still, her limbs so weak that she hesitated to move away for fear she would fall. Her breath came in uneven spurts and her breasts heaved rapidly from the emotional charge that was rocketing through her veins. To the casual observer he would have looked only like an old friend greeting the new graduate, but to Cindy his kiss had demonstrated once again how easily this man could control her.

"And now, I really think we ought to go find your mother. She'll be wondering where we are, and I wouldn't want to put you through an embarrassing explanation."

"I'm not going anywhere with you, Boyd Hamilton! How dare you come here? Don't you know when you're not wanted? Must you infiltrate every aspect of my family's life?"

Cindy beat her fists angrily against his broad chest in its beige mohair jacket. His powerful hands caught her wrists in an iron grip, forcing her to turn her face toward his. His lips were curved in the arrogant sneer she had come to hate and his brown eyes coldly viewed her from their imperious perch above his aquiline nose. His face was the face of a predator, not handsome, but ruggedly attractive, and in all the years Cindy had known him she had never seen it softened by the slightest hint of human compassion. Now the piercing eyes moved over her as if she were some bothersome insect he could eliminate with a flick of his wrist.

"Stop being a child!" he said tightly. "I had expected to find some modicum of civilized behavior on your part, now that you've finished college, but I see you're still the same spoiled brat you always were."

Unbidden tears welled in Cindy's blue eyes. She wrenched her wrists free and turned her back to him, flinging her long blonde hair against his chest while she bit at her lower lip and blinked furiously in an attempt to gather her composure. She despised herself for being so emotional in the presence of this man who interpreted human sensitivity as weakness, a weakness which he would use to overcome and destroy any person who got in his way.

Memories flashed through her mind: Boyd Hamilton, the young electronics genius her father had taken under his wing. Boyd Hamilton, who had charmed his way into the warm intimacy of her family until finally, after her father had died, he had taken over everything . . . business . . . family . . . everything. Her mother's letters over the past two years had been full of Boyd Hamilton and all he was doing to help her. Cindy had become sick of the name; she had never trusted him. He was only out for what he could get; all he wanted was to get ahead in the computer industry, and he had picked her father's company as his vehicle. Unfortunately, she was the only one who had seen through his scheme to control their lives; everyone else had been completely deceived by his charming manner. Now his unexpected arrival had even clouded the bright joy of her graduation day.

His lean fingers caught her shoulders, drawing her gently back against his chest. At six feet two inches, he was a full foot taller than she was and she could feel the inflexible set of his angular jaw as he rubbed it gently against the top of her head. His hands traveled down her arms, pausing momentarily at the gentle swell of her breasts before molding themselves to her slender waist. She allowed herself to lean back farther—why fight him? she asked herself—as the fabric of his mohair slacks tickled the backs of her legs. She could feel his heart beating swiftly against her rigid back and she marveled that such an organ should continue to function in the body of a man who gave no indication that he ever used it.

"Richard is busy with final exams and you know how your mother dislikes traveling alone; I only came as a favor to her. I never thought my presence would have such an upsetting effect on you." His warm breath gently ruffled her hair, which rested uneasily against the open collar of his dark brown silk shirt. "In any case, I think, for your mother's sake, you should try to hide your animosity. After all, she invited me and I'd hate to see her feel guilty about ruining your graduation day."

Cindy nodded and he released her arms, slowly turning her until she faced him. "Now, dry your tears and put on a smile. We're going to find your mother." His arm curved casually around her waist as he guided her through the rows of empty field chairs.

Cindy controlled the bitter resentment that was boiling through her veins and meekly followed his orders—just like everyone else who had ever had dealings with him. And her fury was quickly forgotten when she saw her mother sitting by herself on a field chair, glancing nervously about her like a little lost

11

child. Cindy broke away from her domineering companion and raced to her mother, hugging her with unrestrained affection.

"Mother, I'm so glad to see you! For a while there, I thought you might have changed your mind about coming."

"I almost didn't come," Mrs. Templeton said. "You know how nervous I am about traveling alone. But then Boyd insisted that you'd be disappointed if I didn't attend the graduation exercises and he generously offered to accompany me . . . so here I am. I enjoyed the ceremony so much. I'm so glad I came, but we really owe a special thank you to Boyd. He's been very kind to me since your father died."

"That's all right, Mrs. Templeton; Cindy thanked me most adequately before we came over here to join you. She welcomed me with an eagerness I'll never forget."

Cindy glowered angrily at the mocking brown eyes. How he liked taunting people when they were unable to defend themselves! Well, now that she had graduated from college she would be in a position to put him in his place—and how she would enjoy that! She couldn't wait to see him on the receiving end of things for a change.

Her mother was oblivious to the tension that was building between Cindy and Boyd, and she held Cindy away from her, studying her at arm's length.

"Well, Boyd, what do you think of my little girl? She's become quite a beautiful young lady, hasn't she?"

"Quite," Boyd drawled. "It's easy to see that she's inherited her mother's good looks; now, if only she had her mother's charming manners and cultured personality she might make some fortunate man an ideal wife."

Cindy could barely control herself. She squared her shoulders and tilted her head haughtily. "I intend to do

12

more with my life than just become someone's 'ideal wife.' It would hardly be fair of me to disregard the education my mother has been good enough to provide for me."

"Oh, I shouldn't think your education would be entirely wasted," Boyd replied. "What better preparation could there be for motherhood than being a music major in college? I can't wait to hear you crooning lullabies to a large flock of children."

"Don't hold your breath," Cindy returned without thinking. "I'd never allow you to come near any of my children. You know how easily children pick up bad habits."

Boyd threw back his head and chuckled in amusement, but Mrs. Templeton was obviously both confused and embarrassed by her daughter's behavior. "Cindy, whatever has gotten into you? I'm so ashamed I can hardly speak. Apologize to Boyd this minute."

Boyd stopped laughing and shook his head. "That's all right, Mrs. Templeton. Cindy and I have a unique relationship. We understand each other quite well and there's absolutely no need for her to apologize. She could never do anything to offend me."

Cindy's eyes were charged with anger, but she had to agree with Boyd; it *was* utterly impossible to offend him. He was so arrogantly self-assured that it would take a bulldozer to penetrate his wall of conceit. She smiled at the thought that it was only a matter of time before she would put him in his place. But this was not the time, and any further arguing between them would only upset her mother more. Her silent thoughts of vengeance were interrupted by Boyd's slow, drawling voice.

"Much as I'm enjoying this discussion, I really think we should be preparing to leave for home. Do you want to show us to your dorm so I can start loading your luggage?"

"It's this way," Cindy said, placing her hand on her mother's shoulder and leading her away, leaving Boyd to stand by himself.

Boyd paid no attention to her rude behavior and in a few long strides easily caught up to them as they walked across the campus. But Cindy engaged her mother in conversation and kept the dialogue moving at a rapid pace, not giving Boyd the slightest opportunity to interject any comments he might want to make. To her chagrin, he seemed not at all put out.

When they reached the dormitory, Mrs. Templeton remained downstairs in the dining room, too tired to climb the stairs to Cindy's room. Boyd started to follow Cindy upstairs, but she turned to him haughtily. "I can manage things by myself; why don't you stay down here and keep my mother company?"

"Not a chance," Boyd said, nudging her forward. "I'm quite eager to see where you've been sleeping these past four years."

"Why? Haven't you ever been in a college dormitory before?"

"Not in a girls' dormitory." He grinned. "Things were very prim and proper when I was in college."

"We still have strict curfew rules at this college, so you can just stop thinking what you're thinking."

"Really? I thought the atmosphere would be very relaxed . . . seeing as this *is* an art school."

They had reached Cindy's floor and she whirled to face him. "What you're trying to say is that your narrow little engineer's mind thought I was busy with free love and all that sort of thing. Well, just aim your sordid little imagination in some other direction, because I've never done anything like that."

14

The hard lines of his deeply tanned face softened and his powerful hands cupped her shoulders. "I'm very glad to hear that."

"I can't see what business it is of yours," Cindy said, pulling away from him and walking down the corridor. "You're not my father, you know."

"I've never had any fatherly thoughts about you," he said, following her into her room.

"Good! Just because you've managed to charm your way into my mother's good graces, don't think I'm so easily fooled. I'm well aware of your motives."

"Somehow, I don't think you are," he answered softly.

"You'd be surprised at how much I know about you," Cindy charged.

"Well, I'd be delighted to continue this conversation at some other time," Boyd mocked, "but right now I think we should be getting your things down to the car."

Cindy looked pensively around the room where she had spent the last four years of her life. Her roommate had left to get married before graduation, and most of Cindy's belongings had been picked up by the shipping company earlier in the week, so the room had lost much of its homelike quality. She placed her suitcases by the door and stole one last glance at the now barren cubicle. An uneasy feeling of loss welled up in her, and her eyes glistened with unbidden tears.

She bit at her lower lip in an attempt to stop any more tears from flowing and making her seem so childishly helpless in Boyd's presence. But he had noticed and he touched her shoulders, turning her gently into his arms while cradling her head against the steely strength of his chest. His hand came up to stroke her hair, pressing her cheek into the softness of his mohair jacket. The steady throb of his heart was strangely comforting and she longed to remain in his embrace, although why he was being so nice was a mystery to her.

"It's always difficult to leave home, even a temporary one. The best thing to do is to make the break and be on your way," he said, guiding her to the door and picking up her luggage.

After he had seen the two women settled in the back seat of the sleek black Cadillac, he put Cindy's luggage in the trunk, then got behind the wheel and started the engine.

"Where's Leon?" Cindy asked, surprised not to see the family chauffeur. "Why didn't he drive you down?"

"I told you, I was a bit hesitant about coming," her mother said. "You know how much I dislike traveling. But then Boyd offered to come along, so he drove."

"Well, I still don't understand why Leon couldn't have driven you down. It's his job, isn't it?"

"Not really, dear," her mother said. "I rarely go out anymore. Most of my time is spent at the club and I usually can get a ride with one of my friends. Leon has been working mostly for Boyd these past few years since your father died."

"I see," Cindy said dryly. "Boyd seems to have stepped quite easily into Dad's shoes."

"I could never take your father's place, Cindy, nor would I want to. He was a very special man. I've only tried to relieve your mother of some of her burdens."

"And you have, Boyd. I don't know what we would have done without you. I don't think you realize how tangled your father's business affairs were when he died," Mrs. Templeton said, looking at Cindy. "It was only because Boyd stepped in to handle things that I was able to manage without selling the company."

"Perhaps you should have sold the company," Cindy said. "After all, Richard is going to be practicing medicine and my interests lie in music. It seems that the only person who's benefiting by your not selling is Boyd."

"Cindy, how can you be so rude? I don't know what's gotten into you. Boyd's never been anything but good to this family. I hope I haven't made a mistake by sending you to that art college. Your manners have become atrocious."

"Let's just say I've become a bit more worldly and I'm not as naïve as I used to be."

She lifted her eyes to catch Boyd's expression in the rearview mirror, but he didn't act in the least bit perturbed by her remarks. If anything, his eyes seemed to twinkle with amusement in his otherwise expressionless face. Cindy could see that he wasn't taking her seriously. He was so sure that he would be able to charm her into submission, just as he had her mother. Well, he was in for a surprise. . . .

Her thoughts of vengeance were interrupted some hours later as Boyd moved the car off the freeway.

"Where are we going? I thought you were anxious to get home."

"I am," Boyd said. "But your mother could do with a rest. I think we'll stop here for a while. It's getting quite late and I don't see any sense in pushing ourselves any further." He pulled the car into the parking lot of a hotel fashioned to resemble an old Spanish mission.

"We can have dinner here and then if you feel up to it we'll continue on home; otherwise, I'll arrange for rooms and we can spend the night." He looked at Cindy's mother, and Mrs. Templeton nodded her head appreciatively. Cindy wondered how it was that she had failed to notice the lines of exhaustion in her mother's drawn face, but Boyd's sharp eyes never missed a thing, she would say that much for him.

The hostess seated them at a table overlooking the courtyard, and Cindy watched the water gushing from the fountain and dancing in the misty rays of the multicolored outdoor lighting. Boyd ordered Caesar salad, baked potatoes, T-bone steaks and a Pinot Noir for all of them, and once more Cindy felt his casual domination of her life. He simply assumed that it was his place to make all decisions and never bothered to ask her opinion, even on the choice of food. It didn't matter that she agreed with his selection; it was his smug attitude that she found intolerable.

Boyd excused himself while they were having their chocolate mousse, and when he returned he told them that he had arranged to take some rooms for the night. Mrs. Templeton sighed gratefully, took a last sip of her coffee and asked for the key to her room.

"I'm not as young as I used to be and right now I'd like nothing better than a warm bath and bed."

She let Boyd hold her chair for her but motioned Cindy to stay seated. "I may be tired but I'm not a complete invalid. There's no need for you to see me to my room. You two enjoy your coffee, and I'll see you in the morning."

But Cindy had no desire to remain in Boyd's company any longer than was absolutely necessary and she started to leave the table. Boyd caught her hand as she walked past him.

"Stay. I want to talk to you."

His hand held hers in a viselike grip and there was no way Cindy could leave the restaurant without making a scene, so she sat down and watched silently while the waiter refilled their coffee cups.

Boyd waited until they were alone before speaking.

18

"I wasn't going to tell you this until you'd had a chance to reacclimate yourself to things, but your attitude toward me has made this discussion imperative." He paused and sipped his coffee, watching Cindy's face over the rim of the cup. "Your mother suffered a nervous collapse soon after the death of your father. She didn't want you or Richard to know about it for fear it would disrupt your schooling. Since then, I've seen to it that things are taken care of with the least possible trouble on her part. If you have any consideration at all for your mother, you'll stop this juvenile behavior at once."

"If she can't handle the business, why doesn't she sell it? There's enough value in her stock to provide her with an income for life. The only one who's benefited by her not selling the company is you."

"I'm telling you to stop this senseless vendetta you're mounting against me. It's impossible for your mother to sell the business, and, much as you may dislike the idea, she is very dependent on me—and so are you and Richard, for that matter."

He threw some money on the table and came around to hold Cindy's chair. "It's getting stuffy in here; let's go for a walk."

"I don't want to go for a walk with you. I'm tired and I think I'll go to my room."

He slipped her white linen blazer over her shoulders. "I told you I've had just about all I'm going to take of your foul manners. I said we're going for a walk and we're going for a walk." He grasped her shoulder and propelled her out into the courtyard.

"I know what you want," Cindy said, turning to him as the moonlight gilded her soft blonde hair.

He caught her elbows, holding her immobile in his arms. "And what might that be?" he asked, his voice low and husky as he drew her closer to him.

19

"You're hoping I'll fall under your spell just like my mother has. Well, I won't. I know all about you."

"What do you know about me?" he murmured, his warm breath caressing the top of her head while his hands left her arms and traced a pattern of fire down the length of her back.

"You have a reputation for getting your way with women. People have spoken about your amorous conquests often enough. Now you want to get control of my father's business and you think you can sweet-talk me into going along with your plans."

Her words were little more than a whisper as she spoke them into the steel barrier of his chest. He lifted her chin, causing their eyes to meet, and then took her into his arms. She could feel herself gasping for air and wasn't sure whether it was because of the constricting embrace or the anger that was raging within her. Never taking his eyes from hers, he lowered his lips and pressed them almost harshly onto hers.

His experienced hands began exploring her body, pausing at each intimate point to emphasize his seductive powers. His lips softened, playing a leisurely, teasing game with hers until they finally parted beneath his and she gave him the impassioned response he desired.

When at last his insistent lips released hers and he held her away from him, she felt as if all the blood had been drained from her veins. Tears of shame welled in her eyes as she saw him studying her, grimly, like a wolf who has just snared a helpless rabbit. Indignant pride rose in her throat, driving out all the compliant softness of a moment ago.

"I meant what I said. I won't fall under your spell. You may have the experience to make my body respond to you, but that's all of me you'll ever have."

"It could just be that I'm not interested in anything else. I believe I could be quite content with control over your body. And who knows? Perhaps in time your body will convince your mind that I'm not all that bad."

"Never!" Cindy said, fuming at his casual arrogance. She flung herself out of his arms and raced back toward the hotel.

Only when she had reached the lobby did she realize that she had no idea of her room number. She walked to the registration desk and asked for the key to the room that Boyd Hamilton had reserved for Miss Templeton. The room clerk checked his keyboard and returned to the counter, a perturbed look on his face.

"I'm afraid there's a bit of a problem," he said. "Mr. Hamilton reserved three rooms. Mrs. Templeton is in one of them, but I'm afraid he never specified which of the other two would be yours. Do you by any chance know your room number?"

"No," Cindy said, shaking her head. "Mr. Hamilton forgot to tell me, but I don't suppose that matters. Just give me the key to one of the rooms and Mr. Hamilton can take the other." She lifted a key from the desk and headed for the elevators.

Feeling smugly pleased with herself, she closed the door to her room and shrugged out of her white linen jacket. At least she would be able to get a good night's sleep before seeing Boyd again. Somehow she felt that she needed all her wits about her before she had another encounter with him. She slipped her shoes off and began looking for the small white overnight case which Boyd had given to the bellhop. Her calm satisfaction quickly vanished when she saw the tan cowhide case resting on the luggage rack. Closer scrutiny showed the initials B. J. H. engraved in gold just beneath the handles: Boyd Jeremy Hamilton.

Cindy's only thought was to return Boyd's key to the desk and get the key to the other room, which doubtless held her suitcase. She switched off the light and opened the door to the hallway, preparing to make her way to the elevator, but instead she found that she had walked directly into Boyd Hamilton's broad chest. Thrown off balance, she tilted dangerously backward until his arm reached around her waist and drew her tightly against his hard masculine body.

Wordlessly, he backed her into the room and closed the door behind him, never loosening his grip on her slender waist. His warm breath gently caressed the delicate shell of her ear as he bent to kiss the throbbing pulse of her neck. She turned her head to protest but his mouth caught hers, punishing her with the passionate demands of his kiss.

The hands she had raised to his chest in an attempt to ward him off fingered the buttons of his smooth silk shirt as she unconsciously began a tentative exploration of his body, sliding her fingers inquisitively between the tiny buttons, loosening them and combing through the tightly curled mat of dark hair covering his chest. Desire ruled her and she pressed her body into his, answering his kisses with a passion she never would have believed possible, while a part of her mind reeled in shock that it was Boyd Hamilton who was making her feel this way. Boyd Hamilton, whom she had always hated.

Suddenly he lifted his lips from hers and held her away from him while his glittering eyes surveyed the effect he had had upon her. Her lips were parted as if she were gasping for air and the soft thrust of her breasts rose quickly with each uneven breath she took. His firm hands steadied her as she fought for strength to keep her from falling against him.

"I hardly knew what to think when the desk clerk said you had settled yourself in my room. Needless to say, I'm not a bit disappointed by my reception."

The mocking assurance in his voice brought Cindy quickly to her senses. She tore herself free of his embrace and backed into the room, to sink into a chair while her mind tried to calm the fires raging within her.

"I made a mistake. I thought this was my room. I was on my way downstairs when you forced your way in here."

He switched on the light, staring at her as she blinked to accustom herself to the brightness. His manner was completely relaxed as he leaned against the door. His gleaming eyes mocked her disheveled state and his voice echoed his arrogant demeanor.

"I'm disappointed. I was quite sure you had changed your mind and were beginning to take a more friendly attitude toward me."

"We'll never be friends," Cindy said, turning away from him to hide the flush climbing into her cheeks. "I hate everything you stand for and everything you've done to my family."

"That's a surprisingly hostile attitude, considering that you've been away at school for the last four years and I don't remember that we had much to do with each other prior to that."

"I've heard all about you from my mother. All she's talked about for two years is Boyd this and Boyd that. Well, I can see what you're doing; you've taken over the company, which is all you ever wanted, and it's all too apparent that you've brought my mother completely under your spell along the way!"

"And I suppose you intend to put me in my proper place, now that you've studied music and graduated from college?"

23

"Don't sneer. I learned a lot while I was away at school. I didn't spend all my time in the music room."

A mocking smile crossed his lips. "Oh? I thought you told me that you had led a very moral existence at school."

"Must you reduce everything to your level? I was *not* talking about that kind of knowledge."

"I'm glad to hear that," he drawled, "but I really can't see that any of your other experiences would be of much interest to me."

He uncoiled himself from the doorway and walked languidly toward her. "In any case, this conversation is of no great importance to either of us; what will be will be. Now, as it's getting quite late and we still have a long way to drive before reaching home tomorrow, I suggest we call it a night and get to sleep. I've brought your case with me and I'll take mine to the other room, since you don't seem willing to share this one with me."

He leaned down as he passed her and planted the gentlest of kisses on her forehead. "Pleasant dreams, my sweet." His throaty chuckle haunted her dreams all through the restless night. . . .

Cindy could see that it was pointless to discuss her feelings about Boyd with her mother. Mrs. Templeton had always been shielded from life's realities by her husband, and now she apparently was only too willing to place herself in Boyd Hamilton's protective care. Cindy listened to her mother's incessant chatter on the trip home and wondered if perhaps there wasn't some truth in what Boyd had said about the state of Mrs. Templeton's nerves. She seemed to be hiding her inner tensions behind a shield of nonstop, meaningless conversation.

By the time Boyd had pulled the Cadillac up to the white colonial house where Cindy had been born, she was convinced that she would have to handle things without her mother's help. She watched Boyd take control of the situation, ministering to her mother's needs and issuing instructions to the servants, and she was more determined than ever to deprive him of the powers he had assumed since the death of her father.

Chapter Two

Cindy awoke early the next morning, dressed in a high-necked beige cotton dress which she hoped would make her look more mature and businesslike, ate a quick breakfast of toast and coffee and then told Anna, the housekeeper, that she would be gone for most of the day, attending to some personal matters. She avoided her mother's room; Mrs. Templeton was still exhausted from yesterday's trip and Cindy didn't want to disturb her rest.

The bright red Mustang her father had given her as a high-school graduation present had been driven down from school and was waiting for her in the garage. She approached it like an old friend, patted its white padded dashboard affectionately, turned on the ignition and drove down the long circular driveway.

The tree-shaded streets of Atherton were deserted at this time of the morning and Cindy drove slowly, admiring the stately majesty of the palatial houses in this affluent northern California community. Her childhood had been so sheltered that only when she went away to college had she discovered the charmed unreality of her own life.

She left the private community and headed toward the freeway. The newer houses here were smaller and closer together than those in the sequestered area of sprawling older estates. The acreage edging the Bayshore freeway gradually became more rural as she passed through Mountain View. Then the scenery was replaced by clusters of factories and office buildings as she entered the fast-growing community of Santa Clara. She exited the freeway and drove through the area commonly known as Silicon Valley, so named because it was the home of many prominent computer companies which depended on small silicon chips to bring their technological theories to life.

Her spirits soared when she pulled into the parking lot beside the low granite building with the name TEMPLETON INDUSTRIES emblazoned across its front. Her father had worked long and hard to develop the business from a small manufacturer of adding machines into one of the largest computer companies in the world. Her lips tightened in determination as she silently vowed that Boyd Hamilton would never profit from the fruits of her father's labors once she had taken command.

She knew most of the long-time workers at the plant and greeted them fondly as she made her way to the office of Carl Meredith, who had been one of her father's oldest and dearest friends and who still retained his position as general counsel for Templeton Industries. She was chatting with his secretary when the tall, silver-haired man came out of his office to take her hand.

"Cindy, my child, how good to see you! I heard that you were home from college but I never thought you'd take the trouble to visit me so soon after you returned."

"There are some things I'd like to discuss with you, if you have the time."

"I'll always have the time for you, Cindy," Carl said, leading her into his office. "You're practically like a daughter to me. You know that your father and I were more than just business associates."

"I know that, Uncle Carl," Cindy replied, calling him by the name she had used since childhood. "That's why I'm so glad to be able to discuss this matter with you."

"My, my, you make it sound like very serious business," he said, smiling broadly. "You probably need a bigger allowance now that you're home from school. I'll be happy to discuss it with Boyd."

"That's just it," Cindy said, leaning forward and pounding her hand against the desk. "Why has Boyd Hamilton assumed such enormous control over my father's business affairs and even over my family's personal life? He's only an employee, and I feel he's abused his powers since the death of my father. I don't intend for the situation to continue. If my brother and I can't operate the company then I'd like to sell it and invest the proceeds. There's absolutely no reason for us to hold on to the company merely to provide Boyd Hamilton with a soft berth."

All the color drained from Carl's normally ruddy face as the full impact of Cindy's words registered in his mind. He rose from his chair and walked toward the window, lightly tapping his fingers against the pane as if trying to gather his thoughts. Then he turned back to face her.

"Have you discussed this matter with your mother or Richard?"

"No," Cindy said, shaking her head. "Mother never had a head for business, and Richard is involved in final exams."

"Well, I think you're acting much too rashly," he said, settling himself back in his seat. "My suggestion to you would be to leave things as they are for a while. There are some things you don't know about, and making any drastic changes in the business at this time could stir up a hornets' nest."

"Well, whatever I *don't* know about, I *should* know about," she replied, her voice rising in anger. "You're the company lawyer—surely you're in a position to know what's been going on. Perhaps you can tell *me,* since I seem to be the only member of my family with the time or the interest."

"Very well," Carl said, tight-lipped. "You seem determined to pursue this course of action. What is it you would like to know?"

"First off," Cindy said, settling back in her seat, "I'd like to see the company books."

"I'm afraid I can't oblige you there. I'll have to get Boyd's permission before I can let you see any corporate records."

"Why Boyd's permission? Surely I have the right to examine the company books?"

"Boyd is president and chairman of the board. He's running the company now."

"And just how did he get that position? I don't recall being informed about a stockholders' meeting."

"Your mother gave Boyd power of attorney over her affairs. He was elected unanimously."

Cindy rose and paced the room. She could feel the anger rising within her at the complacent way in which everyone seemed to assume that Boyd had the right to take charge of everything. When she turned to face Carl he saw a hostility glaring from her eyes that he had never seen before, yet her voice was low and controlled.

"Very well. But all that's past history. I'm home now and I'll handle my mother's affairs. Mr. Boyd Hamilton can just find himself another company to sponge off."

"Look, Cindy," Carl said, also rising, "things are just not that easy. As your father's friend I'm willing to help you with your problems, but as general counsel for Templeton Industries I owe my allegiance to the company's best interests."

"Then you won't help me?"

"I *can't* help you, Cindy. It would be highly unethical for me to do what you ask. You've just graduated from college; why don't you relax, leave things here alone and enjoy a peaceful summer?"

"I'm surprised to see that Boyd has succeeded in getting you under his thumb. I thought you had more integrity. Well, if you won't help me I'll find someone else who will."

Tears of rejection mixed with her anger at the injustice of it all as Cindy stormed from Carl's office. She had been so sure that Carl would help her. Now, finding that he, too, had fallen under Boyd's influence was more than she could bear. She brushed away the tears as she headed for the exit. Her mind was spinning in circles of indecision when she heard someone call her name and looked up to see Boyd detach himself from a small group of men and come striding toward her. She stepped up her pace in an attempt to be out the door before he caught up to her, but his hand grasped her arm just as she was about to pass through the exit.

"Cindy, why didn't you tell me you were coming to the plant? I was sure you'd be at home resting today." His welcoming smile turned to a frown when he saw her tear-stained face. He tightened his hold on her arm and led her into his office.

"Let me go," she said, trying to free herself from his grip.

"Not until you tell me what's going on."

"It's no concern of yours."

"Everything that happens in this building concerns me," he ground out, clamping his hand down on her other arm and pulling her toward him. "The sooner you accept that, the better things will be."

"I'll never accept that," she said, "and the sooner you realize that I won't permit you to run things, the sooner you'll see the light and find yourself another job."

Boyd's powerful hands held Cindy firmly before him while his impassive brown eyes roamed her face, carefully studying each delicate feature. She was breathless with anger, but he was clearly in control of his emotions and his disdainfully detached attitude only served to increase Cindy's rapidly mounting rage. She was searching for a fitting insult to hurl at him when the intercom buzzed and he released one of her arms to press the button to answer. When his secretary announced that Carl Meredith was outside, insisting upon seeing him, Boyd told her to send him in.

Carl seemed taken aback when he saw Boyd tighten his grip on Cindy's arm. "I'm sorry, Cindy. I had hoped you wouldn't need to find out for a while yet. Well, Boyd, I suppose you've explained the situation to her by now."

"Hardly," Boyd said. "I haven't the slightest idea of what's been going on, but I'm most interested in finding out."

Hostility flickered in Cindy's eyes as she wrenched free of Boyd's grip and settled herself in the black leather easy chair opposite the huge mahogany desk. With a strength born of necessity she steeled herself for whatever was coming. She could scarcely recognize the cold tone of her own voice as she said, "Yes, Carl, why don't you tell Boyd what I intend to do? And why your 'situation' doesn't mean a thing to me. Then perhaps Boyd can gather his belongings and leave the premises, because I don't intend to have him here."

"You don't know what you're saying, Cindy," Carl charged, his voice cracking with emotion. "I'm following your father's wishes exactly; it's your own response to our actions that has caught everyone off guard."

"I don't understand," Cindy said, a hesitant quaver of uncertainty suddenly muting her voice. "Templeton Industries has always been a family enterprise. Why would my father have wanted Boyd to take over?"

The room was shrouded in uneasy silence as Cindy saw Carl glance expectantly in Boyd's direction. Boyd moved to a large plate-glass window overlooking a small private atrium abloom with colorful flowers. He meshed his fingers together and lifted his hands so the tips of his thumbs stroked the lower part of his chin. Then he turned toward the room and let his gaze rest on Cindy, his face wearing an unusual look of concerned apprehension.

"There's no reason to take your anger out on Carl," he said, moving into the chair next to Cindy's. "It's just as he said. He's following your father's wishes. I was merely trying to make a touchy situation more palatable to you by withholding some information. I see now that I was wrong."

"What are you talking about? What right did you have to withhold any information from me? This is just another example of how you've assumed powers which never belonged to you. You act is if you're a king with the right to issue commands to everyone else."

"This has gone far enough!" Carl said, rising to his feet. "I would be remiss in my duties as your father's attorney if I withheld this information any longer." He turned to Boyd. "I'm sorry, Boyd. I know you wanted me to wait until you had a chance to spend some time with Cindy, but it seems we've reached an impossible point. I'm going to tell her everything, and then the decision will be in her hands."

Boyd nodded his silent approval, never lifting his piercing gaze from her bewildered face. Cindy stared back at him and she could tell that he didn't want her to hear whatever it was that Carl was going to tell her. She assumed that he was disturbed because she was now going to acquire some information which would enable her to put an end to his high-handed ways.

Carl cleared his throat and began to speak. "Your father was one of my best friends, as well as being my first corporate client, Cindy, so you know the high regard in which I hold his memory. He was a fine electrical engineer and he had developed a very profitable adding-machine business, but his knowledge in the computer field was nil. Boyd was an electronic whiz with a Ph.D. degree from Stanford. He knew everything there was to know about computers. . . . He saved your father's business from bankruptcy."

"No! That can't be true. You're lying." Cindy's face was ashen.

"I have no reason to lie, Cindy. I'm an old man and I just want to put all this behind me so I can retire and enjoy some time in the company of my family."

Boyd rose from his seat and came to stand behind Cindy. "Why don't we let this go for another day, Carl? I think Cindy's had enough of a shock for today."

"No, tell me everything," Cindy said, stiffening her body. "I'm not a child and I won't be kept in the dark any longer."

She heard Boyd sigh with exasperation as he moved back toward the window. Carl pursed his lips in discomfort and continued with his explanation.

"These little silicon chips sent the entire electronics industry into a tailspin," he said, reaching into his pocket and studying the minute metallic particle resting in his palm. "This one thin wafer can do the work of a massive calculator. This chip actually contains a complex panel of circuitry, like a series of railroad tracks, constructed one layer at a time in a sterile room. It's a painstaking and error-prone procedure. It was only because of Boyd's knowledge that your father was able to stay in business and develop one of the most sophisticated computers in the industry."

"I never realized," Cindy said, her voice a mere whisper.

"Of course not. There was never any need to bother you with such nonsense," Boyd said, moving behind her and resting his hands on her shoulders. "I liked your father very much. It was my pleasure to work with him. Now, why don't you just forget everything and let me take you home? You look exhausted."

"No," Cindy said, shaking her head. "Tell me everything. There's no point in hiding anything anymore."

Boyd's hands cut into Cindy's shoulders as he nodded for Carl to continue.

"You're an intelligent girl, Cindy," Carl said. "You can see that it made no sense at all for Boyd to continue building a company in which he had no financial interest. With his knowledge and track record any bank would have been willing to finance him in starting his own company. Once he did that, Templeton Industries would have been forced out of business. So when Boyd asked for an interest in the company, your father had no choice. Boyd now owns fifty-one percent of the stock in Templeton Industries. There's no way you can fire him. Basically the company is his."

"I don't believe you," Cindy said, rising from her chair and moving to face Carl. "My father would never have given anyone controlling interest in the company. This was a family business and he was building it for his children and his children's children."

"You're quite right about that, Cindy. John never gave up the idea that the business would pass on to his children, but without Boyd's help there would have been no business to pass on."

Boyd's hands touched Cindy's shoulders as she stood looking at Carl in disbelief. His voice was soft and protective. "As I said before, Cindy, I was happy to do anything I could to help your father. Now, let's leave well enough alone. I'll drive you home and one of the men will bring your car back later in the day."

"Have you told me everything, Carl?" Cindy asked, ignoring the pressure of Boyd's hands and continuing with her relentless questioning. "How could my father possibly have hoped to keep the business in the family once he had signed the controlling interest over to Boyd?"

Carl's eyes flickered up to meet Boyd's. Boyd shook his head and tightened his grip on Cindy's shoulders. "No more, Carl. She knows enough."

"I want to hear it all," Cindy said. "Don't hold anything back. How did my father intend to keep the business in the family when he had given Boyd the controlling interest?"

"Quite simply," Carl said. "It was his intention that Boyd should become part of the family."

"I don't understand," Cindy said, all the color draining from her face. "Surely Boyd is too old to have been adopted by my father."

"Certainly," Carl said. "You father never had any intentions of adopting a thirty-five-year-old man; however, he did think such a man might make an excellent husband for his twenty-two-year-old daughter. Then, of course, Boyd's children would have Templeton blood in their veins and the company would remain in the family."

"My father told you that he wanted me to marry Boyd?" Cindy asked, addressing her question directly to Carl and trying to control the welter of her emotions.

"He did more than that," Carl said grimly. "He put it in writing."

"In writing?" Cindy's eyes widened with shock.

"Yes," Carl said, shaking his head. "He was most anxious to see you married to Boyd. In fact, he probably never would have given Boyd a controlling interest in the company if they hadn't agreed to these terms."

"Exactly what are these terms?"

"Boyd got fifty-one percent of Templeton Industries stock on the condition that he promised to marry you when you had graduated from college."

"You agreed to this?" she questioned Boyd in disbelief.

He nodded.

"There's nothing you won't do for money, is there? You're actually willing to marry me just so you can keep control of the company." She shook her head and sighed. "Well, I don't share your mercenary attitude. I have no intention of being a party to this ridiculous scheme. My father must have been under extreme pressure to have ever agreed to this arrangement."

"It was your father's idea," Boyd said softly.

"Only after *you* had coerced him into it," Cindy stormed back at him.

"It really doesn't matter whose idea it was," Carl said. "This is the situation as it now exists."

"I've just altered the situation," Cindy said. "I have no intention of marrying Boyd."

"Then he gets complete control of the company," Carl said.

"What do you mean?" Cindy said. "I thought he had complete control now."

"He holds the controlling shares," Carl explained. "But your family still retains forty-nine percent of the stock. If you refuse to marry him, that forty-nine percent becomes Boyd's property and your mother will lose her dividend income as well as any moneys which she might make on the future sale of the stock should the company decide to go public."

"My father agreed to this?"

"Don't be too harsh on him; the contract works in reverse as well. If Boyd refuses to marry you, then his fifty-one percent of the stock reverts to the control of your family. I believe this arrangement was your father's method of seeing that all the stock remained in the hands of the Templeton heirs, one way or the other."

Cindy sank down in the leather chair as the reality of the situation finally hit her. If she refused to marry him, the company which her father had started would pass into Boyd's hands, a financial disaster for her mother as well as the end of Richard's medical studies. Her only hope lay in making herself so undesirable to him that *he* would refuse to marry *her*, even if that meant he would lose control of the company. Her overwrought mind began whirling with all the possible things she could say to make him back out of the contract. She smiled sweetly at him.

"I realize now, Boyd, that you must have consented to the bizarre terms of this contract in order to humor my father; but now that everything is out in the open, surely we can work out an arrangement which is more agreeable to the both of us."

"I find the present arrangement perfectly satisfactory," Boyd said softly, his intent gaze resting on her face.

"I think I've explained the legalities of the situation to the best of my ability," Carl said, rising from his chair and walking to the door. "The problem is now a personal one, and I'll leave you two to work it out."

Cindy bit her lower lip as the office door closed behind Carl. She glanced in Boyd's direction and his eyes met hers in a hard, unrelenting gaze, challenging her to convince him that there was any reason not to comply with her father's wishes. She shook her head, trying to escape from the intensity of his scrutiny as much as from the entire situation.

"You can't mean that you'd be willing to marry me just to avoid losing control of the company, Boyd."

"On the contrary, that's exactly what I mean."

"That's impossible," she said, her voice wavering with tension. "Things like that just aren't done anymore. Arranged marriages went out with the Dark Ages."

"Well, I guess I'm just an old-fashioned man," he said, his brown eyes mocking her. "I find the idea entirely acceptable."

"But we hardly know each other."

"Marriage is as good a way as any to become better acquainted."

Cindy felt as if she were drowning and grasped for any excuse to save herself. "I'm not even the type of woman who interests you. Father spoke about your girlfriends quite often. They were all beautiful and sophisticated."

"And they'll continue to be so," his soft voice interrupted. "We were not discussing qualifications for my girlfriends; we were discussing your suitability as my wife."

"I don't understand," Cindy said, her voice growing less confident with every passing moment.

Boyd's cold eyes raked her body mercilessly as he calmly lit a cigarette. "The women I date enjoy the same things I do, but I've never proposed marriage to any of them. We satisfy each other's needs and when we no longer please each other we're quite free to break off the relationship." His eyes narrowed as he saw her cheeks flush pink.

"Your embarrassment at my mere mention of such an arrangement only shows how unsuitable you'd be as a girlfriend." He paused when she lowered her eyes, unable to face the cold glint in his gaze, but he was not about to let her escape so easily.

She never even heard his steps as he moved across the plush carpeting and it was only when her downcast eyes rested on his well-buffed black shoes that she realized he had come to stand only inches away from her. He lifted her chin, exposing her defeated features to his triumphant smile.

"On the other hand," he continued, rubbing his thumb lightly along the fragile contours of her chin, "you have all the attributes a man could desire in a wife. I've watched you grow up and I know no one could have had a better upbringing. A man in my position needs a wife to make a proper home for him, entertain his guests and provide him with an heir."

"You're mistaken," she said, trying to twist her face free from his grasp. "I could never become . . . involved . . . with a man I didn't love.

"Love is an intangible item," he said, turning her face to his and bending. "Let me show you something better."

Previous encounters had taught her the chaotic effect his slightest touch had on her traitorous emotions, and she tried to steel her body against his overwhelming powers of seduction; but when his demanding lips met hers they softened, tantalizing with delicate teasing movements until hers parted in helpless response to his masterful urgency. His arms tightened, slowly moving down the curve of her back as her mindless fingers

39

combed wantonly through his hair, pressing his lips more intimately to hers.

Groaning softly with the strain of his movements, he relaxed his arms and lifted his lips away from hers. His hands gripped her arms firmly, holding her away from him so that he could study her unsettled appearance. She stared back at him through glazed eyes, unable to control the ragged breathing which fluttered her breasts and escaped unevenly through her still parted lips.

"I'm a scientist," he said in a coldly detached voice. "I don't deal in intangibles like love, but it's quite apparent that you don't find my touch physically abhorrent, and that removes any doubts I might have had about my decision to marry you."

The clinical tone of his voice quickly destroyed any shreds of romance which Cindy might have pieced together from the passion of his kiss. Her pride rose to taunt her with the knowledge that Boyd's caresses were nothing more than experimental probings to determine her reactions. She shook herself free and hid her shame behind an angry exterior.

"Let me be the first to inform you that while I may meet your requirements for a wife you don't possess any of the attributes I want in a husband. I have no intention of marrying you."

"Suit yourself," he replied, watching her through carelessly lazy eyes. "You're fully aware of the terms of the agreement," he continued, walking toward the intercom on his desk. "I'll tell Carl to draw up the papers giving me full ownership of all the stock in Templeton Industries."

"Wait!" Cindy's desperate cry rang through the silent office. "You wouldn't really do that, would you?"

He shrugged. "Why not? A deal is a deal."

"But my mother . . . and Richard . . . they'd lose their income without the stock."

"That's right," he said, eyeing her coldly.

"You can't do that. . . . It's indecent."

"On the contrary, my dear child. I'm being more than decent about the entire situation. I'm perfectly willing to live up to my end of the contract; you're the one who's being obstinate. If your family suffers it will be your doing, so don't try to shift the blame to my shoulders. I have no guilt feelings about that."

"You're serious, aren't you?" she demanded, her voice seething with rage. "You have no compunctions about making my family suffer just because I refuse to abide by the immoral terms of this outrageous agreement."

"It's your decision and your family," he said, shrugging his shoulders in a careless gesture.

"All right, you callous brute. I can be just as pigheaded as you. You'll get what you deserve . . . I'll see to it."

"Does that childish outburst mean you've accepted my offer of marriage?" he said, lifting an eyebrow quizzically.

"Indeed it does," she hissed. "But that's the only thing about you I'll ever accept. Once we're married I'll make your life so miserable that you'll beg for an annulment and I'll get full control of the company that you stole from my father."

"Are you promising me a bed of thorns, rather than a bed of roses?"

"I'm not promising you any bed at all," she stormed. "Where you sleep is no concern of mine."

"As long as it's not with you?" he questioned.

"I'd rather die."

He studied her for a moment as if he were formulating a response to her violent outburst; then he seemed to reconsider and held his silence for a moment before speaking.

"Well, there's nothing in the contract that says you have to be happy about the arrangement. All that's required is that you consent to it." He walked toward her and grasped her arm dispassionately. "I suppose we should inform Carl that we've come to a satisfactory agreement. You know, he wasn't entirely happy with the contract your father had drawn up."

"That makes two of us," Cindy said, shrugging away from his arm and preceding him into the corridor.

Boyd's hand circled her arm once again as she reached for the door to Carl's office. "You've made your attitude about this marriage very clear to me, but I don't believe it would be advisable to impart this knowledge to anyone else. Sheathe your claws when we're in public and save your passionate scratches for our private enjoyment."

Cindy turned, meeting his condescending glance with the blazing fire raging in her own bright blue eyes, but she sighed her acquiescence and forced a bland smile to her lips as he opened the door to Carl's office.

Carl greeted their news with relief and promised to take immediate steps to implement the agreement. Boyd accepted his congratulations, then informed him that he'd be leaving for the day to buy Cindy an engagement ring, after which they would tell her mother the good news. He told Carl to see to it that Cindy's car was driven home.

"There's no need to buy me a ring," she said when they were seated in his car. "Let's not make this marriage any more of a farce than it already is."

Boyd's hands tensed on the steering wheel as he let the engine idle and turned to face her. "I told you that I didn't much care about your behavior in the privacy of our own home, but I expect you to conduct yourself like a loving wife when we're in the company of others, and I suggest you include your family in that category.

Naturally I intend to provide you with whatever props you might need to carry off a convincing performance. An engagement ring seems to be of paramount importance."

Cindy shivered at the cold, businesslike tone of his voice, clasping her arms across her chest protectively as she burrowed into the soft leather of the seat. Boyd scowled grimly and moved the car out of the parking spot. Neither of them made any further attempt at conversation, and the tension-laced atmosphere still hung between them when he stopped the car behind a small but elegant jewelry store in Palo Alto.

A somber clerk approached them solicitously as they entered the shop. When Boyd informed him that they were interested in purchasing an engagement ring, he led them to a small seating area at the rear of the store, then proceeded to bring them several trays of rings.

"Exactly what did you have in mind?" he asked, looking directly at Cindy.

"Something fairly modest," she replied. "I wouldn't want to invest too much money in such an unimportant item."

"You must forgive my fiancée's sense of humor," Boyd apologized, bruising her upper arm with his constricting fingers. "I'd prefer something in a diamond. Its strength suggests the permanency of spirit I'd like to impart to our marriage."

The salesman smiled weakly, then lifted several rings out of the tray, placing them on a black velvet pillow. The stones glimmered like faraway stars shining in an ebony sky. Boyd studied them momentarily, then selected one and slipped it onto Cindy's finger. The ring was deceptively plain, its one large pear-shaped stone shining brilliantly between two sleek baguettes. Cindy was fascinated by its appearance as it glistened above her pink-tinged fingernails, but she was not about to let

Boyd know that she admired the simplicity of his choice. She shook her hand in annoyance, making the loose ring twirl on her finger before slipping back to the black velvet pillow.

"It's too big," she said, savoring the triumph she felt in proving the inadequacy of Boyd's choice.

Boyd lifted her hand with a casual gentleness which belied the anger streaming from his eyes. "Have the ring sized for Miss Templeton's finger and call me when it's ready." He handed the salesman his business card. "Charge it to my account."

Tightening his grip on Cindy's hand, he drew her from her seat and led her out of the store.

Chapter Three

"I thought you understood that I wouldn't tolerate your infantile temper tantrums in public," he said, propelling her roughly toward the car.

"If my behavior doesn't suit you, you can always call off the marriage."

Boyd's eyes narrowed menacingly as he settled himself behind the wheel. He inserted the key in the ignition but didn't bother starting the engine. He turned toward Cindy, his aquiline features brooding, as if he were trying to arrive at an important decision and wanted to weigh all the possibilities before reaching any conclusion. Seeing his face, Cindy's hopes began to rise. Apparently he hadn't considered just how unpleasant it would be to be married to a woman who harbored such vehement hatred for him. Perhaps now that he was beginning to experience her anger he was having second thoughts.

"Your behavior doesn't bother me in the least," he said, puncturing her tiny bubble of hope. "I believe that I have sufficient experience and ability to deal with the boorish antics of a child barely out of the schoolroom," he continued, smiling wryly. "I was thinking more of your mother."

"My mother? What does she have to do with this?"

"Your mother and I have always gotten along quite well. As I hinted before, I believe she would be very pleased to learn that somehow we had fallen in love and become engaged. However, if your behavior leads her to discover the true state of our relationship she would be most unhappy."

Without waiting for her reaction, Boyd started the engine and moved the car back toward the freeway. Cindy realized the truth of his statement. Her parents had married for love, and her mother thought that to marry for any other reason was beyond pardon. She would never allow Cindy to marry Boyd if she knew that the marriage was being performed solely for business reasons, even though it would mean economic hardship for Richard and herself.

By the time Boyd parked the car at the front steps of her house, Cindy's tormented mind had rejected all thoughts of a speedy escape and she was convinced that, temporarily at least, she would have to play the dewy-eyed bride-to-be.

Evidently Boyd had said all he was going to say on the subject and had decided to leave in Cindy's hands the matter of informing Mrs. Templeton about their engagement. Casually, he helped her from the car and led her to the front door without making the slightest inquiry about what decision she had reached. She tensed when he removed a key from his pocket, unlocked the door and let them into the house. He had even assumed ownership over the home her father had built. Boyd's sharp eyes caught her expression of disapproval and he grimly answered her unasked question.

"Since you and Richard were away for most of the year, your mother felt it would be advisable for someone close by to have a key in case of emergencies.

I've been saving Anna the trouble of answering the door ever since. She's getting older and there's no point in making her walk any extra distance when it can be avoided."

Cindy nodded in understanding. Anna had been her parents' housekeeper for as long as she could remember; she was almost like a second mother to Cindy. She searched Boyd's face as they stood in the entryway. It was out of character for him to be concerned about another person's welfare. People were objects to him, to be used to his best advantage. Why should he be so anxious to spare Anna the extra burden of answering the door?

"I like Anna," Boyd said, as if he were capable of reading her mind. "And I can be very nice to people I like." His hands lifted to her cheeks, smoothing her hair away from her face and curving it behind her ears. Lowering his head, he let his lips trail a path of fire along the tender cord of her neck.

A quiver of delighted anticipation surged through Cindy's expectant body as his hands caressed her back, slowly drawing her into the circle of his arms. She closed her eyes and arched her neck away from him, but his questing lips followed her every move, granting her no respite from his seductive embrace.

A timid, forced cough echoed through the silent entryway and Boyd lifted his head, turning to an embarrassed Mrs. Templeton, who stood clutching a hand to her pale throat.

Boyd's hand grasped Cindy's as he walked toward her mother. "We were coming to tell you the good news, but it seems you've found out for yourself."

Still holding Cindy's hand, he placed his other arm around her mother's waist and led her to the living-room sofa. "Get your mother some sherry," he said to

Cindy as he sat beside Mrs. Templeton, holding both her hands in his.

Cindy watched her mother slowly sip the sherry. The unstable condition of her mother's nerves had been all too apparent to her after Boyd's earlier revelation. He was absolutely right about one thing: her mother would never be able to survive the shock of learning about the contract her father had made with Boyd Hamilton.

Boyd waited until the color had returned to Mrs. Templeton's cheeks; then he rose to stand beside Cindy, possessively circling her narrow waist with his powerful arm.

"Cindy has made me a very happy man by agreeing to marry me," he said, carefully watching her mother's response. "The only thing missing now is your blessing."

Mrs. Templeton's flustered face was instantly transformed by a joyous smile. She quickly rose from the sofa and kissed them both. "Oh, my dears, nothing could make me happier." Her voice broke as she dabbed a lacy handkerchief to her moist eyes. "If only your father were here to share my joy! He was so fond of Boyd."

Cindy tensed at the mention of her father as she wryly recalled that this entire sordid affair was his doing. Her mother noticed the involuntary tightening of her lips and looked at her inquisitively.

"Is something wrong, Cindy? I hardly thought you'd be marrying Boyd after the way you behaved on the journey home from school."

Boyd's hands dug into Cindy's waist as he smoothly answered her mother. "Cindy and I both have highly volatile temperaments; however, the malicious passion of hate can very quickly change into the tender passion of love. I'm afraid our sudden shift of emotions took everyone by surprise, but I can assure you Cindy knows exactly why she's marrying me. Have no qualms about that."

Having been thus reassured, Mrs. Templeton nervously began discussing all the arrangements which would have to be made in preparation for the wedding. She paced the room, worrying about flowers, invitations, press notices and, most of all, the ceremony and reception.

"There's no need for all this fuss," Cindy said. "We were planning on a very small wedding. We'll probably be married in the courthouse."

"You wouldn't do that to me," her mother said in disbelief. "What will our friends think? You're my only daughter and I've looked forward to your wedding since the day you were born."

"Your mother's quite right, Cindy," Boyd said, silencing the protest that was forming on Cindy's lips. "We have our friends to consider, not to mention the importance of this marriage to our business associates. Everyone will be expecting a large formal wedding and I see no reason to disappoint them."

"I'm glad to hear you speaking so sensibly, Boyd," Mrs. Templeton said. "Cindy's too young to understand the importance of maintaining one's image in the community. It's fortunate that she's fallen in love with such a levelheaded man." She sighed with satisfaction as she resettled herself on the sofa. "Now then, when were you planning on being married?"

"There's no rush," Cindy said. "We haven't even announced our engagement."

Boyd's thumb kneaded the back of her waist, insidiously asserting his right of possession while warning her to be silent. "I'm afraid Cindy's enjoying a bit of a joke. I see no point in a long engagement. We'd like to be married as soon as possible. Plan for two weeks from Saturday."

"That's impossible," Mrs. Templeton moaned. "I'll never be able to get things done that quickly." Once again she started listing all the preparations she deemed necessary.

Cindy took advantage of her mother's preoccupation to cast a triumphant sneer in Boyd's direction. At least she had won a slight delay in her sentence of execution; perhaps, given time, she could find a way to gain a reprieve.

Boyd's lips thinned and he glanced at her with impatience. "Don't worry, Mrs. Templeton. I'll make our entire office staff available to you, and since money is no object I'm sure we'll meet our deadline without too much difficulty."

Deadline, Cindy sneered silently. It was completely impossible for Boyd to think of events in anything other than a business sense. Well, in reality their marriage was little more than a business merger, but somehow she hated to hear him coldly discuss it in those terms. Somewhere deep inside of her a small voice begged for a romantic, storybook wedding, followed by a marriage filled with understanding and love. One glance at the hard determination in Boyd's firmly set jaw jolted her out of her idyllic reverie, swiftly plunging her into the icy waters of reality.

"Do you really think we'll be able to get everything done in so short a time?" Cindy's mother questioned.

"I have no doubt, if we get right on things," Boyd said, moving to the telephone.

Cindy watched as he made several calls and began issuing instructions about their wedding plans without even bothering to make the slightest inquiry concerning her wishes. She felt like a helpless leaf being buffeted about in a series of successively confining circles by a whirling tornado—and standing coolly in the eye of the hurricane was Boyd, calmly directing traffic in a businesslike manner that only made him seem more of an automaton in Cindy's unbelieving eyes.

"I've told my secretaries to start making arrangements for the caterers, the invitations and the florist," he said, directing his remarks to Mrs. Templeton. "I assume you'll want to speak with the minister about the church services."

"You can't be planning on a church wedding," Cindy said. "It just wouldn't be honest."

"Cindy!" Her mother paled once more. "You're not . . . I mean you haven't . . ." She looked at Boyd. "That's why the wedding has to be held so quickly. Oh, my, I never thought . . ."

"Don't be silly, Mother. It's not that. I've only been home from school for a day and I hardly saw Boyd in all the time I was away."

"You're far too eager to be a grandmother, Mrs. Templeton," Boyd said, smiling lazily. "I'll remember that in the future, but, as of now, Cindy has every right to a big, white, lacy church wedding." His hand slid sensuously down Cindy's back. "What Cindy meant was that she felt a church wedding might be inappropriate since it's been quite some time since I've been to services."

"Oh, Cindy, that's no problem," Mrs. Templeton said, her face brightening at Boyd's explanation. "Your father hardly ever attended church before we were married. The minister will understand. Don't worry about that at all."

"Fine," Boyd said, meeting Cindy's angry glance with a complacent one of his own. "What about a wedding gown?"

"Cecile, my dressmaker, would be so hurt if I went anywhere else," Mrs. Templeton said.

"Call her now," Boyd said. "Tell her you'll be right over. I'll drop you off on my way back to the office."

"Just what do you think you're doing?" Cindy questioned as her mother went to make the call. "Why are you rushing things so?"

"Look," Boyd said, ignoring the rage in her voice, "if there's one thing I've learned about contracts, it's that the sooner you implement them, the better it is for everyone. We've agreed upon the terms of the deal, so let's get on with things."

"Boyd, you are really unbelievable. This is just another business deal to you. How can any human being be so cold?"

"I don't see you bursting into flaming passion at the thought of our marriage."

"I have no choice."

"Neither have I."

"Yes, you do! You can start another business. Even Carl said you'd have no trouble doing that."

"Perhaps." Boyd shrugged. "But why bother when your father has made things so easy for me?"

"You're impossible," Cindy hissed. "OK, so you've made a good business deal. But why must you make our marriage even more of a farce by insisting on a big church wedding?"

"Are you so selfish that you can't even understand my reasons for that? I told you your mother has been very despondent since the death of your father. Didn't you see her spirits perk up when she started thinking about wedding arrangements? How do you think she would have felt if I told her we had insisted on going through with a quiet ceremony at the courthouse?"

"I'm sorry," Cindy said. "You're right, of course. It seems you're always right."

"Don't tell me my snarling little tiger has become an apologetic kitten? Compliments like that will only turn my head and make me think that you don't hate me as much as you would have me believe."

"Oh, don't trouble yourself with second thoughts on that matter," she sneered. "I'll never stop hating you. I just appreciate the concern you've shown toward my mother. I do love her, you know."

Any response he might have made was prevented by Mrs. Templeton's reappearance. Her bright, smiling face only reinforced the truth of his previous words.

"Cecile is delighted. We're to come right over and she'll get to work immediately. She promises to get our outfits completed even if she has to drop everything else and work through the night." She hugged Cindy. "I'm so happy." Then a distressed look crossed her face. "Oh, dear, I haven't even told Anna yet. I must do that at once. She'll be ecstatic with happiness." Motioning for Cindy and Boyd to follow, Mrs. Templeton walked toward the kitchen.

Anna's happiness at the news of Cindy's marriage was equal to that of Mrs. Templeton. She insisted upon planning the menu, although Boyd convinced her to let the caterers do the actual food preparation.

For her part, Cindy had become a robot, moving through the day without any expression of emotion. Boyd had returned to the office after having arranged for Leon to drive her and her mother home, and Cecile and Mrs. Templeton placed the blame for Cindy's perplexing behavior on a bad case of prewedding nerves. "It happens to everyone," Cecile explained.

Cindy winced at the small Frenchwoman's carefree remark. This situation was hardly something that happened to everyone—and oh, how she wished it weren't happening to her! But a stolen glance at her mother's animated face convinced Cindy that there was no other course of action open to her. She owed this marriage to her mother and to the memory of her father. They had done so very much for her. On the drive home Cindy tried not to let her mother see how little interest she had in all the plans the older woman was excitedly discussing.

They arrived home just in time for dinner, but it held no appeal for Cindy. She explained away her lack of appetite by claiming to be totally exhausted after so many hours at Madame Cecile's. Anna and her mother exchanged a conspiratorial glance and Mrs. Templeton observed that it was an entirely reasonable occurrence since everything was happening so quickly. She told Cindy to rest for a while and Cindy was grateful for an excuse to get away by herself. The difficulty of pretending happiness about an event that she dreaded was turning her into a tense mass of quivering nerves.

She went into the library, closed the door and stretched out on the pale beige sofa. The deepening twilight shadows, together with the reassuring comfort of her mother's home, helped her forget her problems momentarily and she was soon lulled into the calming security of sleep. . . .

Refreshingly cool fingers stroked lightly across her forehead and her eyes flew open to focus hazily on Boyd's perturbed features.

"I called to ask about the outfit you had chosen, and your mother told me that you weren't feeling well."

"I was just tired," she said, sitting up and moving away from him so that he was forced to drop his hand.

"How are you feeling now?"

"Much better."

"Your mother said that you skipped your meal. I've been working late and I haven't eaten, either. Freshen up and we'll go to dinner."

"I'm really not hungry."

"Come with me anyway. Sometimes just getting out for a while makes you feel better." Smiling, he took her hands in his and pulled her to her feet. "Take a sweater. There's a breeze in the air." With a strange sense of unreality she did as he said.

"Getting hungry?" he asked as the car moved through the center of town.

She shook her head.

His dark brow lifted and the corners of his mouth curved in just the slightest hint of an understanding smile. "You look unhappy, and I know a surefire way to eliminate that worrisome frown." Grinning like a small boy, he turned the car onto the freeway.

"Where are we going?"

"No questions; it's a surprise."

His secretive attitude intrigued her and, temporarily forgetting her animosity toward him, she began peppering him with inquiries, trying to discover their mysterious destination. He shook his head and told her to be patient.

When the car exited at Great America Parkway, she stared at him in disbelief. "You must be joking. We can't be going there."

"Why not?" he asked amiably. "What better place to cheer an unhappy lady than an amusement park?" Smiling smugly, he drove into the parking lot.

She kept holding back, insisting that the entire idea was ridiculous, but he placed his arm firmly around her waist and guided her through the gate, threatening to carry her if she didn't come willingly.

He immediately bought her a large pink elephant balloon and a white straw cowboy hat. Then he stood back, scrutinizing her appearance as if she were a photographer's model.

"See, what did I tell you? You look happier already."

"I feel silly," she said, laughing despite her misgivings.

"Silly but happy," he said, leading her farther into the park. "Now, what shall we do first? Are you afraid of roller coasters?"

"Of course not! Do I look like a coward?"

"OK. I just wanted to make sure." He tightened his arm around her waist and led her to a line of people coiled beneath the undulating tracks of a gigantic steel structure.

Cindy had second thoughts about not being a coward, but she was too ashamed to admit them to Boyd, so she sat docilely while an attendant strapped them into a car. Slowly, they ascended to the crest of a steep hill of track, then shot down with a lightning speed that left Cindy's stomach somewhere on the tracks above. Her hat and balloon drifted into the wind and she ducked her head onto Boyd's chest, letting him shield her with his strong, protective arms as all around them the whistling air vibrated with the excited squeals of other riders.

When their car finally screeched to a halt Cindy was almost too shaken to move. She clung to Boyd as if he were the only steadying influence in her otherwise dizzy world. Laughter rumbled deep in his throat as he held her tightly against his chest, rubbing his gently soothing hands along the small of her back.

"Well, I think we've had enough wild rides for now. Let's find a place to sit down." As she leaned her head against his shoulder, he practically carried her to a small sidewalk café and ordered hamburgers and chocolate malts. "It's the only food appropriate at a time like this. Don't you agree?" His smiling brown eyes moved over her slowly and she looked away, embarrassed by the warmth of his gaze.

When they had finished eating they went for a ride on the double-tiered carousel with its handcrafted wooden horses. This time Cindy was completely at ease and she smiled broadly at Boyd when he helped her down and planted a small, tender kiss on her forehead.

"Time to go home. I have a busy day tomorrow." Pausing only long enough to buy her some cotton candy, he led her to the exit.

Cindy licked the pink spun sugar contentedly, pulling off a small piece every so often and holding it up to Boyd's smiling lips. Somehow, he no longer seemed as frightening as he had earlier. It was difficult to be afraid of someone when you were busily feeding him fluffy wads of cotton candy.

When the last wisp of pink fuzz was gone, Boyd held Cindy's fingers to his lips and kissed away the sticky-sweet remnants. A strange, exciting thrill fluttered within her, and she realized that she was enjoying Boyd's company more than she cared to admit.

She made no protest when he said good night at the door and moved his lips lightly over hers. Her own feelings of pleasurable contentment were so strong that she felt an irresistible urge to place her hands on his shoulders and pull his head down to hers for a deeper, more satisfying kiss.

Before she had a chance to move, Boyd lifted his head, opened the door and turned her away from him into the house.

"Sweet dreams," he said, closing the door behind her.

She stood quietly in the entryway, listening carefully as he hurried down the steps, started the motor of his car and drove away. Feeling too self-satisfied to question the warm cloud of happiness enveloping her, she went upstairs, crawled into bed and began to relive the pleasurable events of the evening before finally drifting into sleep.

After that night, she hardly saw Boyd during the weeks preceding the wedding. He contented himself with conducting the business of Templeton Industries, leaving most of the wedding preparations in the hands of his secretarial staff and Mrs. Templeton. Cindy was only too happy with the current state of affairs and hoped that Boyd's lack of social contact with her would continue after they were married. The evening spent at the amusement park had left her feeling so wildly confused that she wasn't really eager to be in his company if she could avoid it. She had almost forgotten her vows of hatred that night. In fact, she had practically fallen into his arms, and he had been the one to pull away. Remembering how much she had enjoyed being with him, she resolved that nothing like that would ever happen again. She would never win her battle with him if she was so easily defeated by the slightest touch of his hand.

Richard had completed his exams and was able to return home in time for the wedding rehearsal. He surprised Cindy early that evening as she was going through her closet, idly considering what outfit she would wear. She hadn't realized how much she had missed him, and when he opened her bedroom door she flung herself into his arms and hugged him as if he had been away for years.

"Hey, watch what you're doing. I realize you're just showing me an abundance of sisterly affection, but you're practically a married woman and I don't want any trouble with Boyd."

It was only then that Cindy raised her head to see Boyd standing quietly in the open doorway, calmly surveying the scene before him.

"No problem, Richard," he said, coming over to stand behind Cindy, lifting her hair and gently massaging the nape of her neck with his long, sensual fingers. "I'm very pleased to learn that Cindy is capable of such an affectionate display. Nothing would upset me more than to find that I was marrying an undemonstrative woman." He bent to drop a kiss behind her ear, and all the joy Cindy had felt on seeing Richard vanished beside Boyd's authoritative declaration of possession.

Richard was too excited at the news of her marriage to notice Cindy's change of mood and went on chattering casually. "Boyd was in Palo Alto on business and he offered to drive me home so we could surprise you. He said you'd be glad to see me, but I never expected a welcome like this."

"Why not?" Cindy asked. "You and Mom are the only relatives I have."

"That situation is due to change on Saturday," Boyd said. "As your husband I'm sure I can expect to be included in your small circle of family members. I'll look forward to my out-of-town trips, thinking about the warm welcome I'll receive on *my* return."

Cindy reached her hand up in an attempt to remove his from the nape of her neck. As it touched Boyd's, he grasped it and turned her to face him, clasping his hands behind her back to form a cage around her slender body. His eyes searched her face, daring her to respond to his provocative statement.

Cindy breathed deeply, incapable of saying what she wanted to say to Boyd while Richard was present. Boyd waited patiently until the fire left her eyes and she looked away, then drew her closer in a triumphant expression of victory.

"We must be keeping you from dressing," Boyd said in a carefully controlled voice. "I wouldn't want you to be late for our wedding rehearsal. I'll wait for you downstairs."

Cindy watched as Richard followed Boyd out the door. She felt completely drained of energy and fell back on the bed while she tried to calm her racing heart.

She felt so terribly alone. Even Richard had no idea how unhappy she really was at the prospect of becoming Mrs. Boyd Hamilton. There was no way she could tell him the truth about the circumstances surrounding her wedding, yet she desperately needed a friend in whom she could confide. A glance at her bedside clock told her that she had to hurry if she was to be dressed in time for the rehearsal, and with a sigh of hopeless exasperation she dragged herself off the bed.

She chose a slate-gray silk shantung dress with a high collarless neckline and long, close-fitting sleeves. It followed the full curve of her breasts, nipped in at her narrow waist and fell to just below her knees in a softly flaring flow of fabric. After donning matching gray silk pumps, she sat down at her dressing table and drew her hair up into a severe French knot. A light dusting of blusher, some pale lip gloss and a touch of eye shadow completed her makeup.

Boyd was seated alone in the library when she got downstairs. He set aside the technical magazine he was reading and stood up when she entered the room.

"Where's Richard?" Cindy asked. "He said he'd wait for me downstairs."

"*I* said I would wait for you downstairs," Boyd replied, walking toward her and reaching his hand out to lift her chin. "Why have you done that to your hair?"

"Why have I done what to my hair?"

"Pulled it away from your face so that you look like a spinsterish schoolmarm. I don't like it."

"I didn't realize that you intended to supervise my appearance. I hardly think my hairstyle is any concern of yours."

Boyd's arrogant demeanor was unaffected by Cindy's remark. He lowered his hand, slowly letting his sensitive fingers trace a feathery path along her neck. His face grew thoughtful as his fingers lingered at her neckline before slipping beneath the silk fabric to begin a provocative series of butterfly strokes along the base of her collarbone. Although the sensuous touch of his fingers sent icy thrills racing through her body, his mind seemed to be miles away. When he finally spoke, the softness of his voice only emphasized the calm control which always guarded his emotions.

"Don't spar with me, Cindy. I'm way out of your league."

"I don't know what you're talking about," she said, flinging her head back and walking away from him.

"Don't you?"

Cindy shook her head. She sensed him standing behind her long before she felt his steely fingers cutting into her arms. Although he spoke in a whisper, his voice held that frozen tone of command that was so typical of him. He pulled her back against his chest.

"What I mean, darling Cindy, is that I'm not one of your college beaus. Don't try your cute coyness on me."

She tried to break free of his grip, but his hands were like iron bands encircling her arms.

"Let me go," she hissed. "I don't have to listen to this nonsense."

"Indeed you do," he whispered into the curving depths of her ear. "As long as we're going to be married, we might as well understand each other. I for one do not enjoy being exposed to childish schoolgirl sarcasm."

"Then why marry a childish schoolgirl?"

"You know the answer to that question as well as I do," he said. "The marriage will take place, and no amount of bad temper on your part will alter that fact."

He placed one broad hand on her shoulder and turned her gently in his arms while his other hand captured her chin, tilting her face toward his. Dropping a feathery kiss at the corner of her mouth, he blazed a tantalizing path across her lips until he felt her response.

Then, relaxing his embrace, he set her away from him and gazed thoughtfully into her eyes. "My kisses . . . my touch . . . they don't repulse you. If you were truthful you'd even admit that you like them. In a few days we'll be married; can't we try to enjoy each other's company?" His hands laced through her hair and cradled her head while his eyes searched for a response.

She made no attempt to escape his scrutiny. It was useless to deny the attraction that existed between them. His slightest touch aroused responses she hadn't known she possessed, and she found herself thinking about him at the oddest times. Perhaps he was right . . . perhaps they should try to put their relationship on a more compatible level. She raised her arms and stroked her fingers lightly across his shoulders.

A forced cough broke the silence in the room and Boyd dropped his arms, letting one rest lightly on Cindy's waist as they both turned to see Richard standing in the doorway.

"I hope I'm not interrupting anything," he said, smiling broadly. "I could leave you alone for a while longer, but then you'll be late for the rehearsal."

"I'm forced to agree with you there," Boyd declared. "Is your mother ready?"

The presence of Richard and Mrs. Templeton was a soothing influence on Cindy on the way to the church. Boyd's parents had died when he was quite young, so most of the members of the bridal party were Cindy's friends. Boyd had asked Carl Meredith to be his best man.

The rehearsal went smoothly and everyone was cheerful when they met at the restaurant where Boyd had arranged a prewedding dinner. Cindy forced a smile and answered questions with brittle gaiety. Her jaw was aching from the effort when she felt Boyd's fingers perched possessively along her shoulders. She tilted her head back in inquiry and met his obsidian eyes, impassively watching her.

"I think it would be appropriate for the prospective bride and groom to dance with each other. We wouldn't want any of the bridal party to get the idea that we're not deeply in love." He flashed a contented smile at her mother as he led Cindy away from the table.

The melodious tones of a slow fox-trot rose from the small combo at the side of the room and drifted onto the dance floor, surrounding the dancers with a cloud of romantic dreams. The languid tones of the music failed to melt the block of ice that surrounded Cindy's heart, and she held herself rigid when Boyd turned her into his arms. He seemed to take no notice of her discomfort and merely tightened his arms around her. Cindy pressed her hand against his chest, using her upturned palm as a barrier between them. Without missing a step, Boyd reached down, caught her hand in his and raised it to his shoulder. Then he tightened his grip on her waist, clasping her to him until the strong beat of his heart vibrated through the softness of her breast.

"Stop it," Cindy hissed.

"Stop what?" Boyd asked, lowering his hand to her hips and molding them to his firmly muscled thighs, making her fully aware of his superior masculine strength. "There's certainly nothing illicit about a man dancing with his fiancée two days before the wedding."

"You know what I'm talking about," Cindy snapped. "I don't like being held so closely. I can barely breathe."

"You seem to be breathing fine to me," Boyd said, grazing his hand across the curve of her breast and lightly cupping it so that the swift beat of her heart echoed against his palm.

"How dare you?" she gasped, lifting her hand toward his face.

"Easy," he said, catching her hand before she could raise it past his neck. "We wouldn't want our friends to think we weren't getting along. As for the way I hold you when we're dancing, I told you that I'm not an inexperienced college kid. You'll just have to learn to do things my way from now on."

"What about *my* desires? Don't they count for anything?"

"On the contrary, they mean everything. I shall devote all my efforts to satisfying your desires."

Cindy drew back, frightened by the subtly erotic meaning hidden behind his harmless remark. Boyd made no effort to stop her from moving out of his arms, and it was only then that she realized the music had stopped and everyone was leaving the dance floor. Boyd's hand dropped to her waist and he guided her back to the table.

Boyd acted the amiable host for the remainder of the evening. Except for a few languid smiles as their eyes met across the long table, he made no further attempts to communicate with Cindy.

He kept away over the next two days, explaining that he was working overtime to get his business affairs in order so he and Cindy might have a few days to themselves after their marriage. Cindy's heart tightened at the thought of spending a few days alone with Boyd. She had an idea of what his intentions were, but if he thought her contract called for any private display of affection he was in for a rude surprise.

The day of their wedding began with the rosy glow of dawn slowly edging its way across the cloudless blue horizon. Cindy watched it appear and knew that every bit of increasing sunlight reduced her chances of avoiding this disastrous marriage. She drew the sheet up to her chin, unwilling to leave her bed, seeking to delay the start of the day as much as possible.

In a few short hours she would be Mrs. Boyd Hamilton, even if it was a marriage in name only. She bought more time by staying under the shower longer than necessary, trying to gather her courage.

After slipping into her white silk bikini undergarments, she walked into the bedroom where Anna was busily gathering the accessories she was to wear with her wedding dress. Cindy removed the protective netting that had covered her hair to protect the hairdresser's elegant upswept styling from the spraying waters of the shower. Then she seated herself at the dressing table, brushing the few stray hairs into place. She applied the slightest touch of blusher and lip gloss and a hint of eye shadow before rising from the table and walking toward Anna, who was holding the wedding gown.

Cindy stepped into the elaborate confection of shimmering white *peau de soie* and frothy Alençon lace. Anna held the gown while Cindy slipped her arms into the long, close-fitting sleeves, then raised it over her shoulders and fastened the endless series of tiny fabric-covered buttons stretching down the back. The exquisite white lace formed a gossamer web, highlighting the creamy skin of Cindy's slender arms and shoulders. The softly luxurious *peau de soie* rose beneath the sheer lace to curve enticingly over her breasts and waist before tracing the smooth line of her hips and falling to the floor in a satiny profusion of sleekly swirling fabric which ended in a long, skillfully designed train.

Anna knelt so that Cindy could slip her feet into the white silk high-heeled sandals, then rose and accompanied her to the dressing table, where she placed the lace veil over her hair. Cindy stepped back to view herself in the full-length mirror and smiled wryly as she saw the fairylike image reflecting back at her.

"You are a beautiful bride," Anna said. "But then, I always knew you would be."

"She is beautiful, isn't she?"

Cindy turned to see her mother standing in the doorway.

"If only her father were here to see her."

Her mother's innocent comment made Cindy's mouth go dry as she considered her father's influence on the wedding. Without his demands, she wouldn't be getting married today, married to a man she had always hated.

Cindy allowed her mother to lead her down the stairs while Anna walked behind, lifting the long train of her gown so that it didn't drag along on the carpet.

The rest of the morning seemed to take place in a dream, and before she knew it Richard was leading her down the aisle to the haunting strains of the wedding march from *Lohengrin*. Boyd stood before the altar, watching her with cold intensity that made her want to turn and run from the church. But she controlled her emotions and continued walking toward him, feeling her heart sink as his narrowed eyes asserted his possession of her before their lips had even spoken their vows.

She felt like a lamb being led to the slaughter when Richard handed her to Boyd and stepped away, leaving the two of them standing before the minister. Cindy went through the motions of the wedding ceremony as if in a trance, somehow managing to utter the correct responses when the minister turned in her direction. Only Boyd could feel her hand tighten and instinctively pull away from him when he placed the heavy yellow-gold wedding band on her quivering finger.

When the minister had pronounced them man and wife, Boyd turned Cindy into his arms and placed a short but firm kiss on her lips before leading her back down the aisle.

From that moment on, Boyd never left her side. He rode to the reception at the country club in the same car with her. He danced with her; he sat beside her at the dinner she was too nervous to eat. Playing the part of the gracious host, he introduced her to his many friends and business acquaintances, each of whom wished them luck and congratulated Boyd on ending his long years of bachelorhood.

Neither of them had wanted a honeymoon. Cindy felt it would be the height of insincerity to take one, and Boyd didn't think he could spare the time away from work. But she had to agree with him when he dryly mentioned that it would look odd if they didn't make an attempt to follow the tradition, and he had suggested that she join him on a business trip he had to make to Mexico City.

Her mother and Anna accompanied her when she

retired to change out of her gown. Her beige silk suit, with its softly flowered chiffon blouse, seemed to transform her from a delicate white china doll into a well-dressed young society matron. She submitted to the tear-dampened hugs of her mother and Anna as they told her how happy they were that she had married such a fine man.

Boyd had changed into a light gray business suit. He placed his arm around her shoulders and escorted her through the heavy shower of rice and confetti as they dashed wildly toward the waiting limousine. The car began to move as soon as they had seated themselves, and Cindy turned away from Boyd to watch the white satin ribbons, streaming from the car doors, flutter in the late afternoon breeze. Suddenly she tensed as she became aware that Boyd's powerful fingers were cupping the nape of her neck, caressing it in long, sensual strokes.

"Tired?" he questioned, smiling at her as his hands continued their undulating massage. "You'll have a chance to rest once we arrive in Mexico. In fact, it might be wise if you napped on the plane."

"I'll be OK," Cindy said, moving away from him. "It's just that everything has been so rushed. I feel as if I've been on a nonstop carousel these past two weeks."

She received no answer but was favored with a strangely indulgent smile as the car stopped and Boyd waited for the chauffeur to open the door. The smile lingered on his lips, burning into the back of her neck as she preceded him up the steps of the company plane. Once inside, he motioned her toward a small bedroom at the back of the plane.

"Why not stretch out and try to get some rest? I have some papers I want to look over before we land," he said, motioning to his attaché case. "If I don't get these figures straightened out in my mind, I won't be able to discuss the contract arrangements for these computers—and that, after all, is the main purpose of this trip."

Cindy was too tired to be upset by the taunting gleam dancing in the depths of his eyes. She sighed listlessly and closed the door behind her.

Chapter Four

Firm but gentle hands smoothed Cindy's sleep-tousled hair away from her face, and she opened her eyes to gaze into the quietly mysterious depths of Boyd's. She didn't know if she was still under the hazy influence of slumber, but it seemed to her that his face wore a soft, compassionate expression she had never seen before.

"We've landed," he said, his low-pitched voice conveying the same element of tenderness she had previously noticed on his face. "I hate to wake you, but you'll be much more comfortable in the hotel room." He lowered his hand and slipped it behind her shoulders, lifting her off the soft, feathery pillow.

She let him help her to her feet and leaned against his broad shoulders as he rested his hand on her waist and guided her down the steps and out of the plane.

"We've already been cleared by customs," he said, settling her into the waiting limousine. "We'll be at the hotel in a few minutes and then you can really make yourself comfortable."

Boyd was unusually pleasant during the ride to the hotel. He spoke in a friendly but detached voice, sharing his knowledge of the city with Cindy and pointing out the various sights they passed on their way to the center of town. Although his stony air of arrogance had vanished in his attempt at light conversation, his deeper emotions still seemed to be encased behind an invisible wall of ice. Cindy made no response to his remarks. She assumed he had adopted this congenial attitude for the benefit of the chauffeur, who, though mute, appeared to be intently aware of their conversation.

When they arrived at the hotel, Cindy was shocked to discover that everyone greeted Boyd as if they knew him. Entering their suite, she was again surprised to find it fully stocked with chilled champagne, tropical fruits and assorted canapés. Fresh flowers sprang from silver and crystal vases to give the apartment a definite air of elegance. Boyd seemed completely at ease, chattering in flawless Spanish with the manager, the bellhops and all the maids who fluttered about the room seeing to his comfort.

"The staff seems quite eager to please you," she said sarcastically. "I imagine you must be very liberal with your gratuities. I suppose Templeton Industries foots all the expenses for these Central American jaunts?"

"Absolutely right!" he said, calmly watching her while he deftly opened one of the bottles of French champagne. "As a matter of fact, Templeton Industries holds a long-term lease on this suite. We do quite a bit of business in Mexico, and it seemed advisable to have a permanent base where we could entertain our guests and feel more at home ourselves."

"Is the suite available to *all* our employees?" Cindy questioned, refusing his offer of a glass of champagne. "I find it hard to believe that it's in the company's best interest to finance such expensive living quarters just so you can have a luxurious place to stay while you're in Mexico."

"The company maintains suites in various locations," he said, shrugging off her refusal and pouring himself a glass. "Our accounting department did a cost-analysis study and found that, in the long run, this method was much more economical than trying to find a suitable hotel room each time the need arose." He lifted his glass. "Are you sure you don't want some? It's very good."

"No, thanks. I'm feeling too exhausted for anything." She rose from the sofa. "All I want now is a bath and a nap."

"Everything you need is in there," Boyd said, opening a door and gesturing into a room full of beautifully gilded antique white French provincial furniture. "Make yourself at home."

"I will," Cindy retorted. "After all, this *is* being paid for by my company."

"*Our* company," Boyd said, his arrogant mouth curving in a mocking smile.

Cindy sighed in exasperation and slammed the door, but the deep, throaty sound of Boyd's amused chuckles came drifting through to taunt her. She casually surveyed the tastefully decorated room and immediately noticed that both her luggage and Boyd's had been placed on the racks beside the walk-in closets in which their clothing had been hung. Of course, she realized, the chambermaids had assumed that a honeymoon couple would be sharing the same bedroom. Well, she would make some changes in that arrangement as soon as she had showered.

The mirrored dressing area with its pink onyx tub and marble-walled shower stall echoed the opulent elegance of the rest of the suite. Cindy relaxed while the warm water stroked the length of her body. She felt the tension receding from her taut limbs as she massaged the fragrant soap into her skin, almost washing away all her cares.

She felt completely refreshed when she left the shower and slipped into a paisley caftan which fit her so loosely that she had no need for undergarments. She was seated at the dressing table, brushing out her intricate hairstyle, when a light tap sounded at the bedroom door and Boyd entered the room.

"You might have waited for me to answer your knock," she said, turning to stare at him in annoyance. "A closed bedroom door does indicate some desire for privacy."

"Not between a husband and wife. We *are* married, after all."

"This marriage is hardly like a normal marriage. We're both fully aware of the circumstances surrounding our relationship."

"Perhaps," he said, coming up behind her and meeting her gaze in the mirror as he lifted a soft tendril of hair from her shoulders and slowly curled it around his finger. "Nonetheless, we are still legally married and I must presume a certain level of informality between us. After all, we will be sharing a home. *My* home."

When Cindy made no response he continued, "I'll be going out on business. I see you've made yourself comfortable. Why don't I have your dinner sent up to the room?"

She cast a dubious eye toward the clock. "Business . . . at this hour?"

"My, my, don't tell me you're going to be a jealous wife?"

"Hardly," she said. "I just don't like being played for a fool."

"I would never do that, my dear. You may be naïve

but you're not the least bit stupid. However, let me do my bit to increase your knowledge of the world. In Mexico, a country with a Spanish heritage, the people observe the traditional siesta and all activity ceases during the heat of the day. It's not at all unusual to have dinner at ten in the evening while conducting a relaxed business conversation at the same time. It's a friendly way to settle any differences that may arise during negotiations." He dropped a light kiss on her glistening blonde hair and left the room.

Cindy threw the brush down in anger. He persisted in treating her like a troublesome child. How was she to know about the customs of Mexico? After all, she had never been out of California before. She was well aware that Boyd had traveled all over the world and she was quite certain that he would continue to use his superior knowledge to make her feel even more inexperienced than she already felt.

True to his word, Boyd had a delicious dinner of tender steak slices simmered in onions, peppers and tomatoes sent to her room. The spicy aroma of the food tantalized her taste buds and she ate hungrily, recalling how little she had eaten at the wedding reception. But when her hunger for food was satisfied, she felt another sensation begin to grow in the pit of her stomach. It was the uncomfortable void of a hollow loneliness. She walked about the suite, fingering various objects, unable to establish any sense of familiarity which would dispel the gloomy chill of being all alone in a strange hotel suite in a foreign country.

Her desolate feeling made her yearn involuntarily for Boyd's return. At least he was someone she knew, and even if she did dislike him intensely he was still someone to talk to. The softly chiming clock on the mantel indicated that it was already morning. She grew annoyed with herself for pacing the room, eagerly awaiting Boyd's return, and strode into the bedroom, determined to hide her forlorn attitude from him and be sound asleep when he returned.

But one thing was certain, she decided when she saw his dark silk pajamas lying on the coverlet beside her white satin nightgown, there was absolutely no way she was going to share that bed with him. She opened the door to a smaller, less exotic bedroom, one which was admirably suited to her purposes.

Feeling immensely pleased with herself, she returned to the master bedroom, where she changed into her nightgown and matching robe. She glanced at her clothing hanging in the closet and decided she could wait until morning to have a maid move it. Let them draw their own conclusions about why she and Boyd slept in separate rooms.

She hadn't noticed any pillow in the other room and decided to take one from this bed. Apparently the smaller bed had not been made up since the chambermaids had not considered that a honeymoon couple would have any need for it. When she lifted the pillow from the side of the bed where her nightgown had been placed, a small black velvet box came into view. Curious, she dropped the pillow and lifted the box, pressing the small gold catch which opened the lid.

Her gasp was plainly audible in the silent room as she gazed down at the shimmering diamond teardrop snugly nestled against the black velvet lining of the box, revealing just a hint of the thin platinum chain from which it was suspended.

"You weren't supposed to find that until morning."

Cindy turned to see Boyd leaning against the door, one arm raised to cradle his head as he studied her.

"It's my wedding gift to you," he said, straightening

away from the doorway and closing the distance between them with pantherlike ease. "A token by which you can always remember our wedding night."

Cindy blushed with embarrassment as he stood directly before her, towering above her and making her all too self-consciously aware of her bare feet and sheer, low-cut garments.

His eyes never left her face as he silently took the box from her, removed the necklace and carelessly tossed the box onto the bed. The light touch of his fingers burned her skin as he gently lifted the thick veil of golden hair away from her neck while he fastened the chain. His hands stayed on her shoulders and his eyes lowered from her face to the diamond, resting in the valley between her breasts. Throbbing currents of electricity charged through the silent room, and Cindy felt her breath quicken as Boyd's hands began to travel, one to the small of her back, pressing her quivering body against the hardness of his own, the other lifting her chin to meet his descending mouth.

Her senses were reeling and her arms began to move almost of their own volition in an unconscious desire to mold her body's softness to the hardening contours of his masculine desires. She forgot her vow to hate him forever and to constantly fight him with all the strength in her body. Instead, every drop of her energy seemed to be reaching eagerly out to him, imploring him to continue his erotic exploration of her welcoming flesh. She became boneless in his arms, her aroused emotions leaping to heights she had never before experienced, and she clung helplessly to him as he expertly guided her into this uncharted territory.

She breathed deeply, yearning to inhale the very essence of him. She was still clinging to him when the painful pangs of reality came charging through to her muddled brain as the scent of stale tobacco mingled with heavy French perfume attacked her nostrils, reminding her of where he had spent the preceding hours of their wedding night. It didn't matter that she hadn't done anything to encourage him to spend the night with her. Indeed, she had given him every reason to believe that she had wanted nothing more than for him to leave her alone. But there was no way she was going to let him use her to satisfy the desires which another woman had aroused. The thought made her feel cheap and degraded, and her body grew rigid when she recalled the absolute ease with which he had drawn a willing response from her. She shuddered with shame at the vision of what might have been and raised her hands to his chest, pushing him away from her.

His demanding lips softened, releasing hers, but his hands remained clasped behind her waist, preventing her complete escape. His eyes studied her while his ragged breathing echoed through the room.

"Is something wrong?" he asked in a low, husky voice.

"Yes," she answered, her voice sounding strangely hollow as it drifted back to her ears. "This entire situation is wrong. It's unfair of you to try to seduce me with gifts and tender words when you know as well as I do that our marriage is rooted in money, not love."

His arms tightened, making her wince with pain and lift her face to his. He loosened his grip slightly but still held her prisoner in his powerful hands.

"Nevertheless, we *are* married and you're not making the situation any easier for either of us."

"Why?" she said, shaking herself free and placing some distance between them. "Because I won't let you use my body the way you use everything else? Do you think you can come in here reeking with the scent of another woman and expect me to fall passionately into your arms just because you've bought me some expensive jewelry . . . with *my* company's money, no doubt."

"Stop it, Cindy. I told you I was out on a business appointment and that we were conducting it over dinner. Naturally some of the men had their wives and girlfriends along. You would have been there, too, if you hadn't been so tired."

"This entire conversation is ridiculous. Our marriage is nothing more than a business arrangement, and it never will be anything else." She raised her arms, unclasped the necklace and threw it down on the bed. "There's no need for you to buy me gifts for a wedding night such as ours." She retrieved the pillow and started walking into the other room.

Boyd's hand reached out to stop her flight. He drew her to him, placing a muscular arm beneath her knees to effortlessly lift her legs off the floor. She struggled furiously against his granite chest, pounding it relentlessly with her tightly clenched fists, but he strode purposefully to the bed and dropped her unceremoniously upon it.

"A bride should spend her wedding night in the master bedroom. If you don't care to share it with me, I'll find a place where my presence is more welcome."

Casting a derisive glance in her direction, he stormed out of the room. In a few seconds, Cindy heard the outer door to the suite open and close again. Her own breathing sounded foreign to her as she tried to create some sense out of the maelstrom Boyd had created within her body. She hated him and wanted nothing to do with him; why, then, had she felt so miserable when he dropped her on the bed like an unwanted sack of potatoes and went elsewhere to seek his pleasures? No satisfactory answer came to her while she tossed fitfully on the smooth silk sheets, and eventually she slipped into the tortured sleep of exhaustion. . . .

Boyd had not returned when she woke the next morning, and after showering she asked that breakfast be served in her room. The restless sleep of the previous night had done little to restore her vitality and she was grateful for an opportunity to spend a few more quiet hours in the seclusion of her room, free of the tension that Boyd's presence always seemed to generate. After breakfast she dressed in a bikini and stretched out on a lounge chair in the privacy of the terrace off her bedroom.

The sun was much hotter than she had expected it to be and after staying in it for a few minutes she moved to a more comfortable spot in a cool, shaded area of the patio. Her exhaustion and the gentle morning breeze combined to lull her into sleep, and she rolled over and dozed peacefully until she was startled into unwelcome wakefulness by the abrupt movement of a cloth across her naked back. Confused, she sat up awkwardly and stared into Boyd's annoyed face.

"What are you trying to do, burn yourself to a crisp? That sun is hot enough to fry an egg."

"I wasn't in the sun," she said, blinking as the sun's bright glare disproved her words. "I don't know what happened; it wasn't sunny when I first lay down."

"What time did you fall asleep? It's five o'clock now, and the earth changes its position in relation to the sun. Don't you know that? Or didn't they teach you anything of a practical, scientific nature in that artistic institution from which you graduated?"

"Of course I knew that," Cindy said, annoyed at his condescending tone of voice. "I forgot; I didn't expect to fall asleep. I just wasn't thinking clearly."

"That's been very apparent to me for quite a while now," Boyd said, taking her hand and lifting her off the chair. "In any case, I think it's time you went inside and started getting dressed for dinner."

"Are we going out to dinner?"

"Yes. I thought you would be fully rested by now and ready to meet some of the people who do business with Templeton Industries."

He led her to the door of the master bedroom, then walked toward the other room. "I have some last-minute business details to attend to. I'll expect you to be ready in about three hours," he called over his shoulder as he disappeared into the room.

Cindy felt a dull ache across her back and shoulders when she walked toward her bathroom to let the water run into the tub. She wondered how long she had been exposed to the full heat of that strong sun and hoped that she wouldn't have to endure any greater discomfort than the stiffness she was now experiencing. In any case, the soothing warmth of a bath seemed infinitely more inviting than the chilling needles of an invigorating shower.

She approached her closet, seeking a robe to don after her bath, and noticed that Boyd's luggage—and she assumed his clothing as well—had been removed. Well, she thought confidently, at least I've made it quite clear that I have no intention of sharing a bedroom with him. Snatching a robe from the hanger, she returned to the bathroom.

When she lowered herself into the tub the water scalded her back and shoulders. She bit her lips against the piercing pain as she realized her sunburn was more severe than she had first supposed. Her skin was so tender that she couldn't even bear the slippery touch of the scented soap against her flaming body. Agony shot through her as she rose from the tub and gently patted herself dry.

She considered telling Boyd that she was too uncomfortable to go out to dinner, but she quickly rejected that idea when she visualized his belittling reaction to the predicament she had gotten herself into. He already regarded her as a helpless child who could be easily bent to his will, and she was determined not to give him additional evidence with which to reinforce his beliefs.

The black lace dress which had seemed so devastatingly sophisticated when she bought it now seemed totally unbecoming as it flagrantly highlighted the blazing red fire on her back. But she didn't even want to think about enduring the painful exercise of trying to find a more suitable outfit.

She was just brushing her hair back from her shoulders when Boyd entered the room. She sensed an irritated disapproval in his eyes as they casually scanned her body, coming to rest on her face. She had put on more makeup than usual to hide her burn, which covered her left cheek as well as her back.

"You're wearing more makeup than usual, aren't you?"

"Well, this is a rather festive occasion, isn't it?" she lied, unwilling to tell him her real reason. "I thought I'd get dressed up so our business associates would realize I'm not quite the child you seem to think I am."

Boyd considered her silently for a moment, drawing his lips together as if about to make some remark; then he seemed to reconsider and his face was once more shrouded in that cold impassivity that Cindy had come to hate.

"Well, you're free to do as you please, of course, but we should be going; I don't like to keep people waiting."

He sat quietly beside her in the limousine, yet she could not avoid feeling that he was annoyed with her. However, pride prevented her from initiating any conversation which would break the awkward silence, and she kept her hands tightly folded over her black satin evening purse while she turned her eyes away to look out the window.

The nightclub-style restaurant into which Boyd led her hardly seemed the type of place where one could discuss business, and Cindy looked about her dubiously when he guided her to a crowded table in a secluded alcove. Everyone seemed to know him very well and greeted him in an extremely friendly manner, but the polite friendliness they exhibited toward Cindy seemed to be offered only because she was his wife.

Boyd followed the conversation perfectly, speaking Spanish with such ease that it might have been his native tongue. Cindy couldn't blame her discomfort on any inability to speak the language. Her schooling had included enough courses in Spanish to enable her to understand virtually everything that was being said.

Her sunburn was less visible in the dimly lit nightclub, but her skin burned painfully. Although the other women at the table were considerably older, they all exuded an air of well-maintained physical elegance. Their cosmopolitan demeanor only served to increase her distress. Their conversation ranged from clothing to art to a variety of exotic resort areas which she had often read about but never visited. Within her own close circle of friends Cindy had always been considered extremely sophisticated, but now she felt terribly out of place. The informal mannerisms of her California background were no match for the practiced social graces of these women. Each movement they made, whether it was to lift a wineglass or to raise a cigarette to their perfectly outlined lips, made her feel ever more inadequate.

This feeling of inferiority, together with the raw pain of her sunburned skin, made Cindy sink lower in her seat in an effort to be less noticeable and find some comfort within herself. After a while everyone appeared to forget her presence and, except for asking a few questions about whether she was enjoying her steak or if she'd care for another margarita, they left her entirely alone. Every now and then, she'd glance in Boyd's direction and find his eyes resting on her, gleaming with smug satisfaction as if he were pleased to find that she was no match for the sophisticated circle of friends in which he moved.

But if she was an outsider, Boyd definitely was not. It was painful to Cindy to watch the way the men respected his business opinions while the women hung all over him in their efforts to get his attention. The thought struck her that he must have wanted control of the company very much to have married her when he so obviously preferred the attentions of these alluringly beautiful women. Their marriage must be every bit as distasteful to him as it was to her. No wonder he looked at her with such hostile disapproval. She could never compare favorably with the other women at the table, and Boyd was as painfully aware of that as she was.

In the early hours of the morning, when the dinner was finally over, Boyd was bid farewell in the friendliest terms and was issued many invitations to return as soon as possible. Cindy, on the other hand, received polite good-byes and nothing more. She could almost see the pity in his friends' eyes as they wondered how he had ever been persuaded to marry someone so obviously lacking in the social graces.

Boyd maintained his silence in the car on the way

back to their hotel, and Cindy was not about to offer any apologies for her behavior. He must have known what was going to happen, and she wasn't about to sweeten the victory by complaining or looking for pity. She preceded him into the suite and went directly to her bedroom, eager to get undressed and soothe some lotion into her tormented skin.

She breathed a silent sigh of relief as she shut the door, but the sigh became a gasp when the door refused to move and she turned to find Boyd's tall form looming ominously behind her, one powerful hand outstretched to prevent the door from closing.

"What do you want?" she snapped as he softly closed the door and rested his back against it.

"I'd like an explanation of your behavior tonight."

"I don't know what you're talking about," she said, facing him with all the indignation her painful body would allow.

"I'm talking about the cold, disinterested attitude you displayed toward our guests this evening. You were hardly what one might call an asset to the company."

"Sorry about that," Cindy said, tossing her head at him. "If you no longer consider the terms of the contract to be in your best interest, why not just get the marriage annulled? Then you won't have to worry about me or any other 'asset' of Templeton Industries."

"So that's your game, is it?" he said, walking purposefully toward her. "Well, two can play at it as easily as one. If you choose to conduct yourself in a manner calculated to make me want to be the one to break our contract, there's no reason why I can't behave in a manner which will give *you* cause to change *your* mind about meeting all the terms of the contract."

Before Cindy knew what was happening, he had circled her with his arms, pulled her to him and lowered his probing lips to the unsuspecting softness of her own. But even the forceful strength of his demanding lips could not silence the piercing scream of pain that involuntarily tore from her open mouth.

He instantly released her, watching in stunned silence as she crumpled to the floor in a heap of misery. Kneeling beside her, he placed his strong arms beneath her knees and shoulders and lifted her to the bed, placing her gently back upon the pillows and using his clean white linen handkerchief to dry the tears streaming down her cheeks.

His face darkened into a scowl as the cloth wiped away the thick layer of makeup to reveal the scarlet skin beneath it. Then, dropping the handkerchief, he gently raised her away from the pillows and unzipped her dress, slowly slipping it down the length of her body until it slid down her legs and he had removed it completely. Silently, he surveyed her beet-red limbs.

"Why didn't you tell me you were so badly burned? You were in no condition to go out tonight. What the devil are you trying to prove?"

She was too weak to answer and just watched dazedly while he shrugged off his jacket, tossed it onto a chair and walked to the bathroom. When he returned she saw that he had removed a bottle of champagne from an ice bucket and was dipping a washcloth into the chilled water. Wringing the cloth out, he lowered it to her face, bringing relief to her burning complexion.

He continued to run the icy wet cloth over her skin, and the feeling was so welcome that Cindy cast aside the discomforting thought that she was dressed in only the scantiest of lacy undergarments. Boyd seemed so intent on what he was doing that she might have been a wooden dummy for all the attention he was giving to her barely clad body.

By the time he had finished, Cindy felt infinitely more comfortable and attempted a weak smile of thanks. Boyd took no notice of her attempt at friendliness and, shaking his head in annoyance, removed the icy water and washcloth. When he returned from the bathroom he carried with him a large tube of antiseptic lotion. Wordlessly, he pressed some lotion into his palm and began smoothing it onto her face.

The anesthetic in the lotion numbed Cindy's tender skin and she felt contentment flood through her as Boyd continued to spread the thick liquid over her body, moving from her face to her sensitive neck and edging distressingly close to the soft fullness of her breasts.

The languid sense of well-being generated by the cool lotion was being quickly dissipated by the lightly massaging touch of Boyd's long fingers as they sensitively stroked her bare back, lingering tentatively at the lace-covered elastic waistband of her bikini panties.

Cindy's breathing became increasingly ragged as his hands lowered to the backs of her thighs and began spreading the lotion with slow, circling strokes. She looked into his face, certain that he must know the effect his touch was having on her. Her heart seemed to be beating so loudly and wildly that it echoed through the hypnotic silence shrouding the room. She opened her eyes to gaze into his, but his face was absolutely expressionless, as if he were totally unaware of the disturbing effect his hands were having on her reeling senses.

"Am I hurting you?" he asked in response to her dazed look.

She shook her head wordlessly. She did not trust herself to utter a single sound.

"Well, then," he said, replacing the cap on the lotion

bottle, "I think that's the best I can do for you—unless you'd like me to call a doctor?"

"No, that's not necessary. I really feel much better, thanks to you. I just feel so silly at having gotten myself in this ridiculous predicament."

"Well," he said, smiling down at her as he traced his index finger lightly across her cheek, "I have to agree with you. Cruel and heartless as I am, I could hardly expect an affectionate wife under these circumstances. Yet somehow I believe that you don't hate me quite so much at this moment."

"You didn't have to help make me more comfortable. Naturally I'm appreciative of what you've done. I'm not completely heartless, you know."

"But I am? You think I'm a machine, completely devoid of feeling, and that all you're offering me is your appreciation. Well, if I weren't so considerate of your uncomfortable physical state, I could prove that the emotion you're experiencing is not merely appreciation."

"You'd like that, wouldn't you? You'd like to seduce me so you could assert your power over me the way you've asserted it over everyone else. Well, it's not going to work. I may be innocent enough to have my body fall prey to your experienced ways, but my mind will never stop fighting you."

Boyd smiled indulgently beneath hooded eyes as she went on. "If I have my way, you'll never possess any part of me. I hate you with every inch of my being."

"Not quite every inch, my dear," he said, lowering his lips to hers. She tried to turn her head away, but he raised his hands, curling them into her hair and making it impossible for her to break free. His lips were tender as they pressed against hers, softly probing until hers parted in response to his desires. His hands left her face and traced a lightly possessive trail over the soft curves of her body, his touch so fleeting that her sunburned skin never felt it, yet it was enough to set her heartbeat racing and send chills shooting down the length of her spine.

Suddenly Boyd raised his head and calmly studied the effect his tender assault had had on her emotions. Cindy despised herself for letting him observe the ragged breathing which had resulted from his kiss. He had remained in total control of his own emotions and he eyed her as a beast of prey might look at a trapped rabbit. She was nothing more to him than a toy with which he could amuse himself while he remained entirely impervious to any display of human emotions.

"Get out of here," she moaned in an attempt to salvage some of her lost pride. "I never want to see you again."

"I'll go. But you're going to see me again, and next time you won't be shielded by sunburned skin."

The confidence in his voice ate into Cindy as she watched him walk from the room. He moved with the terrifying elegance of a jungle cat, and Cindy was only too aware of the powerful animal magnetism that lurked beneath the well-controlled businessman's exterior. She hated him, hated the marriage he had forced her into, hated the way he so casually asserted his control over her; but most of all she hated her own helplessness when his lips touched hers and his experienced hands caressed her pliant body.

Tormented dreams coursed through her mind that night, leaving her tired and nervous when the early morning light flooded through the window. She sat up and found that although her body still felt tautly uncomfortable when she moved the intense pain had vanished. She ran her fingers lightly across her arm, finding her skin still somewhat tender to the touch, and hoped that she wouldn't find it as uncomfortable to wear clothes as she had yesterday.

She was still checking the state of her burn when Boyd entered the room. His dark hair was damp from his shower and glistened in smooth shadows above the pristine whiteness of his silk shirt. His charcoal-gray business suit concealed the potent maleness that Cindy had come to fear and imbued him with a commanding vigor born of his formidable accomplishments in the business world.

"Are you feeling better this morning?" he said, casually leaning against the bedpost and studying her.

Cindy nodded her head. She had never put on her nightgown last night, although she had discarded her bra to keep it from further irritating her sensitive skin. There was something strangely menacing about having Boyd stand above her, fully dressed, while she lay in bed wearing practically nothing. Shivering more with fear than from any actual chill, she clasped the sheet securely to her body.

"Why are you hiding under that sheet?" he asked. "After last night your body holds no secrets from either my eyes or my hands." He looked inquisitively at her as he bent, retrieved her bra from the carpet and offered it to her, its strap suspended on a lean brown finger.

The sight of her intimate undergarment in Boyd's masculine hand made Cindy color helplessly. "I must have removed it during the night." She reached out to take it from him. "The straps were probably cutting into my shoulders."

"Don't explain. I always prefer to sleep in as little as possible. Excessive nightwear went out with Victorian times, and I'm glad to find that I have a modern wife."

Cindy studied him through lowered lashes. His

teak-brown skin would only grow more handsomely virile under the sunniest skies, and the vision of him in bed, free of any restrictive clothing, made her shut her eyes completely to block out the unwanted thoughts it generated.

"I came to ask you if you'd like to do some sightseeing. I have an early morning business appointment and then I'm free for the rest of the day."

Cindy's eyes flew open as the bed swayed under Boyd's weight and she felt the warmth of his breath only inches from her cheek. His hands reached up to smooth her hair away from her face and his eyes met hers, imprisoning them with his gaze.

"If you keep looking at me like that I'm not going to be able to leave this room and the only sightseeing we'll do will be of each other."

The open desire blazing in his eyes made Cindy acutely aware of the full meaning of his words and she rolled away from him, only to find her escape impeded because he was sitting on the end of the top sheet, imprisoning her. She slid lower in the bed, trying to keep the sheet over the bareness of her breasts.

"I really would enjoy seeing Mexico City. I've never been here before."

"You might enjoy staying in this room with me," Boyd said softly. "I'm certain I could introduce you to some pleasures you've never experienced before."

"Oh, Boyd!" It was almost a plea. "Must you ruin everything? For a minute, I really believed you were trying to be nice."

"Cindy, honey, you have a lot to learn. There's nothing lewd about making love. But I'll have to prove that to you on another occasion. Today I'm quite serious about showing you around Mexico City. I'll go to my business meeting, and then you'll feel free to get out from under that sheet."

He rose and walked toward the door. "But you're really going to have to learn to be less modest in the presence of your husband. Even maidenly chastity has its limits." He glanced back, flashed an enigmatic smile in her direction and left the room.

Chapter Five

Nervously uncertain whether Boyd would decide to reenter her room unannounced, Cindy tugged the sheet free of the bed and, wrapping it around herself toga style, walked to the bathroom. The tepid shower water tingled a bit as it ran over her still sensitive skin but the sharply piercing pain of yesterday was gone. She washed quickly and slipped into a toweling robe before trying to select a comfortable outfit which, while looking attractive, would still meet the demands of both the day's heat and the tender state of her skin.

She finally chose a multicolored floral printed backless sundress with a princess waistline and wide shoulder straps. By the time she had brushed her hair and slipped into a pair of low-heeled raffia sandals, a knock sounded at the door. She answered it to find a waiter with a breakfast tray which Boyd had ordered for her.

The waiter wheeled his service cart out to the terrace, set the food on the round, glass-topped table and bowed politely as he left the room. Cindy was disappointed to find that Boyd had selected a typically American breakfast, rather than letting her sample any of the local dishes. She drank half the orange juice and made a feeble attempt to eat the bacon and eggs before pushing them aside to concentrate on the buttered toast and black coffee which were the usual ingredients of her breakfast. But somehow she had no appetite for even them. Sighing lethargically, she folded her white linen napkin beside the half-empty coffee cup and left the table.

Boyd hadn't indicated exactly when he'd be finished with his business appointment, but she assumed that he expected her to remain in the suite, meekly awaiting his return. She paced the room, haunted by the events of the previous evening and this morning. Whatever else she might think about their peculiar relationship, she couldn't deny that Boyd's mere presence evoked an unbidden response from her body. At times like this, when she was alone, she could calmly and clearly enumerate all her many reasons for harboring a deep dislike of Boyd; but when he entered the room, dominating it with his authoritative masculinity, freezing her with his eyes and tantalizing her with his touch, then wildly turbulent emotions took hold of her senses, sending them reeling and relegating all coherent thoughts to the forgotten recesses of her mind.

She blushed wildly when she remembered the way he had taunted her about his ability to arouse in her a sensuality which she hadn't known existed. It was all too apparent that he was fully aware of her body's involuntary response to his expertly seductive powers, and she realized that it was only a matter of time before he would stop playing with her and claim her body as his own. Her sense of utter helplessness revolved round and round in her brain, pushing her to a state of restless agitation which suddenly made the silent privacy of the suite too much to bear. She needed the company of other people, the sound of other voices, anything that would erase the tormenting image of Boyd's mocking face from her mind.

Slinging her white raffia shoulder bag over her arm,

she fled into the deserted hallway, stepping eagerly onto the elevator when it stopped and riding quickly to the lobby. She decided to station herself in one of the plush red armchairs near the elevators, where she would be in a good position to see Boyd as he approached them on his way upstairs.

For a while she amused herself by studying the different people walking through the crowded lobby. There seemed to be businessmen from all over the world, as well as fashionably attired women who looked as if they had spent hours of time and huge amounts of money in pursuit of such sophistication. Somehow their presence made her mind drift to the graceful women who had hovered over Boyd at dinner last night. It had been painfully evident that they had all found him immensely attractive. Obviously his years of rakish living had imbued him with a potent male magnetism which most women found difficult to resist. And, she thought wryly, much as she wished it were not so, she was no different. His slightest touch made her traitorous body forget the fervent promises of her mind.

She shook her head resentfully as she realized that it was quite impossible to stop thinking about Boyd. Even as she sat here, watching other people, her thoughts drifted grudgingly to him. Annoyance with her inability to forget him made her leave her seat and wander aimlessly about the lobby, searching for some nameless thing that would drive all thoughts of Boyd from her rambling mind.

A softly lit arcade off the main lobby was lined with small, expensive boutiques and she edged closer to them, casually glancing in the shop windows as she strolled aimlessly past. One of the shops featured native carftwork and she stopped to admire the fine basketry and intricately designed silver jewelry, but her

94

eyes were caught and held by a handwoven white batiste peignoir set so simply fashioned that she could not help but admire the gauzy texture of the fabric and the minutely meticulous stitchery which outlined the low V neckline before sweeping below the rib cage to meet and end at the small of the back.

Lightly possessive fingers stroked the nape of her neck and she turned in indignant shock, only to meet Boyd's complacently smiling eyes as he bent his head to place a feathery kiss on her softly blushing cheek. He seemed completely at ease, in contrast to her own flustered embarrassment as he lifted his head and lowered his arm, circling her waist and drawing her to him.

Turning his attention back to the two men with whom he had been walking before he saw her, Boyd said, "Gentlemen, I'd like you to meet my wife, Cindy Hamilton." He smiled at her and nodded toward his male companions. "Señor Diego and Señor Corona; they own the largest insurance company in Mexico and they've just signed a contract to have us computerize the entire operation."

Cindy smiled warmly as each man bowed and kissed her hand lightly in the continental fashion that was the accepted form of respectful greeting in Mexico.

"Now, gentlemen," Boyd said, shaking hands with each of them, "I hope you'll excuse me. I promised to take my wife sightseeing before we return to the States, and apparently she's become so impatient with my absence that she's decided to start on her own."

The two Mexicans smiled perceptively and, after confirming some future meeting dates, walked away, leaving Boyd and Cindy standing alone.

"See anything you like?" Boyd asked as his eyes quickly surveyed the contents of the store window.

"Not really," she replied, yet somehow she was

unable to stop herself from stealing one last glance at the peignoir set.

Boyd's eyes followed hers and he tightened his grip on her waist, leading her into the shop. Speaking rapidly in Spanish, he pointed to the peignoir set and waited patiently while the salesgirl removed it from the display case. Taking it from her hands, he held it up to Cindy's motionless body, his hands stroking the soft folds of the fabric as he outlined the contours of her slender form. Smoky desire clouded his somber eyes as they languidly roamed over her, studying every aspect of her appearance. Almost imperceptibly, a small muscle tightened at the side of his jaw and the dusky passion fled from his eyes, to be swiftly replaced by the cold aloofness to which she had become so accustomed.

He let the nightgown fall away from her body, gathered it up in one hand, nodded his head and once again spoke to the salesgirl in rapid Spanish which was almost totally incomprehensible to Cindy. The salesgirl smiled and took the peignoir set Boyd held out to her while he grasped Cindy's elbow and guided her out of the store. She moved quickly before him, unable to comprehend his sudden change of mood. No wonder she couldn't understand her own feelings about him. His erratic behavior was completely unpredictable. Who could tell where the warm, seductive lover left off and the cold, demanding business tycoon took over? His personality was entirely too complex for her to fathom and she knew she would have to keep her wits about her if she didn't want to end up completely dominated by him.

"Are you very hungry, or can you wait until I take you to a favorite little place of mine that's off the tourist-guide list?"

"I'm not at all hungry," she answered coolly, "and

I'm very eager to do some sightseeing before we return home."

"A rather odd attitude to have on one's honeymoon, wouldn't you say?"

"No more so than spending all of one's time conducting business, wouldn't you agree?"

"*Touché*, my love. I see marriage hasn't dulled your sharp little tongue."

"I should hope not. I'd never stand a chance against you if it had."

"You stand no chance anyway, my sweet. I always get what I want, and any challenge you present only whets my appetite." He smiled rakishly and guided her down a wide, imposing avenue which led to a huge plaza. It was as if she had stepped out of her architecturally modern hotel and into an ancient world, half Aztec and half sixteenth-century Spanish. She looked to Boyd for an explanation.

"The Plaza of Three Cultures," he said. "First we have the reconstructed ruins of the main temple of the Aztecs; then we have the original home of Hernán Cortés and the *Catedral Metropolitania*, legacies of the Spanish *conquistadores*. And, as you have noticed, we've just emerged from a modern hotel complex, symbol of the new Mexico. Quite an impressive cultural heritage, isn't it?"

"You're very knowledgeable about Mexico, aren't you?" Cindy said as he led her to the chauffeured limousine.

"If you want to do business with people you have to understand their country." he replied after he had settled himself in the seat next to hers and issued directions to the chauffeur. "I always try to learn as much as I can about clients before I attempt to do business with them. It's a practice that has made me feel much more secure and has led to my being quite comfortable in most situations."

His glance settled meaningfully on Cindy and she turned away to escape his disconcerting gaze by pretending to watch the passing scenery. Yes, she thought, Boyd did seem to be entirely at ease under most circumstances. Even their travesty of a marriage failed to ruffle his masterful self-discipline. She grimaced at her melancholy reflection in the car window and wondered if he had devoted any time to learning about her so he could handle his unwilling bride without losing his ever-present composure.

"A penny for your thoughts," he said, as his hand slowly came to rest at the nape of her neck.

She twisted in her seat, placing her rigid back firmly against the inside of the car door so that she had drawn herself beyond his reach. "I was just wondering how much you knew about me."

"I know everything there is to know about you," he said, smiling indulgently. "You were only eleven years old when I first came to work at Templeton Industries. Your hair was in pigtails and you had braces on your teeth. I watched the pigtails turn to shining curls; the braces were removed, and the skinny little girl matured into an enticing young woman."

"It's just like you to list my physical characteristics without bothering to mention any mental and emotional attributes I might have."

"Ah, but I'm just now beginning to appreciate those other qualities. Prior to our recent engagement and marriage, I was never aware of your sharp claws and vicious tongue. You see, I was willing to marry you purely on the basis of your shapely little body."

"Liar!" she spat out. "You married me on the basis of a contract which gave you the controlling interest in Templeton Industries!"

"My, but you make me sound mercenary," he mocked.

She satisfied herself by glaring at him and turned back toward the window.

They had traveled south, entering a more open area, and the car pulled to a halt at the edge of a huge lake in a parklike atmosphere. The chauffeur opened the door and Boyd helped Cindy out of the car.

"Lake Xochimilco," he said, pointing to the large island-studded body of water. "The Aztecs created these floating gardens centuries ago. They built rafts on the lake, covered them with soil and began cultivating fruits, vegetables and flowers. The plants gradually took root, anchored themselves to the soil at the bottom of the lake—and the rafts became lush islands."

He led Cindy toward the row of colorfully decorated boats which lined the shore of the lake. The arched roof of each boat reminded her of the covered wagons in which the American pioneers had traveled west. A woman's name curved across the top of each arch and intricately carved curlicues rose above the roof. Boyd walked purposefully, as if he had a definite destination in mind.

"Now, if we can find *Conchita* . . . ah, there she is," he said, hurrying Cindy to a boat with the name *Conchita* colorfully written across its curving top.

"Pedro, so good to see you," he said to the short, swarthy man who came forward to greet them. "I'd like you to meet my wife, Cindy."

Boyd passed Cindy's hand to Pedro, then followed her on board. Pedro led them to a small cloth-covered table at the back of the boat and held out a chair until Cindy had seated herself. For a while, he and Boyd conducted a laughter-punctuated conversation in rapidly spoken Spanish; then he disappeared, returning a few minutes later with a large picnic basket which he placed on the table in front of Boyd. He soon walked to the side of the boat and began releasing it from its moorings.

Boyd started taking food from the basket and Cindy noticed that the boat was beginning to edge away from the shoreline, following a route which would lead them to the flourishing islands at the center of the lake.

"Now," Boyd said, as he poured some chilled sangria into her glass, "we shall enjoy a delicious lunch expertly prepared by Pedro's wife while he guides us through these fabulous floating gardens."

Cindy began nibbling at the fresh melon and spicy chicken. Soon she was enjoying her food with a robust appetite that Boyd obviously found amusing. She held a large garlicky shrimp suspended on her fork while her eyes met his. She was too embarrassed to swallow her food when he seemed to be disregarding his own in favor of studying her.

"Don't stop, Cindy; I didn't mean to stare. I'm just surprised to find you enjoying the food with such relish. Most American women are afraid to try any foreign dishes. I usually wind up buying them a steak or a hamburger."

She placed her fork on her plate. "I like trying different foods, and Pedro's wife is a very good cook."

Boyd's eyes held hers, attempting to communicate the thoughts concealed within their suddenly stormy depths, but he appeared to be debating with himself, unable or unwilling to express these musings aloud. Cindy's skin felt singed, burned to a crisp by his fiery eyes. She blinked her own eyes to break the contact and looked over the side of the boat, studying the profusion of colorful foliage on the island they were passing.

Briefly, her mind registered the flamboyant beauty of the plants, marveling that these spacious multicolored gardens had grown from the small rafts Boyd had described. But then her thoughts returned to more personal matters, mainly the effect Boyd's volatile personality was having on her own seesawing emotions. He could be so charming if he chose to be. When his eyes found hers they made her feel utterly feminine and it became difficult to remember how much she hated him while his manner was so pleasant and relaxed. A small spark at the back of her brain told her that maybe she was mistaken; maybe Boyd wasn't as cold and ruthless as she believed him to be. Then she remembered that he had married her without any thoughts of love. Nothing could be more callous than the contract he had entered into merely to get control of her father's company. She sighed hopelessly at her own inability to find a solution to her problem.

"Tired?" Boyd's softly spoken question brought her out of her reverie.

"Yes, I suppose I am. I think we've attempted to cram too much into this short trip. I know that you came here for business reasons, and I really appreciate your taking the time to do some sightseeing with me."

He reached across the table, resting his hand on hers. "I enjoyed every minute of your company. I'm only sorry that we don't have more time, but this is a big contract and I do have to get back to the office to see that it's correctly implemented. We won't always be so rushed, and then we can spend more time together, sharing experiences and learning about each other."

Boyd signaled for Pedro to return the boat to shore. He thanked him for the lunch and folded several crisp bills into his hand before helping Cindy off the boat and walking back to the car. The wine and the fresh air, combined with the lingering effects of the previous day's sunburn, sent a relaxed lethargy flowing through her veins. She leaned back into the soft leather upholstery of the limousine and closed her eyes.

"Sleepy?" Boyd asked, in a voice so soft that it was almost a caress. Without waiting for a reply, he placed his arm on her shoulder and drew her toward him, nestling her head against his broad chest and clasping her weary body against the bracing strength of his.

"Try to get some rest," he murmured, the warmth of his breath nuzzling her earlobe.

Cindy had assumed that they would be returning to the hotel, but when she felt Boyd gently nudging her awake she looked out the window and realized that they were at the airport. She was still groggy from her short nap and leaned against him for support as he helped her toward the private jet, leading her up the steps and into the rear compartment, where he settled her comfortably into the bed.

She stretched sleepily. "What about our things from the hotel?"

"Don't worry about them," he said, slipping her shoes off her feet. "It seemed foolish to go back just to collect our belongings, so I had the hotel staff pack them and send them ahead to the plane. If you've enjoyed this little trip, perhaps you'd better plan on leaving some clothing in each of our *pied-à-terres*. It makes traveling a lot simpler."

She couldn't answer him. It seemed that he was inviting her to accompany him again despite the fact that she had behaved so poorly when he was entertaining his guests in the restaurant. Why had he decided to give her another chance? Why was he treating her so kindly? Her mind was completely befuddled by all these thoughts and she couldn't find the words with which to reply.

He was looking down at her, silently studying her face while his fingers absently massaged the arch of her foot. "Well, you don't have to make a decision right now. You haven't even had a chance to recover from this trip, and here I am talking about new journeys. You might as well nap on the way home; I have some work I want to get ready for the engineering committee so they can go into immediate action on this new installation." He pressed his long fingers firmly into her foot before dropping it back onto the bed.

It was dark when the plane landed in San Jose. Boyd lifted Cindy in his arms, carrying her off the plane and paying no attention to her embarrassed protests.

"Please put me down, Boyd. I can walk. Everyone is staring at us."

"So what?" Boyd smiled. "You're a new bride, remember? And I'm a groom who enjoys the feel of his bride in his arms."

He tightened his grip until Cindy stopped squirming, only releasing her when they had reached the big gray Rolls-Royce belonging to Templeton Industries.

She colored under Leon's patently amused gaze and mumbled a barely audible greeting when the chauffeur tipped his hat to her. Cindy knew he would lose no time in spreading the word that she had exited the plane in Boyd's arms. Everyone would assume that she and Boyd had been on a romantic honeymoon trip.

She looked at Boyd seated next to her, smiling complacently as Leon drove them away from the airport. Was this all part of his prearranged scheme to convince everyone that they were happily married? Was that why he had been so amiable during the last few hours? This disturbing conjecture seemed increasingly plausible as she watched him sigh contentedly and close his eyes, leaning his dark head against the maroon leather upholstery. He was so pleased with himself, like the cat who had just eaten all the fresh cream. Obviously, he had accomplished his goal.

Meanwhile, she noticed that her stomach was beginning to hurt. Perhaps it was just the result of nervous tension. There was certainly no denying the taut state of her emotions. She hoped that she would feel more comfortable once she had a chance to shower and get into her own bed. Then she looked at the man dozing peacefully beside her and remembered that she wasn't returning to her own home but would, in fact, be going home with Boyd.

The car slowly wound its way through Los Altos Hills, turning in at a private road with fieldstone pillars on either side of the entry and a long fence of wrought-iron railings delineating the property's boundaries. The road followed a winding path through wooded acres until it reached a vale of tranquility set between the sloping hills. In the midst of the glen stood a huge fieldstone castle with massive leaded-glass windows and sharply pointed turrets. Cindy pulled herself upright, opened her eyes wide and stared in disbelief. It was as if she had suddenly been transported from twentieth-century California to medieval England.

But the car moved past the circular driveway leading to the castle and slowly continued on along a much narrower road, finally stopping before a small stone cottage. This house was constructed of the same materials as the larger one but lacked the other's regal majesty; it was a simpler structure which would serve as a vacation cottage or perhaps a cozy home for a small family. The castle had seemed dark and deserted; this house had a warm, welcoming appearance.

Boyd's long brown lashes flickered when Leon came around to open his car door. His lithe, athletic body came instantly alert as he unfolded his long limbs from the seat of the car and reached a strong hand toward Cindy to help out.

"Welcome home," he said as she joined him in front of the house.

Without waiting for her response, he led her toward the front door and turned swiftly to lift her effortlessly into his arms. "I believe it's customary to carry a bride over the threshold of her new home," he said, smiling down at her.

Cindy's head rested against the brawny strength of his chest; her arms slipped instinctively around his neck and she heard every heartbeat and felt every ripple of his sinewy shoulder muscles as he carried her out of the darkness and into the softly lit warmth of the tiny hall.

Leon had deposited their suitcases near the entry and he tipped his hat as he left, closing the door behind him. Cindy waited anxiously for Boyd to put her down, but he seemed in no hurry to release her. For her part, she would be willing to spend forever in the warm security of his embrace, even if he was only prompted to hold her because convention decreed he should do so. She closed her eyes, sighed deeply and turned her face toward his chest.

His arms tightened possessively about her as he carried her through the house. Although she was aware that they had passed several rooms, she saw nothing; her eyes were closed against reality as she reveled in the strength of the arms that were transporting her.

She felt herself being lowered, then released, and her opened palms stroked something soft and warm. With her head resting against a downy pillow, she opened her eyes, strangely disappointed at having lost the protective shelter of Boyd's eager arms.

She turned her head slightly and their eyes met. Boyd gave her little time to reflect on the situation; he had placed her on his bed and was now in the process of removing his shirt and tie, after which he tossed them next to his jacket on the chair at the side of the room.

The bed tilted as he lowered himself to join her. His eyes blazed with desire and she dropped her own so that he wouldn't see the answering passion burning within them. She stared at the broad hair-covered chest plagued by the same uneven breathing that was marked by her own heaving breasts before finally closing her eyes against the sight that was only increasing the inferno raging within her.

His index finger caressed the sensitive cord at the base of her neck while his thumb lifted her chin so that her face was exposed to his penetrating gaze. Then his thumb traced the fine bones of her cheek, moving slowly up her jaw and curving sensually into the pink shell of her ear. She twisted on the bed, moaning as her senses were frantically ravaged by a wild craving she hadn't known existed. His lips settled gently on her temple, following a slow, lingering path down to her shuttered eyes. She was seized by an overwhelming desire to slip her arms around his neck and feel once more the sinewy strength of the powerful muscles rippling through his broad back.

Boyd's lips blazed a seductive trail across the burning skin of her face and grazed lightly against her lips, demanding an immediate response to their butterfly strokes.

Without warning, Cindy's palms pressed against his chest as she pushed him away from her, turned on her side and clutched her stomach, meanwhile moaning in obvious pain.

Boyd stood up, his breathing heavy and ragged as he struggled to find his habitually constant composure. For an instant it seemed that he, too, had lost control over his usually tightly held emotions.

"What the devil is wrong with you?" his hoarse voice ground out. "Is this your idea of some nerve-racking tease? Is this part of your vendetta to get back at me? I warn you, Cindy, you're carrying things too far. I'm going to teach you a lesson about leading a man on—especially your husband, who has a legal right to sample your charms."

He reached out when suddenly she bolted for the bathroom, clutching her stomach as she ran.

"Why didn't you tell me that your stomach was acting up?" he said a few moments later as he combed his fingers through her hair, smoothing it away from her damp, heated face. "I forgot that this was your first time out of the country. My body is so used to sampling native foods that I didn't remember to be more cautious where you were concerned. Pedro's wife is a good cook, but I can't vouch for the sterility of the water she used to wash the fruits and vegetables."

"I'll be all right," she said. "It's just that I never get sick and yet it seems that all you've done since we've been married is administer to my infirmities, first the sunburn and now this."

"Well, I won't claim to be pleased with the situation." Boyd smiled. "It hasn't exactly been a perfect honeymoon, but at least I feel better knowing it wasn't my touch that sent you running. You do seem to become ill at the most inappropriate times."

Cindy realized that the incident had been more disturbing to her than to Boyd. For one tempestuous moment, all thoughts of the wretched marriage contract had vanished from her brain, and if not for the pain in her stomach she would have become a very willing accomplice in Boyd's seductive conquest. But when she looked at him now, all the passionate flames which had seared her body so intently a short while before were gone from his eyes. The sinewy muscles which had tensed above her just minutes ago, tantalizing her wildly careening senses with their invitation to touch, were once again shielded from her sight by his shirt.

"Feeling better?"

She nodded. "Much better. I'm more exhausted than anything else."

"Well, then, why don't we get you settled in for the night?" he asked, shifting her gently while he removed the spread. "I'll get your nightgown. My housekeeper has placed the clothing your mother sent over in these drawers."

The sheer white nylon nightgown he offered her hung from his bent finger by its narrow spaghetti straps. He seemed strangely uneasy as he handed her the extremely feminine garment. She sat up to take it from him but was immediately forced back against the pillows by a recurrence of the queasy feeling in her stomach.

"I'm afraid you'll have to hand it down to me. I'll change into it later when my stomach isn't so jumpy."

"You'll be more comfortable once you've gotten undressed. Let me help you."

"That's not necessary. I'm sure I'll be fine in just a while."

"Don't tell me you're modest?" he mocked. "I thought our relationship had gone beyond that. There was very little of you I didn't see—and, indeed, touch—the other evening."

"It's not the same."

"Isn't it?" He smiled. "I told you then that I had no wish to make love to a woman in pain. When I do take you, darling, the only pain you'll feel will be the sweetly piercing pain of love and the agony of desire."

Cindy was too shocked by the arrogance of his statement to protest when he began slipping her sundress off her shoulders. She was relieved when he gently turned her onto her stomach and in one swift movement seemed to unzip her dress and unhook her bra at the same time. He slipped the dress down to her waist and gripped the elastic of her panties before pulling every stitch of her clothing down over her ankles. His unhesitating expertise indicated that he was well versed in separating a woman from her clothing. She didn't like to think about how he had acquired his experience, and she tried to block out all thoughts of her own nudity as she heard the rustle of her clothing falling on the bedside chair.

A gently inquisitive finger traced the narrow ridges of her spine, broadening to a caressing palm which tenderly stroked the smooth curves of her hip. Then she was turned once more and Boyd placed his hands beneath her arms, lifting her until she was seated upright on the bed. His eyes raked over her body, savoring each minute detail as if committing every line and curve to memory. He sighed and slipped the gown over her shoulders, raising her body as he lowered the garment until it fell to her ankles. He smoothed the sheer material against her skin, lingering over the warmth of her body as if he were reluctant to release her from his touch.

Finally he groaned with barely hidden disappointment and ran his hand down her arm before lifting himself from the bed.

"Hard as it is, I'm going to keep my word. Pleasant dreams. I'll take a cold shower and sleep in the guest room. Call out if you should need me; I'll be right across the hall."

Chapter Six

A soothing warmth stroked the length of Cindy's bare arm as she forced her sleep-shrouded eyes to open, blinking away the fuzzy haze of slumber and focusing them on Boyd's well-tanned face. He lowered his head to place a gentle kiss on her soft, red lips.

"Good morning. How are you today?"

She clutched at the sheet, feeling terribly self-conscious when she saw that, having showered, shaved and dressed, he apparently was ready to leave for work. She tried to sit up, but he pressed her back against the silky-smooth pillow, his thin gold watch gleaming brightly amid the short dark hairs emerging from his crisp white cuff.

"Don't get up. I only wanted to see how you were and tell you that I was leaving for work. Mrs. Gregory, the housekeeper, will be here at nine o'clock to get your breakfast."

Boyd's hands had risen to Cindy's shoulders and he studied her face as he rhythmically kneaded them with a slow, sensuously massaging motion. It had become increasingly difficult for her to resist the forces that surged between them whenever they met. Even when her mind told her that their relationship was based purely on business motivations, her heart responded helplessly to the slightest touch of his provocative hands. Oh, no, she thought to herself. Could it be? Could she actually have fallen in love with her cold-hearted husband? Never, she assured herself, never.

"Do you have to go to work?" She could hardly believe that she had spoken the words.

"Unfortunately, yes. I realize that we haven't had much of a honeymoon, but I promise to make it up to you when things quiet down. Now, I'd better get going or ten engineers are going to wonder where the chairman of the meeting is."

The kiss he planted on her lips this time was as forceful as the man himself. His ragged breathing when he checked himself and drew away from her left no doubt in Cindy's mind that for once Boyd had come close to forgetting his business commitments. She found the thought pleasing and smiled to herself when he groaned and left the room.

She stretched out in the luxuriously large bed, reveling in the cool smoothness of the finely woven silk sheets and the cozy warmth of the fleecy comforter. All the piercing pain of her food poisoning had disappeared during the night, and the bright sunlight peeking through the thin blinds made her anxious to be up and about. She found her blue velour robe and walked toward the adjoining bathroom.

She had just finished showering and was sitting on the edge of the bed changing into her faded blue jeans when the door flew open.

"Boyd . . . I just got back . . ." The words hung in the air as the striking brunette saw Cindy and froze in surprise. "I'm so sorry. I didn't know Boyd had company." She quickly turned and fled from the room.

The shock on Cindy's face was no less than that on the face of her astonished visitor. Boyd had told her to expect the housekeeper, but by no stretch of the imagination could Cindy ever visualize this expensively clad intruder as anyone's housekeeper. Yet the girl had entered the room with the proprietary air of someone who had every right to be there.

Cindy stared at the closed door for several minutes, unable to move long after the woman had left the room. Then anger at her own naïveté replaced the immobilizing astonishment of moments ago. How foolish she had been to let Boyd's deceitful charm lull her into forgetting about his reputation. Just like everyone else, she had fallen under his spell and he had almost convinced her that she was something more to him than merely the means of gaining control over her father's company.

Well, fortunately, the unexpected appearance of one of his many women had brought her to her senses before she had actually fallen prey to his powerfully seductive schemes. Shame at her own abandoned behavior earlier that morning quickly changed to vindictive anger when she visualized the triumphant arrogance that Boyd would have felt after he had made her respond to his touch. And in all honesty she could not deny that it was only Boyd's inflexible dedication to his business commitments that had stopped them from consummating their marriage before he left for work. She had been entirely under his power, with every inch of her being aching for the feeling of his strong arms and the tantalizing touch of his sensuous hands and intoxicating lips. She was certainly glad that the attraction between them was only physical.

For once she was grateful for Boyd's overwhelming devotion to his business affairs. She laughed mirthlessly as she stood up and fastened the waistband of her jeans. He would never know how close she had come to succumbing to the plans he had forged so cold-bloodedly. But that same mercenary streak in his character which had made him marry her also made him put his business commitments first, and now, having been granted a reprieve, she resolved that she would never again be deceived by him.

Determined pride mingled with righteous indignation and her entire body bristled as she made plans for a future which would show Boyd that she was thoroughly repelled by his touch. The thought brought a complacent smile to her lips and she felt more confident than she had in weeks.

Curiosity got the better of her as she pulled a pale blue turtleneck jersey over her head, and she began to wonder about the identity of the beautiful visitor who had beat such a hasty retreat upon finding her in Boyd's bed. Certainly the woman must have been enjoying more than a casual relationship with him for her to have entered the privacy of his bedroom with such apparent ease. This speculation brought an inexplicably queasy feeling to the pit of Cindy's stomach, quickly destroying all the smug satisfaction with which she had been making her plans for vengeful retribution.

Instinct told her that she would not satisfy her curiosity by brooding in her room, and her empty stomach was noisily indicating its immediate need for breakfast. Squaring her shoulders defiantly, she opened the bedroom door and walked into the hallway. The house was still but the strong scent of coffee indicated that someone was busy brewing the delicious liquid. It was easy enough to find the kitchen; she merely followed the pungent odor to its source.

She halted midstride when she approached the threshold of the room. A plump, gray-haired woman stood at the sink beating some eggs in a small white bowl. Cindy supposed that this was Mrs. Gregory, the housekeeper, and bid her a cheery good morning. Then the smile vanished from her lips as she caught sight of the attractive brunette seated at the small, round table.

She went numb, suddenly feeling like an intruder in her own home. Obviously her presence had not upset the girl enough to make her leave Boyd's house, and she apparently was also on familiar terms with Mrs. Gregory. Cindy's mouth felt dry as she groped for words; just how, she wondered, does a wife greet her husband's mistress?

In a smooth feline movement the girl rose from the table and walked toward Cindy, extending her hand graciously. "I'm Lorraine Hanley, a very good friend of Boyd's. Please forgive my intrusion this morning, but I've been out of town and I had no idea that Boyd had taken himself a wife."

Cindy grasped the girl's hand and smiled weakly, marveling at Lorraine's poise and self-assurance. Her own composure was at the crumbling point and all she could think to say was "I'm Cindy Templeton . . . pleased to meet you."

Lorraine lifted her eyebrows and a delighted grin covered her beautiful face. "You are a very recent bride, aren't you? You haven't even adjusted to your new name. Unless, of course, I've been misinformed and Boyd is still up to his old tricks. You *are* Boyd's wife? I mean, your name *is* Cindy Hamilton, isn't it?"

Cindy was saved from responding to Lorraine's icy inquiry by Mrs. Gregory's calm, motherly voice.

"Please sit down, Mrs. Hamilton. Mr. Hamilton left a note saying that you weren't feeling well. He suggested that I let you sleep in, so I haven't bothered you about breakfast. But you do look rather pale and I think it would be advisable for you to have something to eat if you feel your stomach has settled down."

Cindy moved to the dark oak table and seated herself while Mrs. Gregory placed a steaming mug of coffee before her. Lorraine returned to the seat opposite Cindy and held out her cup for Mrs. Gregory.

"My coffee seems to have grown cold; would you mind heating it up?" She smiled sweetly at the older woman, then turned her attention to Cindy. "You're John Templeton's daughter, aren't you?"

"That's right," Cindy replied.

Lorraine took a sip of her freshly heated coffee. "I gather that this marriage gives Boyd additional shares in the stock of Templeton Industries . . . perhaps even control?"

The quizzical smile on Lorraine's lips demanded a response, but Cindy was too unnerved to say anything. She was certain that her voice would crack, betraying her confusion before she had gotten halfway through her reply. Tightening her hand around the warm coffee mug, she slowly lifted it to her lips and took a short sip of the hot liquid.

Mrs. Gregory placed a dish of creamy yellow scrambled eggs and four crisp bacon strips in front of her. Cindy glanced up at her through the veil of steam rising from her coffee cup in time to catch the icy stare the housekeeper had tossed in Lorraine's direction. Although her position as an employee might preclude her from voicing any sentiments about Lorraine's remark, her narrowed eyes made her feelings about the other woman quite clear.

Lorraine puckered her beautifully colored lips petulantly. "There's no need for everyone to act so shocked. I've been well aware of Boyd's desire to be master of Templeton Industries for several years now. After all, it is the most profitable computer company in the area and he does enjoy picturing himself as the king

115

of this little silicon-dominated valley. In fact, except for my childishly impulsive reaction to a silly disagreement we had, my father would have helped Boyd purchase the company and this entire ridiculous situation could have been avoided. However, I'll wait until I've had a chance to speak with Boyd. I'm sure he'll want to have a long discussion with his charming new wife after he hears what I have to tell him." She rose from the table, flung her sleek brown hair over her shoulders and swept regally out the back door.

Cindy watched through the organdy-curtained kitchen window while Lorraine slid behind the wheel of a shiny red Jaguar, started up the motor and navigated her way down the long gravelly driveway with a reckless abandon that sent small gray pebbles flying in all directions.

Cindy tried to concentrate on her food, but the confused jumble of thoughts buzzing around in her brain seemed to fall like a massive lump straight to her stomach. Shaking her head in bewilderment at this latest turn of events in her relationship with Boyd, she pushed back her chair and brought her plate over to the sink.

Mrs. Gregory puckered her lips in disapproval at the sight of the food left on Cindy's plate. "You'll never recover from that stomach upset if you don't start eating again."

"I'll be fine," Cindy said, somehow pleased by the older woman's concern for her well-being. "It's nearly lunchtime anyway. I thought I'd visit my mother this afternoon and I'll have lunch with her."

Cindy's red Mustang had been brought to the cottage along with the rest of her personal belongings. She felt as if she were greeting a long-lost friend when she settled herself behind the wheel and started up the engine. Four years was a long time to be together, she reflected. She was quite sure that she and Boyd would never remain married for that length of time.

Traffic was light on the freeway and she arrived at her mother's home within twenty minutes. After parking her car at the far side of the circular driveway, she used her key to let herself in, then called out to Anna and her mother while walking through to the kitchen.

They were both seated at the small breakfast table and rose to greet her with hugs and kisses. Anna motioned her to a seat between the two of them and began filling a plate with lettuce, tomatoes and chicken salad.

"If I had known you were coming for lunch, I would have prepared something special. As it is, you'll just have to settle for potluck. I thought you'd still be away on your honeymoon."

Cindy picked up her fork and made a small, ineffective stab at the chicken salad. "It wasn't really a honeymoon. There were some business associates that Boyd thought I should meet, and then he had to return for an important conference this morning."

"Hmm . . ." Her mother's slightly raised eyebrows registered her disappointment. "Not a very romantic beginning to your marriage, was it?"

Cindy pasted a bright smile on her face. "I suppose we're just not very romantic people." She quickly turned the conversation to the sights they had seen in Mexico City, and the rest of her visit passed easily.

It was still early afternoon when Cindy turned the car toward the cottage in Los Altos Hills. She shook her head grimly when she considered how distressed her mother would be if she ever learned just what she and Boyd had been thinking when they had planned their marriage.

It seemed impossible for Cindy to remember that just a few short weeks ago she had been a carefree college student. Now she was a married woman, wed to a man whose only interest in her was to control her emotions to the same degree that he already controlled her business affairs.

She slowed the car as she entered the winding driveway and once more her interest was caught by the majesty of the palatial dwelling which dominated the landscape, making Boyd's small home seem insignificant by comparison. Somehow it seemed entirely unlike Boyd to have anything second-rate, and she couldn't understand how he would be content to live in the shadow of this gargantuan castle, dilapidated though it seemed.

Curiosity overcame her inhibitions and she turned the Mustang off the narrow road and onto the circular driveway leading to the massive front door of the huge stone house. She shut off the ignition and studied the exterior façade of the home. Although many windows were boarded up and a section of one tower seemed to have fallen away, the handcrafted beauty of the dwelling could not fail to impress her.

The place appeared to be completely deserted, so she opened her door and began walking around the exterior, hoping to get a glimpse inside.

The main floor of the house was above ground level and in order to look through the windows she had to go around to the back and mount the wide, fan-shaped steps leading to a stone-balustraded terrace. Although the land at the rear of the house was overgrown with weeds, she could see the bedraggled remnants of a formal garden languishing beneath the encroaching greenery.

Cindy shook her head at the sheer waste of it all. The artist in her mourned the loss of such timeless beauty. The artisans who had built this home were a vanishing breed, and even if one could find the craftsmen to reproduce these works of art the cost of duplicating such majesty would be astronomical.

Impressive French doors with small panes of heavy leaded glass separated the balcony from the interior of the house. Cindy used a tissue to wipe the dirt off one of the panes and then pressed her face against the glass, trying to peek into the room beyond. But the view was clouded because the interior of the glass was almost as dirty as the exterior.

Frustration seized her and she hastily jiggled the ornately carved brass doorknob, never expecting to find the entrance unlocked. But the knob turned easily in her hand and the door opened when she gave it a slight push inward. She hesitated for a moment. Much as she wanted to see the inside of the house, she was well aware that she was trespassing.

She decided that it would do no harm if she just stood on the balcony and peered into the room through the open door. The room had faded murals painted on its walls and was crammed with several massive pieces of furniture, protected by the graying white canvas of mildewed dustcovers.

One piece of furniture caught her roving eye and held it. Despite the fact that it was hidden beneath a tattered dustcover, she could distinguish the elegant outlines of a grand piano. The musician in her took over and, without even considering the propriety of her action, she entered the room and removed the protective cloth.

The beautifully patterned rosewood gleamed softly in the dim afternoon light as Cindy's fingers lovingly caressed the old ivory keys. Mesmerized by the beauty of the finely crafted instrument, she pulled the bench closer and seated herself. All thoughts of the outside world vanished as her fingers deftly moved over the keys.

She ended the piece she was playing with a resounding crescendo and leaned her head forward, resting her arms against the rosewood frame. She was drawn back to reality by the soft sound of clapping coming from behind her. Realizing that she had no right to be using the valuable instrument, she quickly prepared a mental apology and turned to face her audience. Instead of viewing some stranger who she had imagined would be the owner of the mansion, she found herself looking into the compelling brown eyes of her husband.

His arm rested on the doorjamb and his head was tilted to one side as he studied her. "I didn't mean to disturb you," he said, lowering his arm and walking toward her. "But you were so completely involved in your playing that you didn't even notice me arrive. I was afraid that you might be startled if you turned and found me watching you."

He reached down, removed her hands from the keyboard and lifted her to stand beside him. "You're really very good," he said, still holding her hands in his while tracing the graceful lines of her fingers with his own.

All Cindy's resolutions could not alter the intoxicating effect which Boyd's slightest touch had on her emotions. A cold chill shot through her body while, inexplicably, her hands began to grow moist with the dampness of perspiration. She quickly snatched them away from him.

"Does that surprise you? That I'm a good pianist? What do you suppose I've been studying all these years?"

"I'm sorry," he apologized. "I didn't mean to antagonize you; that was intended as a compliment. But you're right; I should have realized that you had been studying music and would naturally be very proficient in your field.

"In any case," he continued, "there was surely no need for you to snap my head off."

"I didn't snap your head off. I just resent the condescending manner you have toward me. You seem amazed to find that there's anything I can do well."

"The one thing you are indisputably expert at is turning a pleasant conversation into an all-out argument."

"I never remember having had that disagreeable trait until I married you. However, if we must argue, and that seems to be our destiny, then I suggest we do it in *your* home. I hardly think it would be proper for the owner of this house to find us having a domestic dispute on his property."

She walked away and started to cover the piano once more, but before she could complete her chore Boyd came up behind her and grasped her shoulders, turning her roughly toward him.

"Don't ever dismiss me like that. I'm your husband, not some lovesick puppy of a college boy who'll stand for that sort of nonsense."

"Heaven forbid that anyone should ever think that the great Boyd Hamilton was a lovesick boy. Such thoughts never entered my mind. You're too cold to even know the meaning of the word love. I just didn't think it would enhance your standing in the community if the owner should walk in to find you screaming at your wife."

"It just so happens that *I* am the owner, so that's one thing we don't have to worry about. Now, do you think you could settle down and address me in a more civilized manner?"

"You own this house?" Cindy said in disbelief. "Then why are you living in the cottage?"

Boyd glanced around the room. "This place is hardly

livable right now. Besides, I had no need for such a large home when I was a bachelor. The little place was much easier to get into shape, and at the time it suited my needs admirably."

"Then you don't intend to make any repairs to this house?"

"That's not what I said. Things have changed; I'm no longer a footloose bachelor. Now that I'm married, I'll need a larger home. In fact, I was rather pleased to see your car parked in the driveway. I thought this might be a good opportunity for us to explore the place and decide exactly what changes you'd like to make."

He ignored her protests and led her through the heavy oak doors and into a spacious entryway with a high ceiling. Here, too, the walls were covered with intricately hand-carved moldings and dusty murals. The wide, dark walnut steps of a freestanding stairway swept down to the foyer in a fluidly moving curve from the lofty gallery at the upper story of the house.

"You've already seen the music room," Boyd said, guiding her across the carrara marble floors. "The library and sitting room are really quite similar except for the bookshelves in one and the gilt furniture in the other. The kitchen is a bit out of date, but the architect did a quick study and has assured me that there's plenty of room to install a fully modern one with all the necessary appliances."

He motioned toward the stairway. "Would you like to see the upper floor? The view from the outside balcony is beautiful."

They started up the stairway and once again Cindy was struck by the absolute grandeur of the house. When they had reached the upper landing, she turned to look down. Even countless years of accumulated dust could not obliterate the shimmering beauty of the huge Waterford crystal chandelier. She tried to imagine how the house must have looked when it was well cared for and closed her eyes to enhance the vision.

"Don't tell me the height is making you dizzy," Boyd said, placing his arm around her waist.

The warmth of his hand propelled her into an instant state of alertness. "No, of course not. I was just trying to picture what the entry hall must have looked like when the house was first built . . . you know, when the marble floors glistened and the crystal fixture reflected the sheen of those hundreds of little candles."

Boyd smiled. "Ah, so you did notice that the house was constructed before electricity came into use. Well, I can't promise you the soft glow of candlelight; I enjoy the conveniences of electricity far too much. However, I intend to do everything else in my power to restore this house to the full measure of elegance envisioned by its original occupants."

His arm tightened around her waist. "Come on; daydreaming isn't going to get this place refurbished. I want you to see the rest of the rooms before it gets too dark." He led her down the wide corridor.

All the furniture in these rooms was covered with white muslin dustcovers just as the furniture on the lower floor had been. They seemed to move through an endless number of guest bedrooms. Finally Boyd opened the door to a huge room, dominated by a massive four-poster bed. The heavily embroidered silk curtains were tattered with age, but the graceful opulence of the furnishings had withstood the ravages of time.

Cindy looked in quickly, then turned away, unwilling to discuss the intended use of this room. Leaving the snug circle of Boyd's arm, she walked rapidly to the next room and flung the door open.

Her choice here was no better. The room had obviously been designed as a nursery.

123

Boyd had silently slipped up behind her. "Any thoughts on the decoration of these rooms?" he asked, smiling lightly.

"Not right now," Cindy replied, closing the door. "You'll have to give me some more time."

"Not too much time, I hope. As you already know, I'm not a very patient man."

She began walking rapidly toward the stairway. All the joy which she had experienced when she had first entered the house had now vanished. No longer was it a structure of beauty to be admired for its old-world craftsmanship; now it was Boyd's home, the home he was clearly determined to share with her. The very thought drove any hope of serenity from her mind.

He followed her down the stairway. "You seemed disappointed in the upstairs rooms. I wouldn't worry about it too much. The place has been neglected for a long time, so it naturally looks rather shabby. The architect promised that the basic structure is good and that we'll have no trouble making any changes we want."

She nodded silently as he closed the outer doors and led her to the car. "Leon dropped me off here, so I'd be obliged for a ride home."

She made no attempt to answer him as he slid in beside her. Although the drive to the cottage could not have taken more than a few minutes, Cindy was heatedly aware that his eyes never left her face in all that time. She concentrated on the road and tried not to reveal her tension.

Once inside the house, Boyd walked toward the kitchen to speak with Mrs. Gregory while Cindy headed for the master bedroom, anxious to have a few minutes to herself so she could consider Boyd's revelation that he intended to move into the huge mansion which dominated the property. She wondered how much longer she could be expected to participate in this marriage based purely on cold, financial considerations.

Her thoughts were abruptly interrupted when Boyd strode casually into the room. He tossed his jacket on the bed, shortly following it with his shirt and tie. He seemed totally at ease, completely oblivious to Cindy's presence. She turned from the window, her voice raspy from the dryness of her mouth.

"What are you doing?"

"Changing for dinner," he said, moving toward the large closet at the side of the room. "I hope you don't insist on formal attire at the dinner table. I get so tired of wearing a suit all day that I like to relax when I get home."

Cindy shrugged. "I couldn't care less what you wear. I just don't understand why you're changing in my room."

"*Our* room, my dear." The smile on his face vibrated in his deep voice. "This is the master bedroom, and I am the master, so I assume that this is where I belong."

"I thought you were sleeping across the hall."

"That was only a temporary arrangement since you weren't feeling well. This has always been my bedroom." As if to prove his point, he took a heavy brown velour robe from the closet.

Cindy's lips curled in anger. "Then I'll move my things into the other room."

Boyd's hand caught her upper arm before she could reach the closet where her clothing was stored. "What the devil is going on? This morning you practically begged me to spend the day with you. We've just spent some time walking through the house I hope to have made into *our* home, and now you tell me that one of us has to leave this room."

"I was merely trying to establish a civil relationship

with you. I have no intention of sleeping with you. I thought I had made that perfectly clear."

"The only thing that's perfectly clear is that you're acting like a spoiled brat, and I won't stand for it."

"Then leave. You were the one who insisted that we be married."

All the unbridled anger faded from his face and once more he was the picture of calmly resolute arrogance. "So that's your game. You think that you can provoke me into walking out on you. Well, forget it; I'm not that easily put off."

He pulled her roughly toward him, his dark eyes glowing with determination. She tried to pull away but her strength was unequal to the task and her lips were easy prey for the merciless onslaught of his as they pressed against hers, moving with a ruthlessly insistent obstinacy until she parted hers helplessly in response to his urgent demands.

Without taking his lips from hers, he lowered his arm and lifted her effortlessly, carrying her swiftly across the room. Her frantic mind barely had time to register the softness of the bed against her back when she felt Boyd's hands moving across her body, removing her shirt and expertly unfastening the clip of her lacy bra and flinging it aside.

His lips softened and moved to the edge of her mouth, tracing a languidly exhilarating path over her cheeks before sliding down to the sensitive cord at the side of her neck. She tensed, arching her body to get away from him, panic-stricken at the wild sensations his lips were arousing in her.

His hands continued their exploration of her body, cupping her breasts gently and stroking them, but his face lifted, giving her a brief respite from the ruthless invasion of his tantalizing lips.

Their ragged breathing vibrated through the room in testimony to the potency of the savage passions which, once unleashed, were now soaring rapidly, depriving both of them of any ability to stop what he had set in motion. She opened her eyes, widening them as she saw the sharp determination in the hard masculine features poised above her, the eyes studying her with all the ferocity of a predator inspecting his helplessly trapped prey.

The unconcealed desire burning in his eyes made her push her hands against his chest, moaning a soft refusal as she tried to roll away from him. He caught both her hands in one of his, gripping them tightly, not releasing them until they were once more tightly secured beneath the powerful muscles of his lowered torso. His strong hands framed her face as she moved it from side to side on the pillow, seeking to avoid his lips, which once again hovered above hers, waiting to claim what she was swiftly becoming powerless to protect.

She was breathless, weakened by her struggles and the depths of her own clamoring passion, but some small spark of anger sprang from the crevices of her subconscious, forcing her to voice a final, quiet refusal. "No, we can't do this. Please stop; it's wrong."

"Why is it wrong for me to make love to my wife? You can't deny that you're enjoying it. The only reason you're fighting me is because of that infantile streak of vengeance which you refuse to surrender. But you'll just have to stop it. I won't put up with any more of your childish behavior."

His voice was husky with barely concealed desire. "You're my wife and we're in bed and I intend to put an end to this little game you've been playing with me. You can stop fighting me and enjoy what I can teach you, or you can continue this senseless battle and deny yourself. Either way, I fully intend that from this point on our marital relationship will be physical as well as factual."

"Why? Why are you doing this? You know that ours was a marriage of convenience. We don't love each other. You have no right to expect this of me."

His voice was hard; a definite chill had broken into the heated atmosphere of the room. "I'm fully aware of the circumstances of our marriage. I also know how that devious little mind of yours works." A small, wicked smile creased the corners of his mouth as he continued to study her dispassionately. "Don't think I'm blind to your little game. You think that you can keep our marriage on a platonic basis and then demand an annulment by claiming that it was never consummated. Well, you can forget that ridiculous scheme as of right now. After tonight, an annulment will be out of the question."

Unshed tears clouded Cindy's eyes and she tried to find the words to refute his accusation. But her tongue seemed as weak as every other muscle in her body and her dry lips were unable to produce the words of denial that were whirling around in her brain.

His lips began to slowly caress the areas of her body that were already tingling from the exploration of his hands. She gasped when they reached the crest of her breast and she tried to push his head away, but her hands became entwined in his thick dark mane and began traveling on their own path of grasping discovery, threading through the short curling hairs above his nape until they began frantically probing the unyielding strength of the teak-brown column of his neck.

He seemed to sense victory and moved over her, whispering inaudibly against the softness of her cheek, the curve of her ear, and the throbbing of her throat. But she was oblivious to everything except the raging demands of her own body and barely felt the brief moment when he finally made her his wife. Her passion mounted in a rush of ecstasy until she felt she could no longer bear any further expansion of the delirious pleasure and dug her fingers into the strong, rippling muscles of his back. Shivers of bliss convulsed her body and she cried out, opening her eyes, widening them as her body rocked in ecstasy.

Boyd's face loomed above her, glowing with a passion of possession that seemed to equal her own soaring fervor. Then all strength seemed to leave him and he drew her to him, clinging to her in the same hopeless state of reeling emotions in which she had clung to him only moments before.

Boyd had turned on his back, still holding her within the circle of his arms. His hands continued to caress her body, soothing it as it began the slow, shadowy descent to earth. His touch was gentle, undemanding, seeking only to bring her to a calm bliss she had never yet known in his arms.

Reality seeped into Cindy's cloud-filled mind, and billowing shame quickly replaced the explosive euphoria which moments before had surged through her body. She stole a glance at Boyd. He was staring moodily at the ceiling, a strangely contented calm masking the hard lines of his aquiline features.

Humilation and rage rose in her when she remembered the woman who had come to Boyd's bedroom that morning. Well, there was no way she was going to give him the satisfaction of knowing that she had fallen into his arms just a few short hours after she had met his mistress. She should have mentioned the woman earlier, but she would say nothing now.

She pushed her hands against him, moving herself out of his arms. "I didn't think even you would sink to rape in order to achieve your goal."

Anger flickered momentarily within the depths of his eyes, then vanished, to be replaced by hard lines of determination. "I would hardly call it rape, my dear. You were not exactly unresponsive." He shifted a pillow behind his back and sat against it, leisurely observing her movements as she swung her feet to the floor, clutching the blanket tightly to her breast.

"You knew I didn't want you to make love to me. I've never denied that you were experienced enough to make my body respond to your touch. But I'll never stop fighting you. I'll never forget the lengths to which you'll go to gain control of the company, and you'll never achieve that ambition."

"I already have, my dear." His voice was soft with assurance. "Don't forget that as long as I do everything in my power to ensure our marital happiness Templeton Industries is mine. And I've just proven the extent of my willingness to play the perfect husband, haven't I?"

His mocking grin was more than Cindy could bear. Throwing the blanket togalike over her shoulder, she ran into the bathroom, slamming the door behind her.

Chapter Seven

Cindy let the cool shower stream gently down her body while she tried to regain some degree of control over her emotions. Boyd's musky scent clung to every inch of her skin and she rubbed the perfumed soap against herself with an almost destructive ferocity. But if scrubbing could eradicate the outward evidence of what had transpired between them, there was absolutely no way that she could ever remove the enduring consequences of his ravages.

In more ways than one, Boyd had destroyed her childhood dreams. Well, she thought grimly, Boyd has certainly completed my education. Harsh as the experience had been, he had shown her what it was to be a woman, *his woman*.

She knew that he didn't love her. What he felt for her was purely the desire that a healthy man could feel for any woman. It was certainly not the romantic love she had always dreamed of experiencing one day. Yet she could not deny that Boyd had been right when he said that she had been his willing partner as they made love. Was her own inexperienced flesh so weak that it responded with such passion to a man's slightest touch?

She shut the faucets and shook her head. No, that

was hardly a reasonable explanation. Other men had kissed her, but their touch had been meaningless. Their expressions of affection had meant nothing at all to her.

Was it possible that she had fallen in love with Boyd? The mere thought frightened her as much as Boyd himself frightened her. He was a cold, heartless entrepreneur whose only interest in her was based on the fact that she was the key to the ownership of her father's business. Being a man, he could make his body respond to hers just as it would to any other female form. But for her it was a shattering experience and, much as her mind sought to deny it, every fiber of her being told her that she had fallen heavily and hopelessly in love with Boyd Hamilton, the man who had the power to destroy her entire family. Earlier she had been able to deny it to herself, but after what had just passed between them she could hide from the truth no longer.

After drying herself, she wrapped the towel around her body like a sarong and reentered the bedroom, only to find that Boyd had gone. Sighing with relief, she quickly discarded the towel and slipped into fresh clothes. She was too distressed to give any thought to her choice and absently selected a paisley-printed raw silk caftan from the closet. She had just dropped it over her head and was reaching behind her to grasp the exasperatingly inaccessible zipper when she heard Boyd's voice echo softly across the room.

"I'll get that for you," he said. "I believe it's one of a husband's many pleasant duties."

The relaxed contentment on his face and the arrogant swagger of his walk were more than Cindy could bear.

"I can manage," she said, twisting herself with all the skill of a circus contortionist. "A girl learns to do these things for herself if she doesn't want to appear in public half dressed."

Boyd smiled benignly as he came up behind her, stroking her hands lightly before replacing them with his own. His fingers glided lazily over each small indentation of her spine, melting her bones while he cleared the fabric to prevent it from being caught up in the teeth of the slowly ascending zipper. When he bent to lift the heavy curtain of thick blonde hair away from her neckline, his warm breath caressed her nape and she twisted her head to escape the havoc he was wreaking on her senses. But her slight movement only succeeded in exposing the tender shell of her ear to the merciless attack of his questing lips.

The gentle, moist warmth of his uneven breathing sent icy shivers racing along the length of her spine and she quickly drew away from him while her legs still had the strength to support her body.

"Thank you. I'll be able to manage now," she said, reaching around to hook the clasp at the back of her neck.

She flung her hair casually over her shoulders and turned to find Boyd's pensive brown eyes studying her. Although the caftan was loosely fitted, the supple nature of the silk made it cling to every curve of her slender body, and the look on Boyd's face told Cindy that he was now remembering the hidden flesh that he had tasted just a short while ago.

"What is it you want?" she said, biting her lower lip and turning away so he wouldn't see the heated blush of embarrassment which was slowly creeping up her body.

"You know what I want," he said, a cynical grin quirking the tight corners of his mouth. "But I don't expect that you'd be very receptive to my desires right now, although I'm sure I could persuade you without too much effort on my part."

Cindy's shame turned to raging anger. "You're despicable! Don't you ever come near me again!"

The smile never left Boyd's face. "I thought you'd feel that way. That's why I'm not trying to get what I really want. I merely came by to tell you that Mrs. Gregory has returned and is prepared to serve us dinner. We were quite alone before because she goes home to give her invalid husband an early meal before serving mine. It helps if we don't keep her waiting since she likes to get back to him as soon as possible."

"Why don't you let her leave now? I can serve our food."

Boyd smiled. "I'm sure you can. But I think she would be hurt if she thought we didn't want her services. No, the best thing to do is to be on time for dinner and let her complete her chores quickly so she can leave before it gets to be too late." He grasped Cindy's elbow and guided her into the small, cheerfully furnished dining room.

Pale green wallpaper blended beautifully with the highly polished oak-planked floors, and a brass candelabra-style chandelier hung above the oval mahogany table, its ten small bulbs softly illuminating the gold-edged china, multicolored floral centerpiece and ornately patterned silverware.

Boyd led Cindy to a tapestry-covered Queen Anne chair at the foot of the table and held the back of the chair until she had seated herself. Then he took his place opposite her.

Mrs. Gregory served the shrimp cocktail immediately and waited silently in the kitchen before bringing the crisply roasted duck on a bed of wild rice.

When the dinner plates had been cleared away, Mrs. Gregory served a frothy chocolate mousse with coffee and assorted butter cookies. Boyd wanted to linger over his coffee and Cindy recalled what he had said about Mrs. Gregory's being eager to return home, so she thanked the housekeeper for the delicious dinner, then offered to clear away the dessert dishes herself.

After the older woman had gone Boyd relaxed in his seat and smiled at Cindy. "It seems you've made a friend of Mrs. Gregory. Most unusual; she's usually quite taciturn until she gets to know you."

"Perhaps she feels she knows me already," Cindy said, returning his languid smile.

"Impossible. I imagine it would take years to even begin to understand all those mysterious little quirks smoldering in the depths of your deviously complicated soul."

"Maybe others don't find me as devious as you do."

Boyd sipped his coffee slowly but made no response to her statement. They had just finished their dessert when the telephone rang. Boyd went to the study to answer it, and Cindy began clearing the table. She had rinsed the last cup and was placing it in the dishwasher when she heard Boyd's footsteps moving across the ceramic-tiled kitchen floor. She dried her hands on the linen handtowel and turned to face him.

"We've been invited to dinner," he said, taking the towel from her and setting it down on the pale pine countertop.

"Oh?" she replied, lifting her eyebrows quizzically.

"An old friend of mine has just returned from abroad and wants us to join her for dinner tomorrow evening . . . Lorraine Hanley, or, rather, the Countess di Ferrante as she is now called."

Cindy still said nothing about her earlier encounter with the woman and continued watching him, waiting for some further explanation of his relationship with the Countess di Ferrante.

"Her father is an old friend of mine; we do a lot of business with his bank. They hold the papers on the

135

loans which provided us with the expansion money we needed when we moved into word-processing machines."

So that was where she had heard the name, Cindy thought quickly. Mr. Hanley had been a long-time golfing partner of her father's, in addition to being his banker. Distaste rose in her throat when she remembered her father's grinning assurances that the company loans would never be in danger of recall as long as Boyd kept the banker's daughter happy.

"Is Lorraine married?" she asked, controlling the trembling in her heart so it wouldn't show in her voice.

"She ran off and married an Italian count she had met on a skiing vacation. But I think they've had a little spat and now she's planning on staying with her parents for a while."

"When would she like us to come for dinner?" Cindy asked, keeping her voice as casual as possible.

"Tomorrow at eight."

"I'll be ready. Now, if you'll excuse me, I'd like to go to bed."

"You go on," Boyd said. "I'll work in the study so the light won't disturb you." He moved forward and casually brushed his lips across her forehead.

Cindy turned and ran from the room. Just the slightest touch of Boyd's lips made her blood surge with a yearning that could only be satisfied by throwing herself into his arms and begging him to make love to her as he had done earlier in the evening. He had shown her the heights of ecstasy he could help her reach, and every inch of her being longed to be taken there once more.

But, weak though her flesh might be, Cindy refused to let Boyd use her the way he used everyone else. It was one thing for her to realize how completely she now loved him, but she vowed to herself that she would never let him know how much she cared.

If Boyd insisted on his right to the master bedroom, then she would no longer sleep there. She took her clothes, walked into the guest bedroom and closed the door, turning the lock decisively, guarding herself against her own weakness as well as her husband's desire.

She undressed and slipped between the covers, but tension prevented her from easing into sleep because she knew that no lock would ever keep Boyd from entering her room if he wanted to get in. Her fears increased when his footsteps sounded in the hallway, coming closer minute by minute. The steps halted outside the master bedroom, then shifted to her door, and she held her breath expectantly, not knowing what his next move would be.

The doorknob turned, then stopped as it encountered the resistance of the lock. It turned once more, as if Boyd needed to be convinced that the door was really bolted. Everything was silent for a moment; then his hand released the knob and his departing footsteps indicated that he had returned to the master bedroom.

Cindy breathed a sigh of relief when she heard the door to his room close. She curled up in her blanket and tried to relax into sleep. Unbidden tears flowed from her eyes and as she drifted into a troubled slumber her pillow grew damp.

The next morning, when Cindy entered the kitchen, Mrs. Gregory told her that Boyd had already left for the office. She prepared Cindy's breakfast, then excused herself, explaining that she wanted to complete her housework quickly and take advantage of an early evening since she didn't have to prepare dinner.

Cindy had hoped that Mrs. Gregory would have stayed to chat with her and perhaps tell her more about Boyd and his relationship with Lorraine, because she seemed to know both of them very well. Now Cindy was at a loss as to how to spend the day.

Once more, she was drawn to the deserted mansion which Boyd intended to refurbish as his home. She went directly to the music room and spent the entire day practicing at the piano. Much as Boyd now dominated all her thoughts, she could still forget her problems in the joy of her music. She was lost in reverie when a gentle tapping sounded at the open French doors.

"I'm sorry to disturb you, Mrs. Hamilton, but Mr. Hamilton said I might find you here. I'm leaving now and he thought I should remind you that you had a dinner appointment for eight o'clock this evening and it's six o'clock now."

Cindy waved to Mrs. Gregory as the older woman drove away; then she began walking toward the house. She wanted to be dressed before Boyd got home. Vivid memories of what had occurred the last time he had come home and found her undressed still sent shivers through her body and she wasn't about to chance another similar encounter.

The knowledge that Boyd's former girlfriend was giving the dinner party made Cindy especially nervous about her appearance. She remembered how unattractive she had felt among the elegantly dressed women during their short honeymoon in Mexico City and she was determined that such would not be the case tonight.

She chose a black silk dress which she had never worn before. She had never bought anything like it and she probably wouldn't have purchased this if her mother's dressmaker had not been so insistent. Now, as she slipped its silky folds over her head, she was glad she had let herself be talked into buying it. The top came straight across, curving under her arms and flowing into a diamondlike clasp which pleated the fabric before it was tossed over one shoulder and draped across her bare back so she could catch it like a stole within the crook of her other elbow. It had not the slightest hint of a waistline and molded itself to her slender curves as it fell loosely from the evenly spaced pleats created by the glittering clasp.

At the dressing table she applied a hint of pale pink blusher and lip gloss. A few strokes with her brush settled each fine strand of ash-blonde hair into its proper place and as she turned back toward the closet her face seemed to be surrounded by an ethereal veil of golden silk.

She was slipping into high-heeled sandals when the sound of running water coming from the master bedroom indicated that Boyd had come home and was showering before getting dressed. A sigh of triumphant satisfaction slipped softly from her lips as she realized that she would be completely dressed and waiting for him when he emerged from his room.

Casting a swift glance at her reflection in the mirror, she nodded with satisfaction and sprayed herself with expensive French perfume. She looked every bit as sophisticated as any of the women with whom they had dined while they were in Mexico City. Let Boyd call her a spoiled child now. Flinging her long silky hair over her shoulders, she picked up her black satin evening bag and went into the living room to wait for him.

She settled herself in the fawn velvet Queen Anne wing chair which stood at one side of the unlit fireplace and glanced around the room. The furniture was all antique. A thick, handwoven Persian carpet covered

.the oak floor, adding to the warmth of the room and giving a uniformity of design to the eclectic collection of furniture, each piece of which seemed to have been separately selected for its own individual beauty. She frowned uneasily. Nothing about the cottage suggested the icy personality of its owner. She wondered who had done the decorating. Certainly not Boyd!

Her reverie came to an abrupt end when he entered the room. He was slipping into a black cashmere evening jacket and adjusting the ruffled cuff of his white silk shirt. He lifted his head, his bluntly cut dark hair contrasting with his white collar, and she saw the full breadth of his muscular chest, now covered by the minute pleats of the fine silk shirt.

Cindy tensed. No amount of ruffles or pleats could hide the sheer animal magnetism which permeated every fiber of Boyd's being. He straightened and turned to study her appearance. Only his sudden intake of breath gave any indication of his response to her attire. Then his habitual mask of composed diffidence swung quickly into place.

"You constantly surprise me," he said, walking toward the bar. "This is the first time any woman has been ready and waiting for me."

She smiled sweetly. "Really? And I thought all your women were constantly waiting, at your beck and call." She leaned back in her chair, hoping to achieve a pose of sophisticated ease.

The icy arrogance of his answering smile froze her blood, making her heart skip a beat. "I'm sorry to see that your ladylike gown hasn't stopped your constant stream of childishly catty remarks."

He took some ice cubes from the silver bucket and tossed them into a glass, then swirled some imported Scotch over them. "Can I get you something?"

"Tomato juice with a touch of vodka, if it's not too much trouble."

"Nothing you want is too much trouble for me, my dear," he said, opening the lower door of the liquor cabinet, which had apparently been converted into a small refrigerator. He mixed the drink and walked slowly toward her.

Their fingers touched when he handed her the drink and she clutched the glass, quickly drawing her hand from his as if she had grazed a flame. His brow lifted inquisitively and he moved away to lean negligently against the fireplace mantel.

"I called to remind you of our dinner engagement. You weren't home."

"I was at the other house."

"Ah, I told Mrs. Gregory that you might be there. Were you studying the rooms for decorating ideas?"

"I was practicing some pieces on the piano. You forget so much if you stay away from an instrument for even a short while. This is the first chance I've had to practice since my graduation."

"It doesn't really matter, does it? Now that you're out of school there's no need to drive yourself so."

She placed her glass on the small table beside her chair. "You don't seem to understand. Music is my life. I've devoted years of study to it. I see no reason why I should have to give it up now."

"You have other commitments now which will be placing more demands on your time. I don't think you'll have the luxury of devoting much time to frivolous activities."

"Why is my work frivolous? You seem to place great importance on your own labors."

Boyd set his empty glass on the mantel and came toward her. "My work *is* important. I deal in facts and

141

figures. The machines I design help run the industries of our country. I've never had any time to dawdle over a musical instrument."

"Yes, you're so involved in that business of yours that you'd sell your soul to retain control of it."

Detached amusement curved the corners of his tightly set lips. "You're quite mistaken, my love. I did not sell my soul to gain control of Templeton Industries; I purchased yours."

Shame and anger united in Cindy's veins, sending a red flush of heat racing through her alabaster skin. Boyd's slight smile widened into a broad grin as he reached down to grip her hands and draw her to him.

"Don't you touch me," she said, her blue eyes icy with anger.

His fingers moved casually over her body, stroking her bare shoulders and adjusting the folds of her stole. His warm breath caressed the curve of her cheek as she tilted her head to escape his roving hands. "You don't really mean that," he said, lifting her thick curtain of hair and probing the pulsating warmth of her neck with his fiery fingertips, "and nothing would please me more than to prove just how much you enjoy the physical side of our relationship, but we do have a dinner engagement and Lorraine hates to be kept waiting."

The mention of Lorraine's name only sent Cindy's anger soaring to new heights. She flung Boyd's hand off her shoulder and stormed out the door, settling herself in the passenger seat of his sleek white Mercedes. He closed her door and got behind the wheel.

"Where's Leon?"

"Leon drives the company car; tonight is strictly a pleasure outing. I provide my own transportation on such occasions. I wouldn't want some dissatisfied stockholder to accuse me of misappropriating company funds." He flashed a brief smile at Cindy before heading the car down the driveway.

She sat silently beside him while he drove the short distance to Lorraine's home. His contented humming nearly drove her to distraction, but she knew that there was absolutely nothing she could do to send his emotions reeling the way he so easily sent hers.

The Hanley estate was set on the crest of a towering hill at the end of a long, winding road, ingeniously hidden among countless acres of rolling green hills. Boyd stopped the car at the entrance to the pillared white mansion and handed the car keys to the valet who opened the door. Cindy was helped out by another valet and waited for Boyd to join her before starting up the broad fieldstone steps.

The small uniformed maid had barely opened the door before Lorraine hurried out to meet them. The iridescent beading covering the fabric of her form-fitting scarlet dress flickered enticingly with every sensuous movement of her voluptuous body. Diamonds dripped from her earlobes and sparkled between her breasts, accentuating the deep, plunging neckline of her seductive gown. She moved with the undulating ease of a woman who has been manipulating men since childhood, and Cindy felt herself shrink back as she realized that it would take more than a clinging black gown to elevate her own charms to Lorraine's level.

Their hostess smiled a tepid greeting at Cindy and slithered toward Boyd, leaning forward to kiss him on the lips before linking her arm with his and drawing him into the living room. Boyd's other arm reached back to curve around Cindy's waist as he pulled her to him and stopped short, momentarily halting Lorraine. Her eyes turned toward his in question.

Boyd's expression was as impassive as ever and Cindy

thought that she would never really understand him. "I don't believe you've met my wife, Cindy—"

Lorraine's dulcet tones interrupted him midsentence. "Ah, but I have."

For once Boyd's face registered genuine surprise and it was a moment before he reassumed his usual rigid composure. "You have?" His voice was calm, mildly inquisitive but not overly excited.

"Yes, didn't Cindy tell you? We shared a cup of coffee yesterday morning. You should have known that I'd come to see you as soon as I'd recovered my land legs. I was very disappointed to find that you'd left for the office, but it gave Cindy and me a good chance to get acquainted. You should have told me you were getting married. It came as quite a shock."

"As I recall, you didn't inform me of *your* marriage plans until you had taken the final step."

Lorraine's sharp green eyes daringly traveled the length of Boyd's handsome physique, finally coming to rest as they looked into the lazily hooded depths of his brown eyes. "We all make mistakes. But, fortunately, they can be rectified." She smiled meaningfully and relinked her arm with Boyd's, once again urging him forward toward the crowded living room.

Lorraine's intimate exchange with Boyd had completely deflated Cindy's faltering ego and she entered the living room prepared to spend an utterly miserable evening. She drew back in surprise when a tall, sandy-haired young man came forward and took both her hands in his.

"Cindy Templeton, what a marvelous stroke of good luck! I can't believe my eyes. What on earth are you doing here?"

Boyd tightened his grip around Cindy's waist and shot a hostile glare at the other man. His displeasure was only heightened when she drew away from him and looked excitedly up at the blond man.

"Craig Simmons! I thought you were going to Paris after graduation."

"That's where I've been for the last year. That's where I met the Countess di Ferrante. She talked me into returning to the States. . . . Don't tell me you don't know about the local symphony group that's being formed?"

Cindy shook her head.

Craig turned to Lorraine in disbelief. "Don't you realize that Cindy Templeton is one of our most promising young pianists? She'll simply have to be part of any symphony orchestra that I'm directing."

Lorraine flashed a triumphant smile. "But of course. Why don't we just leave you two alone to get reacquainted and discuss the orchestra?" She snuggled up to Boyd and guided him away from Cindy.

Craig began talking nonstop about his plans for the new symphony group and happily led Cindy into the dining room when he found that they were seated next to each other. It came as no surprise to Cindy that Lorraine had chosen Boyd for her dinner partner. Craig and Lorraine seemed entirely happy with this arrangement and Cindy was too depressed to care one way or the other. But Boyd was watching her every move with such disdainful hostility that she found herself unable to concentrate on either the food or Craig's enthusiastic recital of his plans for the future. It was obvious that her husband had been comparing her with Lorraine and his conclusions had left him anything but happy with her.

When they had finished their dessert and coffee, Lorraine announced that afterdinner cordials would be served on the terrace. Craig placed his hand lightly on

Cindy's waist and began to guide her outdoors, nodding at Boyd and Lorraine, who remained a twosome. "Take a look at our delightful hostess. She's exactly where she wants to be. I'm assuming that's her old boyfriend, the one she had a spat with before she ran off and married the count. Now that she's getting her divorce, she probably intends to renew old acquaintances." He had been so busy telling Cindy of his own plans that he hadn't even asked how she was doing, and obviously didn't realize that she and Boyd were married.

She felt the blood drain from her face as her legs grew too weak to support her body. She leaned against Craig for strength and he drew her closer to him, apparently misinterpreting her weakness as an expression of affection.

They had finally reached the terrace and Cindy sank gratefully into the soft cushions of the redwood sofa while Craig went to get their liqueurs. She leaned back to rest her head and found herself gazing into Boyd's guarded eyes. Lorraine had turned her attention to her father for a moment and Boyd, momentarily deprived of the devotion of the woman he loved, was now studying his wife over the rim of his brandy snifter.

With a movement so carefully controlled that he seemed more mechanical than human, he placed his glass on an adjacent wrought-iron table and walked slowly toward Cindy.

"Get up! We're leaving!"

"Why? It's still early and Craig just went to get me a cordial."

A muscle twitched beneath the taut skin of his firmly set jaw. "Yes, I'm well aware of your attentive beau . . . can't seem to do enough for you, can he?"

Cindy bristled with anger as Boyd's strong hands gripped hers, lifting her from the chair. "He's not my beau; he's just someone I know from school. He graduated a year before I did. He's a fine composer and conductor and I won't have you soiling our friendship with your dirty mind."

"I'm not interested in your beautiful friendship, so smile sweetly and say good night to Lorraine," he commanded in a voice so low only she could hear him.

"Why? Are you afraid that I might offend your mistress?" she whispered with an angry smile.

Boyd dug his fingers cruelly into her side so that she gasped breathlessly as they reached Lorraine's side.

"Not feeling well?" Lorraine said, eyeing Cindy as if she were a bothersome child.

"Yes, I'm afraid that's it," Boyd replied before Cindy had a chance to open her mouth. "It seems my bride is still recovering from the excitement of our marriage. We'd best be getting home."

Lorraine smiled indulgently. "I understand; Cindy *is* still rather young. She's probably not equal to the late hours *we're* used to keeping." Her emerald eyes narrowed intimately.

Boyd smiled cryptically and guided Cindy toward the door.

"Boyd."

He turned his head back to look at Lorraine, who had just called his name.

"Keep in touch. . . . Don't forget your old friends just because you're married." She smiled intimately as she finished speaking.

Boyd returned her smile but continued walking toward the door, his broad hand remaining tight as a vise around Cindy's narrow waist. The valet recognized them as they began descending the wide fieldstone steps and ran to get the white Mercedes.

The drive home was accomplished in complete silence. Cindy was too angry to initiate any conversation with Boyd, and his lips were tightly set in taciturn silence. Nothing improved once they reached the cottage and, after a sharp look at Boyd's unfriendly back while he poured himself a drink at the bar, Cindy swept through the living room to the seclusion of her bedroom. She undressed quickly and prepared for bed, sure that Boyd would never try to force his attentions on her tonight. His former mistress had returned and had been quite effusive in stating her willingness to provide Boyd with all the love he could ever desire. Cindy's place in his life had become more unbearable than ever and she sighed miserably when she heard him enter the master bedroom and close the door behind him.

She had spent a restless night and came reluctantly awake when Mrs. Gregory tapped on the door to tell her that she was wanted on the telephone. She lifted the bedside receiver, expecting to hear her mother's clear voice, but instead was surprised to find that Craig Simmons was on the other end of the line.

"Did I wake you? You left the party so suddenly that we didn't get a chance to finish our conversation."

"Well, I was rather tired and my husband decided that it would be best if we went home."

There was a strained silence on the other end of the line. Then Craig cleared his throat and began to speak. "I'm sorry if I said anything inappropriate last night, but I had no idea that you were married to Boyd Hamilton. Forget what I said about Lorraine and him. That's just a lot of stale gossip."

"Don't concern yourself, Craig. I'm a big girl now. I know what the score is."

"Well, I just don't want to be the cause of any trouble between you."

"Don't worry about that. There's nothing you could do to make our relationship any worse."

Silence shrouded the cable for a moment, then Craig spoke again. "I'm not sure I understand what's going on in your personal life, but I do know I've been hired to put together a small musical group for the local community and it would be a shame not to utilize your talents as a pianist."

Cindy hesitated before replying. "I don't know. Last night was the first time I heard about your plans; let me give it some thought."

"Look, you don't have to give me a definite response right now. Just come to the organizational meeting this afternoon. I won't hold you to anything if you should change your mind."

Cindy agreed to attend the luncheon meeting and was at the country club by noon. An uneasy shiver passed through her body when she recalled that the last time she had been here had been the occasion of her marriage to Boyd. She shook her head in an effort to clear these disturbing thoughts from her mind as she entered the private dining room where the Friends of the Symphony were holding their first formal meeting. Most of the people present were older women, the so-called dowager matrons of the community, but, unfortunately, Lorraine had apparently decided to join the group as well.

She saw Cindy and came forward to greet her, all smiles. "Cindy, I'm so glad that you could make it. I was afraid that you might not have recovered from last night's illness."

Cindy speculated that she might never recover from her "illness," a broken heart, but she smiled just as sweetly and said, "I'm just fine. Thank you for being so concerned."

Lorraine introduced her to the other women and soon the meeting was under way. The informal lunch-time conversation was all of the promising future for the newly formed group, and when they finished their meal Craig stood to address the gathering.

He talked enthusiastically about his plans for the small orchestra, then mentioned that they were most fortunate in having an extremely talented pianist living right in their community. By the time he had finished speaking, Cindy found that everyone had taken it for granted that she was an active participant.

It seemed too much of an effort to deny it—and, besides, she too had been caught up in the ebullient preparations. Why shouldn't she do what she wanted? After all, she had studied toward this goal. Boyd had made it quite clear that he would never let her have any voice in the operation of Templeton Industries, and she was not about to sit home all day, meekly tending to his incomprehensible desires.

For the first time since her graduation she felt in complete control of her own destiny. She told Craig that she would be pleased to be the group's pianist and agreed to meet with him to start rehearsing a concerto he had composed.

She stopped off in the ladies' room before leaving and was running a comb through her hair when she overheard a conversation taking place in the inner lounge.

"Pity that Boyd got married, isn't it?"

"Well, I think Lorraine has no one to blame but herself. Imagine running off and marrying that fortune-hunting count just because she and Boyd had a little spat."

"I suppose it *was* foolish of her. But she wanted to get married and Boyd kept putting it off. He was too involved with his work to think of marriage."

"Well, he took care of his business problems when he married the little Templeton girl. She's no match for Lorraine. Boyd's not about to become an instant homebody, *if* you know what I mean. His wife is going to have plenty of spare time to devote to the musical group, Lorraine will see to that."

Cindy closed her purse and fled the room, glad to get into her familiar red Mustang and leave her humiliation behind her.

Chapter Eight

After entering the estate grounds, Cindy drove past the big house without stopping. She no longer had any desire to see the house which Boyd intended to use as his family home. The conversation she had overheard at the club, combined with Lorraine's openly possessive attitude toward him, left no doubt in her mind that Lorraine was the woman he really loved. He had merely married her to get control of her father's company. Her firsthand knowledge of the heartless way he lived his life convinced her that he was completely capable of installing her in the nearby mansion and forgetting about her while he resumed his romantic relationship with Lorraine.

She wondered what could have caused the argument which had sent Lorraine off to Europe in such a huff to marry a man she quite obviously had not loved. It was entirely possible that, even then, Boyd had determined to marry Cindy as an important part of his scheme to assume control of Templeton Industries. Lorraine seemed to be extremely sophisticated, but perhaps she wasn't blasé enough to stand quietly by while the man she loved entered into a marriage of convenience. She wondered what new plan of action Boyd and Lorraine had contrived to safely eliminate her from interfering with the smooth course of their affair.

These thoughts were still reeling around her mind when she walked into the house. Mrs. Gregory was preparing a salad in the cozy kitchen and looked up as Cindy said hello.

"Ah, I'm glad you've returned. Mr. Hamilton has been trying to reach you all afternoon. You weren't at your mother's and he had no idea where you could possibly have gone."

No doubt, Cindy thought, Boyd had been upset to find that she wasn't staying at home, meekly awaiting the whimsical call of her lord and master, and he had probably asked Mrs. Gregory to do some detective work to determine where she had spent the day. But she wasn't about to give him that satisfaction.

"I was attending a meeting; I didn't think it was necessary to inform Mr. Hamilton of my whereabouts."

Cindy could see that the housekeeper was disturbed by her answer. She was obviously very fond of Boyd and didn't like to see anyone disregard his commands.

"I don't think Mr. Hamilton was expecting to be informed of all your social engagements; I believe he was merely concerned because he didn't know where to reach you." She paused. "In any case, he's going to be working late this evening and won't be home for dinner. I've prepared your food and I'll stay to serve it."

"There's no need," Cindy said. "I'll serve myself later; I'm not hungry now, anyway."

She went to her room and was about to change into a comfortable pair of jeans when the telephone rang. She was certain that it would be Boyd, checking on her once again, and she answered the phone warily.

There was a moment of silence on the other end

before Craig's hesitant voice came through. "Cindy?" he said tentatively. "Are you all right?"

"I'm fine, Craig. Why do you ask?"

"No reason. It's just that you sounded angry . . . not at all like yourself. I thought perhaps you had some problem."

"Nothing is wrong, Craig. I guess I must have had my mind on other things."

"Well, I'm glad to hear that," he returned. "I was wondering if you'd like to join me for dinner this evening. Lorraine told me that she was meeting your husband, so I realized you'd be free. I thought it would be a good opportunity to discuss our plans for the symphony. What do you say? Will you join me for dinner?"

So Boyd and Lorraine were already beginning their little game of subterfuge! Equal parts of hurt and anger rushed through her. Well, she wasn't quite as gullible as he imagined her to be and wouldn't sit docilely at home eating a lonely warmed-over dinner while he and Lorraine pursued their clandestine love affair. "I'd like very much to have dinner with you, Craig. When can you pick me up?"

"I'll be by in about an hour and a half. Is that too soon?"

"That's fine," Cindy responded. "I'll be ready."

When the phone rang again, she didn't answer it. This time she was certain that it *was* Boyd and she had no intention of getting into any discussion with him. How could he have made love to her the other evening when all the time his thoughts were with another woman? That was something she would never understand.

But then, he had never once claimed to love her. His attitude toward her was one of pure passion; love never entered into it. Men were capable of making love

154

without being in love, but women were different; at least, she was. And she loved Boyd as much as it was possible for one human being to love another.

His mere presence in a room made her come alive, and when he left she felt as if a part of her had gone with him. The strength of her love for Boyd gave him complete control over her, whether he knew it or not, and she couldn't bear to think of a life without him. But he didn't return her love, and giving him any indication of her true feelings would only result in more misery for her.

She was glad that she had volunteered to help Craig with the symphony group. At least she would have something to occupy her time and take her mind off the hopeless agony of her love for Boyd. She had always been prepared to devote the greater part of her life to a career in music, and although it now seemed a pathetically empty existence compared to a lifetime of love spent in Boyd's arms she was grateful that it would give her something to do in the empty eternity stretching before her.

Dinner with Craig was pleasant; they ate at a local Japanese restaurant and spent most of the evening talking about music. The only brief jarring note came as they were leaving the restaurant and ran into Carl Meredith. He seemed surprised to see Cindy dining with another man, mentioning that it seemed as if she'd only just been married. But she explained that she and Craig were old friends who were now working together on the local symphony and he seemed to drop his suspicions.

The ride home was as relaxing as the rest of the evening had been, but when they arrived at the cottage she saw that Boyd's Mercedes was already parked in the driveway and a cold shiver of apprehensive fear tickled her limbs. Then she became inwardly annoyed with herself. She had done nothing wrong. Why should she fear Boyd's reaction? After all, the evening he had spent with Lorraine was far more improper than the dinner she had enjoyed with Craig.

"Thanks for showing a lonely bachelor a good time," Craig said as he walked her to the door. "I'll call you tomorrow so we can decide when to get together and begin rehearsing."

Before Cindy had a chance to answer him, the door flew open. Boyd's face was a study in anger, dark brows set over the fiery coals of his eyes, taut lips above a firmly set jaw, and for all the rigid control he was exercising over his emotions, a telltale muscle twitched in the strong brown column of his neck.

The cold knot of fear retied itself in the depths of Cindy's stomach and she whispered a soft good-bye to Craig, squeezing his hand lightly to tell him she would be better able to cope with Boyd by herself. He lifted his eyebrows in inquiry and when she nodded mutely to him he waved good-bye and turned toward his car.

Boyd shifted the ice in the glass he was holding while stepping to the side so she could pass in front of him and enter the house. His muscular body remained tensely motionless, but his piercing eyes followed her over the threshold.

She had reached the center of the living room when the door slammed with such force that she jumped in fear, and before she had a chance to regain her composure his hands gripped her shoulders, spinning her around to face him.

"Just where do you think you're going?"

"I'm going to bed," she said softly, terrified by the rage burning in his eyes.

"Not before you tell me where you've been from this morning until ten in the evening."

She twisted, trying to free herself from his imprisoning grip, but his fingers bit into her flesh and made escape impossible. "I don't have to account for my activities any more than you have to account for yours."

His breath hissed between his teeth and he brought her up against the steel barrier of his chest. "You know perfectly well where I was. If you were any sort of wife you might have come down to the office and met me for lunch instead of flirting with that solicitous college boyfriend of yours."

"I wasn't flirting. We were discussing arrangements for a concert the symphony group will be giving. Craig wants me to play a composition of his for the first presentation."

"And if I object?"

"I'm not asking your permission," she ground out, defiantly staring him in the face.

The minute the words were out of her mouth she regretted them. All the careful control which Boyd had been exerting over his vindictive fury vanished. Wordlessly, he flung his glass into the fireplace and picked her up. Effortlessly, as if she weighed no more than a child, he carried her into his bedroom and deposited her on the king-sized bed.

The savagery pulsating through every fiber of his body sent Cindy into a shivering frenzy of fear.

His hands caught her wrists when she tried to roll off the bed and he lowered his body to pin her helplessly beneath him. His powerful thighs rested against hers, leaving little doubt in Cindy's mind of the manner in which he had decided to exert his dominance over her. The thought sent flickering tongues of shame flaming through her cheeks.

"No!" she whispered breathlessly. "Please, Boyd."

"So now it's 'please, Boyd,' is it?" He chuckled

mirthlessly. "What happened to the independent woman who didn't have to ask me for anything?"

"Please, Boyd . . . don't do this. Let's talk things over like two sensible human beings. You're behaving like an animal."

"I'm through being a sensible human being where you're concerned. Maybe I am nothing more than an animal. After all, I'm not a gentle, creative artist like your friend Craig. I'm an automaton with a computer where my heart should be. Isn't that what you think? Well, right now I'm programmed to make love to my wife and you lack the means to program my thoughts in any other direction."

She turned her head to the side as he lowered his lips toward hers, but he caught her flaming cheeks and stopped her flight. His thumbs curled under her chin and cruelly lifted her lips to meet the brutal onslaught of his. Her nostrils detected the sharp, tangy odor of Scotch as he closed the distance between them.

There was no affection in his kiss. His lips were mercilessly demanding, until hers finally parted from the sheer savagery of his attack. She lay motionless beneath him, incapable of fighting him yet unable to respond to the demands of his body when his touch was so utterly devoid of any indication of love or even gentleness.

He lifted his head, his mouth twisted in disgust. "What's happened to my passionate little sex kitten? Don't tell me that you've so exhausted yourself satisfying your lover that there's nothing left for your husband?"

Cindy became furious at the injustice of his accusation. Without thinking, she shifted and brought the full force of her outstretched palm across his firmly set jaw.

"You're disgusting!" she said, mindless of the reddening imprint her fingers had left on his cheek.

"Maybe so," he replied. "But I am your husband and you won't deny me what you've been so eager to share with your boyfriend."

Once more his lips crushed hers, forcing her to submit to his heartless caress. Then, suddenly, like a gentle wave lapping against the shore, his hand began to move along her body, probing the pulsating cord in her neck, tenderly massaging the slope of her shoulder, until at last he pushed aside her flimsy bodice and explored the soft curves of her smooth white breast. The warm touch of his questing hand loosed an unwilling moan from her captive lips and he straightened, pausing in his attack as he lifted his face to study the desire that was now evident on hers.

The hard lines of his aquiline features softened momentarily as his lips tantalized the area his hands had just exposed. Her trembling fingers clutched savagely at the strong brown column of his neck and her body stirred hungrily beneath his. All the barriers and restraints were removed with the same swiftness of purpose with which Boyd now discarded their clothing, and she felt her own passions rising to a feverish pitch which left him in complete control of the situation.

He teased her enticingly until she rose to a new plateau of ecstasy, losing all count of time and place. Nothing existed beyond the walls of this room and nothing mattered except Boyd and the happiness he was bringing her.

The taut pleasure within her peaked, sending delectable tremors of arousal racing through her and leaving her to drift mindlessly on a tranquil cloud of sheer delight. Boyd's arms still encircled her, holding her tightly against him as if to protect her while she descended from the heavenly apex. Ever so slowly she became aware of his hands stroking her back, molding her to him, reinforcing their unity.

She clung to him desperately, her cheek resting comfortably against the softly curling hairs of his chest. The musky scent of him attacked her nostrils, sending a new stream of love surging through her veins. She longed to see his face, caress the arrogant lines of his jaw and tell him how much she loved him. But she knew that he would only laugh at her. He must have had another argument with Lorraine, and that, combined with the fact that his wife had shown a streak of independence, had made him turn his seductive powers on her. What Lorraine had apparently denied him he had won easily from her. Yet, loving him as she did, she was unwilling to rupture the calm beauty of the moment and resolutely pushed all thoughts of Lorraine from her mind.

The pleasant languor of submission spread through her limbs, relaxing her into peacefully satisfying slumber. No longer caring what he thought, she pressed herself against the firm security of Boyd's muscular chest and dreamed of the endless happiness she would experience if only his need for her had sprung from love instead of from his simple wish to quench his masculine desires.

She awoke when daylight streaked across her pillow and found that Boyd had gone. She snuggled beneath the covers, reliving the events of the past evening, fully realizing that she should feel the painful pangs of remorse, but her heart refused to let her repress the hopeless love she was shielding from Boyd. What on earth was wrong with her? she thought as she turned on the shower. How could she spend her daylight hours reveling in the remembrance of last night's passion?

She lifted her face toward the stream of cool water, hoping it would clear the confusing clouds from her mind and let her see things as they really were. Last night had been nothing more than an expression of sexual desire. Boyd had used her body to relieve the passions aroused by Lorraine. And if that wasn't bad enough, he was the man she had sworn to hate, the man who had stolen her father's business, the man who had married her in order to solidify his hold on that business. And, she thought, unable to stop the heated blush that ran through her body, I was an eagerly willing accomplice in my own seduction.

She could no longer delude herself by claiming that Boyd had forced his attentions on her. She had wanted him every bit as much as he had wanted her.

Self-hatred consumed her thoughts as she stepped out of the shower, grabbing a towel from the heated rack and drying herself. Then she stopped. She remembered that she had allowed Boyd to make love to her because she had fallen in love with him. Much as she still hated his cold, arrogant manner, she had come to depend on him. The reason she relived the moments when he had caressed her body was that on those occasions he had exhibited the traits she cherished most about him, traits she had never before believed he possessed. He was considerate, tender and thoughtful, totally different from the man she hated.

At those times she could forget why he had married her. She could overlook the fact that he loved another woman and could pretend that his kisses were an expression of love rather than mere desire. Dropping the towel, she walked to the bedroom to get dressed. As painful as the thought might be, she had to admit, to herself at least, that he was the man with whom she wanted to spend the rest of her life. She wanted to share his thoughts, his home, his bed. She wanted to bear his children. But were these feelings powerful enough to permit her to continue this relationship based on one-way love, or would her pride and desire to be loved make her leave Boyd and put all thoughts of love and happiness out of her life forever?

She was fastening the waistband of her blue denim wraparound skirt when there was a tapping on the door.

"There's a young gentleman to see you," Mrs. Gregory said. "He said that you were expecting him. His name is Craig Simmons." There was a definite undertone of disapproval in her voice.

"Please ask him to wait," Cindy said. "I'll only be a moment."

She couldn't imagine why Craig had come to the house without calling first. Surely he was aware of her husband's reaction to their relationship. What if Boyd hadn't left for work yet?

Then she remembered her determination to keep this one area of her life—her music—completely separate from him. That was the only thing which would keep her from slipping into a bottomless chasm of loneliness when he no longer cared enough to show her even sham tenderness. She had to remind herself that desire didn't have the lasting power of love, and the time would ultimately come when Boyd's desire for her would no longer be powerful enough to bring him to her side, even for a few moments of shared passion. Then she would have only her music to get her through the empty days and nights. Whatever happened, she must not lose that. Without her music she would find life without Boyd completely beyond her powers of endurance.

Craig was waiting for her in the living room. He was studying the colorful silk tapestry which hung over the fireplace. He turned when he heard her footsteps move across the planked-oak floors.

"That's a very valuable tapestry. I imagine that it's at least two hundred years old. Yet look at how vivid the colors still are. It's been marvelously preserved."

Cindy shrugged. "I can't take credit for any of the things in this room; Boyd handled the decoration. You'd have to check with him to get the history of the tapestry."

Craig lifted his brow. "That's odd. Somehow, I can't imagine Hamilton choosing such lovely things. He strikes me as much more the chrome-and-leather type. Strictly utilitarian, if you know what I mean."

Cindy pursed her lips and lifted her palms. "Boyd is a very complex person. I imagine only he is fully aware of the wide range of his tastes and desires."

Craig made no attempt to reply to her statement. Instead, he smiled and came toward her. "I know I should have called to set up a meeting but I wanted to see the old piano you mentioned last night so I thought I'd save time by coming right over."

"The piano's in the other house," Cindy said. "The large one you passed as you drove down here. Why don't we have some coffee and then we can go there?"

"Fine," Craig said. "I brought the concerto with me so we can start rehearsing immediately."

After they finished their coffee, Cindy led Craig down to the castle and through the French doors leading to the music room, then removed the dustcover from the piano. He stroked his fingers lightly across the rosewood frame, then lifted the top to study the soundboard. He looked at the ornately carved legs and shook his head in disbelief.

"I've seen instruments like this before, but only in Paris, in the homes of the nobility. They had been in the family for years. I wonder how Boyd acquired this one."

"I believe he bought the furniture with the house. I doubt he realizes how valuable it is."

She began playing. Her rendition did not always flow smoothly and her performance was choppy in spots, but this was the very first time she had tried the piece and she knew that she would improve with practice.

Craig was smiling at her when she had finished. "Your playing has gotten even better since I heard you last. You just have to polish some of the more subtle points and you'll have the piece down pat. I'm going to try to schedule the premiere as soon as possible. It won't take you long to prepare and I think the concert will be just the boost our group needs to get the additional financial support which will put us on our feet."

"I hope you're right," Cindy said. "I'd hate to let you down."

"Don't worry; you won't. Now, why don't we take a break? After all, I am new in town and you've lived here all your life. We can spend the afternoon seeing some of the famous tourist attractions."

"There's really not much to see in the immediate vicinity. If you want to play tourist, we'll have to go into Palo Alto. Or we could drive down to San Jose."

"OK. I vote for San Jose."

Craig began studying road maps while Cindy went to tell Mrs. Gregory where she was going.

"What time will you be back?" the housekeeper asked.

"Not too late," Cindy replied.

"Then you'll be home for dinner."

"I imagine so. Will Mr. Hamilton be dining at home?"

"He hasn't called," Mrs. Gregory replied.

Cindy shrugged and walked out the door.

Craig was folding the map and replacing it in the glove compartment when she got to the car. "All set?" he asked, as he started up the engine.

"Yes," she replied. "I told Mrs. Gregory that I'd be sightseeing with you." She quickly turned the conversation to general topics, anxious to leave her personal problems completely behind her for the day.

With the help of the map and Cindy's memory of the various landmarks, they arrived at their destination. "Winchester Mystery House," she said as Craig turned into the tree-shaded parking lot.

"It looks perfectly normal to me," he said as they walked toward the mansion. "Where's the mystery? Don't tell me there are ghosts. Is the house supposed to be haunted?"

"I don't know if it's haunted, but it's anything but normal. Does the name Winchester mean anything to you?"

"Yes," he replied. "It's the name of a gun . . . a rifle, I think."

"That's right. A repeating rifle first produced in the last century, probably the most important gun in the early development days of the American West. Sarah Winchester married the heir to the Winchester fortune."

"I see. And he built this house for her?"

"Only partially. And when he died Sarah was convinced that the evil spirits of all the people who had been killed by a shot from the Winchester rifle would return to haunt her."

"Then the house *is* haunted?"

"Not exactly." Cindy smiled. "Let's join the tour and you'll see what I mean."

The house was huge. It had one hundred and sixty rooms. There were two thousand doors, but some of them led nowhere. Several times the guide would open a door and they would find themselves looking at a blank wall. There were forty staircases, but many of them went straight up and ended in a parapetlike arrangement, leaving the group with no option but to turn back and retrace their steps. Secret passageways were built in the most unexpected places. Although the house contained many old and beautiful furnishings, the oddity of its structure dominated everything else.

By this time Craig had learned the reason for the peculiar architecture. The guide was very familiar with the house's history and enjoyed seeing the shock on the faces of the group as she recounted the story for their benefit.

Craig was laughing when he and Cindy walked to the car. "So Mrs. Winchester believed that she could mislead the evil spirits by building a totally confusing house? Imagine living in a home where even you and your servants needed a map to find the way around. I suppose she had a right to assume that the ghosts would find it baffling."

"Yes, and don't forget," Cindy said, "she also believed that she would stay alive for as long as she kept adding to the house. She thought that once the structure was completed she would die. Actually, all work ceased on the day she died, but not before she had built one of the strangest houses ever seen."

"Where to now?" Craig asked, helping her into the car. "Would you like to have something to eat? We seem to have forgotten about lunch."

"It's getting late, but we could stop for wine and cheese at a local winery."

"Sounds great; I'll feel just like I'm back in Paris."

"Don't let anyone hear you say that. The wine industry in California is anxious to establish an ambiance all its own."

Craig turned the car into a narrow dirt road and drove through acres of vine-covered fields before stopping at a large fieldstone farmhouse. They parked and walked through a wide stone arch, entering a secluded garden with small, round tables.

The day spent with Craig had been a soothing change

for Cindy, so different from her tension-fraught hours with Boyd, and the dry flavor of the Chablis only added to her feeling of contentment. Craig placed some ripe Camembert on a thin slice of toasted sourdough bread and offered it to Cindy.

"You know," he said, "I much prefer the sweet French bread to this tart-tasting relative. How do you ever get used to it?"

"It's part of our heritage." Cindy smiled. "The forty-niners were so busy searching for gold that they couldn't be bothered keeping their bread dough fresh. It turned sour. They baked it, ate it, got used to it. Now it's a San Francisco tradition. No self-respecting Californian would dream of eating that tame stuff you Easterners call bread."

"So we're still in the wild West?" Craig asked.

"Not anymore. Not when someone like you attends our music schools and then returns to organize a symphony orchestra." She nervously checked her watch. "We'd better be going. I did promise Mrs. Gregory that I'd be home early." She didn't add that she was also afraid of a repeat of last night's scene with Boyd.

This time the driveway was empty and Cindy breathed a sigh of relief when she realized that she wouldn't have to offer Boyd any explanations. Craig promised to call her as soon as he had set a date for the opening concert and Cindy said that she'd begin practicing immediately.

The deserted house was silently peaceful and she was still relaxed from her pleasant day. She strolled slowly into the small atrium just outside the living-room door and settled herself on a lounge chair. In a few moments the warmth of the fading afternoon sun combined with the lingering effects of the wine to lull her into a welcome state of slumber.

Somewhere in the distance, a door slammed, bringing her instantly awake. She was blinking her eyes to adjust to the situation when Boyd came storming into the atrium.

"So you're home, are you? I thought you and your boyfriend would make another evening of it. Then perhaps you'd run into someone I know again. How do you think I felt when Carl told me he'd seen you dining with another man?"

"You have no right to speak to me that way! I told Mrs. Gregory that I was taking Craig sightseeing. We went to the Winchester House."

"Oh, were you getting some decorating ideas for our new home? That's what you should be doing, you know. Any other wife would be busy furnishing a comfortable home for her husband and the children she plans to give him."

"But then, I'm not like any other wife, am I? Another woman wouldn't be married to a man she despised, a man who married her only to gain control of her father's company, a man whose girlfriend still occupies more of his time than his wife does."

Boyd reached down and gripped her shoulders, dragging her to her feet and up to his chest. "You don't know what you're saying." Then he stopped short, lowered his head and sniffed at her parted lips. "You reek of liquor. Where the devil have you been? Winchester House, indeed. Since when do they serve liquor there?"

"We stopped off at a winery for some wine and cheese. I only had one glass."

"Wine and cheese. How cozy. Almost like a lovers' tryst."

"What would you know about love?" she charged, tearing herself out of his arms. "I ought to have had more wine. Maybe if I got drunk enough I wouldn't be so aware of how brutally you force your unwanted attentions on me."

Anger glowed deep in Boyd's eyes. "So I'm brutal, am I? I force my attentions on the sanctity of your pure body, do I? Well, don't worry. It won't happen again. I'll offer my attentions where they'll be more welcome." He gripped her shoulders roughly, shaking her until her head spun. "But don't think that you're going to share your feminine charms with any other man. You're still my wife and I don't intend to have you make a fool of me with that musical friend of yours."

"Craig wouldn't stoop to such a thing. He respects me too much."

"Ha! You don't know anything about men—and as far as I'm concerned, you'd better keep it that way. If I so much as hear that you've gone out with Simmons again, I'll have him thrown out of the community. I wield a lot more power around here than the conductor of some ridiculous symphony orchestra."

Tears formed in Cindy's eyes as he groaned in disgust and released her. She had no doubt that he meant what he said. He was totally heartless, entirely capable of ruining Craig's career. She walked to her bedroom with tear-fogged eyes. In a short while she heard the door slam and the Mercedes spin down the gravel road. Painful tears dampened her pillow as she realized that he had gone to see the woman who would welcome his love.

Chapter Nine

True to his word, Boyd did not again attempt to make love to her. For the next six weeks of their marriage he behaved as if they were casual acquaintances who happened to be sharing the same house. On the rare occasions when he dined at home his conversation was polite but meaningless, and when they had finished eating he retreated to his study to work on whatever papers he had brought home from the office. It was almost as if he had erected an invisible barrier between them, a barrier which Cindy's wounded pride would not let her try to penetrate.

She was so desperately lonely that she threw herself into her music. If not for the fact that she had to rehearse for the concert, which was now only a few days off, she was sure she would have gone out of her mind. The rigorous demands of her practicing also helped her avoid the uncomfortable questions that always arose when her mother mentioned the fact that she and Boyd seemed to spend so little time together. Mrs. Templeton's romantic heart would have been broken if Cindy had ever tried to explain that Boyd loved another woman.

One afternoon, two days before the concert, she was

practicing in the deserted mansion and looked up to see Lorraine standing in the doorway. The other woman clapped her hands dramatically and slithered toward the piano.

"That was very good," she said. "Craig thinks that you have quite a promising future as a concert pianist."

"I've always enjoyed music," Cindy said warily. She was sure that Lorraine had some ulterior motive for stopping by.

"I'm glad," Lorraine said. "It will give you something to do after the divorce."

"After what divorce?" Cindy's mind reeled, but she tried to keep her hurt out of her voice.

"Why, yours and Boyd's, of course. Hasn't he spoken to you?" She lifted her eyebrows at Cindy's blank look of disbelief. "Oh, well, I guess he didn't want to trouble you until after the concert. We all know how temperamental you artists are."

"I'm not temperamental. Boyd and I have both been very busy lately. However, there's never been any discussion of a divorce."

Lorraine clicked her tongue and leaned against the piano. "I'm sure you know that Boyd and I were engaged before I ran off and got married. We had a silly disagreement and I went away in a huff; then he married you just to get back at me. Well, luckily, we both realize our mistake. I've gotten my divorce, and as soon as Boyd terminates your marriage we'll be free to take up where we left off."

Cindy clasped her hands tightly in her lap, unwilling to let Lorraine see the fear that was chilling her body. "Why did you and Boyd argue in the first place?"

Lorraine lifted a heavily jeweled hand and tossed her long dark hair over her shoulders. "Boyd is a very ambitious man; he always wanted to be head of his own company. My father and I offered to provide him with the financing he needed to start his own business but Boyd was too proud to accept any help from us. Besides, he had some wild idea about not going into competition with Templeton Industries."

Lorraine walked around the room, lifting the dust-covers and absently studying the furniture. "I can't wait to decorate this house; you do know that I helped Boyd furnish the cottage?" She flashed an evil smile and continued. "He refused to get married until he had satisfied his business goals, and I became impatient, ran off to Europe and married the count in an attempt to show Boyd that I could live without him. It was a terrible mistake."

She completed her survey of the room and turned to face Cindy. "Well, we've both grown up since then. Boyd is willing to let my father provide him with the funds necessary to start his own company or to buy out your interest in Templeton Industries. Either way, the path will once again be clear for our marriage."

"What if I don't agree to a divorce?" Cindy asked in a quavering voice.

"Pointless," Lorraine replied. "California provides for no-fault divorces. If one partner wants out the other can't fight to continue the marriage. Besides, you and Boyd are hardly compatible. I would say that Craig is definitely more your type. He certainly holds you in high regard. Who knows, once you're divorced from Boyd perhaps Craig will make his feelings for you more apparent."

Cindy couldn't answer Lorraine. Somehow the thought of Boyd's divorcing her so soon after their marriage had never entered her mind. Lorraine walked triumphantly toward the door. Evidently she had accomplished her mission. Cindy wondered if this had been Boyd's idea. Obviously he no longer cared enough about her to even ask for a divorce face to face and had therefore delegated this tedious chore to Lorraine.

"I'm so glad we had this talk," Lorraine said as she walked out the door. "It's always better to get everything out in the open."

Cindy sat quietly until she heard Lorraine's car move down the driveway. Then she covered the piano and walked back toward the cottage. If Boyd asked for a divorce she would get full control of the company's stock and her mother and Richard would be financially secure, but what money could ever replace the fiery touch of Boyd's lips against hers?

The concert was being held in the auditorium at Stanford University and Cindy had wanted a chance to practice on the piano there and evaluate its tonal quality as well as the acoustics of the room. After her conversation with Lorraine the thought of facing Boyd again filled her with pain and she decided to drive up to Palo Alto immediately, thus avoiding any personal contact. Craig wasn't in when she called to inform him of her departure, so she left a message with his answering service. Then she packed her bags and told Mrs. Gregory that she was leaving for Stanford.

"Does Mr. Hamilton know?"

"I'll leave a note," Cindy replied, and returned to her room.

She wrote a short note and left it on Boyd's dresser. Painfully romantic memories invaded her mind as she glanced at the bed on which Boyd had introduced her to the joys that love could bring. But their love had been one-sided, and now Boyd's desire for her had vanished so completely that he no longer even wanted her as his wife. Even the company she brought as a dowry no longer interested him. She shook her head to clear her thoughts and fought back the tears that were threatening to fall. Then she picked up her bags and walked to the car.

Her mind was so fogged by misery that she was barely aware of the time it took to drive from Los Altos Hills to Palo Alto. She checked in at a hotel and immediately called Richard to ask him to meet her for dinner. She hoped he would be able to spare the time from his studies. Perhaps his pleasant companionship would take her mind off her hopeless love for Boyd.

Richard was delighted by her invitation and suggested that they meet in her room for a predinner cocktail before going down to the restaurant. He promised to be at the hotel within the hour. Cindy changed into a high-necked knit-jersey dress; the sapphire fabric was almost the color of her eyes and highlighted the pale gold tones of her hair. She grimaced as she noted that she had to fasten her belt one hook over, and her current depression was not improved by this indication that, in addition to her other problems, she was losing her attractively slender waistline. Then she realized that sitting at the piano all day was hardly conducive to keeping one's figure in good shape. Once the concert was over, she vowed she would start playing tennis.

She had just finished applying her lip gloss when she heard Richard's familiar tap. She rushed to open the door, grasped his hands affectionately and drew him into the room.

"Are you here all alone?" he asked. "Couldn't Boyd get away?"

"He was too busy," she replied. "You know how it is."

"I'm going to have a talk with him," Richard said. "He's a real workaholic and that's not healthy. If he doesn't learn to relax he's asking for trouble."

Cindy couldn't risk a discussion about Boyd. Richard

was quite perceptive and she didn't want him knowing that her marriage was on the verge of breaking up—although, according to Lorraine, everyone would have that information soon enough.

"How's school going? Are you happy you chose medicine?" she asked, quickly changing the topic.

"Very. I just wasn't cut out for the world of commerce like Dad and Boyd. It's a lucky thing for all of us that Boyd and you fell in love; Dad really wanted to keep the business in the family."

"Maybe he should have sold the company. I mean . . . what if Boyd hadn't wanted to marry me?"

"Not a chance," Richard said, mixing her a wine spritzer. "The only reason Dad was able to keep Boyd working for him all these years was that Boyd always had his eye on you."

"What?" Cindy's shocked tone was evidence of her disbelief.

Richard smiled. "Didn't Boyd tell you? Why do you think he came to our house so often during your school vacations? He hardly ever visited us when you weren't around."

"But Mom never said anything."

"Mom didn't know. Dad wasn't sure that you liked Boyd and he was afraid Mom would insist on letting you make your own decision. He really thought you might refuse to marry Boyd and then he would leave the company. So, as I said before, it was good news for everyone when you fell in love with Boyd."

Cindy's head began to spin. Was it possible that Boyd had married her because he loved her, or was Richard mistaken? Had her father deceived Richard so that he wouldn't know how she had been forced into marriage? And even if Boyd had loved her when he married her, had her subsequent behavior so disgusted him that he had once again turned his attentions to Lorraine?

Suddenly the confusion whirling around inside Cindy's head flooded her body, filling her with a queasy nausea. She clutched at her stomach and ran for the bathroom.

When her nausea was finally under control and she reentered the room, Richard grasped her shoulders and led her to the bed. He calmly took her pulse while she rested back against the pillows.

"How long has this been going on?"

"A few days. It happens so suddenly . . . I can't seem to control it. I wonder if it could still be that bug I caught in Mexico."

Richard smiled. "It could be something you caught in Mexico, but I'd hardly call it a bug."

"I don't understand."

"Well, it's hard to be absolutely certain without lab tests and a complete examination, but my meager medical knowledge points to early pregnancy. That's the usual cause of dizziness and nausea in a healthy young bride. There are going to be a lot of happy people when they hear the news."

Cindy did some quick mental calculations and realized that Richard was probably right. She had been so busy rehearsing and trying to control her depression over the miserable state of her marriage that she hadn't paid any attention to the physical changes in her body. No wonder she was putting on weight.

Richard was watching her carefully. "I'll have room service send up some food; you'll feel better after a light meal. Do you want me to call Boyd and get him up here? I think this news is important enough to drag him away from the office."

"No! Please don't! He'll be here the day after tomorrow for the concert and I'll tell him then."

"Well, all right, if that's what you want. But I really think you should tell him immediately. This isn't the sort of information a wife should keep from her husband."

Cindy didn't answer Richard. There was no way she could tell him how much she dreaded breaking the news of her pregnancy to Boyd. How terrible it would be if he decided to stay married to her just for the sake of the child! Then she realized that she didn't have to tell Boyd about the baby until after he had asked for his divorce. He would be free to marry Lorraine, but she would have his child to remind her of how much she would always love him.

The thought cheered her, and when she had eaten the eggs and toast Richard had ordered she obeyed his instructions and prepared for bed. Relaxation came surprisingly easily and she fell asleep dreaming about the child she and Boyd had created. . . .

She spent the next day in the auditorium. Craig joined her there at about noon and helped her adjust the pace of the music to the acoustics of the large room. At last he applauded generously and walked toward the piano.

"That sounds as perfect as anything I've heard. You look beat. Why don't we grab a bite of dinner and call it a day?"

She shook her head. "I hope you don't mind, Craig, but I'm very tired. I think I'll skip dinner and have something sent up to my room."

"OK," he said. "I'll see you back to the hotel."

She invited him in to review some final changes in the score, and when the phone rang she asked him to answer it. All the color drained from his face and he held the receiver out to her. "It's your husband."

"How cozy," Boyd snarled. "I called to find out how you were. Richard phoned me and suggested you might need some moral support before the concert. Unfortunately, he's not aware of all the men in your life. I told you to stay away from Simmons and I meant it. I thought you knew me well enough to realize that I expect my orders to be obeyed."

Cindy took a deep breath. "It's not what you think, Boyd. I was rehearsing all day and Craig just stopped by to help me with some last-minute changes."

Boyd spoke as if he hadn't heard her. "I'll see you tomorrow night. Just make sure you're not with Simmons." He slammed down the receiver.

"More problems?" Craig's voice was laced with gentle compassion.

"No," Cindy smiled weakly, "just preconcert nerves."

"What is it, Cindy? I know that you're not happy with Boyd. I just want you to know how much I've come to like you."

She shook her head. "Please, Craig. Don't say any more. I like you as a friend but that's it. I love my husband very much; there's no room for anyone else."

Craig reflected for a moment. "Hamilton's a very lucky man. He doesn't deserve you."

Cindy shrugged. "I love him," she repeated.

Craig shook his head and walked to the door. "Just remember, I'll be here if you ever change your mind."

Cindy locked the door after he had left. She would never change her mind. Her heart, her body and now even the child growing within her belonged to Boyd Hamilton. Nothing in the world could ever alter that. Although her pride wouldn't let her crawl to him, begging for his embrace, she would never settle for any other man's caress.

On the night of the concert she put on a plain black matte jersey gown with a low scoop neckline and long fitted sleeves. It clung to the curves of her breasts and waist, then flowed freely to swirl gracefully around her ankles. She had chosen this simple outfit because she wanted nothing in her appearance to detract from the importance of the music she was offering at this performance.

In a last-minute decision she clasped the diamond necklace Boyd had given her around her neck. Despite her protests he had insisted that she keep it, and now she needed the reassurance of this expensive token of the desire he had once felt for her. It glittered brilliantly against her soft white skin. The simplicity of the gown and her upswept blonde hair only served to enhance the majestic beauty of the fiery jewel.

A string quartet from the university performed first, and then she was introduced. She nodded to the audience and approached the piano. As she sat down and began to play, all other thoughts vanished from her mind. When she had finished she knew that she had interpreted the composition perfectly, and she smiled as she stepped forward to take a bow and receive her bouquet of long-stemmed American Beauty roses.

The smile vanished when she looked down, for the first time, at the front row of seats. Her mother, Richard and Anna were all there applauding her, but the sight of Lorraine, her jewel-studded hand resting possessively on Boyd's strong shoulder, was enough to deprive Cindy of all the joy the performance had given her. She was relieved when Craig stepped forward to address the audience, permitting her to leave the stage. She prayed for sufficient self-control to hold back her tears until she was alone.

But she was not allowed this luxury because Richard came to her dressing room to tell her that they were all going out to a late supper and, since she was the guest of honor, it would be impossible to start without her.

Cindy smiled and got her long black velvet cape. The blue satin lining of the double-ruffled collar nestled against her fair complexion, highlighting her sapphire eyes and giving her features the appearance of finely molded porcelain.

They went to a small restaurant not far from the university. Lorraine monopolized the conversation, talking about her plans for the future of the symphony group, and Richard watched her hands as they lightly touched Boyd each time she wanted to emphasize a point. He raised his eyebrows and looked at Cindy. She turned away, unable to face the question in his eyes.

"That's a lovely necklace, Cindy. When did you get it? I don't believe I've ever seen it before." Her mother smiled at her.

"It was my wedding gift to Cindy," Boyd said. "I don't think she's ever worn it before." His obsidian eyes probed her face intently.

Cindy blushed as her hand rose involuntarily to finger the large diamond. It was foolish of her to imagine that the jewel had any emotional significance; Boyd's feelings for her were as cold as the stone around her neck. His gifts were meaningless if she couldn't have his love.

She was brought out of her reverie when she saw that Richard had asked Lorraine to dance. Apparently he had seen enough of her open display of affection for Boyd and had decided to stop her from embarrassing his sister. Her eyes were still on them when she felt Boyd's hand on her shoulder.

"Do you think you can spare a dance for your husband, now that you're a celebrity?"

Her heart froze for a moment; then, as if to compensate for its lost beat, it began racing wildly. Boyd's hooded eyes studied her unwaveringly as he awaited her response. She smiled and rose. His arm circled her waist lightly as he guided her toward the dance floor; then he turned her casually into his arms.

The sudden ease of his movement caught her by surprise and her eyes opened wide to meet his as his arms became inflexible steel bands, bringing her against the hard, lean length of him. For a moment her limbs grew rigid, unwilling to succumb to his imperious possession. Then a low sound, somewhere between a moan and a sigh, escaped her slightly parted lips and all the fight left her. Her bones became as soft as warm taffy and her body relaxed against his, fluidly melting against the masculine contours of his flesh as if she were slipping into a mold created for her use alone.

She felt a tremulous shudder move swiftly through Boyd's body and his hands slid down her back, caressing her and urging her closer until it was impossible for her to take a breath without feeling it echo deep within his powerful chest.

Her cheek was resting against the black satin lapels of his well-tailored evening jacket and she raised her eyes, anxious to see if his face reflected even a slight echo of the emotions that were coursing along her veins. Her heart filled with an uncontrollable yearning as she saw the tan column of his neck rising above the white silk of his evening shirt. His strong, musky odor mingled with the clean, spicy scent of his aftershave and each breath she took tantalized her nostrils, making her dizzy with desire.

Suddenly the dizziness became real and the room began to spin. Boyd's face was a blurred smudge in an impressionist painting and her world seemed to be slipping away from her. She grasped the collar of his jacket, her fingers clutching at the fabric desperately as she sought some support to prevent her from falling into the dark abyss of nothingness. Then everything went black.

She dimly remembered Boyd lifting her in his arms and hearing a distant buzz of concerned voices, but her eyelids felt like lead plates and she lacked the power to unlock them and readmit the world.

When she finally forced them open, she found herself stretched out on a red velvet lounge. The mirrored walls told her that she was in the outer lounge of the ladies' room. But Richard was holding her wrist in his hand, checking her pulse, and Boyd was pacing the floor like a caged animal. Richard dropped her wrist and stroked her cheeks with the cool, damp cloth which had been resting on her forehead.

"Feeling better?" he asked.

Cindy smiled weakly; his voice was no longer that of her brother but had taken on the solicitous compassion of the professional physician. "I'm fine," she replied, looking up past Richard to Boyd's dark countenance. He was clearly disturbed, but she was unable to determine whether his distress was caused by concern for her well-being or by anger at the realization that she had probably ruined his plans to spend the evening with Lorraine.

"I think she should get right to bed," Richard said. "Why don't you take her back to the hotel? I'll take charge of your other guests and get them settled for the evening."

Boyd nodded his silent agreement. "Thanks, Richard, but stay with her a few minutes longer. I want to make some arrangements with the hotel and have the car brought around so she doesn't have to wait."

Cindy watched as he walked through the door, which had been propped ajar to indicate the presence of men in this women's world. She saw Lorraine walk up to

Boyd, take his arm and move slowly beside him into the lobby. Then she knew that Boyd had not excused himself to make hotel arrangements. He had just needed some time to tell Lorraine that he was being forced into accompanying Cindy back to the hotel. She bit her lower lip to hold back the tears that threatened to spill from her eyes.

Richard was studying her solicitously. "You really must tell Boyd that you're pregnant. He has a right to know. He's worrying his head off about you and there's absolutely nothing wrong with you that time and some dry biscuits won't cure."

Cindy was about to answer Richard when Boyd swept into the room. His presence was overwhelming and once more she felt the paralyzing breathlessness which consumed her whenever he surveyed her with that penetrating gaze of his.

"All set," he said to Richard. "Thanks for helping out with the others. I'll get her into bed, then perhaps you can make arrangements for her to see a physician while we're at Stanford. I know that some of the finest doctors in the world teach here." He bent and lifted Cindy in his arms without waiting for Richard to reply.

Her head rested against Boyd's shoulder all during the short trip back to the hotel. His strong arm held her to him, providing the support which held her upright. His lips were set so grimly that she didn't even consider initiating any conversation. When they reached the hotel he lifted Cindy easily in his arms and carried her through the deserted lobby into the elevator.

"That's the wrong floor," she said, as he pushed the penthouse button. "My room is on the fourth floor."

His lips mocked her, though his eyes were surprisingly tender. "Just be quiet; I know exactly what I'm doing."

He exited at the penthouse floor and unlocked the door to a large suite, similar in size to the one they had stayed in on their honeymoon. He kicked the door closed and carried her through the elegantly furnished sitting room. She got only a brief glimpse of the ornately carved French gilt furniture, skillfully arranged around a carrara marble fireplace.

The huge rococo framed mirror over the bar reflected Boyd's dark virility above her blonde fragility. His purposeful steps were muffled by the thick Persian carpet as he crossed into a dimly lit bedroom dominated by pink satin wall coverings and fragile white furniture. Lifting away the white spread, he placed her on the pink satin sheets, propping her head against the lace-trimmed pillow. Then he began loosening his tie and shrugging off his dark evening jacket. He tossed them carelessly on the needlepoint seat of a bergère chair and walked back toward the sitting room.

"Would you like a brandy? It might make you feel better."

She shook her head. The mere thought of alcohol was enough to send her head spinning again. She breathed deeply, trying to hold back the involuntary churning in her stomach.

Boyd twirled the ice in his glass and walked toward the bed, carrying a white garment in his hand. He laid it next to her. "The outfit you were admiring in Mexico. I looked forward to the nights when you would wear it for me, but it's too late for that now."

He appeared to be more relaxed as he seated himself at the edge of the bed and studied her silently over the rim of his glass. She realized that he had just informed her that their marriage was over. Soon he would ask for a divorce so he could marry Lorraine.

"You're pale as a ghost. You hardly ever smile anymore and now you're beginning to have fits of fainting. Has our marriage done all these things to you?"

Cindy smiled silently. She couldn't deny that her current state of health was a direct result of their marriage. But she knew that Boyd didn't have this interpretation in mind when he asked his question.

When she failed to answer him he rose and walked toward the dressing table, fingering the fragile petal of the long-stemmed pink rose in the cut-glass bud vase. The taut muscle in his jaw began to twitch and his lips narrowed as he pressed them together.

"I'm not the ogre you think I am. *I'll* file for the divorce. Under the terms of my agreement with your father I'll lose my stock interest in Templeton Industries; you'll be free to sell the company or do whatever else you want."

Cindy pressed her tightly balled fists into her sides. She rolled her face away from Boyd so he wouldn't see her misery. Lorraine had been right; she and Boyd had reached an agreement. He was now willing to take a loan from her father's bank and no longer needed Templeton Industries or the woman he had married to gain control of it.

"Do you intend to marry Simmons and pursue a career in music?"

His question took Cindy by such surprise that she had no chance to think about her answer. "No, of course not."

"Why not?" Boyd towered over her, waiting for her response.

"I don't love Craig," she replied. "He's just a good friend. We share a common interest, music, that's all."

Boyd sank onto the bed beside her and placed his empty glass on the night table. His hands circled her face and turned it toward him. "Then what will you do?"

"I don't know. I imagine I'll travel for a while. This area seems too confining. What difference does it make to you? I'll be out of your life."

Boyd's smoldering eyes slowly traveled the length of her body. Then he groaned wildly and his powerful hands pressed against her cheeks as if to crush her while his lips met hers in a brutal assault.

When he finally lifted his head his breath was ragged and uneven. "Does that feel like you'll be out of my life? Do you think I'll ever be able to forget you?"

Cindy caught his hands as he withdrew them from her face. "I don't understand."

"No, how could you?" He laughed mirthlessly. "What sane person could understand how I fell in love with a laughing golden girl who used to come to see her father at the plant? How could you understand what your delightful presence meant to an orphaned young man who had spent his entire life among machines and formulas? You were like my missing half. I wanted you for my own, wanted to share the joy that spilled from your smiling lips, wanted to explore your mind and fill your soul with the passion of my own."

He stopped and looked away from her. She stroked the firm strength of his fingers, imploring him to continue.

"Your father knew all this. He knew that I would never leave Templeton Industries as long as there was a chance that you might marry me. I agreed to wait until you had finished school, but I couldn't take the risk that you might refuse me. That's why I went along with the contract he suggested. It suited my purposes as well as his. I thought I could force you to love me, but I was wrong; people aren't machines. I wish I could program you to make you love me, but I see now that it's hopeless."

186

"What about Lorraine? Don't you want to marry her?"

"Lorraine?" The amazement in his voice was clear and uncontrived. "Why would I want to marry her? I could have had her years ago if she was what I wanted. I won't deny that I've had my share of lady friends; I'm a man, not a saint. But there was no other woman I ever wanted to marry, just you. You are the only woman I have ever asked to be my wife, and now that I've lost you I doubt that I'll ever marry again."

He looked down at her, his arrogant eyes soft and suddenly vulnerable. "Does it amuse you to find that you actually have the power to make me miserable? That's what you've always wanted, isn't it?"

"No . . . perhaps at first . . . before I really knew you." She studied the dark hair curling on his arms. Her long fingers stroked his strong hands lovingly. "I suppose I was always attracted to you. But I was hurt because you were continually surrounded by beautiful, sophisticated women. I guess in my childish way I wanted to destroy what I couldn't have."

His hand freed itself from her grasp, lifting her face toward his. His voice was little more than a breathlessly husky whisper. "What are you saying?"

"I'm saying that I love you. I've known that for a long time, but I thought you only married me to get control of the company."

"Little fool, I only stayed with Templeton Industries to get control of you, to share my life with you. You're all I ever really wanted." His lips pressed into hers, drowning out any verbal reply she might have made, while her body supplied him with a passionate response to his rising demands.

Then his dark head moved away. Flaming desire still raged in the depths of his eyes but he held her from him, exhibiting that iron control with which he ruled his emotions.

"What's wrong?" she pleaded with him. "Don't you want to make love to me?" She hungered for his touch.

"You know I do. But you're still too weak. I'm not certain if it's a result of the tension or the hectic schedule you've been under, but in either case you'd better rest until we find out what's bothering you and set you on the road to recovery."

Cindy smiled and stroked his firmly set jaw. "I'm afraid that there's very little the doctor can do for me right now. Richard says that my condition is quite common among young women who love their husbands as much as I love you." Her hands molded the firm flesh of his shoulder, anxious to know his body with the same thoroughness with which he knew hers. "My father is going to get his wish. Your child will be part Templeton."

His hard features were frozen in wonder. "Are you certain? Why didn't you tell me?"

"I just found out myself. Then I was so sure that you wanted a divorce so you could marry Lorraine. She said she was looking forward to decorating the large house after our divorce . . . that she'd decorated the cottage. I didn't want you to stay with me just because of the baby."

Anger hardened his features. "Lorraine has no part in my life. She offered to help me furnish the cottage and I refused, so why would I let her do anything to the home I bought for us and our children? I'd never consider living there with anyone else. You've made me happier than I've ever been."

He lowered his body to hers, pressing her to him so she felt the strength of his need for her. "Nothing could ever make me stop loving you. My life started when you told me you loved me. Until then I was only half alive."

His lips intoxicated her with their soft entreaties while his hands explored her body, sending her senses reeling into that magic world where only they dwelt. Cindy gave herself up completely, moving her body to unite with his. Her happiness was absolute. What did it matter if Boyd wanted to be King of the Valley . . . so long as she was his queen.

READERS' COMMENTS ON SILHOUETTE ROMANCES:

"You give us joy and surprises throughout the books . . . they're the best books I've read."
—J.S.*, Crosby, MN

"Needless to say I am addicted to your books. . . . I love the characters, the settings, the emotions."
—V.D., Plane, TX

"Every one was written with the utmost care. The story of each captures one's interest early in the plot and holds it through until the end."
—P.B., Summersville, WV

"I get so carried away with the books I forget the time."
—L.W., Beltsville, MD

"Silhouette has a great talent for picking winners."
—K.W., Detroit, MI

* names available on request.

Silhouette Romance

- __#49 DANCER IN THE SHADOWS Wisdom
- __#50 DUSKY ROSE Scott
- __#51 BRIDE OF THE SUN Hunter
- __#52 MAN WITHOUT A HEART Hampson
- __#53 CHANCE TOMORROW Browning
- __#54 LOUISIANA LADY Beckman
- __#55 WINTER'S HEART Ladame
- __#56 RISING STAR Trent
- __#57 TO TRUST TOMORROW John
- __#58 LONG WINTER'S NIGHT Stanford
- __#59 KISSED BY MOONLIGHT Vernon

- __#60 GREEN PARADISE Hill
- __#61 WHISPER MY NAME Michaels
- __#62 STAND-IN BRIDE Halston
- __#63 SNOWFLAKES IN THE SUN Brent
- __#64 SHADOW OF APOLLO Hampson
- __#65 A TOUCH OF MAGIC Hunter
- __#66 PROMISES FROM THE PAST Vitek
- __#67 ISLAND CONQUEST Hastings
- __#68 THE MARRIAGE BARGAIN Scott
- __#69 WEST OF THE MOON St. George

SILHOUETTE BOOKS

330 Steelcase Road East, Markham, Ont. L3R 2M1

Please send me the books I have checked above. I am enclosing $_____
(please add 50c to cover postage and handling for each order). Send
check or money order—no cash or C.O.D.s please. Allow up to six weeks
for delivery.

NAME_____

ADDRESS_____

CITY_____ _____ PROV._____